# Island
## of Fog

## Island of Fog

by Keith Robinson

Printed in the United States of America
First Published: April 2009
This Edition: March 2013
ISBN-13 978-0-9843906-0-1

Visit www.UnearthlyTales.com

ISLAND OF FOG BOOK I

# Island
# of Fog

## Keith Robinson

*Prologue*

The woman handed one of the group a curious object. It was surprisingly light, and looked like a tusk or horn of some kind, about a foot long with spiral indentations along its length.

"If you need me," she said, "just come to this cliff and blow into the horn. You won't hear a sound, but I'll answer immediately."

A strong gust of wind caused the long grass to whip around the legs of the group gathered on the cliff. For a moment the fog was so thick that the woman was engulfed in it, almost completely swallowed up even though she stood a mere few feet away. When the fog moved on, she remained there with her shimmering green silk billowing.

"You'll get used to the fog," she said. "Just be strong."

"Easy for you to say," one of the group grumbled. "I'm not sure I can stand to live like this."

"It's better than the alternative," another argued.

The woman sighed. "You'll manage. Just remember all I've told you. And not a word to the children—just keep your eye on them as they grow."

Still, some of the group were unsettled. "What happens if things don't go according to plan? What if they don't change?"

"We've been over this a thousand times," the woman said. "Let's just keep our fingers crossed." She looked around one last time with her startling blue eyes. "Be strong. I'll stop by from time to time to see how you're doing. Hopefully you'll only have to put up with this fog for eight years or so."

With that, the woman bade them farewell and jumped off the cliff.

*Chapter One*
## A strange discovery

Halfway into the silent woods, Hal Franklin paused before a clump of blackberry bushes and scratched at his left forearm. *Why* was it itching so much today? He unbuttoned his cuff and was about to roll up his sleeve when Robbie called from up ahead, his voice sharp and clear.

"Keep up, Hal! What are you doing?"

"Nothing," Hal called back. He pushed up his sleeve and studied his arm, expecting to see the welt of a mosquito bite or the redness of poison ivy. To his surprise everything seemed normal, and yet it itched like crazy. Irritated, he re-buttoned his sleeve and plunged through the bushes to catch up with his friend.

Robbie Strickland was pacing back and forth at the foot of a steep rise, a tall, skinny boy with dark brown tousled hair and a pointed nose. He was twelve, the same age as Hal but a head higher. Robbie's thick plaid shirt hung off his shoulders as though wrapped around a wire coat hanger, and his jeans ended above his skeletal ankles.

"You got fleas or something?" Robbie asked as Hal approached.

Hal realized he was busy scratching his arm again. "It's nothing. Let's keep moving before it gets dark on us. I don't want to be riding home across the fields at night."

They'd left their bikes and school backpacks in the meadow outside Black Woods, under the sprawling oak.

Together they started up the slippery slope, using thick protruding tree roots for footholds. Hal broke into a sweat despite the chill in the air.

"So where's this amazing thing you were talking about?" Hal asked, panting.

"Almost there," Robbie said, reaching the crest of the hill. He brushed his hands off, then disappeared from sight down the other side.

When Hal reached the top, he too paused to brush the cold wet soil from his hands. The knees of his jeans were plastered with the stuff. *This had better be worth it*, he thought.

He followed Robbie down the other side of the hill, sliding on pine needles and cones. Already at the bottom, Robbie was foraging for something in the bushes. He grinned and held up a long stick, then set off once more, thrashing at poison ivy as he went. No path existed this deep in the woods, but he darted between the trees without hesitation, following some uncanny sense of direction.

Hal followed close behind, stealing glances left and right, sometimes over his shoulder. Daylight across the island was feeble at the best of times, but here in the woods it was dismal. Patches of fog drifted between the pines as if lost and alone.

He scratched his arm again. It had been itching an awful lot lately, now that he thought about it.

Robbie stopped, and Hal almost bumped into him.

"What—?"

"Shh," Robbie said, holding up a hand.

The sound of trickling water permeated through the trees, and Robbie grinned. "We're close," he said, and set off once more, stomping on a bunch of toadstools before picking his way over a rocky formation that poked out of the soil.

Ducking under low-hanging branches, Robbie pushed through a clump of bright green ferns and disappeared. Hal struggled after him, and emerged behind his friend in a clearing thick with fog, where a foot-wide stream gurgled along a shallow rut. The water foamed on smooth rock and poured under thirsty overhanging root systems before meandering off down a gentle slope out of sight. Robbie stood at its edge, looking back at Hal.

"See it?" he whispered.

Hal stopped and scanned the clearing. *See what? Something in the stream? In the trees?* All Hal could see was fog; nothing unusual there, since it was always foggy on the island. On the other hand, it wasn't usually quite this thick in the middle of the woods . . .

Then he saw it. He blinked in amazement. Across the other side of the clearing, almost buried under tall ferns, lay a cave-like opening ten feet across. From this cave billowed a thick column of pure white smoke, rising up through the trees.

"What is it?" Hal gasped. "Is there a fire under the ground?"

He stepped across the stream for a closer look, imagining a raging inferno deep below the surface in some cavern or tunnel. He pulled aside the ferns and saw that the opening was like a giant rabbit warren, set in the side of a shallow slope. The gaping entrance funneled down to a dark, narrow tunnel, and from this tunnel belched the strange thick smoky substance, twisting and turning as it escaped into the air.

Hal suddenly got a face full of the stuff as it whorled over him. He lurched backward, expecting his eyes to sting and his lungs to fill with acrid fumes. But instead the smoke smelled musty and damp, somehow familiar.

Perplexed, he followed the column of smoke upwards, noting how it mushroomed out and filtered through the leaves, yet left no sign of blackening as smoke from a fire might. If Robbie had been here before and seen this, it must have been burning a while . . . and yet there was no heat emanating from the hole, and no stinging, choking fumes.

Robbie came up beside him and planted a foot on the rim of the cave, causing soil to shake loose underfoot and trickle down inside. He was engulfed in thick gloom from the knees up, and when he spoke his voice sounded muffled. "It's not smoke. It's fog."

With a jolt, Hal realized his friend was right. "This is where it all comes from?" He shook his head in wonder. It explained a lot. It had been foggy across the island every day of his life, and now he knew why. "Do you think if we plug up the hole, the fog will clear?"

"That's what I wondered," Robbie said, backing away from the hole and beaming. His eyes shone with excitement. "Can you imagine it? A day without fog? A blue sky? Come on, let's find something to block it up with—branches, leaves, anything will do."

"Wait," Hal said, pointing at the muddy ground nearby. "What are these?"

Around the mouth of the cave were several strange footprints—large, hand-sized prints of some kind of animal.

Robbie circled the prints with a puzzled expression. "That's weird. They weren't here yesterday."

"Why *were* you here yesterday?" Hal asked. "You mentioned a new bug?"

"Yeah. Found a beauty, a blood-sucking butterfly. Look." He showed Hal a red welt on the pale, tender skin of his inner arm. "Isn't it cool?"

Hal didn't think so. He would never understand why his friend spent so much time lurking in dark, creepy woods, studying bugs and plants. "Yeah, great. I didn't know there was such a thing as a blood-sucking butterfly."

"There isn't," Robbie said, looking smug. "So I bottled it to take home. Then I came across this hole." His brow knitted into a frown. "But like I said, these prints weren't here then."

The prints were cat-like, Hal decided; large rounded pads, each with four smaller indentations at the front end.

"Lauren's got a cat," Robbie murmured.

Hal grinned at him. "Trust you to think of her."

"She's the only one of us with a cat," Robbie protested, his cheeks reddening.

"Not for much longer," Hal murmured. "Biscuit is as old as we are, and in cat years, that's pretty old." He studied the prints thoughtfully. "These are far too big for a cat though. It might be Emily's dog, I suppose."

They both stared in silence.

"Well," Robbie said, looking around, "I guess it *has* to be Emily's dog. It must have run away or something, got lost in the woods. There are no other big animals on the island, unless it swam across from Out There."

Out There was the world beyond the island. Hal pictured it as a vast expanse of land, but Robbie argued it was a series of small islands just like theirs. Since the adults refused to talk about their old home, imagination was all the kids had to go on.

"I wonder why it was sniffing around the cave," Hal said. He thought the tunnel probably went deep, maybe as deep as the earth's core. Maybe all this escaping fog was steam from underground rivers that were boiling away under the intense heat of volcanic activity. Hal had once read a book about volcanoes, and could imagine bright red hot magma coursing through the rock far below, waiting to erupt as a river of lava, eating everything in its path . . .

A rustling in the bushes nearby caused both boys to spin around.

Hal scanned the woods, seeing nothing but dense vegetation and gloomy darkness. "Did you hear that?" he whispered.

"Yeah."

They stood in silence, watching and listening. The woods were too thick to reveal much. For all they knew there were a hundred pairs of eyes staring at them from the cover of darkness. Over the constant bubbling of the nearby stream came the faint, faraway sound of a woodpecker hard at work.

A frog croaked and hopped into the stream with a tiny plop. Robbie sighed. "Well, whatever it was, it's gone. Must have been Emily's dog. Come on, let's find some branches and cover this hole. After we get a framework going, we can stuff the gaps with leaves and mud."

They searched the clearing for something suitable to start the framework, but the pines in this patch of the woods were high and the lowest branches far out of reach. "We need a dead tree," Hal said after a while. "One that's dropped a few branches. Or maybe we could come back another day with a saw."

Robbie frowned. "We could follow the stream to the cliff. The trees aren't so high there. They have room to spread out."

They followed the meandering stream, trying to keep close to its edge. But the overhanging vegetation caused them to veer off, and Hal was just starting to wonder if they'd lost track of the stream altogether when Robbie called out, "It's through here. I just stepped in it."

At last the woods brightened and they reached the cliff edge, along which ran a narrow man-made path. The fog was thick here, nudging up against the bordering trees and blurring the fifty-foot sheer drop into the sea. The stream bubbled out of the woods and off the cliff, and suddenly Hal recognized where he was. "Isn't this where Thomas was killed?"

"Yeah," Robbie said. "He fell off that little slope right there."

They edged closer. Patches of grass swayed in a gentle sea breeze, and trees leaned out over the cliff as if on a dare. Far below, visible only when the fog thinned for the briefest of moments, the deep green sea swirled and foamed over jagged rocks. The island was surrounded by them, but sometimes the fog was so thick around the coast it was impossible to see them even from a beach right down by the water's edge.

Hal had a vision of Thomas Patten, a small red-haired boy with a happy face, straying off the cliff path and slipping down the slope, then plunging to his death on the rocks below. It had happened six years ago, but Thomas's desk remained in the classroom, empty, as a constant reminder to stay away from the cliffs. Nine desks, eight students.

Hal shuddered and backed off, glad he hadn't been there at the time. "What was he doing?"

Robbie gave him a puzzled look. "He was six. He wandered off into the woods, got lost—"

"Yeah, I know all that, but what was he *doing?* Playing in the stream? Maybe trying to see the waterfall?"

Hal doubted it was a spectacular waterfall. The stream bubbled down the slope and, from what he could see, fell away over the edge in a fine spray. But he couldn't be sure without crawling down the slope and peering over the edge.

"And where did his parents go afterwards?" Robbie added. "You reckon they jumped off the cliff and killed themselves?"

They'd had this discussion many times before. But before Hal could answer, they heard a crack somewhere in the woods, followed by a rustling sound.

Every muscle in Hal's body tensed. He squinted, searching for a sign of movement in the bushes. But he saw and heard nothing.

"What *is* that?" Robbie whispered. "Do you think it's Emily's dog?"

Hal cupped his hands to his mouth. "Wrangler! Wraaaan-gler! Here boy!"

Silence.

Robbie put his hands on his hips and scowled. "Do you think it's Abigail, messing with us? She's been following us around a lot the last couple of weeks."

Hal felt relief wash over him, mixed with annoyance. Of course! It would be just like that annoying brat, Abigail Porter, to follow them into the woods and spook them. Hal glared into the darkness. "Abi, get lost."

But there was no answer, so they got back to the business of finding decent branches to drag across the fog-hole. "You'd think it would be easy to find a few branches in the middle of the woods," Robbie complained. "Oh, hold on. There's one."

It was long and brittle, but if they were careful it might survive the trip back to the clearing without breaking up. They put it aside and foraged for more. After a while they found another two, each long enough to span the ten-foot fog-hole but not so heavy as to be impossible to drag through the woods. They decided they needed one more, so Hal climbed a tree and edged out along a low branch to the end. It bent under his weight so that Robbie could reach up and grab it. Then Hal swung down and, together, they yanked on the branch until it snapped and tumbled down in a flurry of brown and red leaves.

"That should do," Hal gasped, wiping sweat from his brow.

Robbie picked up one of the heavier branches by the thick, splintered end and set off, dragging it through the dirt. It caught on bushes as he went, but he put his back into it and soon disappeared into the woods. Hal tucked the ends of two thinner branches under his armpits and hauled his load after Robbie. One of them would have to come back for the fourth limb.

They were gasping by the time they arrived back at the clearing. They dragged the branches over the stream to the fog-hole, and then collapsed for a rest.

After a while, Robbie climbed to his feet. "Give me a hand," he said.

Together they struggled with the heaviest branch and laid it across the fog-hole, kicking ferns aside as they did so. It spanned the gap with ease, but on its own did little to stop the fog from billowing out.

"I'll get these other two branches across the hole," Robbie said, "if you'll go back and get the other one."

"Yeah, you do the easy bit," Hal said, rolling his eyes.

He set off, following the drag marks so he wouldn't lose his way. The woods seemed even more silent and lonely without Robbie close by, and he wondered how Abigail could stand shadowing them from a distance—assuming it was her. Or maybe it wasn't her but Fenton. Fenton was big, kind of pudgy and heavy, but strong too, and Hal couldn't imagine him being scared alone in the woods.

On the other hand, maybe they were right the first time, and Wrangler, Emily's faithful border collie, was running loose.

As Hal collected the fourth branch and headed back to the clearing, a nagging doubt crawled into the back of his mind. Wrangler was an old, sturdy dog, but he wasn't big enough to leave footprints the size of those by the fog-hole. And if it was Wrangler out there, why didn't he come running to greet them?

Hal quickened his pace. It was impossible for any other kind of large animal to be lurking in the woods . . . wasn't it? They'd all been on the island twelve years—surely they'd have come across a large animal by now.

When he got back to the clearing he found Robbie sitting on a boulder, knees up to his chin, rocking back and forth. He had laid all three branches across the fog-hole. The fog hardly faltered, and a fourth branch across the hole might not help much either, but it would give the boys a good, solid framework to build on. Cramming the gaps with smaller limbs, twigs, leaves and ferns should do the job.

Hal dragged his branch closer. "You gonna help me or not?" he gasped. Robbie said nothing, so Hal finished the job on his own with a final heave. He stepped back and brushed his hands, nodding with satisfaction. "Now the fun part—"

He broke off and stared at Robbie, noticing something strange for the first time. His friend sat there on the boulder looking forlorn and embarrassed, and his shirt was in tatters over his pale, bony frame.

Hal stared in silence.

Robbie shrugged. "I don't know what happened. One minute I was struggling with that last branch, and the next—I don't know, I just—"

Hal waited, bewildered. "Just what?"

"The branch got caught up and I tripped, and I got annoyed and . . . and then . . . I don't know, I suddenly felt stronger and I just picked up that branch like it was a twig and threw it across the hole." Robbie shook his head. "I couldn't believe my own strength, you know? I fell back into the ferns and just sat there staring. Then I realized my shirt was all torn up. I even popped the button on my jeans."

"Robbie," Hal said, feeling awkward, "what's up with you? Did you lose your temper or something?"

"No, I . . . well, I don't think so." Robbie frowned. "Maybe I did. I was pretty steamed for a second there, and scratched to bits on thorns, and then the stupid branch wouldn't budge, and . . ."

Hal stared at his friend, disturbed by the uncertainty he saw plastered across his face. Was Robbie cracking up? Who got so angry they ripped their shirt apart? It hung on him in tatters. All the buttons were gone, and the arms were ripped open lengthways. That had been some temper tantrum!

"Remind me never to annoy you," Hal said, trying a grin. Robbie seemed to perk up, and the awkward moment was over. "And Robbie, your mom's gonna kill you when you get home."

They turned to finish the job they'd started. The hard work was done; now came the fun part, filling in all the gaps and stopping the fog forever.

Something scampered through the woods toward them. Twigs cracked and leaves rustled, and there was the splash of a puddle. Then sudden silence, and in that silence Hal thought he could hear harsh breathing. Something was right there in the shadows, watching them from behind some bushes.

A high, fluty voice floated out of the gloom. "Where am I? What is this place?"

The voice was so strange and unfamiliar that Hal almost jumped out of his skin. He found Robbie clutching at him.

"You!" came the strange voice. "How did I get here?"

About twenty feet in front of the startled boys, a face came into view around a bush. It seemed to hover out of the darkness, bringing with it a bulky body that

Hal couldn't make out. But the face was clear to see, and it wasn't human: an animal of some kind, with bright blue eyes set in a dark red face, and with what seemed like hundreds of razor sharp fangs lining its gaping mouth.

Robbie turned and bolted. Hal pounded after him, praying that his friend didn't get them both lost. Hal didn't look back, but imagined the hideous creature preparing to leap on his back at any moment. Was that its hot breath on his neck? A snarl inches from his ear?

Black Woods was a blur of scratchy bushes, low-hanging branches and squelchy mud all the way to the outskirts, where the boys burst into an open field and stumbled through knee-high grass. Snatching glances over their shoulders and seeing no sign of a monster, they finally collapsed behind a lonesome bush, gasping, streaming with sweat, and almost crying with relief.

"What was *that?*" Hal panted.

"No clue," Robbie said, white-faced. "Scared me to death though. That voice—and that red face—it was like a cat, but with human eyes and hundreds of teeth."

"Yeah, those eyes," Hal agreed with a shudder. "So bright and blue . . ."

"Evil," Robbie said. "Whatever that thing is, it's not something I'm going to stick around and chat with. But how did it get here?"

"That's what it was asking us," Hal remembered. "It was asking where it was and how it got here. Do you think we should tell our parents?"

They discussed the matter at length, and finally decided not to say a word—for now. For one thing, they were not supposed to be in Black Woods. Since Thomas Patten's death, the woods were off-limits, at least to Hal and some of the others. Robbie's parents didn't seem to care so much, but if the boys admitted to being there they'd also have to explain *why* they were there, and then the subject of the fog-hole would come up.

"It's *our* fog-hole," Robbie said, clenching his fists. "We found it, and we're going to block it up. And when the fog stops pouring out and a blue sky appears, it'll be *us* that everyone thanks."

*That's if we ever get a chance to return*, Hal thought, glancing for the umpteenth time toward the woods. It seemed unlikely they'd be able to finish the job if a strange and frightening creature had taken up residence in the woods.

Tired and disappointed, the boys snuck out from behind the bush and warily skirted the perimeter of Black Woods until they found the sprawling oak where they'd left their bikes and backpacks. They set off across the meadow as fast as they could pedal, Robbie's ragged shirt flapping off his bony shoulders like a flag in the wind.

*Chapter Two*
## Thursday morning class

It was drizzling on Thursday morning when Hal's mom rapped on his bedroom door. He woke bleary-eyed and looked out the window at the thick gray fog. It was a shame he and Robbie hadn't been able to finish blocking the fog-hole. They'd have to return sometime and pack it with smaller branches and twigs, then leaves and ferns, maybe some mud on top to seal it off for good.

With a jolt he remembered the red-faced monster in the woods! He pressed his nose to the glass and scanned the front lawn, half expecting to see a pair of creepy blue eyes staring back at him from behind a tree or hedge. But, thankfully, there was no sign of the creature. Perhaps it was a forest-dweller and preferred to hide itself deep in the woods. That would explain why he and Robbie had never come across the thing before.

Mulling it over, he pulled on his clothes and ambled to the bathroom. Standing in front of the mirror, he dipped his hand in the bucket of fresh water and slicked down his short, sandy-colored hair. Then he brushed his teeth with the last of his mom's homemade mint-flavored tooth powder. It wasn't as good as the toothpaste from Out There, but that supply had run out years ago.

Along the hall came the sounds of his mom puttering around in the kitchen. Hal returned to his room, made sure he had the right school books in his backpack, and then popped his head into the living room to check the time.

His dad was there, a huge man, quite unlike Hal and his mom—black hair, brown eyes, olive skin, broad shoulders, and very tall. He had a thick bushy beard that tended to collect food when he ate. He was standing by the fireplace with the precious clock in his hands, winding it up as he did every morning and evening.

"What's the time, Dad?"

"Morning, Hal," his dad said. "It's just after seven." He hung the clock back on the wall over the fireplace with the sort of loving care Robbie gave to his precious bugs when he bottled them to take home.

In the kitchen, Hal's mom was busy frying eggs, sliced potatoes and onions over the fire. The kitchen fireplace was even larger than the adjoining one in the living room, and over the crackling flames stood a heavy iron framework with hooks for pots and pans, a rotisserie spit that spanned the hearth, and a small iron surface for frying. Above the frame hung an enormous soot-encrusted metal hood that collected the smoke and guided it up the chimney.

"Hey, Mom," Hal said.

She smiled at him, her face red and her forehead moist. Her long sandy-colored hair was streaked with gray, and she stood not much taller than Hal, a slim woman with a weary look in her green eyes. "About ready to eat?"

The family ate together as usual, idle words passing between them as they cleaned their plates. Hal's dad devoured the last of the bread and then kissed his wife goodbye. He threw on a long coat, climbed into well-worn boots, and set off for the farm, leaving Hal to help his mom clear away the plates.

"Be a dear," his mom said, handing him a bucket. "Go and fetch us some water, would you? My shoulder's acting up again."

Hal stepped out into the drizzle and grimaced as the cold damp started to soak though his clothes. He hurried across the lawn to the road, the bucket clanging against his leg. According to his dad, the main road had once been busy with cars, trucks, and motorbikes, the hub of a thriving island community, especially down toward the docks where the old shop fronts were rotting away. Hal found it hard to imagine.

Robbie's house loomed out of the fog on the opposite side of the road. Despite a choice of bigger, better houses tucked away in idyllic spots on the island, in recent years all eight families had ended up huddled together on this small stretch of road. Living near one another made life much easier, and there was a handy freshwater stream they could all share.

Hal arrived at a narrow, humped bridge, under which the clean, sparkling stream flowed. A wooden frame and pulley system had been rigged up, and Hal hung the bucket on the hook and lowered it into the water. The pulleys made it easy to wind the bucket back up, but carrying it back to the house was another matter. Water slopped over the rim as he hobbled along, and the handle dug into the palm of his hand. How did his mom manage this two or three times a day? He was just glad he lived so close.

"Hal, where's your coat?" his mom asked with a frown as he returned to the house and dumped the bucket in the kitchen. "You'll catch a cold."

"Won't," Hal said. He'd never had a cold in his life, and neither had any of his friends.

He pulled on a jacket, grabbed his packed lunch, slipped it into his backpack, and left for school. Packed lunches weren't essential since class ended before lunchtime anyway, but some of the classmates—Hal and Robbie in particular—preferred to eat out in a field somewhere, or perhaps up a tree, rather than go straight home and sit at a kitchen table. Food always tasted better outdoors!

A heavily trodden dirt path led away from the main road and ran alongside a cornfield bordered with a rickety wooden fence. Since all the kids used the same path, Hal often met his classmates along the way. Sometimes they rode their bikes, but on wet, muddy days like this it was better to walk. He brushed past Emily and Darcy as they walked together, and caught up to Robbie.

"Get home all right yesterday?" Hal asked.

Robbie nodded and grinned. "I snuck in the bedroom window, changed my shirt, then climbed out and walked in the front door as if I'd just got home. Mom never suspected a thing."

"Cool."

They reached the top of the hill and started down the path that led into the meadow. An old community hall, now used as a school, stood there with the tip of its narrow bell tower lost in a mist of drizzle, its aged wood siding dark with moisture.

"I wish we could have blocked that fog-hole," Robbie said with a faraway look. "Imagine waking up this morning with no fog, just a blue sky and bright yellow sun."

"It's raining," Hal said. "There wouldn't have been a blue sky anyway."

A voice shouted from behind. "Hal! Shortie! C'mere!"

Hal groaned.

Heavy feet came stamping up and a large hand clamped onto Hal's shoulder. "I'm talking to you, squirt. And you, beanpole."

The hulking form of Fenton Bridges butted in between Hal and Robbie, shoving them apart. He wasn't quite as tall as Robbie, but was built like a bull, with short spiky hair and small, staring eyes. As always he carried with him a faint smell of underarm body odor.

"Teacher's giving us a test today," he said, glaring at Hal. "That means you're going to pass me the answers when I need them. Right?"

"Work 'em out yourself."

Powerful fingers gripped the back of Hal's neck. "Sorry? Didn't quite hear you."

Hal squirmed but couldn't get free. "Get off!"

"Pick on someone your own size," Robbie mumbled.

Fenton turned on him at once, but retained his tight grip on Hal's neck. "Oh yeah? Like who, skeleton boy? Show me a single person our age who's as big as me, and I'll go pick on him."

"Try Out There," Hal said through gritted teeth. "There are probably hundreds of kids your size you can go play with."

"Or try the pig sty," Robbie said.

Fenton released his grip on Hal, and a huge fist lashed out. It caught Robbie on the chin and, in a flash, he was lying in the mud holding his face.

Fenton stood over him, his face red. "Watch yourself, stick insect. Say anything like that again and you'll be fishing around in that puddle for teeth."

*13*

"Leave him alone!" Hal yelled. "I'm not gonna help you cheat, so get lost!"

He was almost yanked off his feet as Fenton grabbed a handful of coat and pulled him closer. "And you watch out too, stumpy, or you'll be joining your bony friend in the mud." Fenton shoved hard, and Hal stumbled backward. "Now remember, when I signal for answers, you better pass 'em across. Or else the beanpole gets it."

He stalked off toward the school.

Hal helped Robbie to his feet. "You all right?"

"Great," Robbie said with tears in his eyes. He brushed them away and scowled. "Why's he always pick on us?"

"Because I sit near him in class," Hal grumbled. "And if I don't do as he says, he'll beat you up."

He looked back along the path and found Darcy and Emily standing perfectly still, clutching each other, watching from a safe distance.

"He's horrible," Emily called out. "Is Robbie okay?"

"I'm fine!" Robbie yelled. "It's nothing. You can stop gawping now." He brushed himself down, wiped some mud off the back of his trousers and elbows, and hurried on toward school, shooting a glance to Hal. "Come on."

The school building was small, with a large room at one end and several tiny rooms at the other. Mrs. Hunter, who was Lauren's mother and the class teacher, used the small rooms for storing school supplies and books. The large room, fitted with windows down the two longest sides, housed nine small desks arranged three by three that faced a larger desk at the front. On the wall over the teacher's desk hung a whiteboard. A nearby clock announced it was nearly eight as Hal and Robbie entered.

Chairs scraped, school bags and backpacks were slung on the floor and unzipped, and books were piled on the desktops and flipped open. Hal's desk was the exact center of the class. To his left, Robbie sat by the window, and to his right sat Fenton, who gave him a warning glare.

Mrs. Hunter waited with a tiny smile on her lips while the class settled. "Now," she said at last, "a history test. You did your homework, yes?"

"Yes!" came a chorus of voices, but Hal heard a small, nervous "No" from Dewey at the back. At least Dewey admits it, Hal thought, throwing Fenton a mutinous glare. Fenton caught him looking and glared back, then slid his finger across his throat and nodded meaningfully toward Robbie.

"Hey, Hal," whispered a girl's voice from over Hal's other shoulder. It was Abigail Porter, who sat behind Robbie by the window. "Psst!"

Unable to ignore her, Hal shot her a look.

She gave a sweet smile, a freckle-faced girl with brown hair tied back in a ponytail. Until recently her hair had been long enough to reach her waist, but in the last couple of weeks she'd cut it short, much to everyone's surprise. Now she twirled it around her fingers in a most irritating way, pulling it around in front of her face and pretending to powder her nose with it.

"Hey," she whispered. "Got something to tell you later. Can we meet after school?"

Mrs. Hunter came by just then, handing out test papers. Hal waited until she'd moved up the aisle, then turned to Abigail. "Can't. Busy," he lied.

"It won't take long," Abigail whispered. "Just ten minutes. Got to tell you something."

"Then tell me now."

"Stop whispering, you two," Mrs. Hunter said.

Hal jumped. He mumbled an apology and glanced over his paper. In her usual neat handwriting, Mrs. Hunter had written a series of history questions.

"Now then, children," she said in her high, clear voice. "You have half an hour, starting now. No talking, eyes down."

A complete silence engulfed the room, at least for the next twenty minutes. Hal worked through the test with a grudge, wondering what was the point in learning the history of a world they'd never get to see anyway. Who cared if some guy called *Columbo*, or whatever his name was, discovered America? What good did it do Hal and his friends? Still, he worked hard to get the answers right anyway, struggling to remember what he'd skimmed through last night during homework.

He heard Fenton clear his throat and decided not to look up. *Pretend not to notice*, he thought grimly.

Fenton cleared his throat again, louder this time, and Hal feigned an expression of total concentration and bent lower to his paper, chewing the end of his pencil.

Then a balled up piece of paper hit him on the cheek, and he blinked in surprise. Fenton was glaring at him, and nodding toward the paper.

With a sigh, Hal unfolded it and read: *your crusing for a brusing buddy. whats number 4, 7, 12, 15 and 24*

Hal studied his own answers. He was up to number nineteen of thirty questions. Fenton had probably skimmed through them all and was now going back to fill in a few blanks. It would be easy for Hal to write the answers on the paper and throw it back—but why should he?

He thought long and hard over his dilemma. Fenton was always picking on him, partly because he sat nearby, but also because Robbie was easy to beat up if Hal didn't do as he was told. Hal felt bad about seeing his friend getting pushed around, so he tried to comply whenever possible.

"Tell the teacher," Emily had once said.

"I'll tell her," Lauren had suggested, "later, at home."

"Don't say a word!" Hal had said, horrified. He didn't know what was worse: running to the teacher for help, or annoying Fenton even more.

So it went on, and once again Hal was faced with the same old dilemma: give Fenton what he wanted, or refuse and see his friend beaten up after school.

He stared at the paper, then at Fenton's stocky profile and those big, clumsy fists. Then he glanced across at Robbie, who was fingering a small bruise on his chin.

With a sigh, Hal copied his answers onto Fenton's creased scrap of paper. He had to jump ahead on his own test to figure out question twenty-four, but it was an easy one. He balled up Fenton's note and, after checking to make sure Mrs. Hunter wasn't watching, threw it back.

Fenton didn't even make an attempt to say thanks, just unfolded the paper and copied the answers onto his test paper.

Twenty minutes into the test, Emily gave a loud sigh, sat back in her chair, and folded her arms. Next to her, right in front of Hal, Lauren was busy trying to scratch her back at a place she couldn't reach. And Darcy, who sat at the third desk in the front row, seemed to be falling asleep.

Robbie was gazing across at Lauren, tapping his pencil against his chin. When he noticed Hal watching him, he reddened and looked away. Behind him, Abigail looked thoroughly bored. She slouched across her desk with her head resting on her hands. And beside her, right behind Hal and as quiet as a mouse, Dewey Morgan was still scrawling away.

Hal twisted around and glanced at the final desk, the ninth, which stood behind Fenton. No one sat there anymore. Before Thomas had died, when they were all young, there had been much swapping of desks and moving around as best friends became nuisances, and sworn enemies became pals. But on the day Thomas died, his desk and chair had become a tombstone, a memorial, and despite several swapped desks since then, his alone remained empty.

Mrs. Hunter's chair creaked and she stood up. "Okay, children, time's up. Pencils down, please." She started moving between the desks, collecting up the test papers, and the class took a moment to stretch and fidget.

Next, Mrs. Hunter gave the class an essay to write while she marked the tests. Hal yawned his way through it, and the morning dragged on. Outside, the rain stopped and the gray gloom brightened to a white haze.

"Very good, Emily," Mrs. Hunter said, nodding with approval. "Top marks. Thirty out of thirty."

Emily grinned and glanced around the class, glowing with pride.

"Also, well done Lauren and Hal, not bad at all, apart from a few silly mistakes. Abigail, you need to concentrate a little more. Very poor score indeed.

As for Dewey and Robbie, well, I suggest you take a little extra homework and actually study this time. I'll re-test you both after school tomorrow."

"Oh, Mrs. Hunter!" Robbie cried, sounding exasperated. He slumped back in his chair, his arms dangling at his sides.

"And Fenton," Mrs. Hunter said, now sounding serious. She gave him a long stare and held up his paper. "Only four right. Or, to put it another way, twenty-six wrong. That's a terrible score by any standards. But what's worse is that you cheated."

"Mrs. Hunter!" Fenton said, sounding like a shocked grown-up. "What do you mean?"

"It was question seven that gave you away: 'What was the name of the great explorer who discovered America in 1492?' Both you and Hal gave the same answer: Columbo."

There was a silence, and then Fenton sputtered, "But—yeah, he copied me, I saw him peeking, and anyway, isn't that the right answer?"

"The answer is *Columbus*, not Columbo," Mrs. Hunter said. "Columbo was just some detective character on television. Hal, I guess you must have heard your father talking about the old days and somehow got the name mixed up."

Hal shrugged.

"But, Mrs. Hunter," Fenton argued, "how do you know Hal didn't copy *me*?"

"Stop it, Fenton," Mrs. Hunter snapped. "You'll stay an extra half-hour after school all next week, and you'll re-take the test tomorrow with Robbie and Dewey. Is that understood?"

Furious, Fenton spent the rest of the class glowering at Hal, as if it were all his fault. Luckily, Mrs. Hunter kept Fenton in during mid-morning break, otherwise he might have pounded Hal into the soggy meadow.

When class finally ended at midday, Hal kept an eye on Fenton. The big boy had a nasty look on his face, a grim determination that caused his surly features to twist into a grimace. But when Mrs. Hunter tapped on Fenton's shoulder and spoke to him in a low voice, Hal seized the opportunity and grabbed Robbie's arm. "Come on, let's go while we can."

"I'm not scared of him," Robbie grumbled, as they emerged into cool but fresh air.

"You should be. He could beat you to a pulp if he wanted to."

Abigail appeared between them as if by magic, much as Fenton had done earlier only without shoving them so hard. "Ooh, looks like Fenton's going to be beating up a certain skinny boy. You'd better run, Robbie."

"Mind your own business," Robbie retorted.

"Ooh, touchy," Abigail said. She nudged Hal's arm. "So can I talk to you for a moment? Alone?"

Hal shook his head and increased his pace. "Go away, Abi. Go play with the girls."

To his annoyance, Abigail broke into a skip and linked her arms though Hal's and Robbie's. "The girls are boring," she said. "All they talk about is hair and homework. Especially Emily. Did you hear her earlier, boasting that she got every question right? Boys are much more interesting. What shall we do? How about going down to the docks and building a raft to escape the island?"

Both Hal and Robbie tried to shake her loose, but she hung on and giggled. "Oh, come on," she pleaded. "Let me come along. I won't be a nuisance, I promise."

"You already are a nuisance," Robbie said through gritted teeth. "Abi, get lost. You're not wanted."

Abigail released them and slowed to a stop. "Be like that, then," she mumbled. "See if I care. But Hal, I really do have to tell you something sometime."

"Why me?" Hal asked over his shoulder. "Tell Darcy or Emily. Emily loves gossip—go tell her."

The boys hurried on, putting distance between them and Abigail. She was trudging along now, looking out across the fields and daydreaming. "Good riddance," Robbie muttered. "What a nuisance she is. What with her and Fenton . . ."

"She's always pestering me these days," Hal said. "Keeps saying she needs to tell me something. Tell me what? What's so important that she can't just come out and say it? Why all the secrecy?"

"I bet I know," Robbie said with a sudden mischievous grin. "She wants to tell you that she's fallen in love with you."

Hal punched him hard on the arm. "Get lost. The only one who's in love around here is you—with Lauren. Why don't you talk to her, ask her if she wants to go bug-hunting or something?"

"Yeah, right," Robbie said, kicking at a stone.

Laughing, Hal shot a glance over his shoulder to check for Fenton. There he was, just emerging from the school building some distance away, looking harassed; it seemed Mrs. Hunter had had a few serious words with him. Lauren's mom was nice, but she had a sharp tongue from time to time, cowing even the likes of Fenton Bridges. That was good; he needed taking down a few pegs. In the meantime, Hal and Robbie had put some space between them and the school, so all they had to do was keep an eye open in case Fenton came pounding after them in a rage. They could outrun him if they had to.

Abigail, last seen staring into space as she ambled along, had vanished into thin air.

*A raft.*

Her silly, foolish suggestion about building a raft to escape the island echoed in Hal's mind. Of course she'd been joking . . . but what an idea! Imagine if it could be done!

*Chapter Three*
## A brilliant idea

" **A** raft," Robbie repeated, staring with growing excitement at Hal. "You really think we can build one? You really think it'll float?"

Hal nodded. "Of course it will. We'll sail Out There, to where our parents came from, and find out what all the secrecy is for. I reckon it's a place much bigger than this island, with lots of people and tall buildings and—"

He broke off, remembering where he was. Mrs. Hunter's Friday morning math class was on break, and Hal stood with Robbie outside the school. It was a bright morning, and the nearest hills stood out clear and sharp against the pure white fog beyond. The hazy glare from the sun made Hal squint. Because it was drier today, Hal, Robbie, and a few others had brought their bikes to school. They were lined up in a neat row against the side of the building, the front wheels inserted into a rusty rack.

A quick glance around assured Hal that no one was eavesdropping. Darcy, Lauren and Emily were huddled together as usual, while Abigail was busy teasing little Dewey Morgan by following close behind him wherever he walked. Every so often he would turn and yell at her to leave him alone, and each time she would stop, spread her hands, and say, "What? What am I doing?"

Meanwhile, Fenton leaned against a wall with a frown on his face. He was prodding around inside his mouth with a pudgy finger. *At least he's not beating on Robbie and me*, Hal thought. But he feared that would come later, after school; Fenton, Robbie and Dewey were supposed to be staying late to re-take the history test. It would be a perfect time for Fenton to pounce on Robbie and pummel him into the ground.

And for what? Because Hal had agreed to help Fenton cheat? He vowed never to give in again.

Satisfied that no one was eavesdropping, Hal turned back to Robbie. "We'll go to the old barn and find the materials we need, and I'll borrow some of Dad's tools. Hopefully he won't notice."

Robbie nodded, his eyes shining. "Let's get started tonight."

"After your detention," Hal reminded him. "I'll hang around for you."

Mrs. Hunter appeared in the doorway. "Break is now over. Come on in."

Everyone filed back inside, the three girls first, then Dewey—with Abigail on his tail—and then Hal and Robbie. Fenton shuffled in last, still frowning.

With a noisy scraping of chairs, the children resumed their seats. Fenton raised his hand at once. "Pweathe, Mithith Hunter? Can I pweathe go home? I've got a toothache."

"Goodness, Fenton," said Mrs. Hunter with concern. She rounded the desks and stood before him. "May I see?"

Fenton opened his mouth a little, and said "Ah" while Mrs. Hunter peered in. She stared for what seemed a very long time, and then cleared her throat.

"That's, uh . . . that's quite a toothache you have there, young Fenton Bridges," she said. "Yes, you may go home. Perhaps you should ask your mother to take you to Dr. Porter. She may have something to alleviate the pain."

Fenton nodded and got to his feet. Without another word he shuffled from the room, quite unlike his usual surly, boisterous self.

Hal stared in amazement, then turned to Robbie. Robbie looked delighted.

"Poor boy," Mrs. Hunter said. She looked across at Abigail. "But I should think your mother can brew something that will help, can't she, Abigail? Like when Darcy broke her ankle years ago. Dr. Porter's healing paste soon eased the pain, and she was walking again in a few weeks."

"Mom's always messing with potions and stuff," Abigail said, nodding. "Most of it smells horrible. As bad as Robbie's breath, actually."

Everyone laughed except Robbie, who swung around and glared at her.

"It's true," Abigail said, spreading her hands and looking around the class. "You know when you step in something that stinks, like in the cow field? Well, Robbie's breath is—"

"All right, that's enough, Abigail," Mrs. Hunter interrupted. "Back to work, children. Robbie, face front. Just ignore her."

Hal couldn't help grinning as his friend returned his attention to the front of the class, his face bright red and his eyes ablaze. Abigail had a way of riling everyone up.

But then Hal noticed something odd, and his grin faded.

Robbie had been holding a pencil in his fist as he swung around to face Abigail in anger, and now that pencil was in two pieces, snapped in half. Robbie noticed it himself just then, and stared at it as if wondering how it had got there.

As Mrs. Hunter resumed scrawling boring math problems on the whiteboard with a squeaky black pen, Hal stifled a yawn and started doodling on his paper. He sketched tiny detailed pictures of rafts, considering what to use for each component. He and Robbie would need a large platform to sit on, say five or six feet across, and something fastened underneath to keep the thing afloat. He couldn't think what to use as floats though . . .

"Hal?"

He jumped and looked up. "W-what?"

Mrs. Hunter was staring at him expectantly. Hal cleared his throat and gazed past her at the problem on the board, frowning as if thinking hard.

"Dimwit," mumbled Abigail from behind.

"Come on, Hal," said Mrs. Hunter, tapping her foot. "Weren't you paying attention? I know math is not the most interesting subject in the world, but it is very important that you grasp the basics. Anyone else know the answer?"

In the front row, Emily Stanton raised her hand like she was trying to touch the ceiling.

"Yes, Emily," said Mrs. Hunter.

"Forty-two," the dark-haired girl said triumphantly. "It's a very easy problem, Mrs. Hunter. I can't think why Hal didn't get it."

Mrs. Hunter shot Hal a glance. "Neither can I, Emily." She returned to the board and started on another problem.

Her voice faded into the background as visions of a raft floated through Hal's mind, a raft bobbing up and down on the ocean waves, forging through the fog and emerging into clear, brilliant light where the sky was blue and the sun was blinding. And on the horizon lay land! What would they find Out There? Thousands of people milling around, cars and motorcycles roaring along the roads? His dad had suggested there was nothing left there anymore, but what did that mean exactly?

That was the trouble with adults: they kept so many secrets. It was as though they were trying to forget their old life Out There, and yet often one adult or another would make a casual remark about the way things used to be. Hal's mother, for instance, as she scrubbed clothes in a bucket of heated soapy water, would often mention "washing machines" and how easy things once were. And most mornings, when she drew up icy cold water from the stream and struggled back to the house with a bucket in each hand, she would arrive red-faced and make some comment about how she used to take running water for granted.

So what had changed? Maybe now, with a raft, he and Robbie would find out.

Class ended at long last, at least for those who weren't re-taking the test. As Fenton had managed to get out of it, Robbie and Dewey were left alone in the classroom with Mrs. Hunter while Hal lingered around the corner by the bike rack. He watched Darcy, Lauren and Emily wander off and wondered where Abigail was.

As if on cue, she emerged from the school and looked around.

Hal ducked down behind the bike rack. The last thing he wanted was for her to be pestering him for the next half-hour while he waited for Robbie.

But then she started toward the bike rack. Hal groaned. What was she doing? Only two bikes were left, his and Robbie's, so she had no reason to be here.

"Hal?" she called.

Hal bolted around to the other side of the building and headed out across the meadow. When he was a safe distance away he threw himself down into the long grass and held his breath. Moments later Abigail appeared, looking around with a puzzled frown on her face.

"Hal? Are you here?"

He remained still and quiet, peering through the grass. The things he had to do to avoid that girl! She stood there a while, searching for him, then continued on around the school. She soon disappeared from sight.

Through one of the windows, Hal could see Robbie working hard on his test, and behind him the tiny figure of Dewey bent over his desk. It would be a while before they got through, so Hal rolled onto his back and stared up into the fog.

It was peaceful lying there alone, and after a while he dozed off. He was woken by his name being called, this time by Robbie. Hal jerked upright and looked around. There was no sign of Abigail; she must have gone home. He trotted around the building to the bike rack.

"Where'd you get to?" Robbie asked, looking puzzled. "I knew you hadn't left, because your bike's still here."

"Dozed off," Hal said. "Come on, let's get going."

They extracted their bikes and set off for the dirt path that led back to the main road. But as they got close, Abigail sprung up out of the grass. "Hi, Hal."

"Ignore her," Robbie murmured. "Just ride past."

"Hal, I need to talk to you."

Hal sighed and stopped. "All right, talk. What do you want?"

Robbie clicked his tongue and slowed. "Come on, Hal."

Abigail brushed herself down and removed some grass from her hair. "You carry on, Robbie. I want to talk to Hal alone."

"Look, Abi," Hal said, "we're busy and don't have time to stand around waiting for you to say what you've got to say. Spit it out."

She frowned. "You're busy? Doing what? Can I come?"

Robbie laughed. "Sure, Abi, if you can keep up with us without your bike."

Abigail raised an eyebrow and tilted her head to one side, looking smug. "Oh, trust me, I can keep up with you, even without my bike."

This made Robbie snort. "So you can run as fast as we can ride, can you?"

"I don't need to run. But I bet I can keep up with you anyway."

Hal and Robbie exchanged a look. Then Robbie shrugged. "There she goes again, being all strange and secretive as if she knows something important. Like we care."

Abigail took a step closer to Hal, her eyes wide. "But I do know something important," she whispered. "Hal, tell your friend to buzz off so we can talk. It'll just take a few minutes, honest, and you'll be amazed."

Robbie snorted again. "C'mon, Hal, we've got things to do. Important things."

Hal paused. Abigail stared hard at him with big brown eyes, and in a flash he found himself curious. What could be so important that had to be kept a secret? And why insist on telling *him?* Maybe he should send Robbie on ahead so he could listen to what she had to say . . .

But, as if reading his mind, Robbie sneered and said, "I'm sure whatever Abigail's got to say is much more important than what *we're* about to do—right, Hal? I mean, Abigail's always got important, useful things to say, hasn't she? Last week she told us Emily's neck was getting longer. And a few days ago she told us Lauren had hairy fingers. Are you sure you want to stop and listen to her, Hal?"

Put like that, Hal had to admit his friend was right.

"It's all true," Abigail said, frowning. "Look, Hal, I know how it sounds, but—"

Hal held up his hand. "Abi, when you learn to stop telling fibs and yanking everyone's chain, maybe I'll stick around long enough to listen to what you have to say. See you."

And the boys rode off together, leaving Abigail standing alone.

"She's so weird," Robbie said after a while, as they cycled down the narrow path that ran through the fields. "So anyway, what's the plan? Get tools first, or what?"

"No, let's go to the barn and see what we can find. We can take it down to the docks bit by bit, and stash it there."

Robbie nodded. "And start building it tomorrow. We have a full weekend ahead of us."

The barn stood alone in a field just beyond the main road, right behind the house that Dewey Morgan lived in. Although Dewey's dad would still be out at the farm on the other side of the island, with all the other men, his mom would no doubt be home, and she had only to glance out the back window to catch Hal and Robbie making off with long wooden planks and materials.

So they would need to break in around the back, as they always did.

They cut through the fields and approached the barn from the rear, keeping it between them and Dewey's house. There at the back was a small door set with a dirty window. This door was always locked, as were the huge double doors at the front, but the boys had no intention of trying to break open the lock.

They worked to remove the window frame. It was metal and very rusty, and the screws that were supposed to hold it in place just popped right though the delicate, crumbling frame. It came away in sections, leaving a sprinkling of rust on the doorstep. Once the frame was removed they pried the glass out of the housing and stood it in the grass against the wall.

The boys climbed though the narrow opening into the dark, musty barn. Great metal racks of shelving spanned the length of the barn, and on them were piled endless crates of supplies. Hal and Robbie wandered down the first aisle, reading the labels on the plastic crates. Here were school items like pens and pencils, notepads, and sticky tape; next to that piles and piles of new clothing to fit all sizes; then blankets and sheets, towels, face cloths, and all sorts of bathroom accessories like soaps and bath salts; and on the end were plates, silverware, pots and pans, and other kitchen utensils. And all of that on just *one* rack.

"How many bars of soap are left, do you think?" Robbie said, trying to peer through a fogged plastic crate. "I bet we run out of that next. First it was the shampoo, then the toothpaste . . . I worked out once that if a family gets through a tube of toothpaste once a month, let's call it fifteen tubes a year, and there were originally nine families—"

"And we've been here twelve years," added Hal.

"—then they must have brought in something like sixteen hundred tubes. Can you imagine sixteen hundred tubes of toothpaste? None left now though."

"They underestimated," Hal agreed. "We're using homemade gunk now. I can't remember the last actual tube we used. Must have been a year ago."

"And don't forget we've been a family short for the last six years," Robbie said. "They planned for nine, but Thomas died and his parents disappeared, so we would have run out of toothpaste earlier if they'd still been around."

"Maybe we weren't supposed be here this long," Hal said, staring into space. "I mean, my dad said this barn was once filled with rolls and rolls of toilet paper, but it all went long ago, like back when we were little."

Robbie nodded. "Yeah, my mom said people used to have toilets in the house that flushed everything out through pipes below the floor to some underground tanks. Can you imagine? A lot easier than the porta-john around the back."

They came to an aisle containing nothing but cans of food. "Dad says most of this canned stuff is past its use-by date," Hal said. "What a waste. He said they filled this rack full from top to bottom just in case we ever ran short on farm produce, but the farming has gone so well that not much of this canned stuff has been needed, so it's been forgotten."

"Here we go," Robbie said, walking past a large, painted sign pinned to the end of a rack. "Construction stuff. Look, some nice planks of wood. Think we could lash some together and make them float?"

Hal stared at the planks. They were eight feet long and a foot wide, and looked heavy. They'd need at least five or six to make a platform wide enough to sit on with room to maneuver. How were they going to get five or six heavy planks down to the docks? It was a long walk, and they'd have to scramble through the fields to avoid being seen.

He sighed. "Now I'm wondering if we should just pilfer something from one of the old houses, the ones near to the docks. Maybe we could just use a door or something?" He spotted a row of gray plastic tubs on the lowest level and bent to read the label. "Primer paint. Five-gallon buckets of the stuff. I wonder . . ."

"We don't need to paint the raft," Robbie said.

"No, I'm wondering if we can use these buckets as floats. If we emptied them and put the lids back on, they should work well enough—say one on each corner of the platform, or more if needed." Hal stood up, growing excited. "We could maybe run a couple of planks crossways to the door, one at the top and one at the bottom, and fix the buckets to the ends. That'll make the raft wider, so it might not rock so much and turn over."

With a plan forming in his mind, Hal began calling out a list of things to take. "Two long planks—we can manage those all right if we each carry an end, and make two trips. Let's take four buckets. There are maybe fifteen here—think four will be missed?"

The five-gallon buckets were far heavier than Hal could have imagined possible. He and Robbie struggled with one and got it all the way to the back door before realizing how awkward it would be to lift it through the window, so they fiddled with the rusted lock until it came loose. The door was jammed solid, but it burst open in a shower of dust when they put their shoulders to it.

After they'd hauled four heavy buckets outside, they removed the lids and poured the thick, creamy white liquid into a rut. They left the buckets upside down to drain and went back inside to fetch a couple of planks and a long length of rope.

About fifteen minutes later they worked on closing the door again, then spent some time refitting the glass and frame. They brushed off their hands and got ready to transport their raft materials to the docks, after first replacing the lids on the buckets. "The paint will dry around the rim and help stick the lids on," Hal explained. "Help me with this plank."

They set off across the fields toward the docks, walking parallel to the main road but some distance from it so as to remain out of sight.

"I'm starving," Hal said as they threaded their way through a small clump of trees. "When we get to the docks, let's have our lunch before going back for the other plank."

When they were well past the occupied houses, they left the cover of trees and rejoined the main road. After several hundred yards it sloped downwards and the boys knew the docks were close. The screaming of seagulls came to them out of the fog, and then the gentle sound of water washing up the pebble beach. The wind picked up, and brought with it the strong, fresh scent of the ocean.

On the coast the fog always seemed thicker. Hal and Robbie hurried down the road with their plank, a wall of gloom ahead of them, but then the docks appeared and the road leveled out. It ended at the water's edge, but a sturdy wooden pier continued out over the swirling green water. Huge black tires hung all along the sides, and a number of narrow wooden ladders were fixed here and there. The tires and ladders had perplexed Hal for years until his dad had told him that boats once moored there, long ago before the island was cut off from the outside world.

A low wooden jetty ran alongside a grassy bank off to one side. The boys descended a short flight of stone steps and walked all the way to the end. "This'll do," Hal said, dropping his end of the plank. "We'll dump everything here, then come back tomorrow and start building."

Robbie dropped his end too, and the jetty reverberated under their feet as the heavy plank fell with a bang. They took off their backpacks and sat down to eat their lunch.

It was calm and peaceful sitting with their legs dangling over the side of the jetty above the choppy green water, munching on sandwiches and sipping water from plastic bottles. Hal started into an apple but found it too soft for his liking, so he hurled it out to sea. Excited gulls swooped in to see what it was, but they didn't seem too interested and flapped away again.

"Think there's a monster out there?" asked Hal after a while. "A sea serpent, I mean?"

Robbie snorted. "Yeah, right. It's just a bedtime story, to keep us from swimming out too far. Maybe our parents are afraid we'll swim right out into the fog and through to the other side, where the sky is blue."

"Or maybe they're afraid we'll get lost in the fog," Hal said. "If only we could have plugged up that hole in the woods. Then we might be able to see Out There."

Well," Robbie said, getting to his feet, "we'll see Out There pretty soon. Come on, let's go get the other plank. Then the buckets, and then we'll have to find a door we can use, and then get some tools and nails and things."

*Chapter Four*
## The raft

Saturday was a busy day. Hal borrowed a hammer, a box of nails, a three-pack of duct tape, and some more rope from his dad's garage and crammed it all into his backpack along with his packed lunch. He set off on his bike to the docks, where he'd planned to meet Robbie. He caught up with his friend halfway along the road; Robbie was wobbling all over the place, trying to steer and pedal while hefting two heavy wood-handled shovels.

Hal grabbed one from him. "Are these our paddles?"

Robbie nodded. "You got the hammer and nails? How are we going to fix the buckets to the planks?"

"We'll figure something out. I brought duct tape and lots of thin rope. We'll lash them on somehow."

The fog was so thick this morning that the houses at the sides of the road were invisible until the boys passed by the front lawns. It was cold too, and Hal wore a thick sweater for a change. Robbie, as usual, seemed unaffected by the cold and wore a thin shirt and jeans that were too short.

They stood their bikes by the stone steps leading down to the jetty. The water looked cold and uninviting as they set to work.

They'd spent the previous afternoon bringing the two planks, four empty buckets, and long rope down to the docks, and then had set off to find a door. With plenty of empty houses and old shops nearby, it hadn't been a difficult task; they'd walked in and lifted one from its hinges, a good sturdy door with a small diamond-shaped window set in the center at eye-level. Getting it to the docks had been a chore though, for it was much heavier than they'd imagined, and seemed to get heavier the farther they carried it.

They crouched on the jetty and arranged the door and planks. They planned to build the raft upside down, so they first nailed the heavy planks crossways along the top and bottom of the door, and then spent a long time lashing the plastic buckets to them. With a combination of rope and heavy-duty waterproof duct tape, the four drums seemed secure enough at last. When they finished, they stood and stared at the underside of their raft with great satisfaction.

Now it was time to turn it right side up and put it in the water.

"Let's eat first," Hal said. "It must be lunchtime by now."

"Yeah, I'm starving," Robbie agreed, holding his stomach.

As soon as they were finished, they got to work turning the raft over. It was heavier than expected. With two heavy planks fixed to an even heavier door, and what seemed like miles of rope holding the buckets in place, the thing seemed to weigh a ton. They strained, but could not lift the raft up to a vertical position so it could fall over onto the other side. Robbie grew more and more red-faced as he struggled, all set to blow a fuse. Hal felt about the same. His face was hot and sweat dribbled from his forehead.

They tried once more, both gripping one end and lifting with all their might. They got it up to knee level, then straightened their backs, bringing it up as high as their waists . . . but again their strength failed them and they just couldn't get their tired arms to hoist it any higher. "Drop it," Hal gasped.

But suddenly Robbie gave a yell of frustration, and Hal found the raft lifting out of his hands. The structure rose to a vertical position, teetered there, and then toppled all the way over. It hit the jetty with a tremendous bang that made the whole platform shudder. Nearby seagulls screeched in fright.

Hal stared open-mouthed at his friend. Robbie stood there, breathing hard, his fists clenched and his eyes blazing. Somehow he seemed bigger, taller, his shoulders wider and filling out his shirt more than usual. "Robbie, what—"

Robbie looked at him, puzzled. "What's wrong?"

And in that moment he shrank down a few sizes, a slow, subtle change that might have been missed by anyone not paying attention. He lost a few inches in height, and his shirt drooped and sagged. In seconds Robbie was his usual beanpole self, blinking and confused.

Hal stood there, speechless.

"You . . . you saw that, didn't you?" Robbie asked, flushing red. He ran a hand nervously through his hair. "Something happened to me again. I felt it—like I got big and strong for a second."

"You did." Hal shook his head. "I think I'm going nuts. That's just not possible. You grew—got a few inches taller—and wider at the shoulders. I thought you were going to bust out of your shirt again."

"It was even worse back in the woods," Robbie said. "I *totally* lost it then, got angry and frustrated. This time I just wanted to turn the stupid raft over, so I tried harder."

"And it worked. Hey, if you can do that at will, you've got nothing to fear from Fenton."

Robbie's mouth dropped open. Then a smile spread across his face. "That would be cool. I could pick him up and throw him halfway across the island!"

Hal's arm started itching at that moment, and he scratched at it with annoyance. "Not this again. It's been itching on and off for days now, like I've been bitten, only there's never anything to see."

29

They got back to work and struggled to get the raft into the water. It meant sliding it sideways, which at least was easier than lifting it up on end. They tied a rope to it first, and then heaved with all their might. The big empty tubs tied to the underside of the planks had squashed a little under the weight of the raft, but they seemed intact; however, dragging the raft caused them to pull at the nails and rope, so the boys tried to lift the heavy structure as much as they could. When it finally toppled off the jetty into the water, for a horrible moment they thought it would plunge straight down underwater and sink forever.

But it bounced and bobbed, then settled low in the water. Hal pulled on the rope so it didn't float away. "The door's got a few inches of clearance below it," he said, pleased. "That's all that matters. The lower it is, the less it will bob around. As long as it doesn't sink too much lower when we get on, it should be okay."

"Let's give it a try," Robbie said, rubbing his hands. He sat on the edge of the jetty and lowered himself onto the raft as Hal pulled it closer. Once it was in position, knocking against one of the jetty supports, Robbie tied it up. Then Hal handed him the shovels and climbed down to join his friend.

"This is going to work fine," Robbie said, peering through the diamond-shaped window to the water below. "If we were a little lower and the door was actually touching the surface, we'd be able to see underwater."

Hal laughed. "If we were any lower, we'd get wet. And anyway, the water's too murky to see more than a few feet. Okay, I'm going to untie us. Ready to start paddling?"

"We're going now?"

"Why not? We've got all afternoon."

Together, without another word, they dipped their heavy shovels into the water on opposite sides and began to paddle. It took a moment to get synchronized, but soon the raft started to move away from the pier. The waves slopped against the underside of the door.

The raft seemed to handle well. As the boys bobbed over the water, paddling with their shovels, Hal glanced back at the jetty and was surprised to note it was already fading into the fog thirty or forty feet away.

Then he spotted someone standing like a statue by the roadside at the top of the stone steps, a girl with long brown hair pulled back in a ponytail. Her hands were stuffed into the pockets of a knee-length black coat. A red scarf covered her mouth and stood out bright and colorful in the gray gloom of the fog.

"Oh no," Hal whispered, his heart sinking. "It's Abigail."

Robbie's head snapped around. He scowled. "She'll tell on us!"

"Where are you going?" the girl called, her voice echoing off the swirling green water.

The raft bobbed and drifted. Hal knew Robbie was wondering the same thing as he: Should they ignore her and go on, or try to include her in their scheme and hope she'll keep her mouth shut about it?

Hal sighed, deciding he'd better say something. "We're going Out There," he called back, trying to keep his voice low so the whole island wouldn't hear.

Abigail didn't appear surprised. She pulled the scarf from her mouth. "What about the sea serpent?"

"There *is* no sea serpent," Robbie retorted.

The raft kept drifting and the fog grew thicker between them and Abigail. Hal tried his best to seem like he was confiding in her, as if she were their best friend. Maybe if she were on their side, she'd keep quiet, at least until they were back. "We need you to keep this secret," he called. "You know how much trouble we'll be in if we're found out. Can we trust you?"

Abigail was now just a faint silhouette. "Obviously not, or you would have let me in on this earlier." She sounded distant now, and at that moment the fog swallowed her up and her disembodied voice floated out of the gloom. "Don't get lost out there. You should have brought loads of string."

"String?" Hal muttered, puzzled. "What does she mean?"

Robbie slapped himself on the forehead. "She's right. We could have tied the string to the jetty and unraveled it as we went. Then there wouldn't be any danger of getting lost."

"I'll be right here when you get back," Abigail's voice called from far away. "And if you're not back by, say, next week, I'll go and get help."

"Oh, you're so funny," Hal murmured through gritted teeth. He stabbed at the water with his shovel, paddling hard. But Robbie fumbled, trying but failing to get the timing right, and the raft ended up in a slow spin. It was a good thing Abigail couldn't see them, Hal thought; she'd have been laughing her head off.

Once they got synchronized again, the raft surged onwards, heading farther into the murky grayness. It was a different kind of fog to what they were used to on land: thicker, colder, somehow menacing. Smoky fingers reached out to touch them, tentative and curious, and Hal had the eerie sensation it was sniffing at them the way Emily Stanton's old dog sniffed at fences as it scampered along the road.

They paddled in silence. A damp, freezing chill seeped through Hal's thick sweater and into his skin. Even the wooden handle of the shovel felt like a shaft of ice. Robbie's teeth were chattering.

Hal glanced back the way they had come and couldn't help but gasp. The jetty, the road, even the pier had vanished from sight, swallowed up in the gloom. The island had disappeared, and all around was silent, rolling mist, and cold water that lapped against the raft. Suddenly Hal's nerves went haywire and his breath came in short, ragged bursts. His arm began to itch.

Robbie stopped paddling and turned to him with a frown. "Are you all right?"

"We . . . we're quite a ways out," Hal gasped, fighting to stay calm. He jabbed a finger back toward the island. "How are we ever going to find our way back? Robbie, this is nuts—"

Robbie's eyebrows shot up. "It was *your* idea."

"I know," Hal said, "but it was a stupid one, all right? We need to think this through better. Abigail's right, we should have brought some string to help guide us back. We could get *completely lost* out here. There's nothing to see but fog. How do we know we're not going around in circles right now?"

Robbie looked around, silent.

At that moment, Hal's left forearm itched like a hundred ants were biting him, and he almost dropped the shovel in his urgency to scratch it. What a disaster *that* would be! They'd really end up going in circles with only one paddle.

"So . . . should we give up?" Robbie asked, continuing to stare into the fog. A hint of disappointment had crept into his voice.

Hal pondered. It would seem a great waste of effort if they just paddled back and never tried again, but there was nothing wrong with thinking things through better and returning later. Apart from bringing some string for guidance, they could tie lines around the shovels in case they got dropped in the water. So it wouldn't be a complete failure if they returned now, as long as they planned to come back out better prepared.

"I think," Hal began, "that if we go back and get some string, then—"

Something bumped the underside of the raft.

Hal and Robbie looked down in unison, then at each other.

"What was that?" Robbie asked nervously. "A rock? Is the water shallow here?"

Hal peered anxiously into the water, but saw no rocks sticking up. The surface of the ocean undulated like a sheet blowing on a clothes line, eerie and silent except where it slopped against the raft's plastic drums. It didn't *seem* shallow . . . but rocks could be lurking just below the surface. What if one ripped the floats apart? "We should head back," Hal said. "Let's plan this thing a little better and come out again."

"Okay," Robbie said, and now Hal detected a hint of relief in his voice.

They switched their grips on the shovels and paddled in the opposite direction. Again it took a second to get synchronized, and the raft began to turn.

"Stop!" Hal exclaimed. "I mean, don't *stop*, but—we've got to keep this thing straight, otherwise we won't know which direction to go in. Wait while I turn us back a little . . ."

"That's too much," Robbie said, dipping his shovel into the water and paddling against Hal's strokes.

Hal ground his teeth together and tried to hold down his temper. "Let's just row together and go straight. We must be turned about right by now. As long as we get back to the island we'll be okay—anywhere will do. Then we can follow the shore until we get back to the docks."

"Right," Robbie said, nodding. "As long as we don't row away from the island and miss it completely."

Something bumped the underside of the raft again, and this time they felt the deck rise for a second. Hal glanced down and glimpsed a flash of white through the glass panel. But then something to the side caught his attention and he searched the water just beyond his paddle.

He gasped and pointed.

A gigantic milky white serpentine body slipped by just beneath the surface, fast and silent, dwarfing the feeble little raft Hal and Robbie cowered on.

"Th-the sea s-ser-pent," Hal stammered.

Robbie brandished his shovel over his head as if batting at the monster might help. "We're dead," he moaned.

It seemed to take ages for the full length of the serpent to undulate past, its girth narrowing to the blunt tip of a snake-like tail as it went. It slid away under the surface and a current tugged at the raft, causing it to bounce up and down.

Hal gripped the shovel in one hand and scrabbled for a secure hold on the raft with the other. Every muscle in his body was taut. He was shivering hard, and his breath came in rasps. He felt powerless. What could they do? That thing could capsize them with a flick of its tail, or chomp them in one mouthful.

"We've gotta paddle," he said. "Ready? Three, two, one, go."

He began paddling, but Robbie was frozen in place, gripping the shovel over his head.

"Robbie, stop gawking and paddle!"

"Can't."

"Yes you can! I can't do this on my own—"

Robbie mumbled something.

Hal frowned. "What? What did you say?"

"It's coming back."

Out of the fog came the monstrous snake, its enormous bulk slicing easily through the water toward them. Its head lifted slowly—three feet wide with glistening white scales the size of fists, long drooping fins that stuck out from behind its lower jaw, and yellow eyes as big as plates. The serpent stared right at them, unblinking, emotionless. Its mouth opened just a fraction, enough for a shining black forked tongue to slip out, quiver, and slip back in again.

Robbie began yelling. He dropped the shovel onto the deck and scrambled back, bumping into his friend. Hal woke from his temporary paralysis.

"Robbie, there's nowhere to go—be careful or you'll—"

Too late. As the raft bobbed to one side, Robbie's shovel slipped off the deck and into the water with a tiny plop, gone forever.

But now the serpent was right over them, glaring down with baleful eyes. Water ran in rivulets down its scaled face and spattered the raft. The serpent's tongue flicked out again and quivered, lingering this time, as if tasting the air. A nasty rotting smell engulfed the frightened boys, and they recoiled as a deep hissing sound filled their ears.

"We're dead, we're dead, we're dead," Robbie was mumbling, his voice muffled. He had both hands over his face and was rocking back and forth.

As Hal stared up at the monster, something strange came over him. Some of his fear drained away, and determination crept into his heart. With a shaky voice, he spoke to the serpent. "Leave us alone. I mean it. Or you'll be sorry."

His fingers tightened around the shovel.

The serpent moved closer, somehow able to tread water and keep its head poised above them. The fins behind its lower jaw hung dripping and limp, and now Hal saw other fins farther along its body, just below the surface, fanning back and forth. Hal imagined the serpent's endless length undulating from side to side below the surface, deep within the murky depths. He shuddered and wished he could erase that creepy image.

The serpent's mouth opened partway, and the rotten stench caused Hal to recoil in disgust. He swung upwards with all his strength, and the shovel caught the monster a resounding smack on the chin.

Hal thought he saw surprise flash across the serpent's huge unblinking eyes as it backed away. It tilted its head once more and stared at him.

"See what you get when you mess with us!" Hal shouted, his face heating up. Panic gave way to the anger that bubbled up from deep inside. He felt breathless. His throat burned and he felt a crawling sensation all over his body. "Come back for some more, you worm!"

To his astonishment, the serpent slipped below the surface.

Hal searched the water. He saw flashes of white, then felt a bump under the raft. "It's going to sink us," he said, his anger suddenly evaporating and horror setting in. Would it pull them under and wait until they drowned before chewing them up? Or would it just *swallow them alive?*

The raft lifted, and both boys made a grab for the deck. Hal's shovel—the last remaining paddle—dropped out of his hands and slid off the deck into the water with a plop. "This is it," he muttered between gritted teeth.

"I don't want to die!" Robbie wailed.

The raft tilted a little to one side but continued to rise out of the water until all four plastic drums were clear. Now Hal saw the monster's broad, flat head below the deck, with its slick scaly skin. The raft wobbled as the serpent began cruising through the water.

Hal's mouth fell open. *What—?*

Cruising through the water? Why wasn't it capsizing them? Why would it lift them up and carry them through the fog? It didn't make any sense.

Unless it was taking them to its lair, or whatever sea serpents called their homes. Maybe it wasn't hungry yet. Maybe it wanted to save them for later, by storing them in its larder. Maybe they'd find the skeletons of other people stored there, people who'd been swallowed whole and their bones spat out.

Robbie was moaning, his eyes jammed shut.

"Hey," Hal said, poking him, "we're not dead yet. It's taking us to its lair. There's still hope."

"There's no hope," Robbie said, shaking his head. "We're dead. We should never have tried this."

The serpent continued to slide through the water, seeming to know where it was headed even though the thick fog revealed nothing.

Then the fog thinned and Hal caught sight of land. He squinted, and his mouth fell open. "Robbie. Robbie, look. The docks."

Robbie's eyes snapped open. "What?"

The serpent slowed as it approached the jetty, then sank out of sight, lowering the raft back into the water. Momentum carried the raft onwards, and Hal and Robbie sat in silence as they bobbed the rest of the way to the jetty. Seconds later they bumped against one of the posts, and Hal instinctively reached for it, his mouth hanging open.

Glancing around, he caught a flash of white, and then the water swelled as massive scaly coils broke the surface and the monster circled around.

The boys scrambled onto the jetty, bumping heads in their hurry to get off the raft. The moment they were clear, the serpent raised its head out of the water once more and descended on them. Hal and Robbie yelled and crouched low, knowing it was already too late . . .

But nothing happened except a loud splash. Hal felt cold seawater spatter over him, and he jerked upright and snapped his eyes open. Where had the monster gone? There—gliding away through the fog, receding into the distance . . . with the small, pathetic raft perched at an angle on its head. In half a minute it faded into the gloom, and everything was quiet.

Hal and Robbie stared in stunned silence.

*Chapter Five*
## Startling news

Abigail came pounding along the jetty, her face white. "The sea serpent! That was the sea serpent!"

Robbie climbed to his feet. "No, really? What, that giant monster in the sea that nearly ate us alive just now? Never!"

"Are you okay, Hal?" Abigail said, ignoring Robbie and looking down at where Hal sat on the jetty. "You look like you're going to be sick."

Hal puffed out his cheeks and got up. "So now we know the sea serpent exists. I just can't believe it didn't eat us."

"What *happened* out there?" Abigail asked. "I couldn't see anything through the fog, but I heard shouts—and was that Robbie screaming like a girl?"

Robbie's face turned red. "I wasn't screaming, just yelling. Hal gave the serpent a whack on the chin, but then it snatched the shovel right out of his hands and crunched it up. So I got annoyed and threw mine at it. Caught it in the eye."

Hal glanced with surprise at his friend, and started to grin.

"Really?" Abigail said skeptically. "And it was so frightened that it decided to bring you back safe and sound?"

"That's what I can't figure out," Hal said. "Why'd it bring us back? You reckon it's some sort of guard, to keep us on the island?"

Abigail turned and gazed at him with an expression he couldn't fathom. "You could be right. And if that's true—why? Is it there for our protection, to keep us from sailing out into the fog and getting lost? Or do you think it's there to keep all of us prisoners?"

"Prisoners!" Robbie looked scornful. "What, our parents too?"

"It explains why they've never tried to leave," Abigail went on, staring out into the fog over the sea. "Yes, maybe we're all prisoners. It fits with another theory I have."

Robbie turned away, shaking his head. "You're crazy," he mumbled. "It's just some giant snake in the water that wasn't hungry. We got lucky."

"And that's why it brought you back to the jetty and took the raft away?" Abigail said. She clicked her tongue. "Come on, Robbie, I know there's a brain in there somewhere. Try using it for a change."

Hal shivered. His jeans were wet and cold, and standing around talking wasn't helping. "Let's go," he said. "Tell me this theory of yours, Abi."

"Don't listen to her," Robbie said. "She doesn't know anything."

However, Abigail looked pleased. "You really want to hear? Okay." She walked alongside Hal, leaving Robbie to tail behind. "We imagine Out There as some huge place full of thousands of people living in tall buildings, right? Like in the pictures we've seen. But the adults don't talk about it, and when they do, they mention stuff like crazy people living in ruins, as if there's nothing left anymore, just some dead place we couldn't ever live in. Well, maybe all that's a big lie to stop us wanting to go visit. And maybe the sea serpent is there in case we ever get it into our heads to try leaving the island."

"I still don't get it," Hal said. "If that's true, it doesn't explain *why* we're here. Why are the adults hiding on this island, cut off from the rest of the world? And why has no one from Out There ever come to visit?"

"Don't know, Hal," Abigail said with a shrug. "But it could be that the adults are not hiding *themselves*, but *us kids*. Maybe they don't want anyone to find us."

Robbie snorted from behind them. "That's nuts. What's so special about us?"

Hal stopped dead, and Robbie bumped into him. Standing in silence, Hal gazed at Abigail through narrowed eyes, a deep frown on his face.

"What's up, Hal?" she asked.

"Nothing," he said, his mind racing with visions of Robbie changing, growing stronger. Did that count as special?

Robbie was frowning too, as if he'd just realized what he'd said and made the same connection.

"I think we should stick together," Abigail said, breaking the silence, "and figure this out once and for all. Together we could—"

Robbie gave Hal a sharp nudge. "Here we go. All this talk of sticking together is just her way of getting to hang out with you, Hal." He brushed past her and climbed the stone steps to the road. "Let's go."

Abigail hung back with Hal. "Your pants are wet," she said with a hint of what sounded like smugness. "I think you were both more scared than you're admitting."

"We weren't—" Hal broke off and felt his face heat up. "Hey, we didn't *wet* ourselves, if that's what you mean. This is just seawater."

Abigail laughed. "It's okay. I won't tell anyone."

Hal fought an urge to argue. But of course she was just teasing him, getting him riled up as she usually did.

They climbed the stone steps. Robbie was already sitting on his bike, drumming his fingers on the handlebars. "Where's your bike?" he asked Abigail.

"Didn't bring it," she said. "I have other means of getting around."

Robbie rolled his eyes. "Like walking, you mean. You always have to make things out to be more than they are. Like a few weeks ago you said you were 'undergoing an important change' . . . all mysterious-like. Everyone was wondering about it. And the next day you came into school with a haircut."

"Do you like it?" Abigail said, pulling at the ponytail behind her head. "Mom said I should leave it long, but I told her to lop some off. It was interfering with my mode of transport."

"What?" Robbie exclaimed, throwing up his hands in exasperation. "I have *no idea* what you're talking about, and neither do you." He shook his head and prepared to pedal off. "Come on, Hal."

"Coming," Hal said. He climbed onto his bike and turned to Abigail, suddenly feeling awkward about riding off and leaving her behind. "Well, I guess we'll see you on Monday."

"Hey, good job with the raft," she said, smiling. "You know, you're quite brave for a short guy. Even if you did wet your pants."

Hal shrugged. "Well, when you've got to go, you've got to go."

Abigail beamed. "You have a sense of humor! Good for you."

With perfectly white even teeth, a smattering of freckles, and deep brown eyes, Hal thought she could be quite pretty sometimes. It was a shame she spoiled it by being so irritating.

As he spun his pedals and started to move off, Abigail's smile faded and she grabbed his arm. "Hal, wait."

Robbie groaned and hung his head. "Oh, come *on*."

But Hal paused, staring in surprise at the white fingers pressing into his arm just above the elbow. "I've gotta go," he mumbled.

Abigail only tightened her grip. "Hal, I still need to show you something. Something important."

Hal waited, eyebrows raised. Abigail remained staring at him intently, and he frowned. "So? Tell me."

She shot a look at Robbie. "Not here. Later. I'll stop by your house after dark. When everyone's asleep."

"More drama," Robbie murmured.

Abigail relaxed her grip on Hal's arm and stepped back. "Well, see you later then."

Robbie tore away, and Hal set off after him, his eyes fixed on the road. It was a steep incline and they pedaled in silence until they reached the top. Panting, they slowed to a cruise and rode side by side through the fog.

Then Hal's arm started itching again. It felt like someone had stuck pins into his skin, and he wobbled all over the road in his hurry to scratch at it.

"Look out!" Robbie yelled as their front wheels nearly touched.

Hal jammed on his brakes and yanked up the sleeve of his thick sweater. Then he froze, his eyes widening. Stretching from his elbow to his wrist was a rash of bumpy, mottled green skin the color of cucumber. He touched it and found it to be thick and tough.

Robbie had turned a large circle and was heading back. "What's wrong?"

"Nothing." Hal wrenched his sleeve back down, but then wondered why he was trying to hide the rash from his best friend. He swallowed. "Well, you know that itch on my arm?"

"You must have fleas," Robbie said with a grin.

"It's not fleas. Look." Hal rolled his sleeve up once more.

Robbie's grin faded and his face went white. He stared and stared, and then pointed at it. "That's not normal, man. What *is* that?"

"I don't know. It's been itching for maybe a week now, on and off. I didn't think much of it until we went to Black Woods the other day. Since then it's been much worse." Hal gazed at the rash, his heart thumping. "I keep checking, you know? To see if there's a rash or bite or something. But I've never seen anything until now."

Robbie was still staring. He backed off a little. "That's just weird. You need to go see Abi's mom."

Hal thought about the funny little doctor with her homemade foul-smelling potions. Dr. Porter worried a lot, and every so often got everyone together to give shots of something or other. But although the adults suffered from colds or other ailments from time to time, not one of the kids on the island had ever been sick. "Wonderful immune systems," Dr. Porter had always said with awe. "You kids are very lucky."

*Or special*, Hal thought.

He prodded the rash. It didn't hurt, but his skin felt taut as if he had gotten something sticky across his arm that had dried and hardened. Could it be gangrene? He'd read about gangrene in a book. Someone had been wounded and infection had set in, and the wound had turned a funny color and stunk. Hal sniffed his arm carefully, but could detect no odor. Still, the rash was an odd color, so maybe it was the *start* of an infection.

Only he hadn't been wounded, so that didn't make any sense.

"Has your mom got any itch stuff?" Robbie asked. "I'm always getting stung or bitten, so ages ago Mom got some itch stuff from Dr. Porter. It's like sludge, and it soothes the itching. You want to try some?"

"Sounds good to me," Hal agreed.

He stopped by Robbie's house on the way back and waited while his friend nipped inside to fetch the sludge. Robbie returned with a small jar containing a strange purple-colored substance.

"You can keep this," he said. "I scooped some out of the big jar we have. Hope it helps."

"Thanks. You doing anything tomorrow?"

Robbie rolled his eyes. "Got to clean up my room before I do anything else. I might just hang around the house and study."

Hal grinned. Robbie's idea of studying was poring over bug books. "See you Monday then," he said, and rode off.

When Hal arrived home and parked his bike outside, he caught the smell of something delicious cooking and hurried down the hallway, his stomach growling. The hall candles flickered as he passed through into the kitchen.

"Ah," his mom said. She was stirring a pot that hung over the fireplace. "The wanderer returns."

Hal caught his breath. "What? What do you mean? I haven't wandered anywhere. We just went down to the docks, that's all."

His mom raised an eyebrow and stared at him. "All right, don't be so defensive. I just meant that you and Robbie have been out a lot recently."

"Oh. Yeah. Been busy." Hal relaxed and stood by the crackling fire next to his mom. He liked the fireplace. Not only was food cooked over it, but it helped to heat the house and provided a nice, cozy flickering orange glow.

His mom dipped the ladle into the pot, withdrew steaming stew, and held it up for him. "Here, see what you think."

Hal cooled it by blowing and carefully sipped on the rich creamy brown gravy. "Mmm," he said, gripping his mom's wrist and tilting it so a small morsel of meat and onion tipped into his mouth.

"Good?" she said with a chuckle. "It's seagull with herbs and onions. We'll have it with fresh baked bread and potatoes in a little while, when your father gets home from the farm." She laughed. "Hal, you're licking your lips."

"I'm hungry. Haven't eaten since lunch."

The fire felt wonderful after the cold fog. Hal turned to dry the damp patch on his trousers as his mom busied herself putting bowls out on the table. On the counter opposite stood a fresh loaf of bread, probably baked that very afternoon at Mrs. O'Tanner's house. Darcy's mom had a specially-made brick oven behind the house, where she baked every couple of days for the island community.

Hal hoped his dad would get home soon so they could eat. All the men worked on the farm across the far side of the island, plowing fields, planting seeds, picking fruit and digging up vegetables, while caring for cows, goats and sheep.

"Hey, Mom?"

She rattled around in a drawer for the silverware. "Mmm?"

"If all the cows die, where will we get milk from?"

His mom stopped and turned, frowning. "The goats, I suppose," she said with a grimace. "Why? Are you expecting the cows to die?"

"No, but . . ."

"Don't worry, honey, we'll manage no matter what."

"But what about the goats?" Hal persisted. "What if they all die too, and the pigs and sheep and chickens? What then?"

She gave Hal a long, thoughtful look before answering. "I guess we'd live on seagulls, fish and vegetables," she said with a faint smile.

"What did you live on before you and Dad moved to the island?"

"Well, whatever we wanted, I guess. We bought it all from grocery stores."

"What's a grocery store?"

Hal's mom sighed. "A place where you buy food."

"What do you mean, 'buy food'?"

"Hal, stop asking questions. Make yourself useful and go and get a couple of candles out of the shed."

"But—"

Seeing his mom's raised eyebrow, Hal sighed and went out to the shed at the bottom of the garden. It was already getting dark, and after the warmth of the kitchen the fog felt colder than ever.

He poked around in the musty shed until he found the box of candles. There weren't many left, but Emily's mom probably had loads more. While Mrs. O'Tanner made bread for everyone, Mrs. Stanton made candles. Hal had watched her make them many times before; the farmers would bring along misshapen lumps of solidified oil they'd extracted from huge piles of heated soybeans, and she'd reheat the lumps and turn them into useable candles with wicks. Sometimes she added nice scents.

Hal's dad said the leftover dried-out soybeans were used as cow food. It seemed everything could be used for something on the island.

Stuffing four long candlesticks into his pocket, Hal stepped out of the shed, closed the door, and returned to the house.

In his room he studied the strange purple sludge Robbie had given him. Then he pushed up his sleeve. The rash was still there, unchanged since he'd last looked, but it didn't seem to be itching now. He applied a thin layer of cool sludge and wondered if he should mention the rash to his mom. But she'd send him straight to Dr. Porter, and Abigail would be there, hanging around and giggling while Hal was examined all over . . .

He shuddered and hoped the sludge would help clear up the problem.

His dad returned home an hour later. "Been planting onions and cloves," he said in a cheerful booming voice. "Every year I think it's not going to work, we're going to get a frost this winter . . . and it never happens. This fog never ceases to amaze me—keeps the winters mild and the summers comfortable. Come spring we'll have another good crop."

Dinner was served and the three of them dug in hungrily, with no sound but the crackling fire and the gentle clash of silverware on plates. It was a good ten minutes before Hal sighed and looked longingly at the remaining slice of bread in the basket. Could he manage another piece?

"So what have you been up to today, Hal?" his dad asked between mouthfuls.

The question seemed innocent, but Hal felt a surge of guilt. "Oh, nothing much. Went down to the docks." He liked to stick to the truth wherever he could, and simply leave out important details rather than lie.

"You didn't go in the water, did you?"

"No, too cold," Hal said. It was true—he *hadn't* gone in the water, just floated on the surface. "Hey, Dad?"

His mom rolled her eyes. "Watch out, George, he's asking a lot of questions tonight."

Hal ignored her. "Is there really a sea serpent?"

"Oh yes, of course," his dad said, nodding. He narrowed his eyes, swallowed a mouthful without chewing it up, and shot Hal a stern look. "So you'd better not be thinking of swimming out too far, or it'll eat you up in one bite. You know the rules, Hal. Stay near the pier."

Hal nodded, reaching for the bread even though he wasn't sure he wanted it. It was a way of diverting attention from his face, which had heated up. "Yeah, I know the rules. I was just curious. I mean . . . why is it there? Has it always been there?"

"What, the pier?"

"No, Dad—the sea serpent."

His mom pushed her plate back and spoke first. "To tell you the truth, Hal, it's a good thing the serpent is there. It protects us from the people on the mainland."

Hal hadn't thought of it that way. "So there are definitely still people Out There?" he asked.

His parents looked at one another in silence.

"If you can call them that," his mom said. She pulled at the scrunchy in her hair and shook her head so that her locks tumbled free around her shoulders. She seemed deep in thought. "Hal, you'll be thirteen this year. I understand that you're curious to know your origins . . . curious to learn about the big wide world. But *you* have to understand that you're here on this island because the alternative is too . . . too horrible to imagine. There's no life Out There for us."

Hal opened his mouth to ask another question, but his mom held up her hand. "No more, Hal. No more questions. I've said enough already."

*No you haven't*, Hal thought. But he sighed and slumped back in his chair.

"However . . ." his mom said quietly.

Another silence fell, and Hal frowned. Something was in the air. "Mom?"

"You don't want that bread, do you?" his dad asked, and plucked it off Hal's plate. He crammed it into his mouth and chewed with his mouth open and head down.

His wife shot him a look. Then she took a deep breath and turned back to Hal. "You'll have a visitor on Monday."

Hal frowned. "What do you mean?"

"A visitor. At school. Mrs. Hunter won't be in on Monday. Someone else will be there instead."

"Is Mrs. Hunter sick?"

"No, it's nothing like that."

More silence, apart from the sound of Hal's dad swallowing bread. He had crumbs in his beard. "So she's having a break?" Hal guessed. "Who's replacing her? Darcy's mom again?"

"No," his mom said. "This isn't anyone you know. It's someone else, a visitor. She'll be taking your class for a few days, talking to you all, getting to know you."

Bewildered, Hal glanced from his mom to his dad and back again. "Mom, who are you talking about?"

"A lady named Simone. She contacted us today and said it was time."

Hal tried to digest this impossible piece of news. *A lady named Simone.* His mouth worked up and down a few times, but no words came out.

After a while his mom smiled. "It's a shock, I know, meeting someone new. You never thought you'd see the day. But you'll like her. Simone is a very special lady, and she's coming to the school tomorrow to talk to you all . . . and to . . . well . . ." She trailed off, looking uncomfortable.

Hal stared in disbelief. "But Mom, you mean this person has come from Out There? But didn't you say everyone Out There was crazy or something? You just said so a minute ago! How can there be someone—"

"Simone's different," his mom explained, exchanging a glance with her husband, who was still chewing. "You'll like her."

Hal pushed his chair back with a scrape, got up, and paced the kitchen, trying to sort out his muddled thoughts. *A person he'd never met. A visitor. Coming to the island.* "But how is she getting here? By boat? But the sea serpent will get her!"

While his dad stared at his empty plate, his mom spoke in a slow monotone, as if reciting a memorized speech. "All will be explained, Hal. Just go to school on Monday as usual, and be polite to Simone. Don't pester her with questions. She'll tell you everything you need to know, when she's ready. Now, go find something to do." She stood and started clearing away the plates, then clicked her tongue at her husband. "And George, *please* brush those crumbs out of your beard. You look ridiculous."

Dazed, Hal trudged down the hall to his room. He wondered if Robbie had been told the news yet. He could nip over there and tell him, talk things over, but right now he just wanted to think. He sat on the edge of his bed to mull things over.

*A person he'd never met.*

Hal was so shocked by the news that he lay back on his bed and stared at the ceiling, with a candle flickering on his bedside table.

*Simone. A new person on the island. Someone from Out There.*

How did his parents know her? Why was she showing up now, after all this time? And what did his mom mean, 'it was time'? Time for *what?*

*Everything's gone crazy*, he thought. What with his rash, and Robbie's amazing feats of strength, and the fog-hole in the woods, and the red-faced creature, and the sea serpent, and now a strange woman named Simone showing up for class on Monday . . .

Hal grew sleepy. Eventually his eyes closed and he drifted off to sleep. At some point he became aware of his mom shaking him gently, telling him it was late and he should get out of his clothes and climb into bed, and he sleepily mumbled, "Sure, Mom." But the next thing he knew, he'd drifted back to sleep.

*Tap tap.*

The soft tapping on the window woke him, and he sat up. It was dark outside, and the candle on his bedside table had melted down halfway. For a moment Hal was confused. He was still fully clothed, lying on top of the bed—oh, yes, he'd fallen asleep, thinking of . . . *Simone!* Yes, he'd been going over everything his mom had told him about the new teacher—

*Tap tap.*

Hal sat up, blinking. Then he saw a pale face staring through the window at him and he almost fell off his bed in surprise.

It was Abigail, standing outside in the cold, her face pressed to the glass.

*Chapter Six*
## Abigail's secret

"**O**pen up," Abigail mouthed from outside the window, gesturing toward the latch. Behind her, the fog rolled in the darkness.

Hal opened the window and leaned out as an icy breeze pushed past him into his room. "What are you doing here?" he whispered. "It's late. And freezing."

Abigail frowned and rubbed her arms. She wore only a light red dress despite the thick cold fog. "I told you I was coming tonight to tell you something. Did you forget?"

"Oh," Hal mumbled. "Yeah. I've had a lot on my mind."

Abigail rolled her eyes. "Come out. Bring a lamp and meet me in your garage."

"But—"

Without another word, Abigail tiptoed off across the gravel driveway toward the squat brick building that stood alone at the front of the lawn, next to the road. She had no lantern so faded into the darkness almost immediately, lost against the black silhouette of the garage.

Hal closed his window with a sigh. He picked up the candle from the bedside table and crept to the door. Popping his head out into the hall, he found more darkness and silence. His mom and dad must already be in bed, which meant it was past midnight.

As he stood there, candle held high, he noticed with a shock that the back of his left hand was covered with the same dark green rash as his forearm. His mouth dropped open. Candle wavering, he pulled back his sleeve. The rash, or whatever it was, had spread fast and now encompassed his entire lower arm. It had crept up past his elbow and was almost to his shoulder. It didn't hurt, but it itched, and Robbie's sludge had done nothing to help.

His heart hammering, Hal knew he'd have to tell his mom about it in the morning—if he dared wait that long. He'd surely have to go see Dr. Porter, for this was no ordinary rash. It felt tough and smooth, and scaly in the center where it had started.

*One thing at a time.*

Steeling himself, he rolled his sleeve down and tiptoed along the hall past the living room, his candle flickering. He grabbed the lantern that stood by the door, lit it, and snuffed out the candle. With a stronger light to show the way, he slipped out the front door and closed it quietly behind him, then crunched up the gravel path to the garage.

He found the side door ajar, and a pitch-black room beyond. Hal stepped inside, and the light from his lantern picked out Abigail standing quiet and still in the center of the room, squinting at him. Wasn't she cold in nothing but a light dress? Where was her coat? And why didn't she have a lantern?

A smile tugged at the corners of her mouth. "Come in, sit down," she said, as if inviting him into her house. She waved him toward an upturned five-gallon drum. "There's a seat for you. I want to show you something."

Bewildered, Hal set the lantern on the floor and perched on the drum, which moved a couple of inches under him and made a horrendous scraping sound. He flinched, glancing toward the door. What would his dad say if he caught him out here in the dead of night?

And with a girl!

Abigail looked tired, but her eyes gleamed in the light. She stared at him, then her eyes dropped to his left hand. Too late Hal remembered the green rash, which stood out bright and obvious next to the lantern. Mortified, he stuck his hand behind his back.

But Abigail had already seen. "What's that green stuff?"

Hal racked his brains for some plausible explanation. Green paint? A grass stain? But it was no good; he'd have to tell her. She'd know soon enough in the morning anyway.

He held up his hand for her to see. "It's a rash or something. It's not poison ivy or any kind of insect bite I've ever known. Maybe it's an allergic reaction to something. I'm going to have to go see your mom in the morning, get some kind of treatment."

He waited for the teasing to start. This was the sort of thing Abigail loved. She'd probably taunt him all night long and for days to come.

Instead she nodded with interest, a serious expression on her face. "I've noticed you've been scratching your arm at school, and now I know why. That's how mine started."

Hal blinked. "You mean . . . you have a rash too?"

"Not anymore. And it wasn't all green like that, either. Mine just itched. That's sort of what I'm going to show you. Are you ready?"

"Uh, sure."

Abigail swallowed. "All right then. Promise you won't go screaming from the garage in a panic and wake your parents?"

Hal nodded, an uneasy feeling settling in.

Abigail turned around. Her red dress was ripped high up between the shoulder blades, a ragged, vertical slash roughly eight inches long, dead center. Her ponytail hung almost low enough to cover it, but not quite. "Are you ready?" Abigail asked again over her shoulder. She sounded nervous.

"I guess."

Abigail stretched her arms wide. In the glow of the lantern she looked eerie, standing there with her back to him, feet together and arms out straight.

The rip in her dress parted and folded back as two giant insect-like wings erupted straight out of her back.

Hal heard himself whimper as the paper-thin translucent appendages spread outwards, buzzing with a vibrant energy. They grew to three and a half feet in length, stretching thinner and thinner. The light from the lantern picked out a network of fine, barely-perceptible veins and capillaries.

Hal watched, stunned, as Abigail turned and smiled at him. Her wings buzzed and became a blur. Then she rose off the floor.

She hovered, bobbing up and down. The constant, heavy buzz reminded Hal of a hummingbird. Abigail turned a full circle, then glanced upwards and frowned. The ceiling was pitched, but the rafters hung low. She dropped lightly to the floor and her wings became still.

"My wings are very delicate," she explained, gesturing toward the rafters. "Better not fly around too much in here."

Hal just stared at her, his mouth hanging open.

Abigail turned around and demonstrated how the wings could shrink and vanish back through the tear in her dress. They sank into her flesh as though her skin was liquid. In the next second they were gone, leaving smooth unblemished skin just visible through the hole in her dress.

"Like magic," she said, turning to face him once more. "But I never quite know when I'm going to use them, so I've had to make holes in a lot of my clothes for my wings to poke through and spread out. And just so no one asks me why I have a hole in the back of my dress, I wear a sweater or coat over the top, which I can take off and carry while I'm flying. I've even had to start washing my own clothes at home, so Mom doesn't catch on." Abigail giggled. "She loves that; thinks I'm becoming a responsible young lady."

Hal stared and stared, still unable to say anything. When he looked down at Abigail's thin red dress, she hugged herself and knelt on the floor, suddenly red-faced. "Brr, it's cold," she mumbled. "Carrying a coat is a nuisance, so I didn't bring one tonight. Thing is, I don't really feel the cold while I'm flying. It's like I'm different, somehow; warmer on the inside, you know?"

Hal didn't know.

"I can see better too," Abigail went on. "When I grow my wings, it's like my vision brightens. All the darkness outside becomes a little less dark and I can see things, like trees and bushes, as if they're lit up by a flashlight that I don't have."

There was a long pause. "Okay," Abigail said finally. "So that's my secret. Now . . . what's yours, Hal?"

"W-w-what?" Hal sputtered. "I don't have one."

"Of course you do. You have green, scaly skin. That means you're turning into something. Now come on, show me what you are."

Hal stared at the back of his hand. "I don't know what . . . It's just a rash."

"It's not just a rash," Abigail insisted. "It's *skin*. The scaly skin of whatever creature you're becoming."

"What?"

Abigail laughed. "Don't worry. If your magic is anything like mine, you can change at will." She pursed her lips and stared at him. "But maybe you don't know what you are yet. My wings didn't happen overnight either. They started out as an itch on my back, and I kept straining to see in the mirror. Then one morning I woke to find I had a couple of red sores. I wanted to tell Mom straight away, but she'd gone out early that morning. Then the sores . . . well, they sort of burst open, and there they were—two wings. They were small and folded at first, drooping and oozing some sort of slimy stuff, but they were definitely wings."

Hal was horrified. "What did you do?"

"I panicked. I ran around the house screaming, with these awful wet things flapping around on my back. Good thing Mom was out, actually. But after a while I calmed down and just stared at them in the mirror for ages and ages. Got a stiff neck with all that twisting around. After a while they sort of dried out and stiffened, and looked like proper wings."

She shrugged. "Anyway, somehow I knew they were supposed to be there— part of me, you know? I realized this was part of the secret. Why we're here on the island." She leaned forward and stared at Hal with big brown eyes. "Hal, don't you get it? We're freaks."

Hal caught his breath. "Don't say that. *You* may be, but I'm not." He glared at the back of his left hand. "This is just some stupid rash, that's all."

Abigail laughed, shaking her head. "Who are you trying to convince, Hal? Look, face it—all of us kids are part of some experiment. You saw Mrs. Hunter's reaction when she inspected Fenton's toothache? He's starting to change too. And what about Lauren? Don't tell me you haven't seen her trying to scratch *her* back all the time? I think she must be growing wings too, and I once saw her fingers stretch and grow hair as she tried to reach that itch. And then there's Emily's neck . . ."

Abigail trailed off, spreading her hands. She looked imploringly at Hal as if seeking his agreement.

*And Robbie*, Hal thought. *Robbie's amazing strength, and his tattered shirt . . .*

48

But the idea of becoming something else, something inhuman, terrified him—and if he accepted that the others were changing, he'd have to accept that *he* was too. "No way," he said, shaking his head. "Fenton's got a toothache, that's all. Lauren's probably got poison ivy or something. And you reckon Emily's neck got *longer* one day? You're nuts, Abigail!"

"Am I? You've seen my wings, Hal. How do you explain that?"

"I can't. But not everyone is a freak just because *you* are. You don't want to be the only one, so you're seeing things that aren't really happening. But I'm not a freak, Abi, and neither are Fenton, Lauren or Emily."

*Robbie is though*, the voice in Hal's head told him.

Abigail leaned forward and stared intently at him, her words flowing fast and smooth as if she'd run over the same things in her mind a million times before. "When Fenton got his toothache and skipped class, he went to see my mom. He was gone by the time I got home, but Mom was all agitated and excited about something. She wouldn't say what. She dug around in a drawer and found an old hollowed-out tusk or horn. Then she went out. She was gone a long time. And tonight she told me a stranger is arriving at school on Monday. I think Mom went to see this stranger, to tell her about Fenton's toothache."

Hal shook his head continuously, mumbling that he didn't care.

Abigail pressed on. "I bet this visitor that's arriving on Monday, this Simone person—I bet she's a scientist or something, a doctor like my mom, and she's going to run all kinds of weird tests on us. I've got it all figured out. The adults keep telling us the world is ruined and we're all that's left . . . but I think we've just been hidden away on some remote island as an experiment. I know how doctors think. If they're anything like my mom, we're just curiosities to them. Remember how Mrs. Hunter made us cut open those frogs once? So we could see inside? Well, we're like those frogs. We've been changed somehow, and now Simone's going to poke and prod us, and stick needles in us, and—"

"Shut up!" Hal yelled, jumping to his feet.

Abigail drew back in alarm. "Shh. You'll wake your parents."

Hal pointed a finger at her, backing toward the door. "Just go, Abigail. I don't know what's wrong with you, but there's nothing wrong with me. Just get lost."

Abigail sighed. "Look, we should stick together. We're both monsters and we should stick together and make sure—"

Hal lashed out with his foot and kicked the plastic drum hard across the floor. It bounced off the wall. "No! It's not true! I just have a rash, that's all. Your mom's probably got something for it, and I'll go see her in the morning and—"

Abigail jumped to her feet and advanced on him. "No, Hal, don't. If you tell my mom, she'll tell Simone. You can't be cured. Neither can I, nor Fenton, nor any of the others when they start to change. *This is who we are.*"

"This is who *you* are," Hal snapped, backing away. "Get away from me!"

Abigail spread her hands. "Hal—"

"Go home!"

"Hal, don't tell my mom about this, or your parents. Don't tell anyone. They're waiting for us to change. That's why Simone's been called in, to see if we're turning into freaky monster things yet. She *knows* we're changing. She's been expecting it. Let's keep quiet until we know what's going on. Otherwise we'll be sent away to some laboratory where—"

"Get out of here!" Hal said, and instead rushed for the door himself. He yanked it open and stumbled out into the darkness, running across the lawn. Tears formed in his eyes and, ashamed, he brushed them away. He ran around the side of the house, clambered over the fence at the foot of the garden, and stumbled out into the field beyond.

He ran and ran, gasping for breath, tripping in the long grass and climbing back to his feet to carry on. He scrubbed hard at the rash on the back of his hand. "Go away, go away, go away!"

Finally Hal stopped and bent over, hands on knees, panting. His hot breath plumed in the air as he fought to regain his composure. In the end he flopped down into the grass and lay on his back, watching the fog drift by, staring at the hazy bright patch where the moon was. An owl hooted somewhere.

*I'm not a freak*, he thought obstinately.

The dew in the grass began to soak into his clothing, and he sat up. Weary, he started to climb to his feet—and his mouth dropped open. He stared at his hands, first his left, then his right, turning them over and over.

The rash was gone.

*Like magic. Now you see it, now you don't.*

The moonlight was weak, but just bright enough for Hal to stare in amazement and relief at his rash-free hand. He studied his milky-white skin for a long while, then sighed and rubbed his eyes, exhausted.

He thought about Abigail. She'd called him a freak, but he *wasn't* a freak!

*Lizard-boy*, the voice in his head mocked. *Abigail's got wings and can fly, Robbie's got enormous strength, and what has little Hal got? Lizard skin!*

Hal got to his feet and trudged home. The side door to the garage was closed. He cracked it open and peered inside.

The lantern remained where he'd left it, glowing from the center of the floor. But the room was empty. Hal closed the door and stared out into the fog. Should he go after her? A crazy image of her buzzing through the air like a dragonfly sprung to mind.

Shaking his head, Hal picked up the lamp, snuck back into the house, climbed out of his clothes, crawled into bed, and eventually fell asleep.

He woke late the next morning. "I thought you were going to sleep the whole day," his mom said as he wandered into the kitchen and started to make himself an omelet. "Are you all right? You look tired. Here, let me make that before you burn yourself."

Soon after breakfast, Hal zipped along the road to Robbie's house and rapped on the door. Mrs. Strickland answered. She was a large woman, bigger than her husband and son put together. "Morning, Hal. Sorry, but Robbie's tidying his room this morning. No distractions until he's done. You can come back this afternoon, if you like."

Hal nodded. "I might. I was just wondering if . . . if he's heard the news."

"Simone, you mean?" Mrs. Strickland nodded. "Yes. Simone made it clear that everyone be told at once, so you kids can be prepared to meet her on Monday." She frowned and stepped out onto the doorstep, pulling the door closed behind her. "Hal, have you noticed anything strange about Robbie lately?" she asked, lowering her voice.

"Uh," Hal said, suddenly feeling awkward. "Strange? How do you mean?"

"Oh, I don't know, anything at all. You're his best friend, Hal. If anyone's noticed anything strange, it would be you."

*Don't tell anyone.* Abigail's warning rang in his mind and he hesitated for a moment.

"Robbie's always strange," he said at last. "He studies bugs and plants. It would be strange if he stopped acting strange."

"Hmm," Mrs. Strickland said, not looking convinced.

Hal turned to leave. "I've got to go. Tell him I'll see him tomorrow."

He headed home, glancing along the road as he crossed to the other side. As usual the thick, musty fog prevented him from seeing much farther than a few houses, from which faint orange glows flickered in living rooms and kitchens.

To his surprise, he spotted Fenton standing on the bridge.

The big boy had drawn water from the stream using the winch, and a bucket stood at his feet, but Fenton was now leaning against the stone wall and staring out over the stream, apparently lost in thought.

As Hal watched from the middle of the road, Fenton did something strange. He leaned out farther and pursed his lips. Then a spout of water arced from his mouth, smooth and clear as if from a watering can. It didn't last long, no more than a second, and then Fenton relaxed and eased back from the wall. *Seeing how far he can spit*, Hal thought—only the bully had spat far more water than seemed possible.

To Hal's astonishment, Fenton leaned out again, and another jet of clear water gushed forth, exactly as before, even though he hadn't taken a swig from any bottle that Hal could see.

Stunned, Hal stood in the middle of the road and watched as Fenton spat water two more times without once drinking from a bottle, or even the bucket, to fill his chubby cheeks. Where was it all coming from?

Then Fenton's head whipped around to face Hal. The big boy strode toward him with a scowl plastered across his face.

Rooted to the spot, Hal was expecting a beating for somehow getting Fenton in trouble at school—or was it Robbie that would get the beating? In any case, Hal was far too curious about Fenton's water-spitting trick to turn and head for the safety of home. So he waited, wondering if anyone was looking out the windows of the nearby houses.

"Hey, squirt," Fenton said as he approached. "What are you staring at?"

"I'm not sure," Hal murmured. "It's not labeled."

Fenton stopped a few inches from Hal's face and breathed his bad breath all over him. "I owe you a pounding, squirt. Or shall I give it to Robbie? I'll let you decide, right here and now."

A large fist appeared next to Hal's left eyeball.

"How did you *do* that?" Hal asked, trying to ignore the threat. "That's a neat trick, spitting water like that. How'd you do it?"

Fenton glowered, and his face reddened. "Spying on me now? That's worth an extra few punches. So who's gonna get it—you or Robbie?"

Then Hal frowned. For a second he thought he'd seen—but no, it couldn't be. "How's your toothache?"

Two large hands grabbed the front of Hal's shirt and yanked upwards. Hal stood on tiptoes, feeling his shirt riding up and exposing his midriff to the cold air. A button popped off.

"Quit stalling, stumpy. You answer my question right now or I'll go ahead and give both of you a beating. Now, who's it gonna be?"

Hal couldn't help but notice that the big boy's teeth had taken on a strange animal-like quality, with sharpened incisors and fang-like canines. They weren't particularly long, just a different shape, but easy to spot at this range, especially when Fenton bared them like a dog.

And as he stood there snarling, his eyes seemed to take on a reddish glow. Clear water suddenly dribbled from the corners of Fenton's mouth and ran down his chin, like he'd sprung a leak.

With a gasp, Hal fought to free himself and found Fenton's grip to be like stone. The bully had the strength of ten men. *Like Robbie*, Hal thought. *Robbie gets strong too, only he doesn't dribble everywhere, or have glowing red eyes.*

"Let go!" Hal yelled. "Get off me!"

"You gonna make me?"

Hal's skin started to crawl and itch, and his throat burned. He felt something stirring deep inside his chest, as if something dormant was awakening, disturbed by the scuffle. If it was possible to take a large magical dose of strength and courage, this was what it would feel like. He recognized the same feeling he'd experienced on the raft when he'd stood up to the serpent, as though he could take on anything regardless of size.

Fenton suddenly frowned, looked him up and down, and released his hold. He took a few steps backward and stared down at his wet shirt, where he'd dribbled all over it. The fiery glare had gone, and now he appeared confused. "What— what's happening to me?"

The powerful feeling within Hal's chest dwindled in an instant, and he suddenly felt drained. He ran a hand through his hair. "Fenton, we should talk. Abi told me stuff last night, and showed me something you wouldn't believe. I didn't believe everything she said until now. We need to—"

"Abi told you stuff?" Fenton said, his voice dripping with scorn. "Been filling your head with trash, has she? And you want me to *listen* to it? You think I'm dumb?"

*Pretty dumb, yeah*, Hal thought.

He must have looked like he was thinking such a thing because Fenton gave him a shove in the chest that sent him reeling. "Right, since you never answered my question, both you and Robbie get it. Watch your backs, because you're gonna get it when you're least expecting it."

With a sudden, eerie grin filled with pointed teeth, Fenton turned and stomped away. He fetched his bucket of water from the side of the bridge and disappeared into the fog.

*Chapter Seven*
## The visitor

T he sun threw a hazy glow through the fog on Monday morning as Hal wolfed down his breakfast and hurried out to his bike, his backpack heavy with books and lunch. "What books should I take?" he'd asked his mom as he dashed around. "What will Simone be teaching this morning?"

"That's *Miss* Simone to you, young man," his mom had said, waggling a finger at him. "And if I were you, I'd take *all* your books, just in case."

So off he went, weighed down by the extra load. He was early, but so were others in the class judging by how many fresh wheel marks sliced through the dirt trail leading to school. Tingling with excitement, Hal almost forgot Fenton's threat the previous day. But he couldn't forget the bully's bizarre spitting trick; that was something he'd have to relate to Abigail and Robbie the first chance he got. That is, if Abigail would talk to him after the way he had shouted at her last night.

With the cool, fresh air in his nostrils, Hal cycled at top speed along the trail and up the rise to the top. When he sailed over the crest and started down the other side, the school building came into sight, for once looking bright and cheerful in the sunny haze. Even the peak of the tower was fully visible today, a rare occurrence. Across the meadow the fog hung in patches against a backdrop of pure white sky.

Despite the lightness of the fog, that morning Hal's dad had stood outside with a frown on his face, sniffing the air. "Storm's coming," he'd said, nodding. "It'll hit us by nightfall."

He'd seemed so sure that Hal had no doubt it was so. Still, it hardly seemed possible that such bright weather could turn bad.

Hal inserted his front wheel into the rack alongside the other bikes—seven of them, meaning Abigail had brought hers too—and paused a moment at the door that led into the back of the classroom. He peered through the small glass pane.

Fenton threw a balled up piece of paper at Dewey. It bounced off his face and he jumped in surprise as Fenton burst into laughter. Emily, on her feet, was waving her arms excitedly as she talked to Lauren and Darcy, while Robbie eavesdropped from his desk by the window on the far side. Hal took one look at Robbie's face and chuckled; Robbie wasn't interested in the conversation—he was watching Lauren with a faraway look on his face.

Abigail sat at her desk directly behind Robbie, staring out the window on the far side. It seemed everyone was a few minutes earlier than normal this morning, and Hal, despite his haste to get there, was the last to arrive. Miss Simone had not yet shown up.

He threw open the door and strolled in. The instant Emily saw him she abandoned whatever story she was telling. "Hal! Have you heard the news? We have a new teacher this morning!"

Hal nodded and turned to Lauren. "So what's the deal, Lauren? Isn't your mom going to be teaching us anymore? She must have told you something about this Miss Simone person."

Lauren shook her head. "I don't know much more than anyone else," she said quietly, "except that Mom said she doesn't know how things will go from here on. Apparently it's up to Miss Simone."

Everyone was silent. Then Emily frowned and glanced out the window as if to check that it was safe to talk. "I think we should investigate this," she said. "I think we should form a club or something, and make plans to find out what's going on around here."

Robbie snorted a laugh. "Form a club? Make plans? And I suppose you'll be in charge, bossing everyone around as usual, *organizing* things."

Emily's face reddened and she drew herself up. "I'm a *good* organizer, and you know it. I organize most things, don't I? Games, hikes, even class field trips! I'm the best person suited for—"

"Can it, Emily," Fenton retorted. "And you, Robbie, you skinny moron. Don't forget what I told you. You're gonna get it."

"Is your toothache better, Fenton?" Abigail said, turning to him and smiling. "Shame. I liked it when you were quiet, especially when you went home early."

Fenton reddened and he scowled. "Watch it, freckle-face."

Abigail feigned a look of horror. "Fenton Bridges! Ooh, what you said!" She rolled her eyes. "My mom said you cried like a girl when you went to see her with your toothache. 'Oh, they hurt soooo much!' you whined. Mom said you nearly fainted."

"Liar!" Fenton shouted, kicking a nearby chair. He was trembling with rage. He started toward her. "If you weren't a girl, I'd punch your face in *right now*. But I'll still get you, girl or no girl. You wait—"

Hal stepped in front of Fenton, blocking the way. For a second it seemed nobody breathed, although Hal was sure the thumping of his heart was booming around the walls. "Leave her alone," he said evenly. "If you want to hit someone, hit me instead. See what you get."

Fenton's mouth worked up and down but no words came out. His face turned a curious shade of purple and a vein in his forehead started throbbing. He seemed to be boiling up inside, like a volcano about to blow its top. At last he erupted and let loose with a torrent of bellowed curses. Everyone flinched, but Hal got the brunt of it as Fenton advanced on him until their faces were mere inches apart.

Hal stood his ground and allowed the fury to ride over him like a blast of strong wind. A few days ago he never would have blocked Fenton's way, certainly not for Abigail. But things had changed. *He'd* changed, at least on the inside. He'd felt something stirring from deep within when he'd stood up to Fenton by the bridge yesterday, and had felt the same stirring on the raft when facing the serpent. Something was *in* him, something strong and powerful, and it seemed ready to emerge only when he faced danger.

Now he wondered if it would happen again.

Fenton finally ended his tirade and stood panting and trembling, his face twisted with rage. "And you're gonna get twice as much—no, *three* times as much of a beating as Robbie. You just wait."

"I'll wait," Hal said, nodding. "Whenever you're ready, bring it on."

Fenton turned, lashed out at Hal's chair, sent it flying, and stomped back to his desk.

Hal picked up his chair and sat down, trying to act nonchalant. But his heart was still thumping hard and he felt quite shaky. Hopefully no one would notice if he sat for a moment and waited for his nerves to settle.

"Well," Emily said in a small voice, "anyway, where were we? Oh yes, we were talking about starting a club."

"*You* were," Robbie mumbled.

"Maybe we'll find out everything we want to know when Miss Simone arrives," Darcy said, playing with her wavy blond locks. "Maybe that's why she's here—to tell us why we live on this dismal island, cut off from the rest of the world. Maybe she'll explain what happened to Mr. and Mrs. Patten when little Thomas was killed six years ago."

"Let's hope we get some answers," Lauren said. "We're nearly in our teens now. I think we have a right to know the truth!"

Everyone nodded and murmured agreement. Dewey Morgan, quiet as a mouse as usual, tapped his pencil on his desk as a somber silence fell across the room once more. After a moment, Dewey realized his tapping sounded very loud, and he stopped.

"Tell them what you and Robbie did on Saturday," Abigail said, looking at Hal. She had that teasing twinkle back in her eye.

At once everyone glanced at Hal, then at Robbie. "What?" Emily demanded. "What did you do? Tell us!"

Hal caught Robbie's eye and threw him a questioning look that said, *Do you want to tell them, or shall I?*

Robbie cleared his throat and launched into the tale with gusto, explaining how he and Hal had built a raft and set out across the water into the fog. There were many gasps at this, and even Fenton stopped sulking when Robbie started embellishing the story a little. "So there we were, being pounded by waves, seawater spraying in our faces, and clinging on for dear life to our raft. We rowed as hard as we could, but the current took us miles away from the island. We thought we were going to get flipped over."

Dewey, Emily, Darcy and Lauren had sidled closer, edging between the desks, eyes wide. "Then what?" Lauren asked, wringing her hands.

As Robbie went on to tell of the huge slithery body below the surface, Hal glanced at Abigail. She was listening to Robbie's tale with the faintest of smiles. Every now and then she'd shake her head.

". . . And I whacked it with my shovel," Robbie said, standing up and swinging his arms dramatically. "Blood sprayed from a gash in its chin, all over me, but I didn't care—all I could think about was saving Hal and me, and the raft. But then the monster sank below the surface, and guess what? It started to carry us across the water . . ."

Just then Dewey whispered, "Someone's coming!"

Emily interrupted Robbie and changed the subject. ". . .Yes, so it would be nice to have bacon for a change, but I'd hate to think of those poor pigs being slaughtered . . ."

The door at the front of the class was thrown open and a woman stood framed in the doorway. She had shiny golden hair and was wrapped in a flowing cloak of dark green silky material that came down low enough to drape on the floor. Her eyes were a startling blue, and her skin a golden tan just like the sunbathers Hal had seen in his dad's treasured collection of postcards from Out There.

Hal gasped. Had the room brightened suddenly?

"Good morning, children!" the stranger said in a high, clear voice. Hal couldn't tell how old she was—clearly an adult, but much younger than his parents. "My name is Simone. It's a pleasure to meet you all."

She walked to the desk at the front of the class, her feet making no sound beneath the robe. "Those of you still standing, please take your seats and we'll get started."

Darcy and Lauren returned to their seats, and Emily turned to face front.

Miss Simone looked around and nodded. "Good. You're all here." Her gaze fell on the ninth desk, where Thomas Patten had once sat, but her blank expression gave nothing away.

She seemed to glide across to the coat stand in the corner. There she untied the sash around her throat, swept off her dark green silky cloak, and hung it carefully on a hook. Hal was captivated by the strange, knee-length dress she wore beneath; a patchwork of green and gray cloth woven together and embellished with hundreds of tiny pearls. The dress pinched in snug around her waist and hung in petal-shaped segments around her legs. Without her long cloak, Hal could see that her feet were bare.

Hal wasn't sure if it was the dress, or her golden hair tumbling around her shoulders, or her startling blue eyes that he found so entrancing. He glanced around and noted that Robbie, Dewey and Fenton were watching the newcomer with wide eyes. He couldn't see the expressions of the girls in the front row, but Abigail was frowning, her bottom lip stuck out. Was she envious? Suspicious?

"Now," Miss Simone said as she took her seat, "we'll start by introducing ourselves. Perhaps you could give me your names in turn. You start, my dear."

Emily beamed, obviously delighted at being chosen to start. She cleared her throat. "Emily Stanton, Miss. It's a pleasure to meet you."

Miss Simone smiled and nodded, then shifted her gaze to the girl in the middle, who said in a small voice, "Lauren Hunter."

"Darcy O'Tanner," said the next.

Then onto the second row. "Er, Robbie Strickland."

Miss Simone's gaze came to rest on Hal. "H-Hal Franklin," he said, and mentally kicked himself for stuttering.

"Fenton Bridges," came the bully's defiant tone, almost as though he was sizing up the newcomer and wondering how far he could push her. But Miss Simone moved on without pause to Abigail.

"Abigail Porter," she said in a monotone.

And, finally, "Dewey Morgan," the small boy behind Hal said.

Miss Simone smiled and nodded. "Thank you. I shall try hard to remember which name goes with which face." She took a breath. "I know all your parents, of course—met them a long time ago, before you were born. Abigail, I was sorry to hear about your father."

Hal froze, and he sensed that all his classmates had frozen too. No one *ever* talked about Abigail's dad. It was one thing to mention Thomas Patten and his parents because they'd all vanished without a trace, but Mr. Porter had left behind a distraught wife and a daughter he'd never had a chance to meet.

"You should all be very proud of your parents," Miss Simone went on, apparently not sensing that she had touched on a taboo subject. "They're very resourceful. It hasn't been easy adapting to life on this island without the amenities they'd grown accustomed to in the old world."

"Amenities?" Dewey asked. Hal guessed he was more puzzled by the word itself than by which particular amenities Miss Simone was referring to.

Miss Simone nodded and smiled. "Running tap water. Motorized vehicles for transport. Electricity."

Hal had heard that last word many times before. His parents had mentioned it in the past, but he had never quite fathomed exactly what it was. It had something to do with wires. "What exactly is electricity?" he asked.

"Think of it as a life force," the visitor said softly. "In the old world, it provided life to machines. Your parents used to have all sorts of machines around the house—such things as cookers, refrigerators, microwave ovens, televisions, music systems . . . the list is endless."

She paused. The only sound was Dewey gently tapping his pencil on the desk.

"Sadly, since the demise of the old world and their seclusion on this island, your parents have had to do without electricity. This has necessitated an enormous shift in their lifestyle, because of course the old world had enjoyed the power of electricity for a hundred years or so."

"What *happened* Out There?" Emily asked.

Miss Simone shook her head and rested her elbows on the desk. "A catastrophe. *A deadly virus created by man.* Most people died, and those that survived . . . well, they're sick in other ways."

"A virus!" Lauren said with a gasp.

"Created by a man?" Darcy added. "Which man?"

Miss Simone's chair scraped as she stood and began pacing around the perimeter of the classroom, her bare feet making no sound. Heads twisted to follow her. "Not a single man," she said. "I meant mankind itself, although nobody has admitted to it. Probably terrorists who allowed things to get wildly out of control. Governments across the world organized shelters for the rich and important people to escape the airborne virus, while millions of ordinary citizens had to survive alone. There was no known cure, and most succumbed to the deadly virus within an hour of contracting it. Those that hadn't yet caught it attempted to flee cities and make for the country and the mountains, so as you can imagine there were mass evacuations as people literally ran for their lives."

Hal couldn't imagine any such thing. He'd only ever known a select handful of people, and the idea of millions of people was beyond him, despite numerous pictures he'd seen while growing up.

Miss Simone stopped at the rear of the room. "The mainland is very close, and there stands a large city, what's left of it. It too was evacuated, but not before many, many people died. There were also those who were infected but didn't die; instead they were disfigured, terribly scarred. They must have suffered intense pain and discomfort—probably still do, if any are left alive."

Hal found Abigail staring at him, and he stared back.

The strange woman turned to gaze out of a window. "Your parents were among a handful that escaped the virus completely, and that's because my own people had already selected them and made arrangements to protect them before the virus spread. We hid them away here, on the island, while the world fell apart. We made the air safe."

Hal opened his mouth to ask what she meant about making the air safe when Emily broke in. "Your people had already *selected* them? What do you mean? Selected them for what?"

"And who *are* your people?" Robbie asked.

Miss Simone continued to stare out the window. "My people live in a secret place that the virus can't reach. But we have problems of our own to deal with, although not on the same scale. I won't go into that now, except to say that a solution to our problem meant our people working with a handful of yours. We had already chosen ten childless couples in your world and were in the process of beginning the project when the virus struck—and our plans were hurried along. Unfortunately the virus put us all in a difficult position, and again I won't go into that right now."

"Ten childless couples?" Emily said, repeating the stranger's words.

"Your parents," Miss Simone said, glancing at her. "They were childless when I first met them fourteen years ago, and still childless when I moved them here to the island a year later." She frowned. "But I don't want to go into all that right now—"

"But *ten* couples?" Emily persisted. "There were only ever nine here. Eight now that Thomas has gone."

"Yes, a shame about the Pattens," said the visitor, nodding. "And the other couple, the tenth—they dropped out very early on, before you were even born."

"Why?" Emily asked.

Miss Simone sighed. "Another time, Emily. What's important, children, is that you are here on this island for a very good reason, and I believe we are going to be seeing some important developments over the next few days. And for that I need your cooperation."

Not a word escaped the lips of any of the children. It seemed everyone had stopped breathing.

Miss Simone smiled and clapped her hands together. "Now, I'm going to speak to each and every one of you in turn, privately, and while I'm doing that the rest of you can be getting on with some class work. I'd like you to write a short story about a boy or girl that has magical powers. That should keep you busy."

Silence.

Miss Simone frowned. "So please get out your pencils and paper."

In slow motion, everyone reached for their bags and backpacks and started delving for pencils, pens and pads of paper.

"Miss Simone?" Abigail asked. Hal glanced at her, noting that she had a challenging expression on her face that he recognized only too well.

"Yes, what is it, dear?"

"I just want to know something: How come the virus is still Out There? I mean, after twelve or thirteen years or whatever . . . it just seems like a long time for a virus to be around. And if it's airborne, well, how come we've never caught it? You said the mainland is fairly close."

There was a long silence before Miss Simone replied. "The virus carries easily through the air. Most viruses die within hours if no host is found, but this one is different. It somehow survives, floating on a breeze, sometimes settling like dust, then blowing into the air again—tiny dormant spores that drift around the world, waiting patiently for new human hosts."

Miss Simone turned to stare out the window once more. "It's all around us. But the fog that you see outside is like a protective blanket across the island. It filters the air and destroys any virus that blows this way."

Everyone turned in unison to gaze out the window. The fog drifted in patches across the grass, letting hazy rays of sunlight shine through in places. So the fog was what kept them all alive? Hal shuddered at the thought of what damage he and Robbie might have caused had they managed to block the fog-hole. Now everything made sense—the serpent blocking their route to the mainland, the red-faced monster guarding the fog-hole . . .

Except one small detail didn't fit: Why had the red-faced monster seemed confused as to where he was, and how he had got there?

"So the virus is still in the air?" Abigail asked with narrowed eyes. "How come you seem to have avoided it when so many have died?"

Miss Simone threw her a glare. "Abigail Porter," she murmured. "Your mother's a doctor. I can see where you get your scientific curiosity. It's a shame your father didn't listen to her."

Everyone stiffened once more at the mention of Abigail's dad. Hal studied her face closely and saw her jaws clench and her nostrils flare. Her hands, placed in front of her across the desk, slowly balled into fists.

Miss Simone came to stand by Abigail's desk. "I don't know what Dr. Porter told you of your father, Abigail, but you should know that he didn't cope very well with life on the island. Right from the outset he pushed for others to go with him back to the mainland, to see if the virus had gone, just as you're suggesting now. In the end, Mr. Franklin and Mr. Bridges went with him, wearing special protective suits and breathing masks."

Hal jumped at the sound of his name, and glanced across at Fenton. Fenton stared back for a moment, then looked away.

Hal tried to imagine the three adults wearing strange suits and masks and venturing out across the water, through the fog. How had they traveled? By boat? Raft?

"The virus didn't get your father, Abigail," Miss Simone said, staring down at her. "But the survivors did. When people are reduced to scavenging like animals, with dead bodies all over the place, some of them their own loved ones . . . the last thing they want to see is a group of what look like *scientists* wandering around studying their handiwork. So naturally the survivors attacked them. Viciously. Mr. Franklin and Mr. Bridges were lucky to escape alive."

As she wandered back to the front of the class, Abigail stared open-mouthed after her. Tears formed in her eyes.

"Let's take a break," Miss Simone said quietly. "Go outside and talk amongst yourselves for ten minutes. Get some fresh air. This is a lot to take in, and I want to make sure you digest everything I've told you before moving on."

After a pause, chairs started to scrape as the classmates got to their feet and filed from the room.

"This is horrible," Darcy whispered.

"At least we're safe here," Emily replied with a shudder. "As long as this fog lasts, we'll be fine."

Hal found Robbie and pulled him aside. "The fog-hole," he said quietly. "If this fog is supposed to make the air safe, well, we might have got everyone killed if we'd blocked that hole up!"

"Yeah, so maybe that red-faced monster in the woods is a guard after all," Robbie said. He frowned. "Although it did say some odd things, like it was wondering how it got there. Still, I'll bet it's a guard, to stop us blocking up the hole."

Hal nodded. "That's what I thought. And the sea serpent is there to guard us too—to stop us leaving the island. It's all starting to make sense."

"No, it's not," Abigail said from behind them, her voice low. Hal and Robbie turned to her. Her eyes were red, and she looked angry. "*None* of it makes sense."

"What do you mean?" asked Hal.

Abigail jerked a thumb toward the school. "She hasn't told us why her people selected our parents and hid them away on this island. And she hasn't told us why each couple then had one baby each—not two babies, or three, but exactly *one*. Why have any babies at all? Don't you think that's odd, each couple having exactly one baby, with the world falling apart around them? And I always wondered why our parents waited so long to have children anyway. I worked it out; they were all in their early thirties when we were born, and we were all born within the same year, within the same few months. We're all exactly twelve years old, give or take a few weeks. Doesn't that strike you as a bit of a coincidence?"

She stopped for breath, and shot a glance over her shoulder.

"And who is she, really? Where does she come from? Why does she talk about *her* people and *our* people as if they're different? Did you notice that she mentioned *her* world and *our* world? And what has any of this got to do with what's happening to us?"

Abigail glanced from Hal to Robbie and back again, her chin jutting and her lips pouting. "As far as I'm concerned, none of this makes sense. But I intend to find out."

*Chapter Eight*
**Classroom whispers**

Despite the brightness of the day, an icy chill seeped through Hal's clothing as he digested Abigail's words.

"We need to make plans," Abigail whispered. "We need to find out what's really happening here, and the best way is to follow Miss Simone when she leaves class today, to see where she goes. Maybe she'll go Out There on a boat, and if so, it'll prove the air is fine and that the whole thing is a lie."

Hal nodded. "Sounds good to me."

"Oh, so we're buddies with Abi now, all of a sudden?" Robbie said. "Abi, we don't need you hanging around and—"

"Shut up, Robbie," Abigail snapped. She glared at him. "We have important things to do, and we'd better stick together. It's what I've been saying all along." Then she softened and gave Hal a shy grin. "Besides, Hal and I have a secret. We need to stick together."

Robbie spun to face Hal, looking puzzled—but then he laughed. "So I was right! You and Abi are in love!"

Mortified, Hal grabbed Robbie's arm. "Keep your voice down! That's not what she means. We're not—look, we talked on Saturday night, and—"

"Saturday night?" Robbie said, his face one big delighted grin. "O-ho! You two got together in secret?"

"Oh, shut up, Robbie," Abigail said again, rolling her eyes.

They stood in silence, Robbie looking like he'd just found out some dirty secret, and Abigail looking mildly embarrassed. Hal, feeling a little red-faced himself, looked to see what his other classmates were doing.

Darcy, Lauren and Emily were deep in conversation again—no surprises there. They were huddled together with faces inches apart as if discussing something important. And maybe they were. Maybe they'd all developed the same strange rash as Hal. Maybe they could all grow wings in an instant.

Fenton was grabbing handfuls of long grass and flicking bits at Dewey, who was staring into space. As Hal watched, Fenton glanced over at him and made a slicing motion across his throat.

Abigail stepped closer to Hal and yanked at Robbie's arm. "C'mere, you two," she said. "Hal and I have a secret, but where Hal goes, skinny Robbie goes too, so I guess that makes us a team."

Robbie at once flared up. "We don't need you to—"

"Stop arguing, both of you," Hal said. "Let's make plans."

"Right," Abigail said, nodding. "After school we'll follow Miss Simone and see where she goes. Then we need to find a way off the island. The three of us. We'll build another raft if we have to, and this time we'll tie string to the docks as I suggested, so we can find our way back through the fog. *If* we decide to come back, that is. We might find that Out There is bright and sunny and that there's no virus at all. Imagine that! A world without fog!"

Hal and Robbie exchanged a meaningful glance. "Actually," Hal said, "we found a hole in the woods where the fog comes from. We started to block it up but were interrupted by a red-faced monster."

Abigail stared at them with her mouth open. "What?"

Robbie started to tell the story in detail, but Abigail stopped him and suggested Hal tell it instead. "I want the truth," she said, "not fairy tales." So Hal told the story, much to Robbie's disappointment. When he was finished, Abigail looked thoughtful. "That's very interesting. And Simone said the fog makes the air clean. I'd like to see this hole. Can you take me there?"

"It's not safe," Hal said. "The monster—"

Robbie frowned. "Wait. We decided the red-faced monster was just a guard, so it's probably not dangerous. Same with the sea serpent; it could have swallowed us whole if it wanted to, but instead it just herded us back to the island. Maybe these monsters are Miss Simone's pets, trained like Emily's dog."

"In which case," Abigail finished, "even if we meet the red-faced monster in the woods, it won't harm us. It'll just try to frighten us off. I definitely want to go and see this fog-hole now. Show me where it is, okay? But first we'll follow Simone and see where she goes. Oh, and I also think we should break into the lighthouse. If we can get to the top, we might be able to see over the fog to the mainland."

Hal frowned. "Why go to the top of the lighthouse? Why not just fly up through the fog right here?"

Too late he remembered Robbie knew nothing of Abigail's secret.

But Robbie let out a sarcastic laugh. "Yeah, we'll *fly*. That would be easier than breaking into the lighthouse grounds through the padlocked gates with razor wire on top, and then busting down the door to the lighthouse. Yeah, let's all fly up into the sky."

Another thought struck Hal then. Here was Robbie joking about breaking through padlocked gates and stout oak doors, when all the while he was just the person who might be able to do such a thing. Hal couldn't help smiling to himself. Abigail could fly and Robbie could break down doors, and yet neither knew the other's secret.

A voice called from the school building. "Could you come back inside now, please? Thank you."

"We'll talk more later," Abigail murmured, a deep frown on her face.

Once everyone had returned to class and settled down in their seats, Miss Simone perched on the edge of her desk. "I'm sure you have a lot of questions to ask. But all will be revealed in a few days. First I need to be sure of something, so I want to speak to you all one by one. Emily, come with me. The rest of you get on with your essays—quietly, please."

Miss Simone swept past Hal's desk, and Hal caught a faint smell of seawater, a hint of salt or seaweed. After her trotted Emily, her chin high as if she had been specially selected for some important task. The two disappeared out the back of the classroom, and Hal heard the creak of another door off the short hallway. Miss Simone had taken Emily into the little office; there was a soft click as the door closed behind them.

Everyone exchanged glances as if wondering what to do. "We'd better get on with our essays," Darcy whispered. "Or at least pretend to be getting on. I doubt she'll even care what we write. She doesn't seem to be interested, does she?"

"But then again," Dewey said from the back, "what if she *is* interested in what we write, and we get in trouble for not getting on with it like we've been told? We don't know what she's like. She might have a horrible temper."

After a brief discussion it was decided they should all at least appear to be writing, although it was difficult to concentrate on anything after all they'd learned.

Something small and light hit Hal on the arm, and he automatically looked across at Robbie. But Robbie was staring at his essay paper, on which he'd written four lines. Hal glanced back at Abigail, who nodded down at the floor next to him where a small, wadded-up piece of paper lay. He reached for the paper, unfolded it, and read:

*You nearly goofed, telling Robbie about me. But I guess we'd better tell him, right? Does he know about your rash? I noticed it's gone now. Did you will it away?*

Hal stared at the message for a while, then turned to her. She sat gazing at him with her head tilted to one side. After a moment Hal scrawled a reply:

*Rash just vanished. Robbie has secret too. So yeah, let's all talk.*

He balled the paper up and flicked it back to her.

Footsteps sounded behind him, and he returned his attention to his essay as Emily trotted back to her desk. Miss Simone's voice came from the back. "Lauren now, please."

Lauren got up and, looking nervous, headed to the back of the class. Hal watched her and Miss Simone disappear into the hallway.

"Psst!" Robbie said, leaning forward and poking Emily on her shoulder with his pencil. "What happened? What did you talk about?"

Emily turned slowly, looking bewildered. Everyone had stopped writing to listen. "It was weird," she said. "She asked me if I had experienced anything strange lately. She asked really carefully, like she was testing me."

"And?" Fenton demanded.

"And nothing," Emily said with a shrug. "I don't know what she meant. I asked her what kind of strange things and she said something about unexpected physical changes. I thought that was a bit personal."

Darcy giggled. "Did you tell her to mind her own business?"

But what Emily said then was lost on Hal as he turned to stare first at Robbie and then at Abigail. They in turn stared back at him. *Physical changes.* So Abigail was right. Miss Simone knew something was going on with them.

Abigail scribbled something and passed the note to Hal without trying to conceal it. Fenton immediately piped up, "Oh! Look at the lovebirds, writing love notes!"

"Shut up, Fatty," Abigail said. "How's your toothache? Going to tell Miss Simone about your fangs?"

Fenton clamped his mouth shut and turned away.

Abigail had folded her latest note in half. Hal unfolded it and read:

*Don't say a word to her about my wings, or about your rash! Not until we know what's going on.*

Hal found Robbie looking at him and decided to give him a similar warning. He scribbled a note on a fresh piece of paper:

*Don't tell Miss Simone about how you get all big and strong. Keep it to yourself for now.*

While Robbie read the note, Lauren returned and Miss Simone's voice rang out. "Darcy?"

There was silence as Darcy left the room, and then Abigail whispered, "Hey, is anyone actually experiencing these physical changes Miss Simone mentioned? I mean, seriously. Fenton, your teeth have changed; they're all pointed now. I've seen them."

"Are they?" Emily asked. "Let's see!"

"Yeah, show us," Dewey said.

Fenton glared at Emily, then Dewey, his face turning red. Then he scowled. "You want to see? Do you? Okay, take a good look." And he bared his teeth in a startling grimace that revealed his upper and lower teeth for all to see.

Everyone stared in silence at Fenton for a long while. His pointed teeth were much sharper and longer than they had any right to be, almost like a dog's. Finally Fenton closed his mouth and turned away.

"Anyone else?" Abigail asked. "How about you, Dewey? Got any secrets you want to share?"

"No," Dewey said, shaking his head vigorously.

Abigail turned to Emily. "Hey, bossy-boots. I know *you* have a secret."

Emily's eyebrows shot up. "Me? What do you mean? I have nothing to hide."

"Are you telling me you've never noticed?" Abigail persisted, her eyes narrowed. "*I've* noticed, and I'm two rows back. I've seen how—"

"Abi," Hal interrupted. He shook his head. Abigail stared at him, looking puzzled, and after a moment pouted and nodded.

Emily looked perplexed, and Hal believed she knew nothing of her secret, if indeed she had one. She certainly didn't look any different right now, but then, neither did Robbie or Abigail. Their transformations were temporary. Fenton was the only one whose physical change seemed to have stuck with him.

What had Abigail said regarding Lauren? Something about hairy fingers? Hal strained to see, but Lauren was seated directly in front and her hands were out of sight. But presumably her fingers were quite normal, otherwise everyone would have noticed. So if Lauren's fingers grew hair, it was only for a brief moment. Did she know it was happening?

"How about you, Lauren?" he asked.

Lauren seemed to stiffen, as if she'd been dreading the question. She turned slowly and glanced around the class. It was remarkable how similar she was to her mom, with the same wavy brown hair, snub nose, and tiny dimples. Only Lauren was twelve and much cuter. No wonder Robbie was so fascinated with her.

"Um . . . maybe," she said, "but I don't want to talk about it. It's kind of embarrassing."

Abigail leaned forward, her eyes shining. "I knew it! Lauren, I won't say anything until you're ready, but I think you should keep it from Miss Simone too. You didn't tell her anything, did you?" Lauren shook her head, obviously mortified by the idea. Abigail nodded, looked pleased. "Good. Let's keep quiet until we know what's going on around here. Just pretend nothing's wrong."

There was a silence at this, and then Fenton grunted, "Easy for *you* to say, Abigail. Everyone knows my teeth are sharp and pointed, including Mrs. Hunter, and probably Miss Simone. I can't exactly hide it."

"Do they hurt?" Lauren asked.

Fenton shrugged. "They did. But they don't so much now. One day I was fine, the next I could hardly talk because I kept biting the inside of my cheeks. They're okay now, though. They just look weird."

"And you keep dribbling," Hal said. "You think that's part of it?"

Fenton glanced down at his shirt. It had a few wet spots on it. He scowled and said nothing.

Darcy returned. "She asked for you next, Robbie," she whispered.

Robbie's eyes widened. He swallowed, then got up and headed to the back of the class.

Abigail called softly to Darcy. "Did she mention strange physical changes?"

Darcy nodded, turning around in her seat to face the class. "I told her yes, of course. I'm twelve, after all. But she said no, *other* changes . . . *unusual* changes. I said I didn't know what she was talking about."

Since Darcy had missed out on the most recent discussion, Emily quickly filled her in. Darcy looked bewildered. "Well, we know Fenton has something going on with his teeth. But Lauren, you have something going on too? What about you, Emily?"

Emily shrugged. "We'll talk later, just us girls."

Darcy nodded. Then she looked at Hal with a hint of amusement in her eyes. "And you, Hal? Any weird secrets? Are you getting taller, by any chance? Abigail, maybe you're becoming less of a nuisance and more polite and thoughtful? And Dewey—well, no, Dewey's just right as he is. He's a little dear." She smiled at him with affection.

"You're funny, Darcy," Abigail said, rolling her eyes. "You, Lauren and Emily are always huddled together these days, whispering secrets back and forth. You shouldn't keep secrets from the rest of us at a time like this. We should all tell each other what we know."

"Oh?" Emily said with interest. "Are you going to tell us all *your* secrets then, Abigail? You, Hal and Robbie are just as secretive as us girls. In fact, I think you and Hal have something going on together."

There were giggles and chortles all round.

No more was said for a long while. Robbie finally returned, looking red-faced. He nodded to Hal. "Your turn."

Hal got up and headed to the back of the class. He entered the short hallway and found the door to the small office standing open.

"Come on in," Miss Simone said from inside. The office was tiny, no more than seven feet across and twelve deep. It contained a desk crammed against the wall, and a bookshelf under the small window. Miss Simone was seated at a chair with castors, and she swiveled around as Hal entered. "Take a seat."

Hal sat in the visitor's chair. The desk had a few items on it—a set of trays jammed with papers in one corner, and a pen holder and blotting pad in the middle. But Miss Simone seemed to have no use for any notes. She eased back in her chair and stared at Hal with her startling clear blue eyes.

"Talk to me, Hal," she said. "I know you have something to tell me."

"I do?"

"Of course you do," Miss Simone said. "Tell me what's happening to you."

Hal stared at her, feigning confusion. "Miss?"

"Come on, Hal, I know all about it. You can't keep it secret forever. I just want you to admit it, and to open up to me. That's the first step to a better future. My hands are tied until all of you open up and tell me about the physical changes you're going through."

Hal swallowed. Did she know about his rash? But how could she? He'd kept it secret except from Robbie and Abigail. Now here was this strange woman turning up out of the blue and claiming to know all about him and his rash.

Maybe she knew because *she had somehow caused it.*

"Miss Simone," he said slowly, "I don't know what you mean. What physical changes? You mean getting older? I'll be a teenager this year, and I've grown an inch in height in the last couple of months . . ."

"Hal," she said, leaning forward. Again Hal caught the scent of the ocean on her. "All the girls have told me their secrets. Robbie too. The fact is, Robbie told me of your secret. I just want *you* to tell me. Or show me, if you prefer."

A feeling of anger bubbled up from deep inside. Hal felt his face heating up. This woman was a liar! He doubted very much that any of the girls had revealed anything to Miss Simone, and he knew with absolute certainty that Robbie hadn't. She was testing him, bluffing in an effort to make him talk. Well, she'd just blown it big time. Now Hal knew Abigail was right—this woman wasn't to be trusted.

He got his anger under control and refrained from scratching at his left forearm, which had started itching at a really bad time. He prayed the rash wouldn't spread down his arm and onto the back of his hand. He slowly folded his arms just in case, and looked thoughtful. "Actually," he said, "something strange *is* happening to me."

Miss Simone's eyes widened. "Yes?"

Hal glanced over his shoulder, then leaned forward. Miss Simone leaned forward too, her eyes bright and eager. Hal lowered his voice to a whisper. "I think I might have a crush on Abigail. I hate to admit it, but she's quite nice when you get to know her. And . . . I think she likes me too." He shrugged. "Weird, eh? I never would have thought it."

Miss Simone stared hard at him for what seemed an age, and then she sank back into her seat. "Send Fenton in, if you would," she said through gritted teeth.

Hal's throat was burning and his entire arm itching as he returned to his desk. He felt the rash spreading up to his shoulder and across his back. *Not now, not now*, he thought. He glanced at the back of his hand, afraid of finding the green lumpy skin there in plain sight—but it was clear, at least for now.

"You next, Fenton," he said, rubbing his painful throat. He flopped down into his seat as Fenton trudged to the back of the class and disappeared through the door.

"Are you all right?" Abigail asked, looking concerned.

Hal opened his mouth to answer, but he felt sudden searing pain at the back of his throat, and he bent forward and choked as if he'd got a red hot pepper stuck in there. There was a brief flash of yellow in front of his face, and Lauren, seated directly in front of him, leapt to her feet with a yelp.

Hal rubbed his throat. The pain had gone, and a smoky smell hung in the air.

He was suddenly aware of a silence. All eyes were fixed on him. "Must be coming down with something," he murmured. "Lauren, did I spit on you or something? I think I had something caught in my throat . . ."

"My chair's all burnt," she said, her eyes wide. "Look, it's all blackened around the edges."

"Fire came out of your mouth," Robbie said, staring at him with awe.

"Shh!" Abigail whispered. She frowned at Lauren, then at the others. "This is exactly the sort of thing Miss Simone is looking for. Hal has something weird going on, and so do I. So do you, Lauren, and so does Emily. And we know Fenton does too. That leaves Robbie, Dewey, and Darcy."

Everyone gazed first at Robbie, then Dewey, and then Darcy. But although a flicker of understanding passed over Robbie's face, the other two simply shrugged and looked mystified.

"This is nuts," Emily said. "There's nothing going on with me. Abigail, tell us everything you know."

"Not here," Abigail said. "Later. But it'll have to wait, because Hal, Robbie and I have plans after school. We're going to follow Miss Simone and see where she goes. But Emily, if you really want to help, maybe I could leave you to organize a mission?"

Emily at once brightened up. Hal smiled to himself. It was funny how Abigail knew exactly which words to choose to get others to do her bidding. "What do you have in mind?"

But Fenton returned at that moment. "You next, Abi."

With a sigh, Abigail got up and strolled to the back of the class. Fenton returned to his seat, looking glum. "Did I miss anything?"

Lauren at once told him, in a quiet voice, how Hal had scorched the back of her chair. She pointed out the blackened edges and Fenton looked astonished.

"You never told me you could do that," Robbie said to Hal, sounding a little put out.

"I never knew I could," Hal admitted. He glanced around. "I've had a sort of rash for a while now. It comes and goes, and I didn't think much of it. Thought it was an insect bite or something. But now . . . I don't know. And this—" He waved a hand at Lauren's chair. "Burning her chair? That's, uh, kind of new to me. I think I would have noticed if I could breathe fire."

71

Not much more was said after that.

When Abigail returned to the classroom, she looked triumphant. She poked Dewey on the shoulder. "Your turn," she said. "Don't you dare breathe a word about *anything*—understand?"

Dewey nodded and disappeared.

Emily approached Abigail. "So . . . you had a mission for me to arrange?"

"Yes." Abigail glanced around, and Hal could almost see the cogs and wheels in her brain turning. Then she leaned close to Emily and whispered in her ear for a full half-minute. Emily listened intently and eventually nodded.

"Leave it to me," she said, sounding important.

It was not long before Dewey emerged from the office, with Miss Simone right behind him. Dewey returned to his seat looking a little shaky and pale. As Miss Simone swept by and headed for the front of the class, Abigail glared at Dewey with a questioning look. He gave a weak smile and a thumbs up.

Miss Simone looked disgruntled. "Get on with your essays," she said, heading for the coat stand to retrieve her dark green silky robe. As she swept it around her shoulders and tied the sash at her throat, she glanced up at the clock. It was only halfway through the morning. "Since you have nothing to tell me today, we'll resume tomorrow. Take your essays home and have them completed by morning."

She gave a curt nod, flipped back her hair, and exited through the door at the front. A silence settled on the class once more, and everyone rushed to the windows.

"There she goes," Emily said, pointing. The stranger was moving at a brisk pace across the meadow, her cloak billowing in a light breeze that had sprung up. Puffs of fog blew between her and the school, and in an instant she was gone.

Abigail swung around. "Quickly, Hal, Robbie—let's go. Emily, I'll leave you to organize things here, okay? See you all tomorrow."

Abigail hurried from the room out the back door, and Hal rushed to catch up, followed by Robbie. The three of them collected their bikes from the rack and cycled around the building to the other side, keeping a sharp eye out for Miss Simone. But she was already engulfed in fog.

"She went that way," Robbie said, pointing. "Let's get after her. Hurry, before we lose her completely."

*Chapter Nine*
## Following Miss Simone

Hal, Robbie and Abigail pedaled through the long grass of the meadow, heading in what they guessed to be the direction Miss Simone had taken. It had been bright when Hal had left home that morning, but now the sky had dulled to a miserable dark gray, and the fog had thickened. Gusts of wind whipped at the grass and blew through the trees standing along the edge of the meadow nearby. His dad had predicted a storm, and it seemed he was to be proven right.

Just as Hal thought they'd lost Miss Simone in the fog, perhaps even cycled right past her, she appeared as a fuzzy shape ahead and to the left. The three of them slowed to a crawl and said nothing, just watched in silence.

Miss Simone moved fast, her silky cloak billowing in the breeze and her golden locks blowing freely. However, the cyclists had to keep stopping and starting to avoid catching up with her.

"She'll see us if she glances back," Hal whispered after a while. "We should walk our bikes."

"Yeah," Robbie agreed. "We'll hang back just enough so she's almost lost in the fog, so we can hardly see her. Then, if she does look back, hopefully she won't see us either."

"Is it my imagination," Abigail said, looking around, "or has the fog gotten thicker since we left school?"

"Storm's coming," Hal said. "I don't know if that has anything to do with the fog, but Dad said a storm's coming later tonight. Wind's picking up already. Come on, Miss Simone's disappeared again."

"And let's quit talking in case she hears us," Abigail whispered.

They walked in silence, pushing their bikes through the long grass and listening to the hypnotic ticking of chains around the gears. They left the meadow and started through a rough field of dry brush and the occasional thicket. Throughout the trek they glimpsed Miss Simone perhaps no more than fifty feet ahead, although Hal swore the gap was closing. The fog seemed to be thickening even more, and they naturally increased their pace to keep the visitor in sight.

They had to stop dead in their tracks at one point because a bank of fog rolled aside to reveal Miss Simone stepping carefully through a hedgerow. She was just twenty feet ahead, and had only to whip her head around to see them standing there gaping at her.

But she pressed on through the hedgerow and Hal let out a long sigh. "That was close," he whispered. "Where are we headed?"

"To the cliffs," Robbie said, frowning. "I'm sure the cliffs are this way, and if we head left a little bit, we'll end up at Black Woods."

They forged on, breathless with anticipation. Would the strange woman lead them to a boat? Would she sail off Out There without a protective suit?

When the smell of salt water hit their nostrils and a strong, persistent wind tugged at their clothes and hair, they knew they were nearing the edge of the island. Ahead, the fuzzy dark figure of Miss Simone faded in and out, her cloak billowing and hair streaming. The walk had become a bit of a slog by now, and Hal's feet were moving on automatic, one foot after the other. He almost failed to notice when the visitor finally came to a halt; he kept on walking until Robbie yanked him back.

Miss Simone had stopped by the cliff edge, where the long grass simply ended and gave way to a wall of fog. Robbie had guessed right. But it didn't make sense; how could she have moored up a boat here?

Abigail leaned close to Hal and whispered, "What's she doing?" Her warm breath tickled his cold ear. "Looking for a boat?"

"Maybe," Hal whispered back. "I don't see one though."

They waited in silence as the visitor stood there on the cliff, peering down. She licked a finger and held it up.

"She's testing the wind," Robbie remarked.

"Maybe she's—" Abigail started.

Miss Simone dove off the cliff.

Abigail stifled a scream as the strange woman pitched forward with her knees bent. As she reached a horizontal position, she pushed away from the cliff with her legs and dove outward, as graceful as a bird, her arms extended and her green, silky cloak billowing behind her.

Then she was gone.

For a stunned moment nobody moved or said a word. Then Hal threw down his bike and raced across the grass to the edge of the cliff. An updraft whipped at his hair as he searched for Miss Simone.

About fifty or sixty feet below, the sea pounded against the cliff face, green and swirling with white froth and bubbles where it sloshed back against fresh waves. There seemed to be no dangerous rocks in these parts, but diving from this height was reckless enough. What if she'd been blown back against the cliff face, or dashed against it underwater? What if there was a current that sucked her down and down until she drowned?

"What happened?" Abigail asked, rushing over to Hal's side. "Did she come up somewhere?"

74

It took awhile for Hal to find his voice. "S-she must have a boat out there somewhere, in the fog. She must have swum out to it. What a nerve, though, diving off the cliff like that!"

Robbie whistled. "She's nuts."

"I wish it wasn't so foggy," Abigail grumbled. "We might have seen her swimming away, maybe even seen her boat."

"If this is how she gets off the island," Hal said, "I wonder how she got *on* earlier. Did anyone see which direction she came from this morning? She couldn't have climbed up the cliff here. She must have arrived at the island somewhere else. But then . . . why not go back the same way? It doesn't make any sense."

Abigail sighed. "*Nothing* makes sense. Come on, this has been a waste of time. Show me the fog-hole. Robbie, didn't you say Black Woods is near here?"

Robbie nodded. "Not far. Let's leave our bikes and bags, though. It gets awkward up ahead." He dumped his backpack by his fallen bike and hurried off along the cliff, veering inland a little. The fog swallowed him up.

"Does he know where he's going?" Abigail asked.

"He knows the island better than anyone," Hal said, throwing his backpack down with Robbie's. "Good sense of direction. You should see him in the woods—just cuts right through as if he can *smell* the route."

Abigail slipped her backpack off too, and together they marched along the grassy cliff top and then up a little rise where the terrain became rockier. Bushes sprouted at random, and hidden in the long grass were little potholes that made them stumble. Occasionally they came across rabbits that froze, stared at them with wide eyes and twitching noses, then bolted into the gloom.

Abigail jammed her hands into her coat pockets and hunched her shoulders against the wind, while Hal's fingers, ears and nose slowly turned numb. He should have worn a sweater or a coat—but then, he hadn't planned on taking a walk along the blustery cliffs when he'd set out that morning. Still, the brisk pace warmed him, and Abigail too, judging by her rosy red cheeks and pink nose.

But no matter how briskly they walked, Robbie managed to remain out of sight somewhere up ahead. "Robbie?" Hal called after a while. "Where are you?"

"Where are *you?*" came a faint retort on the wind. "You still back there?"

Robbie didn't seem very far away. If the fog cleared he'd probably be right there, thirty or forty feet ahead, clambering over rocks as Hal and Abigail were.

The meandering walk up and down short hills stretched on. Hal wished there was a simple path; then they could have brought their bikes and avoided the walk back again later. At that moment his stomach growled, reminding him that his lunch was in his backpack, which he'd left with the bikes. Wishing he could chew on a sandwich right now, he sighed and tried to think of something to take his mind off it.

"Abi," he said after a while, "how do you . . . control your wings? How do you make them appear and disappear at will?"

Abigail seemed to shake herself from a state of deep thought. "What? Oh, well, I guess it's like learning to ride a bike. It's easy once you know how, and then you can't *not* ride one, if you see what I mean. It's the same with swimming. Once you figure it out, you just do it without thinking." She glanced at him and frowned. "You must know how to control your scales now, right? You had that rash on your hand when we met in the garage on Saturday night, but now it's gone. You must have willed it away."

"Uh, not really," Hal admitted. "Well, I suppose I might have willed it away somehow, but only by accident. Or it might have been coincidence that it disappeared right when I was wishing it would go away—"

Abigail snorted. "It wasn't coincidence, Hal. This is how it starts. Whatever you are, it creeps up on you, growing like a pimple or a rash, and when it gets really bad you get angry and tell it to go away. And it does. Then it returns, quicker than before. Before you know it, you're a monster."

Hal slowed to a stop. "A monster."

She continued up the rise a moment longer before realizing he'd stopped. Then she turned and looked down at him. "I was kidding. Do you think *I'm* a monster?"

"No," Hal said, shaking his head. "You're a girl with wings."

"I'm a *faerie*," Abigail said with a half smile and a little gleam in her eyes. She took a few steps to one side and leaned against a huge boulder. "At least, I think I am. First I went through an old book on wildlife, but couldn't find anything remotely like me. There's no such thing as a girl with wings, so the book said. Then I remembered a story my mom used to tell me when I was little, about the Tooth Fairy, a magical lady with wings."

"Yeah, right," Hal said with a smile. Then he frowned. "You think you're the Tooth Fairy?"

Abigail shook her head. "No, but it gave me the idea to look for books about fairy tales instead of wildlife. I found one called *Creatures of Fantasy*. It had all sorts of strange creatures, and I found something similar to the Tooth Fairy—a faerie, spelled differently but basically the same thing—a magical person with buzzing wings, only very small, no bigger than your hand."

Hal gaped.

"Only thing is," Abigail went on, "the introduction on the first page said that all those creatures were 'mythical, magic beings,' or 'creatures of the imagination' . . . which of course I'm not."

She looked skyward for a moment. "There's a thought. Maybe none of this is real and we're all in a dream."

The wind tugged at her ponytail. She hunched her shoulders again and tried to bury her nose in her coat. "Let's keep walking," she said. "Robbie's probably at the woods already."

They continued up the rise and found themselves on another grassy field. The walk was a little easier now, and they hurried along together.

"So," Hal said, "you think you're a faerie, from this book of fantasy creatures? I once read a book that had faeries in it."

Abigail looked surprised. "You did? Where did you find that?"

"On the shelves at school. You've been looking in the reference section, but there are plenty of books on the shelf marked 'Fantasy' that have magical creatures in them—stories rather than just pictures and descriptions."

"That's why I've never come across them," Abigail said. "I don't read much of anything except reference books. I don't see the point in made-up stories. I'd rather learn about real life."

Hal frowned. "You're weird. But Robbie's the same. He's read every bug book there is."

Abigail smiled as they walked together. Darkness loomed ahead; they were approaching Black Woods at last. "So anyway," she said, "I started to wonder if maybe I'm a faerie, even though all the books say they don't really exist. Maybe the books are wrong. And if I'm a faerie, then what are you? And all the others? Are we all so-called fantasy creatures?"

"That's nuts," Hal said. But he had to concede that he couldn't really be sure of anything anymore. "Hey, I meant to ask: Why don't you just fly up out of the fog, or over the water to the mainland?"

"Can't," Abigail replied. "I think the fog dampens my flight somehow. I can fly along low to the ground for up to an hour, but if I try to fly upwards I get all heavy and tired. And I'm nervous about flying out across the sea."

They stopped at the fringes of Black Woods and peered in. The fog seemed thinner here, almost as if the trees filtered out the really thick stuff. However, in its place was an ominous dark stillness, as though the woods were listening for intruders. Somehow the open fields of thick cold fog didn't seem quite so bad anymore.

"Where's Robbie?" Abigail asked, as if Hal would know.

Hal shrugged. "Robbie?" he called loudly.

Silence.

He sighed. "I guess we could try and find our way. There's a cliff path that we could follow, but it would be quicker to cut through the woods here. We should come to a stream, and the fog-hole is in a clearing nearby."

Abigail shivered. "Let's go the shortest route. We'll probably come up on Robbie soon enough."

Hal took a breath and plunged into the woods, with Abigail in tow. Nothing looked familiar to him, but he felt he couldn't go far wrong as long as he stayed roughly straight. "Robbie!" he yelled. "Wait for us!"

Abigail said nothing as she trailed behind Hal through the dense vegetation. Twigs cracked and leaves crunched. Bushes rustled and shook. A wet patch of dirt squelched underfoot, and a rodent ran across Hal's shoe and scurried away. It reminded him of the red-faced monster, and he wondered if they were making a mistake by wandering around in the woods with that thing roaming loose. Then again, it was just a guard, after all, and probably alerted to his presence now that he'd been yelling for Robbie. He mentally kicked himself. No wonder his friend hadn't shouted back—he'd had more sense!

"I think our parents are scared of us," Abigail whispered.

"Scared?" Hal whispered back. He pointed the way around a crop of prickly bushes. "What do you mean, scared?"

"Well, think about it. We're stuck here on this island." She waved her hands around expansively. "I always had a theory that the adults were making up stories about Out There being a dead place we wouldn't ever want to visit. I think they just want to keep us here because of what we are. They want to keep us here to experiment on, but they know we could escape if we really wanted to, so they make up all these stories about diseases and things. They're trying to make us believe they love us and are trying to protect us when all the time they're lying and keeping us prisoners here."

"But . . ." Hal struggled over a fallen tree and got his shirt snagged on it. His mind was racing. Surely his parents hadn't lied to him all his life?

Abigail had found a better place to climb over the fallen tree, and she appeared beside Hal as he pulled at his snagged shirt. "See, if we knew the truth, we'd be angry and would try to escape, maybe even attack them. Imagine what you could do with your fire breath! So they're keeping a lid on things, trying to find out if we're changing without coming out and telling us the truth."

The silence that followed was awkward. Hal set off again through the woods, thinking hard. "And what do you think will happen to us if our parents find out we *are* changing?" he asked.

"The same thing that happened to Thomas," Abigail said solemnly. "His parents got rid of him."

"Okay, that's just stupid," Hal said, getting annoyed. "Thomas fell off the cliff and that's all there is to it. You're so paranoid, Abi. Come on, let's find that fog-hole—if the monster lets us. I bet it won't though. I bet it'll chase us away." He marched off, stomping through the woods as if he knew exactly where he was going.

Just then came a scream.

They stopped dead, and Abigail gripped Hal's arm. It was a long scream, filled with terror, coming from deep within the woods. Hal was certain it must be Robbie screaming, but had never heard him scream like that and couldn't be absolutely sure. It started out high in pitch, then slowly changed, becoming low and mournful, then deep and booming. Another voice joined in the fray, savage and wild, and totally inhuman.

A flurry of other sounds followed: bushes rustling, branches snapping, heavy panting, throaty roars and growls. The noises increased, heading toward where Hal and Abigail stood frozen.

A shadowy shape came into view, darting around in the darkness of the woods. Bushes flew apart and the shadow disappeared for a moment, then reappeared much closer. It was big—bigger than Robbie. It stampeded through tangled clumps of vegetation straight toward Hal and Abigail. They instinctively dove for cover behind a tree and crouched there, trembling with fright.

The huge figure blundered past in a shower of leaves and twigs. Cringing, Hal caught sight of dark brown hair and enormous bulky arms and shoulders bearing down on him, a man-shape at least three times his own height. He cowered, ducked his head, and felt a rush of air as the monster stomped by a mere foot or two away. Then it disappeared from view, and the sounds of its huge stamping feet could be heard for another half-minute before fading into the distance.

After a long silence, Hal let out his breath. "It's gone," he said, trying to keep the tremble out of his voice. "Whatever it was, it's gone." He slowly disentangled himself from Abigail's vice-like grip and found himself inches from her white face.

Her bottom lip wobbled as she tried to speak. "Th-th-that was too close."

"Are you all right?" he asked. His arm had started itching.

Abigail pulled back and got to her feet, looking cross. "Of course I'm all right."

"Well, good." Hal glanced in the direction they had been heading—the direction from which the monster had blundered. "I'm confused. That wasn't the red-faced monster . . . which means it must have been Robbie."

"*Robbie?*" Abigail looked so startled that Hal would have laughed if the situation wasn't so serious.

His heart thumped and a prickly sensation crept over his shoulders. "He has these moments of amazing strength," Hal explained. "That's his secret. Once, he burst right out of his shirt. I guess something must have frightened him and he changed into . . . into that thing that ran past us."

"But what frightened him? The red-faced monster?"

Hal and Abigail stood in silence, listening. They heard a rustling sound in the bushes off to one side, the stealthy creeping of a prowler.

"Let's go," Hal whispered, planting his hands firmly on Abigail's shoulders and turning her around. "Robbie's three times bigger than us but he still ran like a girl. Come on."

They started to retrace their steps, but their path was blocked.

A large cat-like creature sat there licking its paw. Hal had seen pictures of lions, and this thing was as big and powerful as one, only with red fur and a flowing crimson mane. Its broad face was a cross between a lion and a man, but its eyes were distinctly human, large and blue, filled with a stony malice.

The monster grinned, its black leathery lips stretching to reveal more teeth than Hal had ever seen in his life—razor sharp and needle thin, and arranged in three deadly rows.

But most frightening of all was its tail. When the monster yawned and climbed to its feet, a long scorpion-like appendage rose into view, arcing over the creature's head and pointing down at them, shiny red and armor-plated. On the end was a quivering ball of long, thin needles, and from the center of these protruded a huge black stinger oozing yellow venom.

*Chapter Ten*
## Manticore

The red-furred monster stood before Hal and Abigail with its scorpion tail arced high over its head, pointing down at them and swaying from side to side like a cobra choosing its moment to strike.

The creature's fur was clean and shiny, but the thing smelled of rotting meat. "Well, well," it said in a high, fluty voice that contained a hint of scorn. "Look who it is."

Despite his fear, Hal couldn't help noticing how the creature's distinctly inhuman black rubbery lips nevertheless shaped themselves deftly around each spoken word.

"Run," Abigail was saying in his ear. She'd said it half a dozen times already, but he hadn't been paying full attention. He took a step backward as she tugged at his shirt from behind.

"If you run," the monster said, as if reading Hal's mind, "you won't get very far. So don't even try." It stretched and yawned, again revealing three rows of teeth, then shook its armor-plated tail. The needles on the end bristled and quivered alarmingly.

"It's a manticore," Abigail whispered, her fingernails digging into Hal's arm. "Run before it—"

The creature took three rapid steps forward and stuck its face inches from Hal's. Now it could easily snap its jaws and bite off his face. Or it could pounce on him, pin him down, and claw him to pieces. Meanwhile its hot, putrid breath made Hal feel sick. That was where the smell of rotting meat came from, as though it had been eating rodents and had bits of flesh stuck in its teeth.

The manticore glanced over Hal's shoulder. "What's your name, girl?"

Hal surprised himself by inching sideways and blocking the monster's view of Abigail. He faced the monster square on, feeling dwarfed by the broad lion-like face and powerful muscular forelegs.

The creature scowled deeply. "Let me see you, girl."

"Stay there," Hal told her.

But Abigail tentatively stepped around into view, still clutching his arm. Hal felt a familiar prickly sensation beginning to crawl across his skin.

"That's better," the creature grumbled. It stared at her, eyes narrowed. "Abigail, isn't it?"

It seemed as if time stopped for a second. The mention of Abigail's name stunned Hal, and he turned to her feeling almost cheated. Did she *know* this thing? But Abigail's expression indicated that she was as astounded as Hal.

The manticore nodded, looking thoughtful. Its tail slowly sank out of sight. "Yes, I remember you. Dr. Porter's daughter." It glanced at Hal. "I don't remember your name, though. Barry? Harry? Howard?"

"Hal," he croaked.

"Haaaal, yes. And who was your friend? The one who was here earlier?"

"You mean Robbie?"

The blue eyes widened. "Robbie, yes. I remember now."

"Who *are* you?" Abigail demanded. "How do you know our names?"

The monster began pacing around them in a tight circle, so tight its muscular bulk nudged against them. Its nose followed close behind the tip of its long scorpion tail, like it was stalking itself. "I lived here once," it said. "I fell over the cliff outside the woods."

Hal caught his breath.

"Thomas?" Abigail gasped.

"I *was* Thomas, a long time ago," the monster said, continuing its pacing. It left large footprints in the dirt, the same cat-like footprints Hal and Robbie had seen by the fog-hole.

The manticore—not an *it* but a *he*, their very own little red-headed Thomas Patten—studied them one at a time. Then Thomas sat and curled his tail around in front. The quills on the end had flattened, and the stinger had vanished from sight. "I don't remember much. I was chasing a groundhog in the backyard . . . I felt strange, and then I changed, became some kind of animal . . . My mother yelled at me and I ran into the woods." He paused, a distant look in his eyes. "She came after me, shouting. I kept running, got lost, eventually saw daylight ahead and ran toward it . . . straight out of the woods and off the cliff. I fell into the water."

"You didn't hit the rocks!" Hal exclaimed. "Everyone said you hit the rocks and died. But you *missed*."

"Yes, but then something grabbed my feet and pulled me down," Thomas said, the corners of his mouth turning down. "I kicked and swallowed water, but down I went, and everything got dark . . . Next thing I remember, I woke up in a forest, lying by the side of a lake. And the fog was all gone."

A thousand questions were on the tip of Hal's tongue, but before he could single one out, Thomas sniffed and looked around with a scowl. "And now I'm back here again. I went to sleep one night in my den, and woke up the next morning in these old woods. Took me a while to realize where I was."

Hal felt a surge of hope. "Thomas Patten," he said, still hardly able to believe it. "So you changed too! We're *all* changing . . . but you changed *years* ago!"

"And you're a manticore," Abigail said, sounding breathless.

Thomas looked them both up and down. "Yes, I'm a manticore. And I haven't eaten properly in a week."

"A manticore," Hal repeated, nodding. "Well, I've never heard of them. But it's funny, you've got red hair, and you *always* had red hair, even when you were—"

"Human?" Thomas finished. He licked his lips. His tail began to unfold, and the quills puffed up so they were standing on end once more.

"Well, yeah," Hal went on. "Not quite that red, obviously. More ginger-colored than anything . . ." He stopped, realizing he was babbling. He had the distinct, uncomfortable feeling that something in the air had changed. The prickly sensation crawled from his shoulders and down his back.

Abigail squeezed his arm and cleared her throat. "Well, it was nice to see you again, Thomas. We'd better get going now. We'll bring you some food, lots of it. We'll go home right now and see what we can find, then come back in an hour or two. Okay?"

Thomas turned his gaze on her and a slow grin spread across his face.

"And then we'll figure out what to do next," Hal said. He glanced over his shoulder. "Well, come on, Abi. Let's—"

"You're going nowhere," the manticore said. His tail reared up over his head and the ball of needles quivered. The black, shiny stinger emerged once more. "Look, nothing personal, but I have to eat. I have to eat *properly*—understand? Rodents aren't enough for me. I'm a manticore now, and have been since I was six. I've enjoyed this little trip down memory lane, but all I want right now is to eat a good meal and then get home to my den." A blue eye winked. "But I promise you won't feel a thing. I'll go easy on you, paralyze you first, and then sting you—much less painful that way."

The ball of quills swelled.

"Thomas, don't mess around," Hal said, pushing Abigail behind him and backing away. "I'm not sure if you're just joking with us or not, but . . . I mean, you wouldn't, would you?"

The manticore gave a sudden snarl—a deep, throaty snarl overlaid with a thin whining sound, like two separate voices sharing the same space, one angry and savage and the other desperate and helpless. Hal and Abigail stumbled backward in horror. Then the tail flicked and dozens of slender darts shot through the air toward them.

Abigail screamed.

Instinct took over and Hal threw up his arms. Poison-tipped quills thudded into his arms, chest, and legs. He felt a moment of searing pain and then his limbs went numb. He was aware of Abigail spinning and falling beside him.

Hal's vision blurred and his knees buckled. He dropped onto cold damp soil, rolled onto his back, and watched the treetops spin far above. The bright white sky hurt his eyes.

Then the manticore bent over him with hot, putrid breath and three rows of teeth glistening with saliva. A long red tongue slopped out of the gaping maw and rolled from side to side.

Abigail's screams had turned to whimpers. Hal tried to focus on her. She lay on her back, her head turned awkwardly toward his. Her eyelids drooped and spit dribbled down her cheek.

A huge foot clamped down on Hal's shoulder, and claws dug in. He yelled.

Something hovered above the manticore's head—the ball of quills, from which protruded the shiny black stinger. It stretched, extended, and a glob of thick yellow liquid formed on the end. Paralyzed, Hal watched as the glob hung there for a moment, then wobbled and dropped. He felt a sharp sting on his face.

"This won't hurt," Thomas said softly. For a moment, anguish flickered across his blue eyes, as if he were putting down a much-loved pig at a time of great need. Then his stare hardened.

The deadly stinger swooped down.

Hal gave a shout and lashed out with clubbed hands that felt heavy, somehow weighted. He struck something. The manticore yelped and leapt away. Suddenly Hal was free, but his vision blurred again. He rolled onto his stomach, planted his hands in the moist dirt, and tried to get up. His feet slipped out from under him and he collapsed.

He felt strange. His cheek stung, his vision swam in and out of focus, and his hands and arms felt heavy, big, powerful. He paused for half a second, shook his head, and stared.

His hands were enormous, with long clawed fingers. His forearms and biceps were bulging, swelling, and in that moment his shirtsleeves ripped open and hung in rags from his shoulders. Beneath the rags rippled muscles he never knew he had. Skin darkened to a now familiar cucumber green and formed into hard scales. A crested ridge popped out along the length of his forearms and spread up past his elbows toward his shoulders. He felt the strange pulsing, rippling, twitching sensation pour up over his back, heard a tearing sound and felt cool air on his skin as his tattered shirt dropped into the dirt. The rippling moved down his legs and his jeans split apart. His shoes popped open and massive clawed feet expanded outwards.

Panic-stricken and confused, Hal glanced up and found Thomas backing away with blood dripping from a gash across his face. He looked angry.

Then Hal was up and running at the monster with an uncontrollable urge to tear it apart with his bare hands. Thomas turned and fled with a howl. Hal stumbled after him on all fours, tearing through bushes as if they weren't there, his breath steaming in the air before him.

It was a curious, dream-like moment. Hal felt as though his mind had been transplanted into the body of something else, some large, powerful creature with green scaly skin and enormous clawed feet. It didn't seem to matter that he was plowing straight through prickly bushes; the manticore darted around them, trying to throw him off, but Hal plunged straight through, intent only on snapping his jaws around the red-furred hindquarters and biting the thing in half.

Hal stopped abruptly, panting. The manticore tore on, glancing back one more time before disappearing for good.

Alone and dazed, Hal twisted his neck, trying to get a look at himself. A twenty-foot-long dark green reptilian body stood there—the body of a dragon, just like those on the covers of countless books he'd read over the years, with tough, scaly, armor-plated skin, and bulky crested ridges protruding from his arms and shoulders. High up on his back, great pointed slabs of bone ran along his spine like a stone wall, all the way down his tail to the heavy club-like arrow tip.

What did his face look like? He squinted down his nose and saw a long, blunt green snout with flared nostrils on the end. Reaching up to touch, he lost his balance and toppled forward, falling flat on his face. Leaves flew up around him.

He lay there a moment, his heart pounding and hot steam puffing from his nostrils. Then he lifted a hand and looked closely. It wasn't really a hand at all, more like a foot, though he still had a rudimentary thumb. He was a four-legged animal. Panic surged through him. He couldn't stay like this! He couldn't go home looking like *this*, a dragon! His parents would have a fit.

As he started to climb to his feet, he felt the weight of three or more people sitting on his back, and was certain his legs would never carry the combined weight. And yet they did, with ease; he felt he could launch six feet in the air if he wanted. He tried it—head high, neck stretched, powerful hind legs flexing—and for a second felt he was twenty or thirty feet in the air. Then he came down with such a thud that his feet sank into the soft soil up to his ankles.

Hal hunkered there, in the middle of the silent woods, and waited for his heart to stop pounding. He felt an itch on his hind leg and idly scratched at it with a foreleg, again losing his balance and almost falling over. Then he realized it wasn't an itch but a thorn of some kind. He stared closer. It was one of the manticore's quills, broken off but firmly wedged in his flesh. There were others, too; he could feel them. Had they penetrated his armor? No, the quills had been sticking in his soft, pink human flesh before he had changed, and his new skin had simply formed around them.

He tried to claw them out, but his new dragon toes were too big and clumsy. He tried to pluck at them with his teeth, but found that even harder. He growled, and his vocal chords emitted a deep rumbling sound unlike anything he had ever heard.

Despite the shock of his transformation, Hal felt fine. In fact, he felt great. The poison that had brought him down seemed to have lost its effect, and only the quills themselves were bothering him. They were like tiny, annoying splinters. They'd seemed a lot bigger when the manticore had been waving them around.

But then, Hal had been a small boy at the time. Now he was a twenty-foot dragon. In a comfortable standing position his head hung low, four or five feet off the ground—so not much change there, when compared with his old human body. His crested back stood a few feet higher, maybe seven or eight feet overall, taller than the tallest of men. That made him a pretty formidable size—not the gigantic monsters he'd seen in books, but still bigger than anything he'd ever come across before.

If he stretched out his wings, he could—

*Wings!*

He whipped his head back and looked again. As though controlled by a separate part of his brain, his wings unfolded from his back, opening and stretching with a curious creaking, leathery sound. Hal gaped. Funny how he hadn't spotted them before, as if his mind had not been ready to comprehend them. Did they . . . did they work? He wondered how to make them move, and again, as if on cue, they flapped gently, catching the air and causing a strong enough draft to rustle nearby bushes.

Astounded, he extended his wings as high as they would go. They moved exactly as he intended, and yet he had no idea how he was controlling them. *Same way you wiggle a toe*, he thought. *It just comes naturally.*

With his wings spread high, they looked like triple-jointed skeletal arms with long thin fingers, between which stretched thin membranes of skin. Now he stood over twice the height of a man, nearly three times his normal short stature.

Panic surged through him again. Would he ever be human again? Was he stuck like this forever? He spun around in a circle, his breath coming in short, heavy pants. His tail thrashed, whipped around, and obliterated a few bushes.

But then he remembered Abigail's wings. She could make them appear and disappear at will; they just folded up and merged with her flesh when she was done with them. Maybe Hal could change back any time he liked . . .

*Abigail!*

She had been stuck with quills, and was lying alone in the woods.

He launched himself into the bushes. Retracing his steps was easy; he had only to follow the flattened bushes and broken tree limbs. He had really left his mark! He tore back through the woods and came across something dark blue up ahead, hung on a bush.

His jeans were torn to shreds. So, too, were his underpants, socks and shirt. Even his running shoes were splayed open and squashed down into the dirt. This was where he'd changed. But where was Abigail?

As he moved on through the bushes, he began to tremble with anxiety. First Robbie had gone missing, and now Abigail. "Abi!" he yelled—but when a throaty roar erupted from his mouth he realized he was now incapable of human speech. That was going to complicate things further.

He slumped down and put his hands—his enormous clawed paws—over his face. What was he going to do? He couldn't walk back home as a dragon, and if he tried to will himself back into human form, he'd be naked! He didn't know which was worse, or which would draw the most startled exclamations from his parents.

He guessed being a dragon would be worse. But still . . .

What to do, what to do. Should he worry about Robbie and Abigail going missing, or that they had been eaten by the manticore, or that he himself was now a dragon, or that he might have to return home naked?

He groaned in despair.

A buzzing came to his ears, and he looked for the source. "Abi?" he called, rising to his feet. His voice came out as a sort of grumpy growl.

The buzzing increased, and Abigail appeared between the pines, hovering ten feet off the ground some distance away. She had removed her coat and was clasping it tight to her chest. Her wings appeared to be poking through the back of her shirt.

Hal rushed toward her. "You're okay!"

Abigail squealed and buzzed away. Too late, Hal realized his mistake. He resolved to stand still and keep his big dragon trap shut, rather than rush toward the poor girl roaring like a monster.

After a few moments, Abigail reappeared, keeping a safe distance. She hovered and watched for a while, her head to one side. Hal kept still and tried to look as harmless as possible.

*How does a dragon look harmless?*

"Are you okay, Hal?"

Abigail's words were quiet and trembling, but Hal understood them. Even though he was a dragon, and seemed able to speak only in rumbles and growls, he could hear and understand her as normal. He gave a nod.

Abigail seemed satisfied, and cautiously buzzed closer. She landed softly and her wings stilled. But Hal noted she kept them ready, just in case.

"Well," she said, "you certainly showed your true colors. You scared me. And you scared the manticore too. Do you remember whacking it around the face? You sent it flying!"

Hal tried to chuckle, but his voice came out like a wheezing grumble.

Abigail came a little closer. "I got stuck by a couple of quills, but you got most of them. Even so I felt woozy and my vision was blurred. When you chased off after the manticore, I pulled the quills out and just lay there a while. The poison wore off. It was just meant to slow us down."

"Yeah, while the manticore came at us with its stinger," Hal said, remembering the nasty black point that oozed yellow venom.

Abigail raised her eyebrows. "I didn't understand a word you just said, but I think you can understand me. Right?"

Hal nodded.

"Prove it. If you can understand me, swing your tail around."

Hal lifted his tail and swished it through the air. It occurred to him that he did so without even trying, as if he had had a tail all his life.

"Cool," Abigail murmured. She sighed, looking relieved. "Now we need to go find Robbie. He's probably running around in circles wondering why he's turned into a huge hairy ogre. We need to go find him, and then get both of you back into human shape. You can't go home like that; your mom and dad would die of fright. Okay?"

Hal nodded, suddenly feeling as though he was acting in a school play, playing the part of a huge obedient dog.

Abigail looked him over for a moment, her eyes wide. Then she smiled, looking nervous. "Remind me never to tease you again."

*Chapter Eleven*
## What happened Out There

Abigail studied Hal's clothes, lying in shreds and tatters in the dirt. She picked up the shirt and frowned. "I guess we could salvage this. You could wrap it round your waist after you change back."

"Let's get out of the woods first," Hal said, wondering if dragons could blush. But of course his words came out as a series of grunts and growls, and he sighed with impatience, causing steam to blow from his flared nostrils.

He stomped off through the woods, heading back the way they'd entered. Abigail buzzed along behind, making occasional comments such as how his enormous reptilian bulk swayed as he walked, and how his tail whipped from side to side, flattening bushes. When she remarked on how he kept passing wind, Hal snorted with annoyance.

"I'm just saying," Abigail said, laughing. She buzzed over his head and flew in reverse a few feet ahead. "Look, it's not your fault. You're just a dragon."

Hal wasn't sure what to make of that, so he let it slide.

Emerging from the woods into thick fog and a strong breeze, he continued the route back to the bikes, stomping the grass flat as he went. Abigail buzzed alongside, bobbing up and down and circling around as though she had too much pent-up energy.

"Why don't you change behind those bushes," Abigail said, landing on tiptoes and pointing to an untidy clump of brambles. "You can't ride your bike home looking like that."

Hal shuffled behind the bushes with mixed feelings. He wanted to be normal again, or more to the point he wanted to know that he *could* be normal again, but the idea of running around naked in the middle of nowhere didn't appeal to him—especially with Abigail around. He turned in a tight circle behind the bush, trampling weeds and poison ivy while he fretted over his situation. His armored reptilian feet were impervious to the nettles, but he stomped them into the ground and kicked dirt over them just in case. He might be glad of the precaution when he turned back into his normal puny human self. That is, *if* he turned back.

"Finished?" Abigail called, sounding impatient. "You look like a giant dog, turning in circles like that." She glanced over her shoulder and studied her delicate wings. Abruptly they shrank out of sight. "See," she said, turning back to Hal, "that's all you do. Just imagine yourself back to normal."

*Sure, sounds easy*, Hal thought.

He tried, but nothing happened. He imagined himself standing there, a normal human twelve-year-old boy with short, sandy hair. But no matter how much he concentrated, no matter how hard he pictured himself hiding behind the bush, still he felt no change. He began to panic. Was he stuck like this forever? What would his parents do with him? Turn him away? What if the other adults came after him, tried to run him off—or worse, what if they tried to slay him? Isn't that what people normally did with dragons?

With a shudder, Hal closed his eyes tight and tried to clear his mind. He was being irrational. Miss Simone was expecting all the kids to change, wasn't she? That meant the other adults were expecting it too . . . which, in turn, meant it wouldn't come as a great surprise if he turned up on his doorstep as a twenty-foot dragon.

But still . . . when Thomas had changed into a manticore one day, had his parents chased him through the woods out of anger and fear, intent on running him off? Or had they been trying to calm him and bring him home? And when Thomas had fallen off the cliff into the water, and something had grabbed his foot and pulled him under—

"You look so stupid as a dragon," Abigail said suddenly, her voice mocking. "Look at you, standing behind a bush with your stupid long tail poking out one end. And your horrible wings sticking up in the air. How ugly!"

Hal stared at her, taken aback.

"And you can't even walk straight," Abigail went on. "And your stupid fat belly jiggles, and you smell—"

Hurt and embarrassed, Hal shrunk lower, wishing he could make himself small enough to hide his humiliating reptile body behind the bushes. His skin crawled and he felt muscles twitch here and there. How could she say all those things? Just when he'd thought she was turning out to be quite a nice girl she had to go and ruin it by taunting him right at a traumatic moment in his life. He had a good mind to punch her in the face, never mind that she was a girl. Why had he let her tag along with him? He clenched his fists and yelled, "Shut up! You look pretty stupid yourself, with your . . . with your . . ."

He clapped a hand to his mouth. His words had come out clear and human, and not as the throaty roar of a dragon. Amazed and startled, he checked himself over carefully and found he was back to normal—two legs, two arms, pale skin, and no tail. And no clothes.

He peered over the bushes at Abigail. She stood at a safe distance with a smug look on her face.

"I thought that might do the trick," she said. "Nothing like a good insult to make you wish you were someone else. Here's your shirt—catch!"

Hal automatically reached out to catch the thrown shirt, and then realization dawned. That girl was too smart by half, but there was no doubt her insults had done the trick and gotten him back to normal.

Without his heavy reptilian armor he started to feel the cold air on his skin, and he stomped up and down and rubbed his arms. He stepped on a thorn and winced, and then remembered the trampled poison ivy and looked to see if he'd stepped on any. To his surprise he found a number of manticore quills lying in the flattened soil, which must have popped right out of his skin when he changed back. Sore spots on his arms, chest and legs reminded him where they had struck, but they seemed no worse than mild bee stings now. One side of his face felt hot from the oozing venom that had dripped from the manticore's stinger.

Twigs cracked on the other side of the bushes, and Hal tensed. "Abi?"

"Ready yet?"

"No!"

Hal studied his tattered shirt. The arms were attached but ripped open lengthways from shoulder to cuff; still, it meant he could tie the shirt around his waist. He arranged it the best he could and, shivering with cold, stepped out from the bushes.

"You look ridiculous," Abigail said, looking him up and down with a smile tugging at her lips.

"Think yourself lucky you only grow wings."

Abigail laughed. "Take my coat. I can't use it when I fly anyway."

"It's a girl's coat," Hal said with distaste. But as Abigail shrugged and turned away, he snatched it from her.

He slipped into the coat and hurried along with Abigail, ignoring the abrasive feel of the long grass as it caught between his toes. He could deal with that. However, just as he feared, the rocky terrain up ahead seemed impassable with bare feet. He stared in dismay at the loose stones littering the way. "I can't walk over that," he moaned. "I'll have to turn into a dragon again."

"Or," Abigail said, "I could carry you."

"Yeah, right."

Without another word, Abigail spread her wings, buzzed into the air, and nipped around behind him. Hal suddenly found himself caught up tightly under the arms. Her cold cheek pressed against his ear. "Let's see if this works."

For a moment it didn't seem like anything was working. Surely, Hal thought, he was far too heavy for her to carry. But after a moment his feet left the ground and he was carried safely over the sharp stones and rocks.

Buzzing through the air made quick work of the journey, and soon they left the rocky terrain behind and returned to the long grass. Bushes loomed out of the fog ahead.

"Thanks," Hal murmured as Abigail set him down rather roughly.

"Welcome," Abigail gasped. Her face was red, and she took a moment to catch her breath. "I guess faeries aren't designed to carry passengers," she said, rubbing her shoulders.

"You did good," Hal said. He felt as though he wanted to pat her on the back or something, but instead stood by and waited until she had recovered. "The bikes are over that way somewhere," he said, pointing.

The fog was so thick it took some time to find them. When they finally got their bearings and stumbled upon them, they gratefully delved into their backpacks for their lunch. Hal had a thick egg sandwich and an apple, but first he took a long swig from his bottle of water. Then he started into his sandwich as Abigail stared suspiciously at her own apple before taking a tentative bite.

Robbie's bike appeared to be missing. So, too, was his backpack.

"Looks like he deserted us," Abigail said while chewing. "That little creep! Trust him to run off and leave us behind."

Hal knew Robbie better than that. "He didn't desert us," he said, after swallowing a full quarter of his sandwich in one go. "He's probably just, you know, embarrassed that he has nothing to wear. At least I have your coat."

"And a diaper," Abigail added with a giggle.

Hal yelled into the fog. "Robbie! Where are you?"

"He probably went home," Abigail said. "Let's head back."

They picked up their bikes, threw their backpacks across the saddles, and started walking. The gears ticked softly as Hal finished his sandwich and Abigail continued to munch on her apple.

"So Robbie's an ogre," he said at last. "You saw ogres in your book too?"

Abigail nodded. "Yeah. I guess that's what he is. A huge, blundering, brainless ogre. It's no wonder Robbie's such a goof."

Hal peered into the fog. He couldn't see more than twenty paces in front. A chilly breeze whipped across the hill and his arms prickled with goose bumps.

Abigail threw her apple core away and climbed on her bike. "I'm cold. Let's ride." She gave Hal a sudden cheeky grin, sprouted her wings through the hole in the back of her shirt, and with a buzz of activity rose up off the saddle, still grasping the handlebars. Then she freewheeled off into the fog, propelled by the buzzing of her wings.

"Hey," Hal complained, pedaling furiously to keep up. His bare feet hurt on the rough pedal treads. "Look, you go on ahead. I'll see you tomorrow. Do you want your coat?"

"Keep it," Abigail said. "Give it back another day. Bye!"

She disappeared into the gloom, and Hal wondered how she knew where she was headed. Maybe she didn't.

Hal rode alone, suddenly exhausted. The transformation into a dragon had really taken it out of him, and now, thanks to the fog, he was pretty sure he was heading off course. It didn't matter though; the main road ran right across the island from the docks on one side to the lighthouse on the other. As long as he found the road, he could just follow it home.

Sure enough he ended up back at the familiar road, although much farther along than he'd anticipated, right down the other end near the lighthouse. He turned and headed home, grateful for the paved surface after all that long grass.

Shivering with cold, and shattered nerves, he finally picked out a faint glow in the fog ahead. Then the dark, square shape of his home took form. The light came from the fireplace and oil lamp in the kitchen.

Hal got off his bike and wheeled it around to the side of the house. His dad would be out at the farm, but his mom would be in, unless she was visiting one of the other moms. He hurried to his bedroom window around the back. It was so miserable and dull outside that his room was in near-darkness. He slid the window up, hoisted himself onto the sill, and clambered into the room.

After he'd dressed and hunted out some more shoes, he climbed back out the window, got on his bike, and made a show of arriving noisily up the garden path as if he'd just got home from school. "I'm back!" he yelled, throwing his backpack down in the hallway and sauntering into the kitchen. But his mom wasn't there.

"Goodness, Hal," his mom called from the living room. "Shout a little louder, why don't you?"

Hal found his mom on the sofa, looking through some old photographs that she kept in a shoebox. She frowned as he entered. "Why are you wearing those old shoes? What's wrong with the sneakers you had on this morning?"

"They don't fit anymore," Hal said, throwing himself down in the armchair. "They were a bit tight, so I got rid of them."

"So you took a spare pair to school?"

"What are those pictures of, Mom?"

"Don't change the subject. So you took a spare pair to school?"

Hal nodded slowly, then shook his head. He was going to have to fib. "No, Robbie lent me these. Miss Simone let us out early and we went back to Robbie's, and while I was there my feet started hurting so I borrowed some of his shoes."

His mom put down the photos and Hal feared she was getting ready to quiz him further. But instead she asked after Miss Simone. "How did it go today?"

They spent the next half-hour discussing the enigmatic visitor. Hal explained in great detail all she'd told of Out There, and when he got to the part where three adults had gone across to the mainland to see if the virus was still present in the air, his mom looked sad and nodded slowly.

"A terrible thing," she said, staring at the hardwood floor. A silence followed, and Hal listened to the fire crackle and spit. Finally his mom nodded again. "Simone had it all worked out. She found this island and wanted to buy the whole place, said she had unlimited funds . . . but it was decided the process would be too complicated and time-consuming even if she could get the rights. Too many questions asked by authorities. So, instead she bought all the properties on the island under various names."

With a laugh, Hal's mom shook her head and ran both hands through her hair.

"She offered the residents so much money that they couldn't refuse. Well, most couldn't, anyway, but some had lived here all their lives and couldn't bring themselves to start up anywhere else, no matter how much money they were paid. But somehow Simone convinced them. I don't know how on earth she did it, but one day she called a meeting and told us all that everything was set. 'Six months,' she told us. That was when everyone would be gone from the island and we could move in.

"Everything seemed fairly simple, then. There were ten couples involved in the project, including your father and I, and over the next few months we sold our own properties or gave notice to landlords, so we could move to the island. We quit our jobs. That was the beauty of it, you see—not only did we get to live on an island, with our pick of any property we wanted for free, but we were to be paid a modest salary too. For life. And we didn't have to do a stitch of work."

Even though Hal possessed scant knowledge of Out There, he recognized that his mom was talking about the deal of a lifetime. He could sense it in her voice, and in the way she gently shook her head in disbelief.

"If anyone else had told us that we'd get to retire from our jobs and live on an island for free for the rest of our lives, while being paid every month . . . well, we'd have laughed. But Simone is a very persuasive person, and she showed us a few things that blew our minds. Things that belonged in dreams."

"What things?" Hal asked.

But his mom just smiled. "Never mind. Anyway, we were convinced. Convinced beyond a doubt that this woman was someone very special, and that what she was telling us was the truth. And . . . you have to understand, Hal . . ."

She looked directly at him then, her eyes tearing up. She took his hand.

"Ten couples. We were *chosen*, Hal. We were all roughly the same age, and all childless. All us women were in our early thirties, and time was running out."

A shiver went down Hal's spine. "Time was running out?"

"Yes. You see, for whatever reason, none of us had been lucky enough to have any children. Simone picked us because of that. Because we were childless, and because time was running out for us. Because we wanted children and were getting desperate. So when Simone offered a special treatment . . ."

She trailed off, but the words echoed in Hal's mind.

"So, of course we all agreed to the project. It was all explained very carefully, and it wasn't a decision we took lightly. But, Hal . . . a virtually private island to bring you up on, a small community of other kids your age, financial security for life . . . and of course the fact that you might not have been born otherwise. Do you understand?"

She seemed beseeching somehow, as if pleading with him to say *yes, that's fine, I understand.* Did she feel guilty?

As if hearing his thoughts, she pulled him to her and hugged him tight. Hal felt very uncomfortable. He'd always been close to his mom and hugs between them were frequent, but this was something else. Something different and unusual.

Regaining her composure and wiping her eyes, his mom continued in the same quiet tone as before. "Everything was going along nicely. We moved to the island and started to settle in. It was lovely, so quiet, as if all our worries had been left on the mainland. You could see the mainland quite clearly from here, you know, when there was no fog. On a clear day you could see tiny cars glinting in the sunlight as they drove along the coastal road. But it was all far enough away that you couldn't hear anything, except perhaps at night—then you could hear occasional police sirens in the distance, helicopters flying over, that sort of thing."

Hal could not imagine the sounds she referred to.

"Then the virus struck," she went on, sounding tired now. "Everything went wrong. We heard about it on the news, saw TV reports from cities farther inland. It was spreading across the country. It hadn't reached the east coast yet, but it would. It was awful. It seemed that all our dreams were shattered, that life as we knew it was over. We just gathered together and spent night after night crying. The men were strong, telling us that everything would be all right, but we all knew it was a matter of time before the virus reached us here on the island. And then . . . and then Simone saved us."

The window rattled at that moment, and they both looked at it in surprise. Outside, the fog revealed nothing but the trailing branches of an overhanging willow tree, blowing hard in a strong gust of wind.

"Simone visited us and told us not to worry," Hal's mom went on. "She had a solution. She said the project would go ahead, but warned us that life would be very different from what had been planned. She told the men to go into the city and arrange trucks—she gave us stacks of cash and suggested we hire some help, as if anyone would be willing to help at a time like this! But she was right—there were actually people willing to earn some quick cash to drive trucks to the island and back." She shook her head. "Even with death approaching from all around, people still want to earn a quick buck."

"What was on the trucks?" Hal asked—but he already knew.

"Food," his mom replied. "Supplies. Everything we could think of. Simone told us to work out what essentials we would need to survive on the island without ever going to the mainland. She said we could start farming and she'd teach us how to be self-sufficient, but she said it would be easier on us if we get supplies anyway. We asked, 'How long for? A month? Six months?' Simone told us eight years."

"Eight years!" Hal exclaimed. The funny thing was that he knew that already. He'd seen the stores in the old barn, had worked out that there was enough there for a decade. But to be told the story was something else. The final confirmation that his parents had actually *planned* to be secluded on the island for eight years or more came as a shock, no matter how much he thought he'd prepared for it.

"That's how long Simone thought it would take," his mom said. Before Hal could ask how long *what* would take, she hurried on. "Anyway, then the fog arrived. It just appeared overnight. And, soon after, there was no TV signal, no radio, no nothing. No electricity either. No phones. Our mobiles didn't work. *Nothing* worked. We were plunged into silence, and outside there was this fog, silent and thick. Simone said it was there to filter the air, to keep the virus from reaching us, but as a side effect it caused electrical currents and radio frequencies to stop working. 'No matter,' Simone told us. 'Everything will stop working soon anyway.'"

Hal's mom gave a forced smile. "She wasn't exactly gentle when she pointed out that our world was about to end."

"And that was the last you saw of the world?" Hal asked.

"For most of us, yes. There was one couple who couldn't stand it though. The Osbornes. After a few weeks of being utterly cut off from the world, they wanted to leave the island and see what was going on. We all tried to reason with them. We even went up to the top of the lighthouse—it looks out across the mainland and actually sticks up above the fog—but it was impossible to tell what was happening. It looked quiet out there. So the Osbornes packed a few things and left. Said they'd be back."

Hal nodded. "But they never came back."

"Which left nine couples," his mom agreed. "We got on with the project." At this she waved a hand as if to brush off the details. "Anyway, months later we were all expecting."

"Expecting what?"

Hal's mom laughed. She pulled at his hand. "*You*, silly. We were all expecting babies. It was wonderful when we found out, but sad too, as we knew our families were still out there. Were they alive? Dead? We just didn't know, and could hardly stand it. Mr. Porter finally cracked—he just had to know more, so he put on a chemical suit, got in the boat, and went off to the mainland. Your father went with him, along with Mr. Bridges. It was awful for those left behind, waiting anxiously for the three men to return."

"But only two came back," Hal murmured, thinking of poor Abigail's mom.

"That's right. Only two came back. We never saw Mr. Porter again."

There was a long, drawn-out silence. Outside the wind picked up once more. The storm was coming.

## Chapter Twelve
### A stormy evening

Hal's mom started putting the photos into the shoebox, shuffling them into tidy stacks. "Since the fog arrived, we've never seen the sun or a blue sky," she said. "It was terrible at first, living with no electricity. Even the water was cut off, because the pumps weren't working. We noticed that batteries still worked though, so we made use of the cars for a while. Until we ran out of gasoline." She sighed. "No power, no running water . . . and no sun. Everything was so *damp*. Couldn't do a thing with my hair, and as for my skin—" She chuckled and shook her head. "Listen to me, worrying about hair and skin when you've never seen the sun in your life. One day you'll feel its warmth on your face, Hal, and your skin will slowly tan a lovely golden color. We'll all have to be careful at first, and use sun block . . ." She trailed off and looked thoughtful. "But that's all for later. What else did Miss Simone tell you?"

Bringing himself forcibly back to the present, Hal thought hard and chose his words carefully. "She asked us if we were changing. She called us one by one into the office and told us to tell her about anything strange happening."

His mom stared at him, her face expressionless. "And?"

"And what?" Hal asked, suddenly feeling as though he were facing off against some great enemy. This was Simone's project, whatever *that* meant, and he didn't trust the mysterious stranger. Not yet anyway. But his mom apparently did, and anything he told her would get back to Simone eventually. *Be careful what you say*, Abigail's voice warned at the back of his mind.

"Are you . . . changing in any way?" his mom pressed.

Hal put on his best bewildered face. "Into what?"

His mom was frozen in place, one hand inside the shoebox and the other holding a small handful of photos. "Hal," she said after a while. But then she faltered. Finally she dumped the rest of the photos in the box and swept a hand through her hair. "Hal, if anything is happening to you—or if anything should happen in the future—you *will* tell me, won't you? Or Miss Simone."

Hal leaned forward. "Mom, what are you talking about?"

Something in the fire popped and a spark flew out. It smoldered on the floor and turned into a tiny black speck of charcoal.

Hal's mom got up and went to poke at the fire. She jabbed at it with the long wrought-iron poker as if trying to spear a fish. "We know about Fenton's teeth," she said with her back to him. "He's changing, Hal. That's the sort of thing we need to be told of. It's important."

"But why?"

Hal waited for his mom to respond, but she said nothing.

"Mom, what's going to happen to Fenton now that his teeth are all sharp and pointed?"

She jabbed again, then bent to toss in a half-log from the small woodpile. "He'll be leaving. He and his parents will move on to another place."

Stunned, Hal was speechless for a long while. Then he swallowed. "A *better* place? Or . . . or a prison? A laboratory?"

His mom swung around, her face a mask of astonishment. She still held the poker, and a fine wisp of smoke trailed from its smoldering end. If anyone had walked in at that moment it would have looked like she was attacking him.

"Hal, wherever did you—why would—" She shook her head, replaced the poker on the side of the hearth, and returned to the sofa, where she clasped her hands together and stared long and hard at Hal. "A *prison?* What gave you that idea? Fenton will be moving to a *nice* place, where the sun shines. It's what we've all been waiting for, Hal. The changes are long overdue. We should have moved away from this miserable island years ago."

She sighed. "Thomas was the first to change, when he was six. It came as a shock, even though we were half expecting it. About eight years, we were told, and he changed at six. But it all went horribly wrong, and he ran away, fell off the cliff, and was killed on the rocks."

Hal opened his mouth to disagree, but closed it again. *Let her speak.*

"Mr. and Mrs. Patten couldn't deal with the loss, couldn't live here anymore. They decided to take their chances on the mainland, so took the boat and left. We never saw them again. From then on we kept a close eye on you all, waiting to see if anyone else was on the verge of changing . . . but years passed and still nothing happened. Now you're all twelve, and our stocks are running low. Some things have already run out, as you know, like the toothpaste, the soap . . . and the shoes will run out soon too, if you keep growing out of them so fast."

The window rattled again as a gust of wind hammered against it. A draft slipped through the frame and the curtains moved. Both Hal and his mom listened to the wind whipping through the willow tree outside in the yard. Earlier they had seen the long, trailing branches dragging in the wind, but now they saw nothing; the fog pressed against the glass like it was trying to smother the house.

The wind died away, a temporary lull, and Hal's mom slid the box of photos onto the shelf under the coffee table.

"I'm not supposed to be telling you any of this," she said with a shrug. "All us parents agreed to say nothing, otherwise there would always be one in your class knowing more than the others, and that would lead to problems. So rather than confuse things, we agreed to say nothing, to keep what we knew under wraps. But now that Fenton is experiencing changes . . . well, now we need to know if it's just *him* experiencing changes, or *all* of you."

Hal nodded.

His mom waited, one eyebrow raised.

Still Hal said nothing. He wanted to tell her, "I'm a dragon! Abigail's a faerie! Robbie's an ogre!" But then what? Obviously they were freaks of nature, or some kind of horrible experiment. Either way they were sure to be locked up and studied for the rest of their lives, or worse, put down like sick animals. But would his mom really allow such a thing? And lie to him that way?

"Hal?"

The problem was that she didn't even know the whole truth herself. She thought Thomas had been killed on the rocks, but he'd survived, despite being pulled underwater by something and nearly drowned. Did Miss Simone know this? Thomas said he'd awoken by a lake and lived the next six years as a manticore, with a blue sky and bright sun. There was no lake on the island, so he must have been washed up Out There, perhaps in some cove or inlet. That explained the blue sky and bright sun, but it also meant the virus had gone—or it never existed in the first place.

Which meant Miss Simone was lying about the virus.

Then again, Hal and his friends had great immune systems, or so Dr. Porter had always told them. They'd never had colds, measles, or chicken pox . . . so perhaps Thomas had simply been unaffected by the virus.

"Hal, what's on your mind, honey?"

Hal focused on his mom. Tell her, or not? He *wanted* to, but that would betray his friends. And so many things didn't quite add up. He needed to talk to Abigail and Robbie first, tell them everything his mom had said, and take a vote on what to do next.

Gritting his teeth, Hal shook his head. "Nothing, Mom. Unless you can tell me *why* we're all supposed to be changing?"

She frowned. "It's a lot to take in, Hal. Some of you might not . . . I mean, it would be terrible if only a few of you . . . well, what I mean is, sometimes it's better not knowing—"

"Never mind," Hal said, getting to his feet. He stalked toward the door and shot her a scowl. "You're not the only one who can keep secrets, Mom."

"Hal! Don't talk to me that way. Come back here."

"I'm going over to Robbie's," Hal said, trying to keep the tremble from his voice. Ignoring his mom's protests, he grabbed a coat, slammed the door behind him, and ran off along the road.

The wind whipped through Hal's coat as he banged on the door to Robbie's house. It was only late afternoon, but the sky had darkened to a dirty gray and the fog twisted and turned in the wind as though confused. No rain yet, but it was on its way.

"Hal," Mrs. Strickland said as she opened the door. "I'm surprised you're out in this weather. You know there's going to be a storm?"

"Yeah, I just wanted to hang out for a while," Hal said, shrugging.

Robbie appeared, peering around his mom's shoulder. He looked perfectly normal, with no sign of the monstrous ogre he'd become earlier that afternoon. "Hal! Come on in."

As Mrs. Strickland stepped aside, Robbie turned and led the way down the hall to his room. Closing the door softly, he turned to Hal with shining eyes.

"I changed. I mean, *really* changed."

"I know," Hal said, nodding. "I saw you. You nearly ran me down."

Robbie stared at him, his forehead creasing. "I did?"

Hal sank into an old armchair in the corner and stared at the shelf above Robbie's unmade bed. Small jars lined the shelf, each containing bits of grass and dry leaves. Hal knew a few of those jars had bugs crawling around inside; the lids had been pierced to allow fresh air in so the helpless insects wouldn't suffocate.

A bizarre vision popped into Hal's mind just then: *eight children trapped in huge jars, being studied by scientists in long white coats.* Some of the kids kept changing into strange monsters, and this caused considerable excitement among the laboratory staff.

"Did you know you were an ogre?" Hal asked.

"A what?" Robbie sat on the edge of his bed and absently ruffled his messy hair. "Look, I don't know what happened exactly. I just remember walking into the forest alone. You and Abi were back there in the fog somewhere, talking, and I didn't want to interrupt." He gave Hal a big, meaningful wink. "Anyway, I walked for maybe five minutes, and then I heard a noise and turned around. And there was this . . . this . . ."

"Manticore," Hal said helpfully. "Abi says it's a manticore. She read about it in a book."

Robbie nodded, looking a little puzzled but accepting the information anyway. "Well, when it raised its tail, and I saw those quills, I yelled and . . . well, I just . . ."

"Ran?"

"No, I charged it."

"What?"

Robbie nodded, his face reddening. "I know. Crazy. I don't know what came over me. I just . . . I just wanted to rush over and tangle with it, you know?"

Hal remembered a similar feeling when he was changing into a dragon.

"I remember thinking how stupid I was," Robbie went on. "I mean, as if I could tackle something like that! But there I was, beating on it with fists that weren't mine. Big, hairy fists. And the manticore didn't seem so big anymore, so I hit it over and over again. And then, well, it lashed out with its tail and stuck me with a bunch of quills. They hurt!"

"Yeah," Hal agreed.

"So I turned and ran, and I kept going until I found the bikes. I thought I'd see you there. But you weren't around."

Hal spread his hands. "You rushed right by us."

"Did I? Well, I was confused. I just assumed you were waiting by the bikes. Anyway, I started calling for you, and then thought, 'Wait a minute, where are my clothes?'"

Hal laughed quietly. "And you had this horrible idea that Abigail would see you naked, so you took off."

Robbie shuddered. "Yeah. I don't know exactly what happened today, but I had to leave. Fast."

"And you came home and climbed in the bedroom window."

Robbie nodded, a wry grin emerging. "Got some clothes on, then sauntered into the kitchen. Frightened Mom half to death, because she didn't hear me come in the front door."

"That's why I climbed back out the window," Hal murmured. "Got back on my bike and rode up to the front door as if I was just getting home."

Now Robbie looked confused. "Wait a minute—you lost your clothes too? But why—" His face suddenly lit up. "You changed as well, didn't you?"

Hal launched into his tale, revealing how Abigail had come by his house late on Saturday night and showed him her wings. Robbie's eyes nearly bugged out of his head at the idea of her buzzing around in the air. "She wasn't kidding!" he said, shaking his head. "When she said she could keep up with us even without her bike, she actually meant it!"

"Yeah," Hal said, nodding. "She teases a lot, yanks our chains, but she's not all bluff. And she makes a lot of sense too. She thinks we're all freaks, and that Miss Simone wants to take us away and experiment on us. Thing is, I'm beginning to believe her. A couple of things don't add up—like Thomas being killed on the rocks. He wasn't killed at all. But even my mom thinks he was killed, which means all the adults must think the same way . . . which means either they all just assumed he was dead, or Miss Simone lied and *told* them he was dead."

Hal paused a moment, feeling breathless. "And where does she come from anyway? She tells us there's a virus Out There, that it's still dangerous to breathe the air, and yet she must live there." He remembered something. "Unless she lives on another world altogether, as she hinted in class?" Hal sighed. "Nothing makes sense. Oh, but I have some stuff to tell you. Stuff my mom just told *me* . . ."

For the next ten minutes Hal recounted what his mom had told him. Robbie listened intently, not saying a single word.

When Hal had finished, Robbie fell back across his bed and lay there looking up at the ceiling. There was a long silence. After a while he cleared his throat. "So, uh . . . you're a dragon, are you?"

"And you're an ogre," Hal said.

There was another long silence.

"And Abigail's a faerie," Robbie said quietly. "What about the others?"

"Haven't thought about it," Hal said, mildly surprised. "There's too much going on. Look, what should we do next? Abigail suggested getting on the raft again and going Out There. You know, tying string to the docks so we can find our way back again."

"I don't think that'll work," Robbie said with a sigh. "I don't think the sea serpent will let us. If it's really there to guard us, to stop us leaving, it's not going to let us get very far, is it? No, I think we should give that up and go plug up that hole where the fog comes out."

"Well," Hal said slowly, "I like that idea better too. But what about the manticore? What if it attacks us again? It might take us by surprise next time. And even if we change and fight it off again, that'll be another set of clothes down the drain. And what if . . . what if the fog really does filter the air and keep us safe from the virus?"

But Robbie appeared not to hear that last part. He sat up and tapped a finger absently on his nose. "What if we tell Miss Simone or our parents about the manticore? Maybe they'll get rid of it. Shoot it with those long rifles they go hunting with."

A horrible thought entered Hal's mind just then. "If they kill the manticore . . . and then roast it . . . we'll be eating Thomas Patten for dinner."

"Oh, gross!" cried Robbie, and threw a pillow at Hal.

There was another long silence. "Anyway," Hal went on, "if our dads go out hunting in Black Woods, they might find our clothes lying around, ripped to shreds."

"And they'll start asking even more awkward questions," Robbie said, nodding. He grimaced. "There must be *something* we can do!"

"Well, Abigail also suggested breaking into the lighthouse."

Robbie nodded. "Yeah, she wants to go to the top to see if we can see out over the fog."

"Which we can," Hal said, growing excited. "My mom said so. If we can get to the top of the lighthouse, above the fog, we might actually see Out There. And if we can see Out There, then we might spot people walking around. If everything looks normal, well, then we'll know Miss Simone and all our parents are lying to us. But if we see a bunch of crazy people running around, then—"

"Then Miss Simone might be telling the truth," Robbie finished.

Hal's brain was starting to hurt. "You know manticores and dragons and ogres and faeries are make-believe, right?" Seeing Robbie's puzzled expression, Hal nodded. "Yes, they're all fantasy creatures, nothing but myth and folklore."

"But . . . they *are* real," Robbie said.

"Right. As real as that blood-sucking butterfly you found. That's something else that doesn't exist, according to all the books on wildlife I've ever read." Hal groaned. "I can't think straight anymore."

Outside, something blew over with a thud, and together they glanced outside. There wasn't much to see; Robbie's room faced the rear garden, but the fog was so thick and dark they couldn't even see the surrounding hedges and trees, just a bank of clouds that drifted fast across the grass.

Then a rumble of thunder sounded in the distance. Hal grinned at Robbie. "Cool. Haven't had thunder in ages."

"Mom'll freak out," Robbie said. "She hates storms."

There was a sudden spatter of rain on the window, and Hal wondered if he should go home before it really got started or wait and see if Robbie's parents would offer dinner. He glanced at the clock on the wall, and frowned.

"It's stopped," Robbie said, following his gaze. "Forgot to wind it. Hang on, I'll check the time in the living room."

"Hey," Hal called as Robbie reached for the door. "Think I can stay for dinner? Then we can watch the storm and talk all night, otherwise I'll have to get back before it starts pouring down out there."

Robbie nodded and disappeared from the room. He returned a minute later, grinned and said dinner was fine, then took the clock down from the wall. He wound it and set it to four-fifteen.

"Is that all?" asked Hal, surprised. "It seems later. So much has happened this afternoon, and it's so dark out."

"Yeah. Come on, we'll watch the storm from the deck, out back."

They went out back to the large screened-in deck that filled the corner space formed by the L-shaped house. The roof had been extended so the space was completely protected from rain.

They sat in lightweight chairs facing the garden and stared across the lawn. Visibility was very poor—there wasn't much to see at all except the spectacle of fast-moving fog, and the occasional spatter of heavy raindrops on the grass. There were a couple of bright flashes, and then the thunder boomed loudly.

"It's getting closer," Hal said.

The familiar smell of musty storm air wafted through the screens. Strong gusts of wind tugged at Hal's hair. Then the rain started hammering down, and another bright flash of lightning lit up the fog in a ghostly white glow.

"Cool," Robbie said over the noise of the rain. "Wouldn't like to be out in it, though. We'd be soaked in seconds."

The rain was coming down so hard now that the edge of the deck had turned a shiny black, and large drops were bouncing toward Hal and Robbie. They backed their chairs out of range.

Thunder cracked and rumbled, dying away slowly. Lightning flickered, and suddenly a tremendous crash of thunder shook the deck and almost deafened the boys. They whooped with delight.

Robbie's mother poked her head out the door. "Hal? Your mother knows you're here, right?"

"Yes, Mrs. Strickland," Hal said.

"Well, good. Dinner will be ready soon." She disappeared back inside.

Another blinding flash lit up the garden, and the thunder boomed once more. The wind began howling now, and the fog twisted and spun as if performing some kind of weird smoky pirouette on the lawn. It was mesmerizing, especially with the lightning flickering every few seconds.

Impossibly, the rain came down even harder, driving sideways under the force of the wind, luckily away from the deck or the boys would have been forced to finally retreat inside. The roof rattled, and an old slate tile suddenly worked loose and slid off, flipping over the gutter as it went. It landed with a plop in the mushy grass. Although he couldn't see beyond the fog, Hal could clearly hear the trees swaying at the foot of the garden. And, somewhere out in the street at the front of the house, a metal bucket went skittering along the paved surface.

Then Hal heard shouts from somewhere, and he glanced around. "Hear that?" he called over the wind and rain. Robbie said something, but the thunder crashed just then and drowned him out. The boys stared wide-eyed at each other and listened carefully.

More shouts—a woman's voice, followed by a number of low, deep voices. Hal couldn't make out anything they were saying. Perhaps the storm was wreaking havoc with someone's house. It certainly was a wild one.

Then there came a panting, snorting sound, and heavy footfalls mingled with the squelch of sodden turf and shallow puddles.

Hal leaned forward in his chair, searching the twisting fog and sheets of rain. And then, out of the fog, a shadowy figure emerged. It slowed to a stop and stood restlessly at the far end of the lawn.

"Look!" Robbie said, pointing.

"I see it," Hal replied, squinting. "What *is* that? A horse?"

As the lightning continued to flicker, the boys saw that the figure was large, and at first glance it did appear to be a horse, with a man or woman on its back, hunched forward as if cowering from the rain. One of the men back from the farm, perhaps? But something was wrong. If only the lightning would flicker again.

"Oh!" Hal exclaimed, stunned, as a flash of light lit up the garden for half a second. For that brief moment the horse and rider were silhouetted side-on, a sleek, powerful shape trotting across the far end of the lawn.

Only it wasn't a horse and rider.

"A centaur!" cried Robbie with excitement, jumping to his feet. "Look! A man with a horse's body!"

*Or a horse with a man's head*, Hal thought absently, staring into the darkness. The night sky lit up again, and the creature—the *centaur*—glanced around furtively, a stout figure whose black, rain-soaked flanks gleamed in the sudden glare of the flashing lightning. More shouts came, closer now, and the centaur's man-head snapped around, panting steam.

The night was plunged once more into foggy darkness, but the centaur seemed to retain traces of discharged energy and its body glowed with a faint luminescence. It reared up, and then, with a stamping and splashing of hoofs, galloped away into the woods.

Astonished, Hal could only stare after it in silence. Robbie turned to him, his face alight with excitement, but before he could say anything, Hal jabbed a finger into the fog once more. "Look!"

A woman had appeared, running after the centaur with a long robe billowing behind her. Her movements seemed eerily disjointed as the strobe lightning effect caught her in various poses across the lawn. Her voice suddenly pierced the hammering rain and blustery wind. "This way! I can smell it!"

It was Miss Simone, her long blond hair plastered over her shoulders and her face glistening wet. In a moment she was gone, and behind her came what seemed like a hoard of children—but there were six, eight, maybe ten of them, all heavyset and stout, grunting and occasionally shouting with deep, guttural voices.

Hal and Robbie watched as they stampeded across the garden. Then they were gone, and the thunder drowned out any further sounds.

It was several minutes before Hal spoke. He leaned over and whispered as loudly as he could, trying to make himself heard over the storm but suddenly fearing that Robbie's parents might hear. "Robbie, tell me you saw all that too!"

Robbie nodded, his eyes wide. "A centaur," he said, "being chased by Miss Simone and . . . and . . ."

"And some short people," Hal finished, puzzled. "I couldn't see them very well, but they were too short to be adults and too big and heavy to be the other kids."

"And there were too many of them," Robbie agreed. "I counted maybe ten."

They stared into the flickering darkness once more, half expecting something else to come bounding out into the open. A vision of the manticore popped into Hal's head, looming out of the fog with a grin on its face, and that terrible tail curled up and over its head, swaying in the air with quills bristling.

Hal shivered, suddenly realizing there was nothing to stop the creature from leaving Black Woods and roaming all over the island. What if it was lurking in the nearby bushes right now? Worse, what if it leapt on him as he headed home later in the evening?

"Where do you think it came from?" Robbie asked suddenly.

Hal blinked. "What, the manticore?"

Robbie looked puzzled. "No, the centaur. And those funny short people."

Hal shrugged. "Same place the manticore came from, probably. Same place Miss Simone came from this morning, and went home to after school. We've got to get to the top of the lighthouse. I think that's the safest plan. We'll do that first, and then we'll talk about blocking up the fog-hole."

"Straight after school tomorrow," Robbie agreed.

## Chapter Thirteen
## Farewell picnic for Fenton

Hal arrived at school the next morning at eight on the dot, having suffered through a breakfast full of curious stares from his parents. On several occasions, one or the other had started to say something, only to clam up and continue eating in silence. Hal guessed they had been trying to ask him about physical changes, but seemed unable to phrase the question.

It was strange that they didn't just come out and ask, *Are you turning into a monster?* But on the other hand, what if they believed he was telling the truth and was *not* undergoing odd transformations? How would an ordinary twelve-year-old boy take to a question like that, if he really knew nothing of dragons, manticores, ogres and faeries?

As he headed to school, deep in thought, Hal realized that Miss Simone's project had a great deal of uncertainty attached to it. It had taken longer than expected for most of them, excluding Thomas, to start changing, and perhaps this had led Miss Simone and all the parents to believe that the project was not going well. If Fenton's physical change was considered a "successful result," and Miss Simone was to take him away somewhere, then what would happen to the rest of them if they never changed? He supposed nothing at all would happen—they'd simply remain on the island forever, scraping up the last of their supplies and doomed never to see a blue sky.

So were his parents hopeful that he would change so they could move on to wherever Fenton was headed? His mom had said it was nice there, with sunshine and blue skies—a better place, she had said. But what if Miss Simone had lied about that too? What if there was no such place? What if Miss Simone just wanted to keep up the pretense until the children started changing, and then do away with the parents and steal the children for experiments?

Hal felt a chill as images of doctors in white coats filled his mind, standing there on the other side of glass walls, holding clipboards and writing notes and nodding to each other as Hal found himself changing into a dragon . . .

With his head full of dark thoughts, he trudged into school. Miss Simone was already there, and she watched like a hawk as Hal entered the classroom and made for his seat. Most of the others were there too, sitting in silence at their desks. Miss Simone's presence killed any chance of conversation, so Hal contented himself with a few wordless glances toward Robbie and Abigail. Dewey and

Darcy filed in a few moments later, and after the scraping of their chairs ceased, absolute quiet fell on the classroom.

Then Miss Simone spoke, her voice pleasant enough but her eyes hard and cold. "Good morning, class. I trust you finished your homework? I'll collect your essays in a moment."

There was a momentary shuffling as each classmate retrieved a single sheet of paper from his or her backpack. Hal had finished his essay just before going to bed—he'd almost forgotten it, but had hurriedly scribbled some words on the paper, keeping his writing deliberately big to fill the space. Miss Simone had wanted them all to write a quick essay about "a boy or girl who has magical powers." Yeah, *right*. As if Hal was going to give the game away and write about being a dragon at a time like this! Miss Simone's little plan was as transparent as the glass in the window frame.

"Now," Miss Simone said, remaining in her seat with her hands clasped on the desk, "today I've decided not to discuss the past. I know you're anxious to learn of the world your parents came from, and why you're all here on the island today. But if I discuss the past, I might also hint at the present and future, and I can't do that unless I know for sure that . . ." She paused. "Well, you see, great things will come to those who confide in me their secrets. Fenton, for example—"

She rose and padded across the floor, barefoot as she had been yesterday. *Does the woman not have any shoes?* wondered Hal.

Miss Simone stopped behind Fenton's desk and put her hands on his shoulders. He looked uncomfortable with the contact. "Fenton here is undergoing a few remarkable changes. You're all aware that his teeth have completely altered, yes? Well, as insignificant as this may sound, his teeth are of the utmost importance to me. They signify something far greater than you can imagine."

Hal smiled to himself. *I think I can imagine pretty well, thanks.*

"This will be Fenton's last day on the island," Miss Simone went on. There were a number of gasps. "You see, Fenton is moving to a better place, where the sun shines and there are many, many people to welcome him and his parents."

A vision of doctors in white coats filled Hal's mind again. Fenton's struggling parents were secreted away in the night, to be tossed off a cliff . . .

Hal shuddered as Miss Simone continued innocently. "His family is ready to start over in a new place, far from here. And all because of his teeth."

She paused for effect. Hal caught Abigail glancing his way, and he wondered what she was thinking. She had that defiant look in her eye.

"Please, Miss?" asked Emily, raising her hand. "Are you saying he's going Out There?"

Simone shook her head. "If you mean the mainland, then no. There's another place. It's . . ." She thought for a moment, then shrugged. "It's just elsewhere."

"Elsewhere," Emily repeated quietly.

Miss Simone flashed a smile of white teeth around at the class, and in that moment she looked radiant, entrancing. "So you see, children, it's in your own interest to, ah, confide in me. The quicker we leave this island, the better."

There was a long silence. Miss Simone looked around carefully, her gaze resting on first one and then another classmate. But nobody said a word. Silence reigned. Her broad smile faltered a little, and then began to fade altogether.

"Miss?" asked Abigail.

Miss Simone's head whipped around eagerly. "Yes, Abigail?"

With that mischievous gleam in her eye once more, she said, "What if we have nothing to report? I mean, none of us have teeth like Fenton's. I think we're all perfectly normal." She looked around. "Aren't we?"

Everyone nodded vigorously.

Miss Simone said nothing. She stood there with her hands still on Fenton's shoulders. Her face slowly reddened. Hal could almost feel the atmosphere thicken, and could have sworn the room grew darker. Although Fenton couldn't see her face, it was obvious from the way he flinched that he detected the change in her mood. Or perhaps Miss Simone's fingers were digging into his shoulders.

"Children," she said finally, through gritted teeth. "Why do you test me so? Everything I've done here has been for your benefit as much as mine. The only reason I'm here at all is because of you. Why don't you trust me?"

Nobody said anything for a while. But then Hal cleared his throat. "Um, Miss Simone? Perhaps if you told us a bit more, then we might feel ready to trust you. Even if we were, um, changing—like Fenton I mean—well, what would happen to us? What's going to happen to Fenton?"

"I told you—he's going to a better place." Miss Simone looked puzzled. "Why don't you believe me? Why would I lie? Look, you were only supposed to be here eight years. Eight years is normally how long it takes. But it's been twelve years already and my people are getting desperate—"

She broke off, biting her lip.

"You may be our last hope, you know," she murmured, her gaze turning to the window. "Communications are failing badly, people are dying as a result . . ."

With a sudden angry toss of her golden locks, she turned and grabbed a sheet of paper from Dewey's desk—his essay—then moved on and grabbed Abigail's, then Robbie's. As she whipped Hal's off his desk, the strong scent of ocean wafted under his nostrils and he had a split-second vision of her diving off the cliff and plummeting to the sea below.

"Get on with some work," Miss Simone commanded. She thought for a second, then shrugged. "Open your history books and copy the text from any chapter onto paper."

Hal wasn't the only one who found this a very strange request. He glanced around and saw a number of puzzled looks. Emily dared to put her hand up. "Um, please, Miss? May I ask why we—"

"No, you may not," Miss Simone said shortly. She was scanning the essays and her face was reddening even more. "What *is* this nonsense? Darcy wishes she could read minds, Hal would like to invent a potion that makes him small so he can 'crawl under a rock and stay there,' and Abigail—" Miss Simone snorted with derision. "—Abigail wishes she had 'the power to make little blue pimples appear all over Robbie's face because that would be really funny.'"

There was resounding laughter, and even Robbie turned to give Abigail a big grin. It was more than just funny though, Hal realized. It was a sense of camaraderie between them all, a friendship that had been taken for granted up until recently. Now, with the arrival of Miss Simone, an untrustworthy stranger who was threatening to take them all away from everything they'd ever known, it was a clear case of 'us against her.'

The next few hours passed without incident. Miss Simone seemed bewildered and frustrated that the class wasn't coming forward with tales of amazing transformations, and tried several different approaches to get them to talk throughout the course of the morning. After she had thrown the ridiculous essays into the trash and calmed down, she turned on her friendly smile again and went around the class, sitting on the corner of each desk and trying to sweet-talk one classmate or another into letting her into his or her secrets. "You can tell me," she whispered, leaning so close that her blond locks tumbled into Hal's face.

When this didn't work she tried emotional blackmail. She made out that all the parents were worried sick and that they'd have to remain on the island forever, and even tried to convince the children that some of their parents had reported symptoms of a virus. "It's breaking through the fog," Miss Simone said, putting on an anxious voice and frowning deeply. "If we could only leave here . . . but of course only Fenton can leave, because he's the only one who is experiencing physical changes."

Abigail spent much of the time rolling her eyes at Hal, and he had to agree that Miss Simone was making a fool of herself. Did she really think her feeble lies were convincing? Clearly she had spent very little time with children before, and completely underestimated their intelligence.

Later, Miss Simone tried a matter-of-fact approach. "Okay, let's level with each other," she said. "I'll tell you something about this place Fenton and his parents are going to, and in turn one of you agrees to be honest."

This was actually quite an interesting proposition, and the class listened carefully as Miss Simone explained that her world—which Emily insisted on labeling Elsewhere—was full of rolling green countryside, huge forests with trees reaching high into the sky, lakes and rivers of crystal clear water, and plenty of sunshine: blue skies, little puffy white clouds, and a brilliant sun that rose round and orange in the morning and cast perfect rainbows during showers. She told of the wildlife too: horses, cows, and sheep just like on the island, but manymore creatures besides, *fantastic* creatures that had once roamed both lands, thousands of years ago.

"Many of the creatures I take for granted are extinct in your own land," Miss Simone explained. "The ties between our worlds have long since been severed. There used to be holes linking the worlds, like doorways, but now there are just a few left in existence. That's why this island was chosen; along its eastern shores are a few holes that allow passage between my world and yours."

This was of enormous interest to the class, particularly Hal, Robbie and Abigail, who had seen Miss Simone diving off the cliff into the sea. That had been along the eastern shore.

"Do you have a boat, Miss Simone?" asked Robbie. "To get to your land?"

"No, I don't need one," she replied. "I'm a good swimmer. I arrive on the island through a hole out in the ocean, and swim ashore. But this hole is along the south eastern shore—quite a walk to the school in the morning, I can tell you! So I leave another way, a much quicker route. Unfortunately it means, uh, jumping into the sea from fairly high up, so it's sort of an exit route only. There's another hole I know of too, but I can't use it."

This was truly some useful information! Hal exchanged glances with Robbie and Abigail. Finally Miss Simone seemed to be explaining things. And telling the truth, by the sound of it.

But here she stopped. "Now, it's your turn. Someone—anyone—please be honest with me. Has anyone experienced anything strange lately? I don't have to explain to you what I mean by strange. If something was happening, you'd know about it. The structure of Fenton's teeth changed overnight, which is frankly impossible in most humans. How about anyone else?"

There was a long pause. Hal wondered why, directly in front of him, Lauren was wriggling her shoulders and squirming in her chair. He hoped she wouldn't give anything away.

"Anyone?" Miss Simone urged. "Please. Fair's fair. I told you a little about my land. Now tell *me* something."

Lauren squirmed some more, and she reached behind her, trying to scratch an itch on her back.

Miss Simone's face was growing red again. "Stop fidgeting, Lauren," she snapped. She glared around the class. "Somebody talk to me. Right now."

But nobody said a word. Everyone did a very good job of looking bewildered, although to be fair Emily and Darcy probably *were* bewildered.

Hal happened to glance at Lauren just then. She had finally reached the itch on her back, but in doing so, something startling happened that almost made Hal jump up in surprise. He quickly looked away in case Miss Simone saw him watching. If she saw what Hal was seeing, then the game would be up for Lauren.

* * *

They made it to the end of class without being strung up by the hot-tempered stranger. Hal eagerly got together with Abigail and Robbie and herded them outside away from Miss Simone. He led them under the low-hanging oak tree and kept his voice down.

"Did you see Lauren's thumb?" Both Abigail and Robbie frowned at him, perplexed. "It changed!" Hal said.

Abigail nodded knowingly. "Ah."

"It grew," Hal went on, "and she sprouted hair from her knuckles. She was trying to scratch an itch, and it must have happened without her realizing it."

"Hair?" repeated Robbie doubtfully.

"And a long, curved nail. It was bizarre. I wonder what she's turning into."

"Could be anything," Abigail mused. "I've seen it happen too. But a long thumb and fingernail with a tuft of hair isn't much to go on."

"Hair," Robbie mumbled.

Abigail turned to him, her face developing a huge grin. "Robbie can't face his girlfriend having hair sprouting from her knuckles."

"Shut up, Abi!"

Hal laughed. "Bet she's right, though. Not a very appealing image, is it? A girl with hairy knuckles. But maybe she's another ogre. Then she'd be a perfect match for you."

Robbie huffed and made a face, reddening.

Most of the classmates had walked to school because it was so muddy after last night's storm, but Fenton, Dewey and Lauren had brought their bikes. There was a moment of confusion when Fenton, silent and broody, swung his around and got his front wheel tangled up with Dewey's pedals. He pulled at it roughly and ended up yanking Dewey's bike right out of his hands. It fell in the grass and Dewey backed off as Fenton scowled at him.

Hal feared trouble from the big boy, but Fenton seemed out of sorts. He looked around at his classmates, as if unsure what to say. Finally he managed to squeeze out a few words. "Looks like that's it, then," he said gruffly.

"Are you really leaving, Fenton?" asked Emily. "I mean, Miss Simone said you were, but I don't believe it."

"I don't believe *anything* Miss Simone says," Abigail agreed.

"It's true," Fenton said, sticking a fat finger in his mouth and prodding at his teeth. "Mom and Dad said so last night. We've been packing."

There was an awkward silence. It seemed unbelievable that Fenton would not be there the next day. None of the children knew how to say goodbye to anyone. The only practice they had had was when Thomas supposedly died years ago. But standing in front of a tombstone mumbling words of remembrance was hardly the same thing.

"Well," Fenton said, turning his bike around. "See you."

"Um . . ." Darcy said.

Fenton looked at her, but she said nothing more. Nobody said anything. It was all too much to take in. How could Fenton *not be there* tomorrow as usual, annoying them all, bullying them? Nobody particularly liked Fenton, but he was one of them, after all.

Hal found his voice. "Are you . . . are you looking forward to leaving?"

"No."

Another long silence.

"Well, see you soon," Fenton said finally, and cycled away before anyone could say anything else.

They all watched him go. *Seven left*, thought Hal. But what fate awaited Fenton Bridges? Was he really going to a nice place . . . or a laboratory somewhere? Was Miss Simone lying to everyone? To the children and their parents? Or, worse, were their parents *in cahoots* with Miss Simone and actually *knew* that a ghastly fate awaited the children once they started transforming?

Nothing seemed certain except for one thing: Miss Simone didn't always tell the truth.

"Is it worth following Miss Simone again?" asked Robbie. "If so, we need to do it right now, because she left a few minutes ago."

"Nah," Abigail said. "Hey, Emily, did you organize things as I asked you to yesterday?"

Emily beamed. "Of course I did." She took out a notebook and starting flipping through pages.

But Abigail didn't give her a chance to speak. "That's fine. Okay, let's make a few plans. Huddle round, gang."

Darcy was lost in thought. "I can't believe Fenton's really leaving. He was a bully, but still . . . we've known him all our lives. He can't just *go*."

"Pay attention, Darcy," Abigail said.

Everyone faced Abigail in a small circle—Hal, Robbie, little Dewey with wide saucer eyes, Lauren absently scratching at her shoulder, Emily with her notebook open and pencil poised, and Darcy, who kept stealing glances over their heads as if trying to find Fenton in the fog.

Abigail was in full command. Even Robbie was hanging onto her words. "Okay. We're going to go home as usual, and then we're going to steal some food and cram it into our backpacks or something."

"Steal some food?" Emily interrupted.

"Yes, because we might not be back for dinner and we'll get hungry. What we're going to do is likely to keep us out late."

"So why not just tell our parents we're planning a picnic, and then we won't have to steal anything," argued Emily. "Then we won't even have to worry about being late for dinner, because our parents won't be expecting us."

"Yes, yes," Abigail said impatiently. "Yes, fine, that's a good idea. A better idea. Okay, so we plan a picnic somewhere, and then we meet up at the lighthouse. Don't tell anyone we're going to the lighthouse, or anywhere near it. Understand? Let's say we're meeting in the field by the old mill."

Emily scribbled in her notebook. "Picnic. Lighthouse. Old mill. Okay, good. Abigail, is this why you wanted Darcy, Lauren and I to bring blankets to the lighthouse?"

"And bolt-cutters," Darcy said.

"And an axe," offered Lauren. "We got everything you asked for. It's all there, outside the lighthouse gates, hidden in some bushes."

"And the binoculars?" Abigail asked, glancing down at Emily's notebook.

"We got everything," replied Emily, looking indignant. "It wasn't exactly a difficult task to organize, you know, although sneaking everything out was a little tricky."

Lauren and Darcy both nodded in agreement. "I actually got caught with the axe as I came out of the shed," Lauren said. "I just said I was tidying up a bit, and—"

"Hey, Lauren," Hal said suddenly. "I saw you scratching your back earlier."

She flicked her hair over her shoulders and cocked her head to one side. "Your point being . . . ?"

Abigail pointed at Lauren's hands. "Hal saw your thumb grow long and hair sprout out. I've seen it happen too."

Lauren stared at Abigail long and hard, and then at Hal. Her cheeks reddened. She turned away with a self-conscious laugh. "You guys," she said.

Robbie cleared his throat. "Um, it's okay if, you know . . . I mean, if you're changing and stuff."

"This is what we've got to talk to each other about," Abigail agreed. She glanced around at each of them in turn. "I vote we stop keeping secrets from each other and just come clean. That's why I thought it would be good for us to meet after school—all of us, on our own away from the parents. Then we can talk, maybe even *show* each other what we are."

Hal immediately felt a flutter of embarrassment. "But, Abi . . . our clothes . . ."

Abigail smirked at him. "Don't worry, I have it all planned out. That's one reason I said to bring blankets. We can cover ourselves with blankets and take our clothes off, then change without ruining them."

Emily's hands flew to her face. "Take our . . . take our clothes off? Are you crazy? What *is* this?"

"It's not what you think," Hal said hurriedly. "Maybe this is a complete mystery to you, Emily, as you and Darcy seem to be the only ones who aren't experiencing anything strange. But the rest of us are. Including you, Lauren."

Abigail nodded. "Let's discuss it later. Are we all agreed? Go home, get some food together for a picnic, and head up to the lighthouse. Meet there at three o'clock. Okay?"

"I think Fenton should be included in this," Darcy said. "One of you boys should knock on his door, see if we can get him to come along. You could tell his parents it'll be like a last meal with his friends."

"Not me!" Dewey piped up.

"That's a great idea, Darcy," Abigail said, beaming. "Actually, we could tell all our parents the same thing. They'll never question us then."

So it was agreed, and everyone set off for home. Hal, Robbie and Abigail walked together for a while, and the boys took the opportunity to relate to Abigail the events of the previous evening. She hardly said a word as Hal reported what his mom had told him, but nodded constantly, as if her own theories were being confirmed. She stopped in amazement when Hal got to the centaur they'd seen at the bottom of Robbie's yard, chased by Miss Simone and what seemed to be a legion of short fat people.

"A centaur?" she repeated. Her eyes were shining. "What does this mean? Is this a centaur from wherever Miss Simone comes from? Or . . . or is this centaur one of us?"

Hal suggested that the centaur had been male. "At least I think it was," he said. "It was dark out."

"It looked male to me," Robbie agreed.

"Which means . . . it must have been either Fenton or Dewey," suggested Abigail.

"Not Fenton," Hal said, remembering what he'd seen by the stream, where Fenton had been spitting water. "He's something else entirely. No, it must have been Dewey. He's being very coy, isn't he?"

"He's a dark horse, for sure," Abigail said, and the boys groaned at the pun. "Well, I'm going home," she said, indicating the shortcut back to her house. "See you at the lighthouse. It's gonna be fun!"

'Fun' was not the word Hal would have chosen. Definitely not.

He and Robbie decided to visit Fenton together. This was such a rare occurrence that they felt extremely awkward walking up the overgrown driveway to Fenton's house. Hal knocked, and the boys waited.

Finally the door opened and Mrs. Bridges stood there. She looked surprised. "Oh, hello. Are you looking for Fenton? I'm afraid he's busy packing a few things. We're leaving tonight, as you know."

"I know," Hal said. "We've organized a picnic, a sort of farewell meal for our buddy. Can he come along?"

"Oh," said Mrs. Bridges, looking troubled. "Well, that's awfully thoughtful of you, but really, Fenton has things to do, and then we're supposed to be meeting all the other folks to say goodbye. I really can't let Fenton go off on a picnic today."

"But if it's not today, it's never," Robbie argued. "Please, Mrs. Bridges, can't you spare him for an hour or so? We're meeting at three o'clock at—well, some place we've agreed."

Mrs. Bridges seemed torn. "Well . . . perhaps it'll be all right. If the other parents agree, then it's okay with me. While you children are having a picnic, we parents can meet and talk privately. Mmm, maybe this is actually a good idea. Just for a short while though, all right? Make sure he's back by four-thirty at the latest. Where are you meeting?"

At this, both Hal and Robbie balked. They couldn't say 'the lighthouse' because that was supposed to a secret. But if they told her 'the old mill,' as they'd agreed, then Fenton would go to the wrong place! "Uh," Hal said, "perhaps we could talk to him? Find out where'd he like to have his farewell picnic?"

This tactic worked well. Mrs. Bridges went inside and, moments later, Fenton appeared. He looked suspicious. "What's up?"

Hal quickly explained the plan. "So we'll meet you at the lighthouse," he whispered. "But tell your mom we're meeting in the big field near the old mill at the opposite end of the island. Three o'clock, okay?"

Fenton still looked suspicious when the boys left, and Hal wondered if he'd even bother showing up.

## Chapter Fourteen
### The lighthouse

The island was shaped like a pear and the lighthouse stood at its narrow south eastern tip, facing toward the ocean where, in days gone by, it could warn ships about the treacherous rocks along this part of the coast. There was just one route to the lighthouse; anyone that came this far along the main road had only one destination in mind: The Point.

The bike ride along the smooth, paved road was fast and breathless. By the time they reached the lighthouse, Hal's eyes were watering and his nose was freezing cold. Alongside were Robbie, Abigail and Lauren, each looking equally red-faced and chilled. Hal had joined up with Robbie and Abigail fairly early on, as they had all left their homes around the same time, but they'd caught up with Lauren on the final stretch of road. Lauren had been ambling along, her backpack stuffed full. When the three whizzed by her, she sped up and tore after them.

The lighthouse loomed out of the fog as the foursome approached the gates. A high wall circled the grounds, and the only way in was through the set of iron gates. But these were heavily chained, and around the top of the walls and gates ran vicious-looking barbed wire. Hal had often considered gaining access to the grounds via the sea—all he needed to do was swim out a short distance, past the fence that protruded into the sea, and then swim back up the pebbled shore of the lighthouse grounds. But that involved getting wet. Besides, the rocks by the lighthouse were jagged, and the sea rough—one strong wave and he'd be bashed against the rocks.

The lighthouse stood gleaming white, a smooth, round tower with a doorway at its base and a number of small dark windows running up the side. Above the fifth window the structure faded into the thickening fog. As far as Hal knew, none of the children had ever seen the uppermost portion of the tower, since the fog had always been too thick to penetrate.

Hal stopped beside Abigail and glanced back at the others. Robbie was panting but Lauren seemed fairly composed. The air was a little more moist than usual and her bangs were matted against her forehead, her long brown locks bedraggled. Abigail's hair, tied up in a ponytail as usual, seemed unaffected by the fast ride, but her cheeks were bright red and her breath plumed before her face.

She got off her bike and went to hide it in the long grass. The others followed her example and made sure the handlebars and wheels were carefully hidden, just in case an adult came along. It was doubtful though; the children's impromptu picnic coincided quite luckily with the similar meeting planned by the adults, so while the children would be together at the lighthouse, their parents would be deep in conversation at Fenton's house.

Abigail stepped up to the iron gates and fingered the heavy, rusted chains that looped through the railings. "I guess we'd better wait for the others. But in the meantime, Robbie, we could either use the bolt-cutters to get through this chain, or . . ."

Robbie nodded. "You want me to break through."

"You see, I can easily fly over the top," Abigail said, "but these gates are pretty high and none of you will get past that barbed wire on top. But Robbie could probably just break this chain quite easily. Or, as I said, we can use the bolt-cutters."

From the mumbled way she suggested the bolt-cutters, it was clear Abigail didn't want to use them at all. She'd arranged for Emily to bring them before she'd known about Robbie's transformation trick.

Not fully understanding the conversation, Lauren was already heading over to a clump of bushes at the side of the road. "Everything is right here," she called. She disappeared for a second and emerged with a long-handled tool with a small, sharp pincer on the end. She came back to the gates, holding them out for Abigail. "Here you go."

"No thanks," Abigail said, shaking her head. "Tell you what, though: Get the blankets. Then we'll wait for the others."

They waited in the road, lounging around on a pile of old blankets. There were four of them, each fairly thick and tattered at the edges. Folded and arranged neatly on the paved surface, they made a halfway decent place to rest.

They didn't have to wait long. Emily and Darcy arrived together, puffing and panting as they rode along the road. Dewey arrived shortly after. But there was no sign of Fenton.

"Should we wait for him?" asked Emily.

"No, let's get started," Hal said. "I'm getting cold sitting around doing nothing." He glanced at his watch. He hardly ever wore it, but had decided it would be prudent today. He'd had it as long as he could remember, and had only changed the tiny battery a few times. "It's three fifteen. If Fenton was going to show, he'd have been here by now, wouldn't he?"

They all agreed, and decided to get started. Feeling somewhat awkward, Hal handed a blanket to Robbie. "I guess you're up," he said. "Get us through these gates."

As Robbie grimaced and took the blanket, Emily look confused. "Where's he going with that? We have bolt-cutters right here."

*119*

"Just watch," Abigail told her with a wink. "This is going to be a shock for you, Emily, and you too, Darcy, but Robbie's going to show us what we're all here for."

Robbie disappeared behind a bush. The others stood and waited in silence.

After a minute, Darcy sighed impatiently. "I don't get it."

"Give him a moment," Hal said. "This is all new to us, you know."

"Hurry up!" Abigail yelled. "Have you got your clothes off yet?"

Robbie stuck his head up over the bush, his face beet red. He had the blanket wrapped tightly around his skinny frame. "Just hold on, will you? I don't know how to do this at will. I normally only change when I get angry or frustrated."

They waited a bit more. Emily and Darcy exchanged a bored look, while Lauren watched with interest. Dewey's face was expressionless.

Robbie's head popped up again from behind the bushes. "It's not working," he said. "I'm not changing. How am I supposed to will myself to change? Maybe I'm not really—"

"Do you want me to come over there and explain it you?" Abigail asked calmly.

"No! Stay away!"

"Oh, Robbie, Robbie, I'm sure you have nothing to hide. Go and see if he needs help, Lauren."

Lauren actually took a step toward the bush before checking herself. But Robbie saw her and ducked down with a yelp.

"That's right, Lauren," Abigail said, winking at the others. "Just peer round the bush and grab his blanket."

In the next moment a huge, bulky monster seemed to topple sideways from behind Robbie's hiding place. It sprawled on the grass and blinked at the sky, a hulking mass of muscle covered with thick, long, coarse brown hair.

Everyone gasped. Whether they expected this or not, to see this enormous brute appear out of nowhere was a great shock!

The ogre climbed unsteadily to his feet, stood still for a moment, and shambled toward them. He was huge, three times Robbie's original height, man-shaped but with unusually long arms like a gorilla that hung down to his knees. But the similarity to a gorilla ended there; Hal had seen apes in picture books, but he'd never seen one with a face so elongated that the huge square chin hung down to its chest. The big brown eyes were sunken, the nose wide and flat, and the mouth seemed large enough to accommodate a couple of soccer balls at once. Robbie licked his lips, and Hal saw uneven blunt molars.

The giant stomped closer, seeming almost shy. He smacked his lips and let his tongue loll lazily from his open mouth. He stood before them and slouched there, his knuckles resting on the ground and his knees slightly bent.

Hal glanced at Lauren and was surprised to see how composed she was. Emily and Darcy, however, were clutching each other, wide-eyed. Their mouths were working but no sound was coming out.

Dewey nodded thoughtfully, apparently unfazed by the transformation. Hal thought of the centaur again, convinced it was little Dewey he'd seen that night.

Then the screams started. Emily and Darcy seemed to have found their voices, and they turned and ran for their lives. Abigail yelled at them to come back, but they didn't hear her. They disappeared from sight, their screams dying away as they fled.

"Idiots," Abigail said. "Robbie, break the chain while I go after the girls."

She flung off her coat and sprouted her wings in one single, practiced movement. Before Lauren and Dewey could even react, Abigail had buzzed off after Darcy and Emily.

Robbie's gigantic mouth hung open. This was the first time he'd seen Abigail fly, and his open surprise was almost comical. "Close your mouth," Hal told him, "before bugs fly in."

Lauren turned back to stare up at the ogre. "Robbie?" she whispered.

Robbie turned his enormous head to her and displayed a tiny, almost human-sized ear. "Hunh?"

"Can you . . . can you understand us?" Lauren said.

Robbie nodded and grunted.

"Let's get these gates open then," Hal said.

Robbie grinned a wide, toothy grin and launched himself at the gates. In a single powerful leap he smashed into them where they abutted, and they busted inwards with a tremendous racket. The chains snapped and flew off, and a padlock whizzed over Hal's head. The gates wobbled and rattled in a faint cloud of rust and dust, then became still.

Hal took one look at the twisted, buckled gates and slapped himself across the side of the head. "I meant open the gates *carefully!*" he yelled at Robbie. "How are we supposed to close them afterwards and look like we've never been here?"

Robbie's small eyes darted back and forth across the gates and finally back to Hal. He shrugged.

Hal turned to Lauren and found that she was clutching at Dewey. Or perhaps Dewey was clutching at *her*, but either way they disentangled themselves and went to inspect the damage.

At that moment Abigail reappeared, walking now, holding Emily and Darcy firmly by the elbows and leading them back to the road. They both looked pale and frightened, and Emily was moaning something under her breath.

Abigail stopped short when she saw the gates. "Imbecile," she muttered. She strode past Robbie. "But at least we're in. If we're going to get into trouble over this, I'd rather get into trouble *after* we've seen what we've come to see. So, come on in." She paused and turned to Emily. "Hey, bring the binoculars, will you?"

As Abigail headed toward the lighthouse, Hal cast a look at Lauren. "You all right, Lauren? You're very quiet."

Lauren shrugged. "A little surprised that Robbie's a huge monster and Abigail has wings, but yeah, otherwise fine." The hint of a smile played on her lips. "I have a pretty cool secret of my own, you know."

Abigail led the way, followed by Hal, Lauren and Dewey, and after them the shambling ogre with huge fists dragging on the ground. The group headed for the lighthouse door. At the rear, keeping their distance, Emily and Darcy trod warily.

The lighthouse grounds were situated on an outcrop of rocky land against which waves crashed and frothed. The road sloped upwards to a large, flat circular plateau. In the center stood the lighthouse itself, much dirtier up close than it appeared from a distance. Nearby stood a run-down brick building, not much larger than a shed. It had a rickety pitched gray roof, aged white-painted siding, and boarded-up windows. A short set of rotten steps led up to a chained and padlocked door. This was the old generator room. According to Hal's dad, the island had once been powered by electricity from the mainland, but a lighthouse needed to be self-sufficient in case of power outages, so it had its own generator too. Hal remembered his dad's explanation verbatim, but still had a little trouble understanding exactly how electricity and generators and even batteries *worked*.

The group marched past the generator building and straight up to the lighthouse door. Hal and Abigail stood together and stared at the chains, which were threaded through the door pull and looped around iron rings set in the old oak door frame. They glanced at each other, shrugged, and stepped back. Hal pointed. "Robbie. Chains. Go."

Lauren had to jump aside as Robbie's massive arms reached forward and grabbed the chains. He gave a quick tug and the links exploded into fragments. Not only that, but the door handle they were threaded through popped off too, and the iron rings embedded in the door frame twisted and split the wood. Without hesitation, Robbie pushed on the door with one huge, meaty hand and opened it— the wrong way. It splintered and cracked and fell inside, busting off the hinges.

"Oops," Robbie said. Hal glanced up in surprise, but realized the word might be common between ogres and humans. Maybe it wasn't exactly 'oops' but something similar. But the meaning was clear, and Robbie put a hand to his mouth as if he'd done something really naughty.

"You don't know your own strength," Hal said. "But good job anyway." He suppressed a shudder at the amount of damage and tried to ignore visions of his father's furious face. What kind of punishment would they receive for this kind of vandalism? They had all stepped way beyond a simple grounding.

Abigail, Hal, Lauren and Dewey filed through the doorway, then stopped inside, glancing back. Robbie stood outside, peering in, his hulking shoulders far wider than the broken door frame.

Lauren tittered. "Hey, Robbie, go and change, then catch up with us."

Hal looked nervously around the room. They were actually *inside* the lighthouse. There were no windows at ground level, but a wrought iron circular staircase wound up the inside of the tower past various narrow openings with decorated leaded glass. The staircase appeared at first glance to be wrapped around a central pole nearly a foot thick, but on closer inspection the pole turned out to be the rounded inner-ends of triangular-shaped steps, stacked one on top of another as they wound up and around. It was a simple but very effective design, and Hal stared in awe at the ingenuity of the builders.

Tucked under the staircase were four dust-covered wooden crates, each three feet square and laid out end to end.

"Ugh, smells musty," Abigail said. "Come on, let's go to the top."

She hurried to the bottom of the staircase and pounded up the iron steps. The staircase rattled as she went. Hal followed close behind, his nerves jangling. *What were they doing?* But it was far too late for second thoughts. The gates were buckled and the door was in pieces. They were in *big trouble*. Yet at the same time he felt they were on the verge of something extraordinary.

Lauren cast a glance back at the door as if waiting for Robbie. Then she started up the steps.

"Last one up's a fat old goblin!" Abigail called from above, giggling.

Hal wished she would keep her voice down. He pounded up the stairs after her, around and around. With no window at ground level, the first was as high as a bedroom in a two-story house. The second was higher than he'd ever been before, and excitement turned to mild anxiety as he passed the third and fourth. From outside, the lighthouse was only visible up to about the fifth window, so as he passed that small opening and saw the fog pressing against the glass, Hal knew they were ascending into the realms of the unknown.

The fog outside the sixth window was just as dreary as the fifth. But, even before he got there, Hal could see a bright patch of square light on the wall opposite the seventh and final window. Sunlight! Climbing those last few steps and approaching that window, he had to squint a little in the brightness. It was still a white haze of nothingness outside, but it was the brightest white haze of nothingness he'd ever seen.

He caught up to Abigail, who stood on a wrought iron platform looking up at the underside of a wooden floor. The steps had run out.

At this height, eight floors up including the windowless ground level, the diameter of the tower had halved. The small, circular room at the top felt small and claustrophobic, a mere seven or eight feet across. Above them, stout oak beams formed the underside of another level. A ladder led up through a square opening, through which bright light flooded.

Lauren and Dewey joined them, and together they huddled on the platform. Far below, the sounds of more echoing footsteps sounded as Darcy and Emily came hurrying up. Hal wondered briefly whether Robbie was having any difficulty changing back into his normal self.

"A hundred and sixty-eight steps," Abigail said breathlessly. "Only a few more to go." She started up the ladder and disappeared through the opening. Seconds later, she let out a high-pitched squeal. "You've *got* to see this!"

Hal clambered up after her, his heart thumping.

The first thing that went through his mind was: *Bright! Very bright! Dazzlingly bright!* He shielded his eyes and glanced around, taking in the detail of the room through fluttering eyelids. Windows lined the entire perimeter except where there was a narrow doorway leading outside. In the center of the room stood what looked like an enormous bicycle lamp set on an ornate iron pedestal bolted to the floor. The space around it was tight and, blinking furiously, Hal rubbed shoulders with the windows as he circled around after Abigail.

She spun and squinted at him, one hand held like a visor at her forehead to shield the brightness. "Look at the view!"

"I'm trying," Hal said. "It's so bright up here that I can't—"

Lauren appeared behind him. "Oh my gosh, it's so warm!"

It *was* warm. Sunlight streamed in through the windows, and the heat in the glass-walled circular room was intense. Together, Hal and Lauren started opening the old black-framed windows, peering through slatted fingers, still unable to take in the view but getting hints of blue. How come Abigail's eyes had adjusted so quickly to the glare?

"Let's go out this door to the balcony," Abigail said, pulling on the doorknob. She struggled for a moment, and then the door squeaked open. A strong draft breezed across the room as she stepped outside.

"It's a gallery," Dewey said absently, who had stuck his head into the room.

Hal and Lauren jostled in the narrow doorway, and Lauren won. She stepped outside and gasped, then pressed herself back against one of the windows.

Hal followed her out, and his feet clanged on a metal grid floor. Breathing hard, he grasped the black iron railings. His leg muscles tightened and his knuckles turned white as he edged around the gallery. Dewey came out after him.

There stood Abigail, squinting hard under the shield of her hand. She was basking in bright yellow sunlight, her dark brown hair shining like it had never shone before. She turned to him, a huge grin across her face. "Out There," she said, and pointed.

The four of them stared out over the fog. It rose like steam off a wet road on a warm day, only a thousand times thicker—an impenetrable whiteness that smothered their island and obscured fields, forests, hills, and houses. It filtered up through the iron grid flooring, smoking around their feet as they stood and stared. It was hard to believe they'd spent their entire lives groping around in that suffocating stuff, breathing it in, oblivious to the bright blue sky above, with its hot yellow sunlight. They'd been content with the murky fog for so long, always dreaming of a blue sky but never expecting to see it. And now here they were, for the first time feeling its warmth, breathing in its fresh, clean air.

How could they ever be content with gloomy surroundings ever again?

Perhaps that was the point. If they'd really understood what was Out There, seen its beauty firsthand, then how happy and content would they have been growing up in such a dreary, damp environment? *Not content at all*, Hal guessed. Now he fully understood one aspect of the adults' secrecy: why they never talked about Out There. The children couldn't very well miss what they never had.

Beyond the wispy perimeter of the fog lay a narrow band of clear, glittering water that separated them from a land mass that spanned the horizon.

Out There.

Hal's worries slipped away as he contemplated the deep blue sky, the rolling green hills, and the serenity of the bay. It was hard to fret over incidental things like breaking into a lighthouse when faced with such stunning, natural beauty.

He remembered how he and Robbie had taken the raft out into the fog. They'd been paralyzed with fear about getting lost. Looking down on the clear blue sea now, he wished and wished they had been able to keep rowing, to emerge suddenly from the fog and to see the mainland ahead. But of course, the sea serpent would never have let them.

Hal glanced sideways at Lauren. Her hair blew gently in the breeze, and as he watched, she closed her eyes and breathed deeply, a smile playing across her face. To his other side, Dewey looked as though he'd been slapped hard across the face—dazed and silent, his mouth open.

At that moment, Emily and Darcy came out onto the gallery, gasping and squinting. Darcy was mumbling something over and over, while Emily's reaction was quite a bit noisier. She screamed and squealed, jumping up and down while holding onto the handrail. It hurt Hal's ears, but he couldn't help laughing.

And finally Robbie arrived, back to his normal self and fully clothed. Hal couldn't quite see his reaction because Dewey, Darcy and Emily were in the way, but he imagined Robbie was as excited and stunned as the rest of them.

*If only Fenton were here*, he thought. Perhaps something like this would have mellowed Fenton for life. It seemed a great shame that he should miss out on this adventure.

*Chapter Fifteen*
**Discoveries**

"**P**ass me the binoculars, Emily," Hal said, suddenly remembering that she had brought them along.

Emily's gaze never left the spectacular scenery as she slowly removed the binoculars from around her neck and passed them to Dewey, who in turn passed them to Lauren, nudging her first to get her attention. When Lauren blinked and looked down, she seemed surprised to find the binoculars in her hands. Hal gently plucked them from her.

Lauren looked like someone had just eaten her last cookie. She pouted and looked longingly at the binoculars as Hal took them. "I'm next after you," she said firmly.

The binoculars were large and heavy, with a handy leather strap. Afraid of dropping them, Hal slung the strap around his neck, then brought the glasses to his eyes. After a bit of focusing he found himself on a beach over on the mainland. "Wow!" he exclaimed. "These things are amazing!"

Hal followed the sandy beach slowly, trying to identify the junk that was strewn all over—the remains of old campfires with broken bottles and empty cans scattered everywhere, an old fisherman's boot, a couple of small rowing boats propped up with rocks and sticks to form a make-shift shelter, even an old rusted car sunk into the sand.

Tracking upwards a little, Hal found a road running alongside the beach. It too was littered with junk. Cars stood abandoned, many of them twisted and dented from collisions, some blackened from fire, all with flat tires and broken windows. Weeds had grown up around them from cracks in the paved surface. One car had a small tree growing out of its open hood.

Beyond the road and spreading up a gentle incline into the hills, houses of all shapes and sizes stood silent with doors standing wide open or hanging off their hinges. Many windows were broken, and tattered curtains hung fluttering in a breeze. Whatever small front lawns these homes once had were now so overgrown with weeds that they looked like a series of miniature forests separated by short picket fences. Hal had seen plenty of this kind of thing on the island already, with all those empty houses down by the docks, but on the mainland there were literally *hundreds* of houses, maybe *thousands*.

"Are you finished yet?" someone asked him.

Hal was so engrossed that he wasn't even sure who had spoken. "Nearly," he said. "One thing's for sure—no one lives Out There that I can see. The whole place was abandoned long ago, just as Miss Simone said."

Further south was the city center. Hal knew what it was because he'd seen pictures of cities before—impossibly tall buildings towering into the sky. He didn't need the binoculars to see these buildings, but the glasses showed him that the surrounding roads, in particular one huge elevated highway that swept around in an arc, were as still and silent as the coastal road.

With a sigh he handed the binoculars to Lauren. "It's a mess," Hal said. "Can't see a sign of life anywhere."

"That doesn't mean there isn't any," Abigail said. "The city may be dead, but there could be large groups of people living somewhere. Maybe they wouldn't spread out all across the city, but collect together like a small community—sort of like us here on the island."

"On the other hand there might not be anyone left alive at all," Lauren said quietly. She handed the glasses to Abigail. "Here, take a look. It's pretty grim."

"I just thought," Robbie said, "that since we're standing up here above the fog . . . does that mean we're breathing contaminated air?"

There was a long silence.

Darcy spoke first. "If we are, it doesn't seem to be affecting us."

"Not *yet* anyway," Emily said. "It might take a while."

"Or maybe we won't be affected at all," Abigail said, passing the binoculars back down the line. "We've never been sick in our lives. My mom's always saying how we have excellent immune systems. I wonder if that's something to do with how we can change into monsters. Perhaps our bodies are somehow able to repair themselves when they get sick."

"Or perhaps there's no virus at all now," Hal mused. "Hey, speaking of monsters . . . Lauren, when are you going to show us what you can turn into?"

Suddenly all eyes were on Lauren. She blushed. "Well, right now, if you like. As long as you don't look at me like I'm a . . . um . . ."

"Freak?" asked Abigail. "No, you're not a freak. None of us are. We're just special." She gave a smirk and rolled her eyes. "I don't know what we are, but I think we should all find out for ourselves before we let Miss Simone get her clammy hands on us. Maybe together we'll be in control of the situation, rather than being scared witless by what's happening to us."

There was a murmur of agreement.

"Okay," Lauren said, sounding nervous now. "Um. I need all of you to go away, though. Why don't you all go downstairs and stand outside? I'll be down in a minute. I need to, um, undress."

Hal nodded, fully understanding. "Come on, guys."

They all took one last look Out There and hurried downstairs, leaving Lauren alone. With seven pairs of footsteps pounding down the noisy, rattling spiral staircase, it was a wonder the whole thing didn't come loose and collapse.

Outside, the fog felt more cold and damp than it ever had before. Just a few minutes outside in the sunshine had shown them what they were missing. Hal was determined to block up that fog-hole in Black Woods now. He was convinced that, together, they could easily overcome the manticore. Together they could overcome *anything*.

They all stood waiting for Lauren, listening hard for her footfalls on the staircase. But no sounds came. Was she still on the gallery? Or in the lamp room?

"How long do you think—" Hal started to say—but at that moment there was a scream from above, and they all looked up just in time to see a figure plummeting out of the fog.

*Lauren's fallen off the gallery!* Hal thought in horror. His heart froze as the figure fell like a stone. *Was* it Lauren, though? It was a snowy-white blur, arms and legs flailing. But at the last moment, huge white wings snapped open and the figure somehow arced out of the dive and soared low to the ground, barely missing it. It looked like an eagle about to pounce on its prey, and for a moment Hal felt sure *he* was the prey as the figure hurtled toward him with yellow eyes, a white-furred face, and enormous, powerful wings like that of a giant snowy owl.

The creature soared over their heads so fast and low that they all ducked and caught a great whoosh of air. They heard Lauren's familiar laugh, and Hal slowly rose to watch as she gently flapped and angled her great wings so that she circled the grounds at a colossal speed. She whooped as she came back over their heads, causing another powerful downdraft.

When she circled around once more, slower this time, Hal and the others were able to get a proper look at her. She had burning yellow eyes, sleek but muscular shoulders, and slender arms with long, bird-like hands and fingers. A shaggy white mane covered her upper body, shoulders, hips and thighs, but below the elbows and knees the hair thinned to short cropped fur. In place of her shiny brown hair, white locks streamed from her head.

She swooped closer and then upwards, coming to a graceful stop in mid-air about twenty feet off the ground, wings outspread, before dropping lightly onto bird-like feet. Her wings folded behind her.

"That was so cool," Abigail said finally. "Honestly, Lauren, you're—"

"I had a bit of a fright though," Lauren said in her normal voice, with just a hint of a rasp. "I've flown around before, swooping here and there, but have never been able to fly very high. It's like I grow all heavy and my wings can't hold me up. This time I thought it would be neat to fly down off the lighthouse. But for a second there my wings didn't do anything at all—I just dropped like a stone."

"We saw," Hal said. "I nearly wet myself."

"I thought you were a goner," Robbie agreed. He was looking a little pale.

Abigail nudged him with her elbow. "Aww, Robbie. Did you nearly lose your sweetheart?"

"Shut up," he snapped, the color flooding back into his face.

"So what *are* you?" Hal asked. "Some sort of bird-girl?"

Lauren shrugged, and the fluffy feathers of her wings shook. "I have no idea." She glanced up at the lighthouse. "One of you is going to have to go up and get my clothes. I don't think I can fit through that doorway and up the stairs with these wings."

"I'll go," Robbie said, taking a step forward.

But Emily stopped him. "You will *not*," she said crossly. "I'll get them."

Robbie looked so baffled that Abigail squealed with laughter. "Robbie, *Robbie*. A girl must maintain some degree of modesty, you know. And that includes keeping her clothing, and especially her underwear, out of the hands of boys."

Lauren seemed amused. Her white furry face was still human in structure and her smile was the same as ever—complete with dimples. Her teeth were a little different though, with a few vicious-looking fangs that had no business being in the mouth of such a sweet girl.

"Who's next?" Abigail said, looking around. "You've all seen my faerie wings—not as spectacular as Lauren's though. Robbie's done his ogre thing. Your turn now, Hal. Let's see what you can do."

But before he could say anything, Emily called from the lighthouse door. She hadn't even made it up the stairs yet. "Hey, look at this! Come and see."

They hurried over to the doorway. Emily stood there holding up some strange green garments. "Look familiar?"

She was holding a one-piece dress or frock made with some fine silky material and decorated with hundreds of tiny sparkling gems. The dress had short sleeves and buttons on the front, and the hem was a patchwork of different color greens in a complex pattern of leaves. It was very organic in nature.

"Looks like Miss Simone's dress," Darcy said, fingering the hem. "A bit like it, anyway. Same sort of material. Why do you suppose it's here? It can't be hers—it's too small."

"There are lots of dresses," Emily said, jerking a thumb over her shoulder. "Those four wooden crates in there are full of clothes just like this—not all dresses, but boys clothes too. And all of it is for children, not adults."

Everyone but Lauren rushed inside and started pulling garments out of the crates. Every item seemed at first glance to be the same, but each was different in subtle ways—a whole wardrobe of clothing to match Miss Simone's.

"This stuff must be for us," Emily said, her eyes shining. "I can't imagine why, but it's like Miss Simone brought clothes from Elsewhere for us to wear."

"Let me see," Lauren called from the doorway. Emily threw her a dress.

"Nice pants," said Dewey, holding them up.

They were the same patchwork of greens as the dresses, only without the glitter. Hal agreed with Dewey—they actually looked pretty cool. He searched through a crate for similar pants and a shirt to match.

"There must be hundreds of things here," Emily said, obviously delighted with her find. "They're all different sizes though—look." She held up two dresses, one that looked like it would fit her, and another that was several sizes smaller. "I suppose Miss Simone had to allow for our growth. I just wonder why nobody gave these clothes to us. They're beautiful!"

"This is weird," Lauren said from outside the doorway. "Look at this." Her huge white wings pressed against the frame as she leaned inside to show them. She held up the dress in front of her and turned it around and around. "See? Completely intact? Now watch." She pulled the dress closer to her body, and suddenly, inexplicably, a gap appeared in the back, a sort of tear down the middle of the green fabric that widened to an oval. "Hey presto, a hole!"

As if performing a conjuring trick, Lauren's bright yellow eyes gleamed and she grinned a toothy grin. "But that's not all. Watch again."

She slowly moved the dress away from her body, pushing it out to arm's length and letting it hang so they could all see the mysterious opening at the back. As the dress moved away from her, the hole closed and sealed itself up.

"What?" exclaimed Hal and Robbie together.

Abigail grabbed the dress from Lauren's hands. "There's no sign of damage."

"Do that again!" said Dewey.

Lauren did so, over and over, with the same effect each time. When she drew the dress close to her body, the gap appeared in the back; and when she pushed it away, the gap closed. She tried different dresses with the same result. She even tried a boy's shirt, and the same thing happened.

Yet nobody else could perform this trick.

They spent some time going through the clothes and testing them to no avail, and came to the conclusion that Lauren herself was causing the effect. On a hunch, Abigail stepped outside with Lauren and sprouted her own wings. Then, astonishingly, the trick worked for her too.

Everyone exclaimed in unison as light dawned. "These are *smart* clothes!" Hal said. "Somehow they know when we change, and they adapt to fit."

"Yes!" Emily squealed with excitement. She clapped her hands together. "That's it! Both Lauren and Abigail have wings, so if they were wearing these dresses, big holes would appear in the back to allow their wings to grow."

Lauren took a dress and hurried away to the back of the generator building, calling over her shoulder, "Back in a minute!"

The others returned to the crates and picked out something they thought would fit. Moments later, Lauren returned, human again, and wearing her dress. It fit her nicely, and she looked comfortable with her light, knee-length attire. "It works!" she said, her face red with excitement. "Look."

She screwed up her face in concentration. In the blink of an eye, fine white fur erupted from her skin, her shoulders bulged, her arms stretched, and her wings sprouted once more. Her green dress appeared to remain unchanged . . . and yet, curiously, it must have altered its cut to fit Lauren's substantially larger shoulders, for there was no evidence of tightness or stretching. The hem, also, was different—no longer in the pattern of leaves, but in a fine weave of feathers, a very subtle design change that seemed to serve no purpose. But the most important change was at the back; when Lauren turned around, there was the hole again, perfectly sized and shaped to allow her wings to protrude unencumbered.

When Lauren changed back into her human form once more, the dress closed up at the back and visibly tightened in the shoulders and around the waist. The leafy pattern returned, and the hundreds of tiny gems sparkled.

"That is *so* amazing," Darcy said, her eyes wide.

"Wait," Emily said, delving into one of the crates. She fished out a small wooden box and opened it. Inside was a thick pile of transparent plastic sheets cut roughly in the shape of a foot.

Darcy pulled one out between finger and thumb. It was flexible. "Is it a shoe sole? Do we put these inside our shoes?"

"What would be the point of that?" Emily said thoughtfully. On impulse she dropped one of the soles on the floor and removed one of her shoes. Then she placed her bare foot directly on the strange plastic sheet.

The sheet came alive. Although Emily's foot was substantially bigger, the sole stretched to fit, then slowly wrapped around the contours of her heel, arch and toes. Emily squealed and began hopping around in circles, trying to dislodge the thing, but it was stuck firmly to her foot.

Hal laughed. "Smart clothes *and* smart shoes."

They all grabbed a pair of soles, eyeing them curiously.

"Let's all get dressed up," Abigail said, her eyes shining.

But Robbie was puzzled. He stared at his own chosen garments, a pair of green and gray trousers with a large shirt that he could just pull on over his head without having to worry about buttons. "I wonder how it works for me," he said. "I mean, I'm three times taller when I'm an ogre."

"Go and try them on," Abigail urged. "Then you'll find out. I'm going to change too. See you all in a minute."

They all rushed off to find suitable hiding places—behind a bush, or around the side of the generator building. Emily stayed in the lighthouse, while Dewey ducked around the back.

Hal found himself a large bush and yanked his clothes off. Should he leave his underwear on? He had to ponder this for a moment, and in the end decided he would keep them. The clothes were kind of cool looking, but they didn't look very suitable for a cold fog! Oddly enough, after he'd dressed, he stood looking down at himself and realized that he felt comfortably warm. He should have been freezing by now, with his thin shirt, thin trousers, and bizarre transparent shoes that left the tops of his feet and toes bare . . . and yet, here he was, as warm as when he had been standing in the bright sunlight at the top of the lighthouse. To his surprise he found that his feet were warm too, as if the soles were generating heat. Even better, he barely felt the rough ground beneath. He stood on a stone to test it further, and was amazed to find it didn't hurt in the slightest even when he put his full weight on it.

What would happen to his new clothes if he changed into a dragon? There was only one way to find out.

He scrunched up his face in concentration, as Lauren had. She had made it look *so* easy. Abigail, too—that girl could sprout wings at will! *So how was it done?* He stared at his hands for a moment, imagining the large, reptilian claws he'd grown in the woods. But just staring at his hands wasn't enough—absolutely nothing happened. Where was that familiar itching he got when he was beginning to change? Or was that itching associated only with first-timers? Perhaps now that he'd undergone a full transformation in Black Woods, there would be no more unexpected itchy rashes or flashes of fire from his throat. Perhaps now he was in control of the dragon within him, rather than the other way round.

It was no good, though. He just couldn't seem to change at will. He left his clothes in a neat pile and returned to the lighthouse, where Emily waited just outside. Her dress was very similar to Lauren's, with some minor differences in pattern and color. And here came Dewey from the back of the lighthouse, wearing the same style pants and shirt as Hal.

Dewey looked pleased with himself, but wouldn't say why. "Just wait and see," he said with a grin.

Eventually Darcy returned with Abigail, both of them barefoot. Abigail gave a thumbs-up when she saw Hal, and immediately sprouted her wings and came buzzing over. Her dress seemed to sparkle a little more while she was flying, and the green fabric shimmered with a silvery glow. She looked more like a faerie than ever. "It works!" she called. "No more torn dresses for me!"

To demonstrate she landed just in front of Hal, turned, and retracted her delicate wings. They were still buzzing as they disappeared into her bare back, and Hal could hear a curious high-pitched whine that sounded like a mosquito. Then they were gone, and in a flash the convenient opening in the back of Abigail's dress closed up. At the same time, her dress lost its glittering, shimmering effect, as if its energy had dissipated.

Robbie returned to join the group, and they all stood together in a circle outside the lighthouse, each clad in matching greens and grays, and each barefoot except for their curious plastic soles. They eyed one another in silence.

Finally Abigail, her eyes dancing with excitement, spoke in hushed tones. "Okay, gang. I think we can safely say that these clothes were designed for us. They're enchanted or something, so we can change back and forth without our ordinary clothes getting ripped and torn. Lauren and I have proved that."

"That's easy for you to say," Robbie said with a frown. "You two just grow wings. What happens to me when I grow three times larger? Or Hal when he turns into a dragon?"

"Well, stop asking stupid questions and show us," Abigail said shortly. "No time like the present."

"Yeah, but what if—" Robbie argued.

Dewey, for once, interrupted him. "It's okay," he said boldly. Everyone turned to him in surprise. "Look, I'll show you."

He had always been small, only a little shorter than Hal but of lighter build. An easy target for Fenton, the class bully. Perhaps *too* easy, which explained why Fenton normally picked on Robbie instead. At least Robbie answered back, and in doing so gave Fenton more of a reason to beat him up. Dewey, on the other hand, was normally very timid.

But not this afternoon. Now he seemed self-assured, as if he had quietly matured a few years in the space of a few hours. He was still in the same small body, but he seemed larger somehow. Dewey appeared to know it too. His eyes had a certain twinkle, his grin a new-found confidence. Hal wouldn't have been surprised if Dewey had stood up for himself and talked back to Fenton, if Fenton were here to bait him.

Then Dewey showed them all where this new-found confidence came from. He reared backward, arching his back, and in the next instant exploded into the size and shape of a horse standing on its hind legs—short brown hair all over, long and muscular legs, jet black tail. For the briefest of moments Dewey staggered there, unbalanced, but then the horse's front legs erupted out of his torso and kicked wildly at the air. Dewey came down heavily on all fours.

But Dewey was not a horse. As Hal and Robbie had guessed, he was a *centaur*, part horse and part human. He was all equine except that, where the familiar neck and head of a horse should be, a human torso grew instead, with human arms, shoulders, neck and head. Thick black hair flowed all the way down his back. The short brown hair that covered the centaur's horse-like body became a finer coat of hair all across his human skin. Even his face was fuzzy, and his eyebrows were extraordinarily bushy.

Dewey's small face had flattened out, become harder and wider, his nose flat with flared nostrils. His eyes were unchanged, but his ears stuck out from his thick mane of hair, curiously pointed at the top. With his darkened skin, his even white teeth gleamed when he grinned.

"Well, here I am," he said proudly.

"There you are," Hal croaked, awe-struck. He realized that he, like the others, had backed up several feet to give Dewey room to maneuver. Dewey seemed unable to keep still; he kept turning and stamping, and whipping his head around to face them. Hal had the strangest feeling he was watching a boy astride a restless horse, and perhaps Dewey felt that way too, being new to his centaur body.

"Oh! Look at his clothes!" Darcy exclaimed, pointing.

It took a moment to see them, but there they were—the trousers and shirt had somehow combined and reshaped into the form of a green-gray cloak, fastened with a sash. When Dewey turned, the cloak billowed this way and that.

"So the clothes just shape themselves around the body," Emily said, clapping her hands together. "That's so wonderful! But I'm not sure I can stand anymore of this body-changing today, guys. My heart is about to thump out of my chest."

Abigail smiled up at the centaur. "I'm proud of you, Dewey. You're . . . well, magnificent! It's funny, but you have the *shape* of an adult horse, all solid and muscular, but you're shorter. I wonder if that's because you're still young?"

Hal realized she was right. The old horses used on the farms to plow fields and pull carts were quite a bit larger. Dewey was impressive, but stood next to a real horse he was probably a couple of feet shorter. Or should that be several *hands* shorter? Hal seemed to remember his dad saying that horses were measured in hands.

Abigail tapped Hal on the shoulder. "Okay, just you left, Hal. Then that'll be all of us except Emily and Darcy, who say they have nothing going on. Now, I happen to know Emily has *something* going on—I've seen it." She narrowed her eyes thoughtfully. "I wonder if we can somehow force her to change . . ."

This made Emily look very uncomfortable. "I don't like the sound of that. I mean, what's happening here is wonderful, but it's also frightening. I can't imagine changing into anything myself. And I certainly haven't noticed anything strange. No sharp teeth, no itches, nothing."

"Nor me," Darcy agreed. "Absolutely nothing at all."

"There's also Fenton," Robbie said. "We still don't know what he is. I wish he'd shown up. He's a big fat tub of lard with hardly any brains, but he's still one of us."

At that moment, a heavy deluge of water fell on Robbie's head from a great height. Gasping and spluttering, he swung around, expecting someone to be standing behind him with an empty pail. But no one was there.

Everyone else was looking up. Hal had seen the water fall out of the fog—a thick clear stream aimed directly at Robbie's head just as he had finished insulting Fenton. He knew instantly that the big boy was here after all. But where?

It took a moment to spot him, but there he was, clinging to the side of the lighthouse, four or five stories up, barely visible in the thick fog. How he was clinging to the smooth, rounded lighthouse wall was anybody's guess. There was nothing to grab hold of.

But Fenton was there, stuck to the side of the tower, a dark, mysterious figure hanging upside down with stomach flattened against the wall, arms and legs spread wide. Was that a long, thin tail stretching around the curve of the wall? What *was* he?

Hal couldn't help thinking of gargoyles, those ugly stone figures that were built into the sides of old buildings. They were supposed to direct rainwater away from rooftop gutters by way of a water spout, so it looked like the statue was spitting. It fit Fenton's description perfectly.

As Hal pondered, he became aware that the creature's eyes were glowing red in the fog. Fenton—and Hal was positive it was him—stared down at them, silent and menacing.

*Chapter Sixteen*
## Transformations

T he creature hanging high off the lighthouse wall remained motionless in the bleak fog, red eyes staring down at them.

Hal felt his skin crawl. "Fenton, is that you?"

There was no answer, nor the slightest indication that the thing had even heard him. Everyone remained silent, except for Dewey, who couldn't seem to stop himself from stamping and turning in circles like a nervous horse. The clip-clop of his hoofed feet echoed around the lighthouse grounds.

"Well, we can't stand around here all day," Abigail said at last, sounding irritated. "Fenton, if that's you, then come on down and talk to us."

"Maybe he's chicken," Robbie said loudly, wiping his face dry. "Man, this water stinks."

Even Robbie's challenge had no effect on the creature. It was like a statue stuck to the side of the lighthouse. *Just like a gargoyle*, Hal thought again.

"You know," Abigail said, "seeing Fenton up there reminds me that time is pressing. Anyone got a watch on?"

"It's nearly four-thirty," Hal said.

"So what?" Darcy said. "We're on a picnic. We can take as long as we want."

"Yes, but Fenton's supposed to be back home by now," Abigail told her. She cupped a hand to the side of her mouth and shouted, "Come down here, idiot!" Clicking her tongue, she muttered, "I had hopes of blocking up the fog-hole in Black Woods before he left."

"We still can," Robbie said. "Doesn't look like he's going anywhere."

Abigail considered. "Mmm. You know, we stood at the top of the lighthouse in fresh air. It seems clean now, don't you think? So if we block up the fog-hole and all the fog goes away, we'll have plenty of blue sky and sunshine and there'll be no reason for *any* of us to leave the island—despite what Miss Simone wants."

"You're assuming," Robbie said slowly, "that our parents *want* to stay here, even with good air."

"Look, whatever Miss Simone has in mind for us—experiments, testing, whatever—I think our parents are only agreeing to it because they think there's no choice. If they let Miss Simone take us back to her world, they get to leave this foggy island at last."

There was a silence.

"That doesn't sound right," Hal said. "When this project was first started all those years ago, the air was just fine. Everything was sunny and bright. Our parents agreed to work with Miss Simone *before* the virus broke out, so even back then they must have been prepared to move to Miss Simone's world eventually, once we were all old enough and starting to change. I don't see why taking the fog away would change the way they think *now*."

"My head hurts," Emily said.

"Mine too," Dewey agreed. He clip-clopped around in a full circle and then made a great effort to stand still. "Look, if Miss Simone made a pact with our parents, then our parents are morally bound to honor it."

Everyone stared at him in surprise.

Dewey looked mildly embarrassed. "It's, uh . . . it's what centaurs would do."

"Made a pact?" Abigail repeated. "Morally bound? What's got into you?"

Emily placed her hands over her head and closed her eyes. "No, guys, I really mean my head hurts," she said quietly. "I've been getting a lot of headaches lately, and this is a bad one."

Darcy put an arm around her and peered into her face. "Do you need to sit down? You look pale."

Abigail sighed. "Look, why don't we talk on the way to Black Woods? We can leave our bikes. We'll change and try out our new bodies. How about it?"

Hal could see there were some mixed feelings between his friends. He suspected the idea of Black Woods and the manticore was the cause of most of the doubt. On the other hand, despite Abigail's flawed logic, the idea of blocking the fog-hole still appealed to him. "I don't know why Miss Simone's people are still pumping that fog through," he said, "but I'm convinced the air is fresh here on the island and I can't see why we shouldn't block the hole."

So it was that the seven of them returned to the broken lighthouse gates. Dressed in their 'smart' clothes, as Hal called them, they were ready and eager to try out their alternate identities on a journey across the island. Black Woods lay forty-five minutes away on foot . . . only they weren't all going on foot.

They stuffed their ordinary clothes, shoes and all, into their backpacks and organized themselves. Abigail and Lauren would fly, of course, but they felt they were unable to carry passengers very far. Dewey offered to take a passenger on his back, so Emily, with her headache, gratefully accepted that seat after first grabbing hers and Dewey's backpacks and all four blankets.

"Ooh, Dewey," Emily said, as soon as she had mounted. "I hope you don't throw me off." She tentatively put her hands on his waist.

Hal knew what was coming next. Either he or Robbie was expected to transform and carry Darcy, who would otherwise have to walk. "I don't even know how to change!" Hal said. "I haven't figured it out yet."

"Try," Abigail said shortly. She reached for her backpack and buzzed away, taking the lead. "Come on, gang. To Black Woods!"

Like the sound of an umbrella opening, Lauren changed in a flash and spread her wings. Then she launched herself after Abigail. Her method of taking off wasn't as simple as Abigail's; she had to bend her knees and jump, and it seemed a bit of a struggle to get off the ground. But, once airborne, she soared past Abigail effortlessly. However, the fog dampened her flight; she could clear small thickets easily, but had to skirt around taller trees. Hal suspected she'd end up taking a number of detours on her way to Black Woods, choosing open fields even if it meant going a longer way around.

Lauren had completely forgotten her backpack, which was stuffed with her hastily retrieved clothes. Robbie went to get it for her. His own backpack had fallen open and almost spilled its contents, so he quickly shoved everything back in—the thickest sandwich Hal had ever seen, a few cookies, an apple, and a bottle of water.

Dewey looked almost apologetically at Hal, Robbie, and Darcy, then kicked himself into action and galloped away, plunging through a thicket and disappearing into the fog. Emily gave a squeal as they went, but it was difficult to tell if it was a squeal of excitement or terror.

Robbie turned to Hal. "Okay, I think I get how to change. Lauren whispered it to me earlier. She said the trick is not to try and think too hard about turning into something else. She said to imagine you're *already* something else, and act like you *know* it. She said that if I want to knock a door down, I should just go and punch it, and then I'd find that I was already an ogre."

"Sounds easy," Hal said doubtfully. "Show me."

As Hal and Darcy watched intently, Robbie walked over to the buckled lighthouse gates and stared at them. He closed his eyes. Then he opened them and, in one swift movement, he punched one of the gates hard.

In the next moment he was yelling and holding his hand, doubled up with pain.

"Guess that didn't work," Darcy said, trying to stifle a giggle.

Robbie, red-faced and clutching his hand, glared at her. In a fit of anger he lashed out at the gate with his foot—and in the blink of an eye he was an ogre, fifteen feet tall and a mass of shaggy hair and muscle. The gate flew off its hinges and scraped across the paved ground, taking part of the stone wall with it.

"Well, I guess it *sort* of worked," Hal told Darcy. She giggled again.

Robbie turned to them and gave a massive shrug. Even with his vastly different features, Hal could tell Robbie's anger had left him as quickly as it had come. The monster made a rumbling sound and turned to leave.

"Hey," Hal called. "Don't forget your bag. And Lauren's."

Robbie looked blankly at the two backpacks, then picked them up by the straps. He tucked them into his belt, and at this, Hal did a double-take. Robbie's 'smart' clothes had transformed into a thick green belt, tied with a strange, complicated knot.

Finally, Robbie stomped away with backpacks dangling from his belt. He crashed through the nearby thicket as Dewey had done, and when he was out of sight, Hal listened as his friend demolished anything that stood in his path. The cracking and crunching and snapping slowly receded.

"Well, just you and me," Darcy said. She forced a smile. "You know, we can just walk if you prefer—if you can't turn into a . . . a dragon."

Hal felt useless. He picked up his backpack and handed Darcy's to her. "Yeah, let's walk a bit. I might be able to change as we go, but there's no point standing around while I try and figure it out."

So they walked, following Robbie's trail. At least it was a clear path! Bushes were either pulled up and tossed aside, or completely flattened. There was even a small tree that Robbie hadn't bothered stepping around—he'd simply shoved it sideways and now it lay there, roots exposed and clods of dirt strewn everywhere.

"So you really haven't noticed any physical changes?" Hal asked as they walked.

Darcy shrugged. "None." She played with her blond hair for a moment, pulling it neatly into a ponytail and feeling for the scrunchy in her pocket before realizing that her clothes were jammed into her backpack. She let her hair flop down again and they walked in silence for a while longer. Then: "We forgot about Fenton. Was he still up the lighthouse when we left?"

"Can't say I noticed," Hal said, trying to remember.

"Well, I hope he doesn't go all weird on us. You said Thomas tried to kill you? Do you think that's because he was a vicious animal and it was his natural instinct?"

"No," Hal said, shaking his head firmly. "I'm certain we all know who we are after we've changed. I know *I* do. None of us would ever try to kill one another. Thomas . . . well, he's been a manticore for six years, probably living in a forest somewhere in Miss Simone's land. He might have, you know . . . gone crazy."

"Maybe Fenton has, too," Darcy said quietly, her face white.

A short while later, Hal stopped. He put down his backpack and went to stand in a clear spot away from Darcy.

"What are you doing?" she asked him.

Hal closed his eyes and cleared his mind. He wasn't Hal the short human boy; he was Hal the dragon. He knew that when he opened his eyes, Darcy would be staring at him in amazement. *This journey is much faster as a dragon*, he thought. *I can already feel the wind rushing through my wings as I run. See? I'm a—*

He snapped his eyes open.

Disappointed, he sighed. "This isn't easy," he said to Darcy. "Why do the girls make it look so easy? Even Dewey made it look easy."

"I think the problem is that you don't really believe you've changed," Darcy said. "You tell yourself you have, but *pretending* you believe it is not the same as *actually* believing it. I think it'll get easier for you, but at the moment you're not convincing yourself properly."

They stood in silence for a moment.

Then, Hal blew his cheeks out. "Well, maybe you're right. But how do I make myself believe?"

"You don't. You can't *make* yourself believe. That's the point. You either believe, or you don't." Darcy thought for a moment. "That's why you changed when the manticore was about to kill you. Instinct took over. Instinct doesn't have time to question whether you believe something or not—it just takes over and does what needs to be done. Right now there's no natural instinct needed, so the only way you're going to change is to really *believe* you can change. Like Robbie—he didn't believe properly when he first punched that gate, but then he got angry and went to kick it, and in his fit of anger he truly imagined that gate flying through the air—he knew he would kick it off the hinges, and he did."

She paused for breath, and looked almost surprised at herself.

Hal nodded slowly. "That all makes sense," he said. He eyed her curiously. "How come you figured all that out when you can't even change yourself?"

Darcy shrugged. "Come on, let's keep moving."

They walked for another fifteen or twenty minutes, according to Hal's watch. He realized that he would have broken the strap if he'd changed into a dragon earlier. He made a point to take it off before his next attempt.

They had walked in a gentle arc, heading inward for a while, through clumps of wood and over fields, but now they were heading back out toward the sea. The distant sound of waves could be heard, and eventually they arrived at what Hal considered a very familiar part of the cliff.

"This is where Miss Simone took a dive," he said, gesturing. "Black Woods isn't much farther."

He found a plastic bottle in the grass and stopped to pick it up. It had Robbie's name scrawled on it. Plastic bottles were in short supply on the island and it had been careless of Robbie to drop it, not to mention irresponsible. "Litterbug," Hal muttered, sliding the bottle into his backpack. The stern voices of his parents echoed at the back of his mind: *Who's going to pick up our trash if we don't?*

Hal and Darcy decided to eat while they walked, munching on sandwiches and apples as they picked their way through the long grass. No doubt the others had arrived at Black Woods long before and were sitting around having their picnic. Hal hated being the one to hold them up, but he felt that if he put too much pressure on himself to transform, it would only get more and more difficult.

They came across a hilly, rocky patch. Hal and Darcy stopped. It was in this same spread of harsh terrain that Abigail had carried Hal through the air, coming from the opposite direction after their adventure in the woods. He remembered that walking on these vicious, jagged rocks was almost impossible with bare feet.

Except now they had cushioned smart soles!

"Well, let's put these things to the test," Hal said, stepping up onto the rock. "But be careful."

Darcy was already jumping up and stamping on the rock. "It's fine," she said. "It's like wearing shoes. I can jump and skip and—OW!"

"Told you," Hal said.

Darcy hopped back to him, grimacing. "That really hurt. I scraped my toe. Look, it's bleeding."

"Here, sit down a minute," Hal said.

Darcy sat, grumbling about 'stupid magic clothes,' and shrugged off her backpack. She unzipped it and started rummaging around for her real shoes.

Hal gazed at her scraped foot. It was bleeding near her big toe. He stared at the red smudge and watched as a tiny trickle leaked out. He had a sudden, inexplicable urge to sniff at it. The thought both repulsed and intrigued him; the idea of sniffing at blood was weird and twisted, and yet another part of him felt it was a perfectly natural, normal thing to do . . .

Before he could stop himself, he got down on hands and knees and leaned in closer, eager to take in the scent of fresh, warm blood.

And Darcy screamed and leapt backward as his huge green snout came at her. For a moment Hal was taken aback, shocked at her reaction, but then realization hit him. *He'd done it!* He'd turned into a dragon once more! And all it had taken was the sight of blood.

As appalled as he was at the idea of sniffing Darcy's foot, his heart soared with delight. Finally! "Look, Darcy! At last!"

But Darcy screamed again. Too late Hal remembered that his words came out as throaty roars. Now Darcy was climbing to her feet and, not looking where she was going, stumbling backward towards the jagged rocky ground. If she tripped and fell, she might crack her head open.

Hal took one leap and swung a huge green paw around behind her. She instinctively lurched backward and fell against it. Trapped, her eyes widened further as Hal's snout came within six inches of her face. To avoid scaring her— *how exactly does a dragon look harmless?*—he immediately backed off and lay down flat on the rocky ground, trying to be still and submissive.

*141*

Watching her out of the corner of his eye, he was pleased to see that she was managing to get control of herself. Her breath was coming in short gasps, and her face was white, but she wasn't trying to run.

"I . . . I know you're Hal," she said after a while. "I'm just being silly. You gave me such a scare. I knew you were a dragon, but . . . but I didn't know you were *really* a dragon—a real one, I mean, so big and dangerous and—look at those claws, and those teeth . . ."

She lapsed into a stream of mumbling that Hal couldn't make out. She seemed to be commenting on everything—his green scaly skin, his huge feet with curved claws, his gigantic leathery wings—but he was only catching bits and pieces of her commentary. He was more interested in her smell. He'd never noticed before, but she smelled nice, a scent of roses. He assumed this was some of that girly bath soap or shampoo that all the moms made.

"Okay," she said, sounding like the Darcy he knew. "I'm ready to move on now. Can I . . . can I climb up on your back?"

Hal grunted a dragon's version of "Yes" and waited while she collected both backpacks and scrambled up on his back. He caught another scent then—a faint trace of blood. He sniffed the air and searched the ground, and saw faint red smears where Darcy had walked.

"Your bag straps broke when you changed," she said, dangling his damaged backpack in front of his left eye.

Hal groaned, reminded of his watch. He finally spotted it lying pulverized on the rock, its strap broken. He'd had that watch for as long as he could remember, and now it was ruined. His underpants also lay in full view, ripped open.

"Oh, look!" Darcy said. "Your clothes!"

For a second, Hal thought she was referring to his underpants and felt a flush of embarrassment. But no, she was talking about his 'smart' clothes, which seemed to have transformed into a handy set of reins, somehow looped around his neck with a little slack in them. He doubted they were *supposed* to be reins, but they certainly were useful. He felt Darcy grab hold of the reins and tug on them. Then she tightened her legs around his neck. She was ready.

At any other time, Hal would have marveled at the idea of Darcy, or *any* girl for that matter, holding on so tightly to him. But as a dragon he hardly felt a thing, just a gentle presence and a slight pressure where her legs pressed into his scaly skin.

He carefully stood and began the march to Black Woods. One day he'd learn how to fly. How had Abigail and Lauren been able to master this stuff so easily? He'd figure it out soon enough, but right now he was content to stomp. The rocky ground might as well have been soft grass for all the difference it made to his tough hide, and he marched without delay until he reached the grassy fields again.

Gradually, he picked up the trail left by Dewey and Robbie, hoof prints and large foot-shaped craters pressed into the soft soil where the grass was thin. There was also a strange whiff of animal, which could be either of his two friends.

Black Woods came into view, looming out of the fog like an impenetrable wall. As they neared, the fog dissipated a little and the blackness of the woods deepened.

"There they are!" somebody said.

Abigail's 'gang' came out of the fog from the direction of the cliff. "Hey," Abigail called. "I see you finally got it together. We thought you'd never make it!"

The group stopped a short distance away, and Hal suddenly felt self-conscious as his friends stared open-mouthed at him for what seemed ages. They were all in their human form, and with their simple green-gray clothing and bare feet, they looked to Hal like a band of shy forest-dwelling elves.

One by one they came closer, Abigail and Robbie first, then Dewey, Lauren and Emily. Abigail patted him on his shoulder, or at least what he thought of as his shoulder. "What kept you?"

"It took him a while to change," Darcy said from her perch behind his neck. "I had to cut my feet open first." She handed Hal's backpack down, and then her own, and Robbie went to stack them on top of the others in the long grass.

"Ooh, Darcy," Emily said, coming forward. "Oh, your poor feet! You're bleeding."

"I know, my toe really hurts. A warning to you all—these plastic shoe things protect the bottoms of your feet, but not the tops! I think I'm going to stay up here, Hal, if that's all right?"

Hal gave a grunt and a nod. He wanted to say, "Okay, let's get this done," but knew he'd end up roaring like the monster he was, so he simply gave another grunt and began marching into the woods. He stopped once to see if the others were following, and then plunged ahead.

He flattened the bushes easily. His thick scales seemed impervious to even the scratchiest of brambles. He remembered this section of the woods from his last trip, and soon came to the exact spot where he and Abigail had met the manticore. There were the remains of his old clothes, ripped to shreds, and his shoes trampled into the dirt. From here on he was unsure of the way, but he plunged ahead, hoping to get it right, and aware that his friends were following his lead.

A pungent stink came to his nostrils. He seemed to have developed a strong sense of smell since becoming a dragon, and this was one smell he could do without. He recognized it as the foul stench of the manticore's mouth. Hal imagined all those rodents Thomas must have scavenged for in the last few days, and all that meat getting caught between three rows of needle-sharp teeth. He shuddered inwardly. But the stink was useful; it told him the manticore was near, a little off to his left.

Hal couldn't think of a way to warn his friends verbally without returning to his human form—something he didn't want to mess around with right now. He needed to remain a dragon. An idea came to him, though. He reached up and, with his teeth, gently grabbed an overhanging branch. He snapped it loose with one quick twist of his neck, then repositioned the branch in his mouth and used it to write in the dirt. He wrote one simple, very untidy word:

*manticore*

Darcy, peering down from her perch, called back to the others. "Hal says the manticore is near."

Immediately there was a flurry of activity behind Hal, and he turned to watch. His friends had been trooping along behind him in single file, some of them carrying blankets. At Darcy's warning, Dewey immediately transformed into a centaur and turned around, stamping the ground, while Lauren, Emily and Abigail huddled closer to each other. Robbie tensed up and put on a deep frown of concentration. Like Hal, he seemed unable to master the ability of transforming exactly when he wanted to, but clearly he wanted to be an ogre at this moment.

A noise ahead of Hal alerted him to a presence. He snapped his head back around to the front and narrowed his eyes, trying to spot Thomas. His nose told him the manticore was close. He wasn't afraid of him at all, but was deeply concerned for his friends, particularly the girls, who were the most vulnerable. Emily had nothing to transform into as far as she knew, and neither did Darcy. Abigail could at least buzz away faster than she could run, but that assumed she wasn't stuck with poisoned quills. Even Lauren, who could fly like a bird in the open fields, was in danger here in the dense woods.

It was up to Hal and Robbie, and perhaps Dewey, to protect them from the manticore if it dared to attack. Surely it wouldn't, though. Surely Thomas had the sense to steer clear when he was clearly outnumbered.

The stench of manticore grew closer.

## Chapter Seventeen
### Attack in the woods

With a howl, the red-faced manticore erupted from a clump of bushes and pounced. Hal thought he was ready for it, but he badly misjudged how the creature would attack. He had half expected it to leap straight at one of his vulnerable friends and dig its claws and teeth in, bringing down its prey under rugged muscular bulk. Hal was ready for that—his rear end was pointed toward his friends, and the heavy club on the end of his tail was already sweeping the air and taking out a small tree or two. Had the manticore tried such an attack, it would have been knocked senseless in mid-flight.

Hal had also entertained the idea of a remote attack, with hundreds of quills flying through the air at them. He couldn't have blocked all the quills, but he might have used his leathery wings as a shield and caught most of them.

But the manticore took him by surprise. It leapt out of the bushes and went for his belly. *His belly!* In the blink of an eye the manticore was under him, burrowing like a rabbit and squeezing into a gap that wasn't quite big enough. Hal first tried to step aside, but the creature moved with him. So Hal jumped high, hoping to come down heavily on the thing and trap it under his clumsy, clawed feet, or squash it under his body. But as he came down he felt a stabbing jab in his soft underbelly.

As Hal reeled from burning pain, the manticore shot out from under him and made another bold move, leaping at Dewey's throat. The centaur reared at once and lashed out with flailing hoofs. There was a knock loud enough to echo through the woods, and the manticore jerked sideways. It landed badly, stumbled, and spun around. It shook its head and a few drops of blood flicked from its jaws.

All this happened in an instant while his friends screamed and yelled. As Dewey's hoof connected with the manticore's face, Hal turned and leapt into the fray, prepared to bury his snout in the creature's bushy mane and find a throat to lock his teeth into. What he would have done then was anybody's guess, but as it turned out, Hal's body didn't behave the way it was supposed to. Instead of reaching the manticore in one single bound, he fell short and landed with a splat in the mud, his wobbly legs giving way under him.

The pain in his belly was searing hot, and he felt a wave of nausea and dizziness as his vision blurred. The screams and yells continued, and the manticore joined in with fluty, shrill laughter. Hal tried in vain to get to his feet.

Dimly he saw a huge shape appear out of nowhere, a great shaggy mass of brown hair and muscle. He blinked to clear his vision and watched with relief as Robbie, in his ogre body, punched the manticore in the face and sent it staggering backward into the bushes.

The manticore was on its feet in a flash, and up came its scorpion tail, arcing over its head. With a savage flick, poison quills shot out and flew at Robbie, who threw up his arms and ducked his head. Hal's vision blurred once more as the pain in his belly spread fast. Anger and frustration suddenly bubbled up and he roared at the manticore. A great flash of hot yellow flame spouted from his throat.

The manticore screamed and tried to dart out of the way, but Hal—in one continuous fiery roar—turned his head back and forth as if he were blowing out candles on a birthday cake. The red-furred creature had no choice but to back off into the woods, with bushes catching fire all around. Overhanging trees blackened as the manticore gave a parting snarl and ran off.

But not for long. As Hal's lungs emptied, he took a gasping breath and the flame cut off. The moment he did so, the manticore stopped running and turned back. Its eerie bright blue eyes shone through the dark, foggy woods. Then the creature whipped off to the side, ducking and diving through the undergrowth like a dog hunting a rabbit.

Trying hard to focus, Hal shook his head and, as if he were emerging from a dream, became vividly aware of the ruckus going on around him. Both Emily and Lauren were knelt in the dirt, holding each other tight and screeching. Abigail was hovering fifteen feet up, not quite out of range of the manticore's quills or vicious stinger, but high enough to be the least likely target. Dewey was dancing in circles, nostrils flared and eyes wide, kicking up clods of dirt with his hoofs.

Robbie, stuck all over with what seemed like hundreds of quills, was staggering around. He tilted sideways and dropped to his knees.

For one horrifying moment, Hal wondered where Darcy was. She was missing! But then he remembered that she was riding on his back. *Or was she?* He twisted his neck, trying to see. But either she was clinging tightly to the back of his head and twisting *with* him, or she wasn't there anymore. "Darcy?" he called. His voice came out as a hoarse growl.

He wiggled his toes. They had some feeling in them, but not much. His belly stung all over. Grimacing, he writhed and managed to get his feet under him, then hauled himself off the ground. But the moment he lifted his head, his balance left him and he collapsed again.

Some help he was! As a dragon he'd felt certain he was more than a match for a manticore. He outweighed the creature, had bigger claws and teeth, and had a powerful club-like tail that could knock down a small tree. Yet the manticore had outwitted him with the ease of a skilled hunter.

Which was, of course, *exactly* what Thomas was.

Hal groaned, partly with pain but also with the realization that his friends had very nearly been killed. If Dewey hadn't got lucky and kicked the manticore in the face . . . and if Robbie hadn't finally managed to transform and lash out at the creature . . . and if Hal hadn't used his fire-breath at the last moment . . . well, who knows what might have happened.

And Thomas was still out there, flitting from one bush to another, taking stock and awaiting his chance to attack again.

Hal felt unable to walk anywhere feeling the way he did and wondered if he'd be better off turning back into his human self so he could ride on Dewey's back. They couldn't just hang around here, that was for sure. As far as he was concerned, the mission to block the fog-hole was abandoned. They had to get away from that evil manticore before it struck again.

He twisted his neck. *Was* Darcy still on his back? He couldn't see her, and suddenly felt certain she had fallen and been crushed under his weight.

Panicked, he swung around and scanned the ground, half expecting to find her squished into the dirt. But she was not there. He peered into the dark woods all around, looking for some sign of movement, or a frightened face looking back at him from under a bush. He sniffed, trying to catch the scent of her rose-scented bath soap. "Darcy! Darcy, are you—"

He blinked in surprise as he heard his own voice coming from his lips. He realized he was human again, dressed in the same green-gray clothes as before. And as he gaped in wonder at the ease and speed of his transformation, the wave of nausea and giddiness faded. He yanked up his green shirt, expecting the searing pain on his belly to be a blackened, blistering burn, but the pain was fading too, and there was nothing out of the ordinary to look at.

"Darcy!" he yelled, glancing around. Where was she?

A scuffling in the woods alerted him and he swung around, looking for the manticore. He could no longer smell the creature's rank breath, and that scared him. Now he had to rely on his eyes and ears instead of his nose, and somehow he felt more vulnerable than he ever had, especially without his claws and fire-breath for protection. *How could he ever get used to being a mere human again?*

"Thomas is still out there somewhere," he warned the others. "Did anyone see where Darcy went?"

Emily and Lauren climbed shakily to their feet, wide-eyed and white-faced. Dewey stilled his restless hoofs and looked angrily into the woods, while Robbie sat and plucked poison quills out of his hide. His fingers were too fat though, and in the end Lauren offered to help.

Abigail buzzed down to the ground. "I didn't see what happened to Darcy," she said. "She was there one moment, gone the next. You don't think . . . ?"

"That Thomas got her?" Hal shook his head. "I don't think he'd be sticking around if he had. He would have made off with his kill."

"Don't say that," Abigail said, a hand to her mouth. She peered into the woods. "What are we going to do now? I honestly thought we'd be able to take care of ourselves. I thought Thomas wouldn't dare attack us with you around."

The manticore gave a fluty laugh from somewhere in the foggy darkness.

Hal touched his stomach once more. "You know, the exact moment I changed back, the pain left. I'm fine now." He stared at Abigail, an astounding notion forming in his head. "This means we can't really be harmed. If transforming somehow heals us . . . well, we have nothing to worry about."

"Except dying," Abigail said shortly. "I doubt we can transform if we're dead first."

Lauren plucked another quill from Robbie's massive shoulder. She winced as it came out, but Robbie hardly seemed to notice. But he looked groggy, and his head kept lolling from side to side.

Hal quickly explained to him—quietly, in case the manticore was listening—that transforming back into his human shape might allow the quills to simply drop out. "That's what happened with me," he said, remembering. "They just fell out and I was fine afterwards. Hurry though. Darcy's missing."

It was at the exact moment Robbie managed to transform back into his small, thin frame that the manticore attacked again. Hal was transfixed by the sight of Robbie's poison quills falling into the dirt, but he jumped with fright when he heard the sudden rush of an animal though the woods. The cracking of twigs and heavy panting sent a chill through his body.

He needed to be a dragon again. *Now!*

But then he frowned, listening as the sounds of the manticore stopped abruptly with a thin, reedy wail of anguish. More scuffling, some urgent grunts, and then a sinister hissing that sent another chill through Hal's body.

"What's happening?" he whispered to Abigail.

She gripped his arm in fingers so strong they left red marks in his flesh. "I have no idea," she whispered back.

Emily, Lauren, Dewey and Robbie stood silent, watching and listening, as Hal took a deep breath and stepped into the thick undergrowth, circling some bushes so he could see what was going on. Abigail, still gripping his arm, tugged at him for a moment, but then relented and followed. Together they fought their way through a tangle of ferns and vines, and stopped in surprise.

Thomas was there, belly to the ground, spread-eagled in the dirt like a rug of deep red fur. His odd human face was a mask of shock. Straddling him was a creature nearly twice his length and even more frightening—a jet black serpentine thing with sinewy legs and a long neck. Its head was elongated and pointed, with a dragon-like crest rising over its brow and running the length of its neck and body. Two rows of even white fangs grinned maniacally, and a black tongue slipped out and quivered before slipping back in with a wet slopping sound.

The creature had its claws buried in the manticore's hide, but its tail was doing most of the work. It was the longest, thinnest tail Hal had ever seen, like a ten-foot shiny black snake had taken a bite of the creature's backside and was unable to let go. The tail was wrapped three times around the manticore's midriff, squeezing so hard that Thomas was gasping for breath. Thomas's own tail, that dangerous scorpion appendage, flailed weakly.

"Darcy?" Hal said, his voice coming out as a rasp.

As Hal and Abigail stared in disbelief, the black serpent opened its mouth wide and water gushed forth all over the manticore's face. Thomas moaned, screwing up his eyes and grimacing as the water dribbled into his mouth.

"No," Abigail said into Hal's ear. "That's not Darcy. That's Fenton."

The serpent took a long, deep breath and hissed noisily. As it did so, the water that matted the manticore's fur thickened into a glue-like substance. The manticore struggled but the serpent had him pinned down. More water gushed, and then came another hiss. In moments the manticore's eyes were glued shut and it was having difficulty breathing through its nose.

The serpent seemed satisfied with its work and uncoiled itself, releasing the manticore. The red-furred creature leapt to its feet and shook itself furiously. It rubbed its face in the dirt, grunting and whining, but its eyes remained glued shut.

Finally it gave a howl, turned, and stumbled away, crashing through bushes and bumping into trees as it went.

As silence descended on the woods, the black serpent swung around to study Hal and Abigail. Red eyes glowing, it remained as motionless as a statue. Then it tilted its head to one side and crouched, and somehow Hal knew that his old school friend—the class bully, Fenton—was in there somewhere.

"Fenton?" he said. "Nod if you can understand me."

The serpent creature gave the smallest of nods.

Relief washed over Hal. "How did you *do* that? The water you spat out—it turned to glue when you breathed on it. That's—"

"Wait," Abigail interrupted. "Look, it's great to see you, Fenton, but let's talk about this later. Right now we have a problem: Where's Darcy?"

*Chapter Eighteen*
**The fog-hole**

They spent the next fifteen minutes calling for their missing friend. With the manticore safely out of the way for now, all but Fenton spread out and hunted through the undergrowth, wondering if she had been knocked unconscious in some unseen scuffle. Fenton remained in his shiny black serpentine form, creeping around in near silence, half walking and half slithering. At one point he passed by Hal a mere five feet away, and yet Hal hardly heard him; the bushes moved and a solid black reptilian body slipped by, as thick as a tree trunk. Hal caught a glimpse of a scrawny back leg, and then came the long, long tail, growing thinner and thinner until it finally ended in a point no thicker than a pencil.

"Dar-CY!" Emily yelled from somewhere nearby. She had been calling the most. "Oh, where ARE you?"

"I just can't understand it," Robbie said, sounding almost indignant. "How could she just *disappear?* She was sitting right there on Hal's back, and then— *wham!* Gone."

"Wham?" Lauren repeated. "She disappeared with a *wham?*"

"You know what I mean."

Hal foraged under some ferns, hoping to find her lying unconscious somewhere. *Better unconscious*, he thought, *than dead.*

A sick feeling had come over him early on in the search. The woods were quiet, and it was extremely unlikely that Darcy had taken to her heels and run so far that she was out of earshot. Perhaps she had run and banged her head on a tree, and was lying dazed in a heap somewhere. Or perhaps she was so terrified that she had curled up into a ball and was refusing to utter a word of reply. Either scenario was better than the one that kept slipping into Hal's mind. He refused to voice it, but it kept rearing up and whispering to him, telling him that the manticore had stung her too, and she had stumbled away and died.

He shuddered. Not Darcy. Not *any* of his friends.

It was strange, though, that none of them had found her. There were six of them—seven counting Fenton, if indeed he was actually looking—and they had made sure to spread out from the point they had last seen Darcy riding on Hal's back. Wary of the manticore, they were peering under every bush and up every tree, then doubling back and searching again and again, never straying too far from each other. Fenton seemed to understand that Lauren was unable to fly this deep in the woods, and Emily had nothing to transform into, so both were vulnerable. Fenton stuck close to them like a sinister watch dog.

"Darcy!" Hal yelled, his throat dry.

There was nothing but silence in the woods.

They finally rejoined, each as somber as the next. Emily was crying.

Dewey, standing tall as a centaur, shook his head slowly. "If she ran away, then she really could be anywhere by now. She's had time to run all the way home, I should think."

That was an exaggeration, Hal knew, but he had to agree that Darcy could well be too far away to hear them yelling for her. "So what now? Keep looking? Leave the woods and get help?"

There was a long silence.

"I'm going to keep looking," Emily said, wiping her eyes. "Even if it takes me all day and night. Fenton will protect me. Right, Fenton?"

Hal jumped, suddenly noticing Fenton for the first time since they'd regrouped. His black serpentine body was hanging from the tree over their heads. His tail was coiled around a branch and he hung upside down with his lizard feet planted on the tree trunk.

After some discussion they decided to split up. "Go do what you need to do," Emily told Hal and Robbie. "Block that fog-hole you talked about. Do it quickly, and then come back and help us search."

Abigail moved to Hal's side. "I'll help the boys," she said. "Dewey, why don't you help Emily and Lauren? You can help Fenton protect them in case . . . you know."

With heavy hearts, Hal, Robbie and Abigail took the blankets and set off for the fog-hole. They said nothing, and Hal knew that each was wondering the same thing: Where on earth could Darcy be? Blocking the fog-hole seemed unimportant compared to finding her, yet somehow Hal knew it had to be done. And faced with the prospect of having to return to Black Woods another time, he was determined to see it through now rather than later.

They came upon the fog-hole a few minutes later. The column of thick, belching fog was utterly silent as it poured up out of the hole in the ground. Some of it puffed sideways and engulfed them, but the rest twisted and turned through the trees above.

"It's amazing," Abigail said, her eyes wide. "This is really where the fog comes from!"

"Let's get it done," Hal said shortly. He studied the branches lying across the hole. These were the few that he and Robbie had managed during their first visit. How long ago that seemed now! "Robbie, we need your ogre strength."

Robbie didn't need to be told twice. He frowned, stared at the ground, and suddenly grew to three times his normal height. The transformation was instantaneous and silent, and Hal felt a pang of envy. Everyone but him seemed able to change at will now.

Robbie stomped over to a tree and reached up to the nearest branch. The branch was thicker than Hal's leg, but the ogre simply snapped it off with one hard wrench. He dragged it over to the fog-hole, and Hal and Abigail jumped out of the way as the trailing end of the branch swept by, littering the ground with leaves and the remnants of an old birds' nest. Robbie heaved the branch unceremoniously over the hole and, without delay, returned to find another suitable limb to snap off.

After a couple more branches had been laid across the hole, Hal decided there was enough of a framework to support the blankets. He and Abigail unfolded and draped them over the branches. When all four blankets were in place, completely covering the hole, they pinned them down around the edges with stones. Just for good measure, in case a gust of wind should happen by, Hal instructed Robbie to throw on a couple more smaller branches, and then the three of them scooped dirt and soggy leaves on top. They stood back to admire their handiwork.

How quickly they had accomplished their task! With Robbie's ogre strength, laying branches had been easy, and the blankets neatly finished the job. Hal half expected the blankets to rise up with the force of the fog trying to get out, but they didn't even ripple. The fog had been cut off without any effort.

Already the air seemed clearer where they stood. The fog no longer billowed and puffed out of the hole at them, and no longer poured up through the trees. How long would it be before the fog lifted from the island? An hour? Half a day? Would it be clear before dusk, or would they have to wait until morning to see a blue sky?

"Well," Abigail said, dusting off her hands, "I guess that's done. We should go and look for Darcy again."

"Okay," Hal agreed. "Come on, Robbie. Job's done."

Robbie returned to his human form and the three of them set off back through the woods. On the way, Hal wondered aloud where the fog actually *came* from, and what was producing it.

"Do you think the fog-hole could be one of these 'holes' Miss Simone was talking about? Do you think it leads to Elsewhere?"

The idea was intriguing, and Abigail glanced back as if she wanted to go and investigate. "We could climb down into the hole," she said, "and follow the tunnel. We might come out in Miss Simone's world."

But the suggestion was meant lightly. Not one of them relished the idea of following a tunnel filled with fog! Hal wasn't sure whether that much concentrated fog would cause breathing difficulties, but he was sure it would be a difficult, if not impossible journey through unknown territory.

"That tunnel could narrow to the size of a rabbit warren," he said, "or it might be too steep to climb down. Maybe one day we can have a better look, but right now we need to find Darcy."

They regrouped once more in the exact spot where Thomas had attacked them. *Not Thomas anymore*, Hal corrected himself. *The manticore. Thomas is long gone.*

Emily looked forlorn, and she sat on a log with Lauren, staring at her dirty feet. Dewey had finally reverted to his human form, and he looked smaller than he ever did. He stood behind the two girls, shuffling his feet. Fenton, still in his serpentine body, loitered in the bushes. His head and body were motionless, his feet planted firmly in the dirt. Only his tail gave a sign of life where it flicked slowly back and forth.

"She's dead," Emily said miserably. "I can't believe it. She's actually dead."

"Don't be silly," Hal said. "You don't know anything of the sort. She's around somewhere, you'll see. Just not *here*, that's all. We'll find her. The question is, should we go and get help, or continue looking ourselves?"

"It must be getting late," Dewey said, sounding nervous. "Does anyone know what time it is?"

"My watch broke," Hal said.

"Look at the state of my feet," Abigail murmured. "All this tramping around in the woods without proper shoes . . ."

"At least you can fly," Emily said, still staring at her own feet. "All of you can change except Darcy and me. And now Darcy's dead, and I'm—" She broke off and her hands flew to her face. The sobs came good and hard now, and Lauren tried to comfort her with an arm around her shoulders.

Hal refused to believe Darcy was dead. Still, her disappearance was a mystery. He wondered if he should turn into a dragon again, and track Darcy using his nostrils, much as a dog might. He should have done that before, now that he thought about it, but having lived all his life without such a keen olfactory sense, it was easy to forget he had one.

It wasn't too late though. "Hey, guys, I think I'm going to turn into a dragon and see if—"

"Oh, my head," Darcy said, sitting up. "I have a lump the size of a stone."

As everyone stared at her in disbelief, she parted her disheveled hair and fingered the bump on her head. Then she frowned. "Why are you all looking at me like that?"

Everyone was speechless. Hal rubbed his eyes and looked again. Yes, she was really there! Darcy O'Tanner was sitting there in the dirt right before them, only she looked different. Although human, her skin was a curious mixture of colors that blended in so well with the surrounding bushes that she was difficult to see. Her face was a mottled green-brown shade, her hair much the same, and the top half of her dress seemed to be the color of a rotten log that lay behind her. Her hands, placed in the dirt as she leaned back, were the exact same shade—a dark blackish-brown that spread all the way up her arms and faded to pale green near her shoulders. As for her legs, at first Hal thought she was buried in dirt and leaves up to the waist, as her legs seemed to be missing. But then she drew her knees up and Hal could see the outline of her legs even though they were all but transparent.

The curious thing was that the color of her skin and dress *changed* as she moved, continually blending in with the surrounding area. No, Hal corrected himself, not just the surrounding area, but the *background*. He wasn't sure what the others were seeing, but from his own point of view, it was as though he could see right through her. That log behind her, for instance—it seemed to be painted onto her dress and part of her arm. And yet he knew without asking that the others were seeing a different effect, for they were looking at her from a different angle.

Darcy's camouflage was perfect, so perfect that she had been lying here unconscious all this time and none of them had seen her.

"Oh—!" Darcy said, holding her hands in front of her face. She stared down at her legs. "I—what—"

Now that he knew she was there, Hal could see her quite plainly, transparent or not. But, he realized, it was only because she was awake and moving. When she remained still for even a split second, the camouflage was so perfect that she blended completely into her surroundings and simply vanished from sight.

Emily found her voice at last and threw herself at her friend. "Oh, Darcy, we thought you were dead! We thought you'd been eaten by the manticore! We've been looking for you for absolutely ages!"

As the others gathered around her, Darcy climbed unsteadily to her feet and held on to Emily for support. "I remember the manticore coming out of the bushes," she said. "I was sitting on Hal's back, and he jumped and I lost my balance. I slipped off into the dirt. The next thing I knew—" She shuddered and closed her eyes, then tried again. "The next thing I knew, the manticore was standing over me, and I saw his big nasty face swinging round to look at me."

"And then?" Robbie asked.

"And then . . . and then I just wished I was invisible," Darcy said, frowning. "And it worked. The manticore stood there for a second or two, looking around, inches from my face, and it *couldn't see me*. Then it leapt away."

She stared at her hands once more. From where he stood, Hal could almost see right through her hands to her face. He blinked, unable to focus properly on her. *Not so much transparent as translucent*, he thought. Her face and hair seemed solid enough and he could make out her familiar features quite clearly, and yet at the same time the tree that stood right behind her showed in half her face, as if someone had painted a line from her forehead to her chin and shaded one half the color of bark. It was unsettling. Hal found himself blinking constantly. When he looked around, he noticed that all the others were too.

"Then," Darcy said, fingering the bump on her head again, "I went to sit up and got hit by something heavy. I think it was Hal's tail, but I'm not sure. I went out like a light. That's all I remember, until I woke up just now."

"So you've been lying here all this time," Abigail said in an awed tone, shaking her head. "What a defense mechanism!"

"What does this mean?" Dewey asked in a small voice. Now that he was back in human form, he seemed diminutive in both size and personality. "What exactly *is* Darcy?"

Everyone stared at her. She stared down at herself.

"Well," Abigail said slowly, "she might be some sort of wood nymph."

That rang a bell at the back of Hal's mind. "A wood nymph," he repeated. "They're shy creatures, aren't they? They just sort of hang out in the woods and keep to themselves."

"Very shy," Abigail agreed, nodding vigorously. "Almost impossible to find, from what I read. They blend in so well with the woods that ordinary people can't see them, even though they might be just a few feet away. I seem to remember reading that their smell is masked, too."

"I don't smell," Darcy protested.

A distant crack in the woods reminded them all that the manticore was still out there somewhere. Everyone glanced around nervously.

"I vote we get out of these woods," Hal said. "We've done what we came here to do. Now let's go home and . . . and see what happens."

The uncertainty of what lay ahead was almost as tangible as a blast of winter cold air. *Whatever should they do next?* All but Emily had managed a transformation of some kind—exactly the kind of transformation Miss Simone was looking for. A revelation of this magnitude would ensure that Fenton would not be the only family leaving the island that night! But what, then, of Emily? What if Miss Simone refused to let her come with them until she showed a sign of change? Nobody wanted to leave her behind. For that matter, nobody wanted to go anywhere at all until they knew where they were supposed to be going!

Besides, *the fog was lifting*. After a lifetime of fog on the island, Hal for one wanted to wake up to a blue sky the following morning.

On the other hand, if they said nothing and kept their transformations a secret for a bit longer, then Fenton and his parents would be leaving tonight—alone.

There seemed to be a bit of a dilemma: either let Fenton go on ahead, or leave Emily behind.

"Or we could make a stand," Abigail said in a determined voice as they left the woods and marched toward home. They had collected their backpacks but had, for now, decided to remain dressed in their magical clothes.

Just in case.

"What do you mean?" Dewey asked, trailing at the back of the group and giving sideways glances to Fenton, who was slithering through the long grass on his belly, pushing himself along with thin, muscular legs. His black reptilian body looked cold, slick and moist, but in fact was dry and curiously warm, as Hal had found out when Fenton had bumped against him back in the woods.

Abigail turned and walked backward as she spoke. "I mean we should tell everyone who we are, *what* we are, but tell Miss Simone that we're *not going anywhere unless we all go as a group*. Including Fenton."

Fenton was the only one of them who refused to change back into his human form. Oddly, Darcy had had no problem at all changing back; she had simply frowned, looked askew for a moment, and solidified. She made it look so easy, Hal thought with a pang of jealousy. But then again, her transformation seemed quite a bit simpler than his own. And since Fenton's new lizard-like body was not too far removed from Hal's own, he quietly understood that Fenton might be having some difficulty switching back.

Or perhaps he just preferred to stay as he was. It was hard to tell what was going through Fenton's mind.

Darcy hung back with Emily and Lauren, while Robbie stayed up front with Hal. Abigail, a few steps ahead, continued walking backward, stumbling once in a while.

"You see," she said, "earlier I suggested not saying anything at all about what we are. Well, now I think we should tell our parents *everything!* We'll tell them what we are, and show them too. Then we'll tell them about blocking the fog-hole, and perhaps they'll understand that there's no reason to leave the island anymore. Or, if we have to go, we can all go together. Including Emily. And if Miss Simone doesn't let Emily go, then we'll tell her that we're not going either."

Robbie rolled his eyes. "You make it sound so easy."

"It *is* easy," Abigail exclaimed. She sprouted her wings and buzzed into the air. "Look at us! In our class we have a dragon, an ogre, a faerie, a wood nymph, a centaur, a bird-girl, a gargoyle-lizard kind of thing, and . . . well, whatever Emily is going to turn into next. If we stand united, how can they refuse our demands?"

"Demands!" Robbie scoffed. "All right, so we stand up to Miss Simone. But what about our parents? What if they're on Miss Simone's side? Are we going to stand up to them too?"

"I can't really see that an extra day or two on the island would make a difference to Miss Simone," Hal said thoughtfully. "Surely she and our parents would agree to wait for Emily to change, since she's the only one left. It's just a matter of time."

"Yes," Abigail said, "and I've *seen* Emily change, at least partially, so I know she's got it in her."

Emily shook her head. "I haven't changed at all, Abigail."

"You have too! I saw your neck get longer in class one time."

Hal marveled at how their conversation had so dramatically evolved in the last day or two. Just a week ago, talk of a neck getting longer would have been scoffed at. Now it was a perfectly natural comment to make about a classmate.

They discussed the matter all the way home, arguing reasons for and against a complete unveiling of their newfound abilities. In the end Abigail won—as usual, Hal thought with a wry smile. Darcy and Lauren were in favor of Abigail's suggestion. They felt sure Miss Simone wouldn't make them leave without Emily and her parents. Dewey and Robbie were against the idea. Dewey felt that he'd rather just keep quiet about the whole thing, keep it all a secret and hope that Fenton wouldn't actually have to leave, although Hal suspected Dewey wouldn't mind too much if the big boy *did* leave. Robbie, on the other hand, was just being rebellious. He simply couldn't bear Abigail making all the decisions.

What Fenton thought, nobody knew. Perhaps he didn't care anymore. In his broody, slithery body, he had the air of a creature who didn't much care for anybody or anything as long as it didn't get in his way.

Feeling a pang of guilt for going against Robbie in his vote, Hal agreed with Abigail's suggestion. He was sick of all the secrecy and the guesswork involved with trying to unearth Miss Simone's great plan. The quicker everything was out in the open, the better.

And so it was that the classmates crossed the foggy fields and made their way to Fenton's house, where the adults were engaged in a somber farewell party.

* * *

The children didn't know what time it was when they finally gathered outside Fenton's house, just out of sight behind an overgrown hedge, but it was very dark already, and the glows from the lanterns inside the house looked extremely inviting.

"I wonder if they've missed us yet," Hal murmured.

"More to the point, I wonder if they've missed Fenton," Abigail said, glancing at the serpentine creature loitering in the street. Fenton had slithered up a long-dead street lamp and was now hanging upside down by the tail, his four feet gripping the post. If he looked out of place in the long grass of the meadows, he looked like something out of a nightmare here in the street outside the houses.

Robbie looked up at Fenton. "Are you ever going to change back, or what? You can't just walk in looking like that. We should probably warn them all first."

Abigail gave a sudden giggle and looked at Hal with a glint in her eyes. "I don't see why," she said. "Hey, they wanted to see some changes, didn't they? Why don't we just show them!"

Hal shook his head. "I don't want my mom having a heart attack," he said firmly. "What if I go inside and try to explain things? And then they can come out and . . . and see Fenton. If we're going to show them what we are, we'll have to do it outside anyway."

Robbie looked fierce. "I'll come in with you," he said.

"Me too," Abigail agreed.

Robbie immediately glared at her, but said nothing.

Hal sighed. "Let me do the talking then. Don't just blurt things out. Okay?"

The three other girls and Dewey seemed relieved at the prospect of staying outside, despite the chill in the air. They sat together on a low wall and prepared to wait patiently. Nearby, Fenton remained utterly motionless hanging from the lamppost.

Hal stepped up to the front door and found it ajar. He pushed the door open and crept inside. The sounds of murmured voices came to him, and he recognized the deep tones of his dad although he couldn't make out the words that were being spoken. Then he heard Fenton's mom saying something in response.

Motioning for Robbie and Abigail to follow, Hal took a deep breath and walked down the hall to the living room. The room was jam-packed with adults, some sitting but most standing in a large circle so that, as Hal entered, he had to stop behind a wall of men and women.

". . . be long before we're all sitting outside getting sun tans," one of the women was saying—Darcy's mom, by the sound of it. "Don't worry about us. We'll be along shortly."

Something cold and wet touched Hal's hand and he almost jumped out of his skin. But it was just Wrangler, Emily's dog; evidently Mr. and Mrs. Stanton had brought him along too. Hal ruffled his head absently, listening to the conversation.

"I *do* worry, though," Mrs. Bridges said. "But we've been over this already. Right now I'm more worried about Fenton. I think we should go look for him."

"Well, maybe," her husband said. "It's not exactly late, but you told him to be back by—what, four? Four-thirty?" He sighed. "It's after six now. I'm sorry, Simone. The kids probably just lost track of time."

"It's all right," came Miss Simone's voice, sounding like it was not all right at all. "But the darker it gets, the harder it is to find our way across the island."

Someone gave a sudden exclamation, and the two men standing in front of Hal swung round to face him. He was suddenly the center of attention as all adults in the room, including Miss Simone, noticed him standing there. Wrangler seemed to sense the shift in the atmosphere and slunk off to a corner.

"Hal!" his mother said. "Where's Fenton? He's late."

"Outside," Hal said. Robbie and Abigail appeared in his periphery as they stepped up. "We're all here. Um, sorry we're late."

"Well, *you're* not late," his dad said. "But Fenton was supposed to be back earlier. We were getting worried. Miss Simone needs to get home, and . . ." He trailed off and frowned. "What on earth are you wearing?"

"They've been to the lighthouse," Miss Simone said coldly. Her silky green cloak was wrapped tightly around her neck and body. It draped all the way to the floor and hid her feet. "They've been snooping." She glared at Hal. "How did you get in?"

Hal had almost forgotten his strange attire. He self-consciously crossed his arms and found himself trying to hide his bare feet by curling up his toes.

"We found a way," he said vaguely. Abigail nudged him sharply. "Look," he said, trying to ignore Miss Simone and speaking directly to his parents, "we came to tell you that things are different now."

There was a silence in the room, broken only by the crackling of the fire in the hearth. The weight of all those adult eyes on him almost squashed Hal into the floor.

He shook himself and turned back to the golden-haired stranger from Elsewhere. "Miss Simone, if you're going to take Fenton away, then you're going to have to take all of us," he said boldly. "Or none of us."

The silence lengthened, this time accompanied by a number of stern expressions.

Miss Simone's eyes narrowed. "I beg your pardon?"

Hal gulped. He felt this wasn't going as well as planned. "We . . . that is, uh, me and my friends—"

"My friends and I," Mrs. Hunter corrected him. Lauren's mom would always be the teacher no matter what.

"My friends and I," Hal went on, "have decided that, um, we should stick together and, uh, well, not go anywhere unless we *all* go. And that includes Fenton. And Emily."

"What on earth are you talking about, son?" his dad said under furrowed, bushy eyebrows. "Where did you get those clothes? Have you been to the lighthouse as Miss Simone said? How did you get in?"

"This isn't a game, boy," Miss Simone said sternly. "Those clothes are not for playing in."

"What *are* those clothes?" Mrs. O'Tanner asked, looking Hal up and down before moving on to Abigail. "They're really very pretty. Abigail looks like a doll."

"They're special clothes," Miss Simone said. "They were supposed to be for when the children started changing. I brought all different sizes because I didn't know when . . ." She shook her head. "Well, anyway, that was then and this is now. All I'm interested in now is getting Fenton into my world where he can go to work." She glanced at Mr. and Mrs. Bridges, reddening slightly. "And you too, of course."

"We busted the gates down," Robbie blurted.

Again that awful silence. Now there were a number of suspicious glares, coupled with a few worried gasps.

Hal turned to Robbie and gave him a look of his own. His friend looked defiant but nervous at the same time. It was almost as though he were looking for trouble.

Abigail seemed to take Robbie's announcement as a cue to switch on her own vocal chords. "Yes, it's true," she said sweetly, a hint of glee in her voice. "Robbie simply shoved the gates off the hinges. Then he punched the lighthouse door in. We went all the way to the top of the lighthouse and out on to the platform."

"Gallery," Hal murmured.

"We saw the blue sky for the first time," Abigail went on, despite the widening eyes all around. "And felt the sun on our faces. It was wonderful. And we couldn't help noticing that we could see Out There too—the city across the water, with those huge buildings and empty houses. It was deserted, just as you said it would be." Abigail's voice hardened. "But we breathed the nice clean air above the fog and felt the warmth of the sun on our skin, and it was *lovely*. And we couldn't help wondering: Why have you never let us up there before? Why have you never let us see the blue sky before? *Why?*"

"Oh, Abigail," her mom said, her hands flying to her face. Dr. Porter came forward with her arms out, but Abigail backed off.

"We just want the truth," Abigail demanded. "It's time you told us everything. *Everything.*"

## Chapter Nineteen
### Miss Simone talks

There was an outcry of whispers and annoyed grumbles at Abigail's outburst, a mixed reaction from a surprised circle of adults. Miss Simone pushed her cloak back over her shoulders and stepped into the center of the room, raising her hands to calm everyone.

Then she turned to Abigail. "Young lady," she said firmly. "You are not old enough to make demands of your parents, or indeed me. Kindly tell us how Robbie was able to break down the gates of the lighthouse. What did you mean by that?"

She stared intently at Abigail, as did everyone else in the room. After a moment, Abigail swallowed and spoke evenly. "Hal wants to say something. So please listen, or he might get angry."

Hal jumped and swung around to her. She gave him a quick nod of encouragement, and a wink.

*Might get angry?* What on earth was she thinking now? Hal wished he'd made her and Robbie stay outside.

Now the center of attention again, he took a deep breath. "What Abigail means is that we're tired of being kept in the dark about everything. So we've . . . well, we've sort of been meeting in secret and discovering a few things." One of Miss Simone's eyebrows shot up. Hal forged ahead. "And one of the things we've discovered is that the fog comes out of a hole in the ground in the woods."

He waited for a reaction from his parents. From any of the parents in the room. But they just stared at him.

"We know that, son," said his dad softly.

"Oh." Hal faltered. Of *course* they knew that. "Well, we discovered it last week and thought it would be a good idea to block it up."

"What?" Miss Simone exclaimed. She looked aghast and seemed to reel on her feet. So did all the other adults. "You thought *what?*"

"Oh no!" cried Mrs. Stanton, her hands flying to her face. "What did we do with the chemical suits?"

"But there was a manticore," Hal went on hurriedly, losing his grip again. "It chased us away so we didn't get a chance to finish the job and then we had this idea to make a raft and leave the island but there was this huge sea serpent, just like you said, Dad, and it brought us back and took our raft away, and then Abigail showed me her wings and called me a freak and Robbie turned into an ogre, and then—"

"Whoa," his dad said, holding his hands up. "Slow down, Hal. You're not making any sense."

But Miss Simone, surprisingly, had developed a smile that might almost be called pleasant. "Oh, I think Hal *is* making sense—finally." She had switched on the charm now. "Hal, are you telling me that some of you have experienced some changes? Is that it?"

"You could say that," Hal agreed. "So there's no need for Fenton to leave tonight. He can stay another day or two, can't he? And then we'll all be ready to go together." He glanced at his mom. "That is, if we really *must* go."

His mom looked stunned, and she reached for her husband's hand.

Miss Simone nodded. "I think I understand now," she said. "Hal, how about I give you all another day. The morning after next I'll be back to take with me whoever is ready to go. But I'm afraid whoever is not ready will have to stay here until they are."

She glanced out the window, but it was too dark to see anything.

"Is everybody outside?" she asked. When Hal nodded, she clapped her hands. "Good. Let's step outside then, and talk some more."

Since Hal, Robbie and Abigail were blocking the door to the hallway, they turned and led the way outside. Abigail gave Hal's hand a squeeze and smiled. Surprised and pleased, Hal returned a grin. But truthfully, he felt a little dazed by the conversation in the living room. He'd blurted it all out in a haphazard fashion and couldn't even recall exactly what he'd said. But at least Miss Simone seemed agreeable to waiting an extra day.

The cold air outside felt good after the stifling living room. Hal hadn't realized how hot he'd started to get. He led the way out to the street, and almost tripped over Wrangler as the border collie hurried past. Hal found Dewey, Emily, Lauren and Darcy still sitting on the low wall. Emily remained seated as Wrangler found her and licked furiously at her face, but the others jumped up and looked fearful at the sound of many pairs of adult feet tramping down the path.

Hal looked for Fenton. He was still there, hanging from the lamppost, barely visible in the dark.

"Hi, Mom," Emily said, waving. "Dad."

Mr. and Mrs. Stanton just stared at her in surprise, studying her curious clothing, as the other children greeted their parents. Hal saw worry in the eyes of many adults—or was it suspicion? Perhaps not even that, but resentment? Hal wasn't entirely sure *what* he saw written on the adults' faces. His mom was wringing her hands, and his dad was scratching at his beard. Signs of worry? But worry about what, specifically? Simply Hal's health and well-being, or something more than that?

Miss Simone looked around. "Fenton's missing," she said.

Abigail said shortly, "He's around."

There was a long, expectant pause.

Hal felt goose bumps on his arms. His magical clothes seemed to do a good job of keeping him warm in the cold, foggy evening air, and even the parts of his body that weren't covered felt oddly comfortable. The goose bumps on his arms must be something to do with the situation at hand, he decided—something to do with the way the adults were staring uneasily at their children, and the way Miss Simone had an almost hungry look in her eyes.

Hal cleared his throat. "Miss Simone, tell us why we've been stuck here on this island all our lives. We know about the fog. We know it's *supposed* to keep the virus out, if the virus is still Out There. But why couldn't we just go to your world from the beginning, instead of staying here?"

Abigail nodded with satisfaction. That had evidently been her burning question too.

Miss Simone looked for a moment like she was going to argue, but then she sighed and nodded. "All right, Hal. The reason is that . . . well, the project . . ." She searched for words.

Hal's mom broke in gently. "Hal, you and your friends are all very special children. We love you no matter what. But we're in Miss Simone's debt. Without her, you wouldn't exist. Without her, you would never have been born. None of us were able to have children, but Miss Simone made it possible. And the reason she gave us this wonderful gift is because the good people of her world *need* you."

"But only if you can change," Miss Simone said. Then she glanced at Hal's mom. "Sorry, Mrs. Franklin, I didn't mean it that way. Of course you're all welcome in my land regardless of whether the children are shapeshifters or not." She turned back to Hal. "But you're only *needed* in my land if you can change. Otherwise," she said with a shrug, "you're just a bunch of ordinary kids."

One of the men cleared his throat. "But no offense intended, right, Simone?"

She reddened. "Uh, no, sorry. No offense intended. I'm not very good with children."

Abigail clicked her tongue. "But you still haven't explained why we had to stay *here*, on the island. Why couldn't we have grown up in *your* world, this nice warm, sunny place you keep talking about, instead of this boring, depressing, foggy island?"

"Ah," Miss Simone said. "That's a technical matter. You see, for thousands of years our doctors have been working with willing parents to breed shapeshifters. We need shapeshifters in our land, and thus the parents of shapeshifters are thought of and treated like royalty—land and property in a beautiful countryside, a comfortable lifestyle forever . . . Trust me when I tell you that your parents will soon be retiring in great luxury."

"And what about us?" Abigail asked, that defiant edge once more creeping into her voice. "What happens to *us* while our parents are living a life of luxury? Locked up in some laboratory, I suppose. Being stuck with needles and tested."

Several horrified gasps filled the air. "Oh, Abigail!" Mrs. Porter said, her eyes filling with tears. "Is that what you think?"

"What are we *supposed* to think, Mother?" Abigail snapped, quivering with anger.

Hal tentatively reached for her hand, feeling awkward. "Let them explain," he whispered.

Miss Simone's eyes were wide. "Oh dear," she said. "I seem to have given the wrong impression. I never was good with children. I'm a doctor, you see, and . . ." She looked at each of the classmates in turn. "Children, in my world, shapeshifters are heroes. There's a diverse population of intelligent creatures there, each more dangerous than the next. Your own world has a diverse population too, a wonderful variety of animals, but none of the animals is smart or tenacious enough to be a threat to humans. You don't see elephants ganging up to take over a village in India, laying claim to the land just because it's a nice spot. You don't see crocodiles charging tolls for use of boats on their rivers, just because it's an easy way to make money. In your world, animals are humble and generally have no need for domination and power. Humans, on the other hand, feel they own the place and can do exactly as they wish, wherever they want, and if animals are driven out of their natural habitat in the process . . . well, so be it."

There was a silence.

"You see," she continued, "in my world there are perhaps just as many dumb animals as in yours, and these are no threat. But, unlike you, we also have a large number of *intelligent* species. In your world, humans always enjoyed being the only smart animals on the planet, but in ours, we have to share our world with numerous other creatures that are just as smart as us, if not smarter."

She paused, looking around at her captivated audience. The goose bumps were prickling Hal's arms again. He suddenly realized he was still holding Abigail's hand, and she hadn't even appeared to notice. Suddenly embarrassed, he gently let her hand drop.

"Sharing a world with all these smart creatures," Miss Simone said, shaking her head, "is, frankly, very difficult. It humbles us, too. We humans strive to make peace and keep to ourselves. We try hard not to encroach or trespass on land occupied by others, even though sometimes contact is inevitable. For instance, we try to have an understanding with our neighbors, the centaurs, because we must share the same natural resources—the fresh water from the mountain stream, the excellent soil for crops, the shelter of the valley against the elements—but sometimes there are misunderstandings and we end up arguing. Many humans simply don't like to share with so-called *inferior* species, never mind that centaurs are far smarter than us in many ways. But when it comes to settling issues and making pacts, centaurs are notoriously stubborn and simply *will not* negotiate over the smallest of matters, and tempers tend to flare quickly and frequently."

Sighing with obvious frustration, Miss Simone began to pace in a slow circle before the children.

"Worse is our ongoing feuds with the dragons and the harpies, who refuse to leave us alone. One thing we humans and centaurs have in common is the fear of a dragon attack, which are often swift and vicious, resulting in a death or two. Or a harpy raid, where literally hundreds of harpies fill the air, their screams deafening. When harpies swoop, it's mayhem—a mass of white feathers and yellow eyes and pungent smells, and when the chaos ends and the harpies have gone, we find most of our small livestock missing, crops ruined, clothes stolen from wash lines."

*Harpies. White feathers, yellow eyes.*

Hal thought of Lauren and glanced across at her. Clearly she had made the same connection because she had shame written all over her face. Shame and embarrassment for what she was—a harpy. But Hal, despite being a dragon, felt nothing. He wouldn't be joining in any attacks on villages, no matter what! And he very much doubted that Lauren would either.

"As for the manticores," Miss Simone continued, "they're just downright evil. They're far more intelligent than dragons and harpies, and can hold a deep and meaningful conversation if the mood strikes them, but right afterward they're liable to kill you. Still, we try to reason with these creatures. Even manticores have some degree of respect for a human wishing to negotiate terms of some kind. But not much. They'd sooner eat him than talk with him."

A glimmer of understanding came to Hal. Dragons, harpies, manticores . . . it wasn't just a coincidence that Miss Simone happened to mention these particular creatures. "You need our help to . . . to *talk* to them?"

Miss Simone stopped pacing and stared first at Hal and then at his classmates, one by one. "Yes. I need your help to negotiate with these creatures, these other species. You, my children, are emissaries of the human race. Not only will you be able to talk to them in their own language, you will feel *empathy* for them, and that will go a long way to helping us *understand* them and, in turn, will allow them to trust us a little more. For thousands of years we've been breeding shapeshifters to help keep order in our land. You are our next generation."

There was a long silence. Finally Emily spoke, her voice cutting clearly through the still, cold air.

"But you *still* haven't told us why we're here on this foggy island instead of in your nice, sunny world."

"Oh," Miss Simone said. "Unfortunately, we can't breed shapeshifters in my world. The air in your world is roughly twenty-one percent oxygen, a little less than our own. The lower oxygen in your world slows development, which is essential in the breeding of shapeshifters. If you had grown up in my world, you would have changed into dragons or ogres or harpies around the age of two and stuck in that form, essentially becoming those creatures and losing your human identities. The lower oxygen in your world does a fine job of slowing the process, allowing your minds and bodies to mature before the creature within manifests."

Emily snorted. "You're saying we've been stuck here on this foggy island because of a slight difference in oxygen? I don't believe you."

"Actually," Robbie said, "I read about this in one of my bug books. Three hundred million years ago there were dragonflies two-and-a-half feet long, and the reason was because there was more oxygen in the air back then—"

"It was around thirty-five percent," Miss Simone said, nodding. "Scientists in both our worlds have uncovered many, many fossils of huge insects from that era. But such enormous bugs are not feasible in a world with only twenty-one percent oxygen, which is why bugs today are so small."

Robbie nodded. Then he frowned. "Could that be why your world has more intelligent species than ours?"

"That's the general consensus," Miss Simone agreed. "Increased oxygen means better and faster development of muscles and organs. Even brief tests have shown that. Apply that logic to millions of years of evolutionary development and you can see why even a slight variation in the oxygen level might make a fundamental difference to life on the planet. In your case, growing up here in your world—on this island—dramatically slows the manifestation of your alternate identities, giving you time to grow into your human bodies."

She paused for thought. In that moment, Hal realized how utterly silent the night was. Even the bullfrogs had stopped croaking.

Hal had a sudden nagging feeling that something was very wrong. He looked sideways at Abigail, but for once she seemed at peace with what Miss Simone was telling her. *The truth at last.*

"There's something strange though," Miss Simone continued. "We discovered long ago that a sudden change in oxygen levels midway through the process somehow messes things up. There are many documented reports about this, and I have a very good friend who is living proof. He's a shapeshifter too, a strapping six-foot man who can transform into a flying horse. Only he can't fly. When he was eight and first began to show signs of transformation, the scientists were impatient to introduce him to my world to study how he interacts with the elusive flying horses. In their haste they brought him across too soon, before he had learned to fly. The scientists figured that he had already undergone a full transformation, wings and all, so all that was left was to actually learn to fly. And yet he never did."

"Why?" Emily asked.

"Nobody knows. It's a mystery. Of course, one case alone isn't anything to go by. But this has happened repeatedly in history. Almost every similar developmental failure can be attributed to haste."

Miss Simone glanced around at them all.

"You can imagine my horror when the virus struck this world. I thought to myself, why did this happen on *my* watch?" She sighed heavily. "Well, we developed the fog very quickly and started pumping it through to your world, and it did a very good job of keeping the virus away. It still does. But we were always unsure of the effect it would have on you children over a period of years. We feared that it might prevent you from changing. Only time would tell. To our surprise, young Thomas changed a little earlier than expected, at age six." She lowered her gaze to the road. "It wasn't the most successful of transformations—in fact it was a disaster, as you know. But it gave us hope that we still had a group of young shapeshifters on the way."

Hal thought about Thomas falling off the cliff, being pulled under the water by unseen hands, waking in a strange place. Had Miss Simone been part of that?

"We were extra vigilant from that day forward," Miss Simone went on. "But nothing happened to the rest of you, and you all turned eight and then nine without a sign of change, and then more years passed and still nothing happened. You can imagine our increasing frustration and worry—you're now four years late!"

"It's not your fault, though, children," Hal's mom called from the ring of silent adults.

Miss Simone shook her head. "No, not your fault. But my people are worried sick. People are being killed through misunderstandings with neighboring communities. Just recently the naga folk thought we were deliberately diverting a river away from their neck of the woods. Actually a rock slide blocked it, and we were in the process of clearing it when the naga sent someone to investigate."

"Naga?" Emily asked, with Wrangler lying happily across her bare feet.

"Snake folk," Miss Simone said. "Half snake, half human . . . Anyway, naturally they got the wrong end of the stick. They're a prickly species anyway, and this just enraged them. So they sent a forest's worth of snakes into the settlement and . . ."

She broke off and fell silent at last.

"If you could have communicated with them properly," Abigail said, "you might have been able to explain the situation and avoid an ugly scene. Is that it?"

Miss Simone nodded. "A simple conversation. That's all we needed. It's the same with the ogres. They're lovely, docile beasts, not an ounce of malice in them. Yet they cause so much trouble for us, and for other species too, just because they blunder around the land and don't stop to think." She snorted. "They're intelligent enough to be talked to and reasoned with in their own tongue, but too dumb to be a real threat. They're like oversized four-year-olds. You can lead them away from danger and trouble by coaxing them, dangling a carrot on a stick—but if you upset one, you'd better run."

Hal nudged Robbie and grinned. Robbie scowled back.

Miss Simone frowned, catching the private exchange. But she said nothing. Instead, she turned slowly in the street and made a final chilling statement that caused Hal's goose bumps to rise again.

"Because of this man-made virus," she said in hushed tones, "which has effectively wiped out most of the population of your world, I fear for the future. I fear that your world is lost forever, and because of that I fear that my *own* world may be on its way to chaos and war with other species.

"You, my children, may be our final generation of shapeshifters."

*Chapter Twenty*
## Monsters in the street

The evening was growing colder by the minute, Hal decided as he stood outside in the street under the feeble moonlight. Even wearing his magic clothes, or 'smart' clothes as he still thought of them, he was beginning to shiver. Now he understood why Miss Simone wore a cloak; there was only so much cold these garments could keep out. The glow of lanterns from inside Fenton's living room once more looked welcoming.

But Miss Simone had no intention of going inside now. Around her stood all the parents. Feet shuffled and eyes darted. There was an air of expectation. Enough had been said; it was time for a demonstration.

Hal looked at Abigail. "Want to go first?" he asked. "Since you were the first of us anyway."

Abigail pouted for a second, and then shrugged. "Sure, why not." She stepped away from Hal and Robbie and moved to the center of what suddenly seemed like a performing stage in the middle of the road. She glanced at her mother. "Ready?" she said softly.

Dr. Porter hugged herself and nodded stiffly.

Hal wondered what was going through the minds of his own parents. What must it be like for them, knowing that their child was about to turn into some kind of monster? How often had they worried about this night? Did they even know what kind of monster Hal was?

As he was debating this question, Abigail sprouted her wings. They just popped out in an instant, her dress parting obligingly at the back. As several adults gasped, she began buzzing and lifted easily off the ground.

"Oh!" her mom said, hands flying to her face. Tears were welling up again, but she was smiling with joy.

Abigail flew closer and then buzzed quickly around the road, obviously showing off. Now the other parents were smiling too, and to Hal's amazement, they actually started applauding.

Encouraged by the positive vibes, Abigail buzzed over heads and spun in mid-air. She had a beam on her face.

Finally, she stopped in front of Miss Simone and bobbed up and down. Miss Simone was nodding with approval, hands on her hips.

"Very good," she said. "Very, very nice."

"I'm a faerie, right?" Abigail asked.

"Yes," Miss Simone said, nodding. "Although in my world they still use the word *fae*. The fae folk are everywhere, and there are many species, so simply calling yourself a faerie is not very precise. It's rather like cats; there are many kinds of cats, you see, including lions, tigers, cougars, and so on."

*And manticores*, Hal thought. *Do they count as cats?*

"Still," Miss Simone said, nodding again, "we'll stick with faerie for now." She reached out and brushed Abigail's hair aside. "Hm. Your ears aren't pointed. How strange. And you're much too big to be a real faerie. Can you shrink?"

Abigail landed abruptly and her wings went still. "What?"

Miss Simone cleared her throat. "The fae folk are tiny," she explained. "About the size of my hand." She held it up palm upwards, fingers straight, in case her point wasn't clear enough. "I wonder if perhaps yours is only a partial transformation."

Abigail shot a glance to Hal. "Um . . . well, I don't know anything about that. This is all I know."

"Oh. Well, perhaps it'll come to you in time." Miss Simone glanced around. "All right, who's next?"

Somewhat deflated, Abigail came and stood by Hal again. He nudged her and whispered that she'd done well. "You just need to practice on the size thing, that's all," he finished. "And your ears aren't pointy enough."

He laughed at Abigail's snort.

Robbie stepped forward. "Okay, my turn. Ready, Mom? Dad?"

Mr. and Mrs. Strickland both looked delighted. It was clearly enough for them to know that their son could change, regardless of what he would become.

Robbie's transformation came as quickly as Abigail's, only it was far more dramatic. Almost everyone in the circle took a step backward when the ogre exploded into being. With Abigail there had been looks of delight; with Robbie it was awe, mingled with touches of concern. Wrangler, who had seemed only mildly surprised at Abigail's sudden transformation, now laid his ears back and tensed as Robbie loomed over him.

As a ripple of applause echoed through the night and Miss Simone began speaking, Hal looked for Fenton. There he was, still hanging from the lamppost, watching everything but remaining absolutely motionless. In the dark of the night he was now a blacker-than-black shape, with just his tiny, glowing red eyes giving him away, and even then because Hal was looking in his direction and knew he was there.

"Wonderful, wonderful," Miss Simone said, sounding bright and cheerful. Gone was her icy attitude; now she was as warm and pleasant as the sun had been that afternoon at the top of the lighthouse. "A fine specimen, if I may say so!"

Robbie shifted from one foot to the other, looking oddly confused, like one of his bugs wondering how it had got caught in a jar. After a while he returned to his usual skinny self and gave an exaggerated bow to the now delighted crowd.

As the applause died, Mrs. Bridges called out. "Where's Fenton?"

In unison, Hal and his classmates turned to Fenton. There was silence for a moment while the adults searched the darkness, following the collective gaze of their children, trying to find the missing boy. And then Dewey's mom gasped and pointed, and one by one the adults saw the black, serpentine creature hanging from the lamppost.

"I'm not sure I'll ever get used to this," Mrs. Bridges murmured.

Miss Simone gave a grim smile. "Just don't faint like you did the first time you saw him like this," she said quietly. "He's still your son."

Hal caught this private exchange and was startled. So Mr. and Mrs. Bridges, as well as Miss Simone, had already seen Fenton's full transformation? He supposed that was logical; after all, Miss Simone wouldn't have arranged for Fenton to leave the island otherwise! But it proved that Fenton could change back and forth and wasn't 'stuck' in his present form, so why he remained so was a mystery.

"Come on down, Fenton," Darcy called. "Show us what you can do."

It seemed for a moment that Fenton hadn't heard—either that or he was ignoring them. But then, slowly, he began to move. He gripped the post tighter, hugging it closer to his sinewy torso, and then his impossibly long tail slowly unwound from the overhanging lamp, and his slender, reptilian body eased down the post.

Apparently noticing the creature for the first time, Wrangler started barking frantically. Emily hugged him and whispered in his ear, trying to calm him.

Fenton slithered across the paved surface, lazily pushing himself along with his gangly legs. It reminded Hal of his and Robbie's short journey on the raft a few days ago, when they had stood on the platform and paddled gently with shovels. Fenton slid across the road with the gracefulness of a raft on calm water.

His red eyes gave no hint of recognition or humanity. Even Hal, himself a lizard-like creature, shuddered at the sight of the black serpent as it eased into the center of the audience. But the fact that Fenton was here, obediently presenting himself for inspection, proved that *the boy was still himself.* His human mind was in there somewhere, however mysterious and menacing he appeared.

Finally Emily managed to calm Wrangler. The border collie seemed very unhappy, crouching low and baring his teeth. A low, continuous growl came from his throat.

Meanwhile the adults were quiet. Almost *too* quiet. Hal wished they'd say something. The last thing he wanted was for Fenton to feel like some kind of freak. The idea of the boy bolting in shame and ending up like Thomas filled Hal with fear. A deranged manticore was bad enough!

"Fenton, do the water thing," Hal said, breaking the silence.

Fenton swung his head to look at him. Then he swung back to look at the adults. Hal thought he saw a momentary flutter somewhere in Fenton's elongated body, like a muscle spasm, and in the next moment water spewed out of Fenton's mouth in a perfect stream, pooling on the road before him. The audience parted as the puddle spread. Wrangler couldn't help letting loose a high-pitched whine.

Then Fenton stretched his neck and, with a sinister hissing sound, breathed on the puddle. The water solidified, thickening and turning a dull translucent gray.

Miss Simone grinned and nodded, then leaned down to touch the solidified puddle. It yielded under her touch like soft putty. When she took her finger away, the dent she'd made slowly smoothed out.

"Fenton is a very rare species," she said quietly. She knelt and gently patted Fenton on the head as if he were a pet. "There are only two that we know of in our entire land, both ten times bigger than Fenton."

Hal gasped. Ten times bigger . . . !

"Fenton is so rare that his species doesn't even have a name," Miss Simone went on. "He's a cross between a dragon and a serpent—a water dragon, or perhaps a serpent dragon. Dragons typically live on land, while serpents live in water. Fenton is amphibious, like a frog or a newt. He breathes air but can spend great lengths of time underwater."

Fenton's long tongue flicked out.

"What's remarkable about Fenton is that he has a couple of extra stomachs for holding water. Many animals have four stomachs—cows and giraffes, for example—and camels have three. But normally they're for storing and processing food . . ."

Miss Simone seemed to be lost in a world of biology, and the intent look on her face was a little disturbing. Hal decided she was exactly the sort of scientist Abigail had described on numerous occasions, the sort who would stare with morbid fascination at a creature in a cage, poking it with needles and making notes, seemingly unaware or uncaring of the subject's feelings. The only difference was that Miss Simone wore a green cloak instead of a white coat.

"But where cows regurgitate food into their mouths and continue chewing on it," the scientist went on, "Fenton regurgitates water and spits it out." She pointed at the solidified puddle. "It's a defense mechanism. The water from Fenton's stomach contains all sorts of strange chemicals, and it dries very quickly after being spat out, turning into a glue-like substance. Breathing on it seems to speed up the drying process." Miss Simone looked almost awestruck. "This is a fearsome weapon against predators."

Her face was red with excitement as she stood once more. She looked around and realized that her audience of mystified adults and horrified children were not quite as enthralled as she.

"I just thought he was a gargoyle," Hal said.

Miss Simone nodded. "Remember that the two adult creatures in my world are ten times bigger than Fenton. One attacked a village recently. Nobody knows why; it just appeared and started spitting water at people, and breathing on them. You can imagine how horrible that was."

"How awful!" Emily cried.

"There's a story," Miss Simone said, "about one of these creatures crossing into your world. It ended up in the Seine River, in France. The locals, of course, were terrified at the sight of this monster, which apparently flooded the land with the foul-smelling water spat from its mouth. These stories are always exaggerated and twisted, of course, but there's some truth to it. You see, the creature's stomach holds a limited amount of water, and while that water is stewing in the creature's belly for several hours, it develops its strange glue-like characteristic. When it spits out that water and breathes on it, the water solidifies. Once the stomachs are emptied, the serpent dragon can drink more water and spit it right back out again, but of course freshly swallowed water won't turn to glue when breathed on. So the creature, frantic to escape, ended up swallowing and spitting ordinary water—lots and lots of it. That's what it was remembered for in your own history books: the *Gargouille*, as it was named, a bit like *gargoyle*, the name of carved statues that have water spouts."

"Is it me, or is the moon brighter?" someone asked. It was Mr. Morgan, Dewey's dad, a big bearded man with a strange accent. He rarely spoke, but when he did, his voice boomed. He was Welsh, if Hal remembered correctly. Whatever *that* meant.

Everyone glanced first at Mr. Morgan, and then up at the night sky. Hal had to admit he had a point. Perhaps the fog was finally starting to clear!

And that was when he had that awful nagging feeling again, that something was very wrong. Yes, the fog was clearing, and while this fact was exciting, at the same time he felt that he and his friends had made a terrible mistake. In that moment he realized he should mention the fog-hole to Miss Simone. He should tell her that it had been blocked and the fog was lifting. Should they be worried about the virus? Surely not. Surely it was long gone by now.

*But what if it wasn't?*

Miss Simone had already moved on to the next performer, leaving Fenton to sidle away. As fascinating as Fenton's transformation might be, nobody could shake the sinister air of menace that followed him. As he moved into the shadows by the side of the road, several eyes followed him warily, including Wrangler's.

Even Fenton's parents, Mr. and Mrs. Bridges, seemed on edge, and they stood in silence as they watched their son slither past.

Lauren was next in line to demonstrate her transformation. Her change was dramatic and, it seemed, extremely welcome after Fenton's eerie presence. As white fur sprouted in an instant and her impressive bird-like wings snapped into place, applause once again broke out. Lauren looked relieved at the positive reaction after hearing all those tales of harpy raids.

In an effort to show off, Lauren took a few long bounds and launched into the air, flapping hard. Heads ducked as she soared overhead. She arced around and came at them again, swooping and putting on a show to a ring of delighted faces. Even Wrangler appeared excited now, his tail wagging gently. Perhaps his mood was directly affected by that of the audience. He seemed confused, but if everyone was happy, well, perhaps this enormous bird-like thing was all right.

Mrs. Hunter was overcome with emotion, her tears flowing freely. She kept saying, "My little girl," over and over. Her husband, a broad grin across his face, was clapping the loudest of them all.

Miss Simone's face was a curious mixture of scientific interest and approval for her successful experiment, but personal disdain at what she must think of as a loathsome creature.

Meanwhile, Hal was only half watching the show. He was more intent on the thinning fog and cooling air. Again he wondered about the virus. It hadn't harmed him or his classmates when they stood at the top of the lighthouse, but it had long ago been established they had good immune systems. What if the unfiltered air was harmless to the children, but remained deadly to his parents?

"Yes, Lauren, you're a harpy," Miss Simone was saying as Lauren flapped gracefully to the ground. "The harpies don't like that name though. They simply call themselves winged people. They insist they're human, and in history have felt insulted that humans refused to accept them as such. Well, the prejudice is thousands of years old and the damage is done; the bird people shun humans and will gleefully pick a fight. The word *harpy* is, by definition, insulting and should never be used in their company."

"Why can't I fly up into the sky?" Lauren asked, looking breathless. "I just can't seem to fly higher than a rooftop."

Miss Simone nodded sagely. "There's a chemical agent in the fog," she explained. "We put it there for exactly that reason. The agent is lighter than fog but heavier than air, so it hangs over the island and dampens flight. It affects birds too." She paused suddenly and looked up. Her brow furrowed.

*Tell her*, Hal urged himself.

"Who's next?" Lauren asked, as she changed back to human form and allowed her parents to hug her. "Dewey—your turn!"

Dewey's change was met with a cry of recognition. "A centaur," many voices said at once. "My handsome son!" cried Mrs. Morgan. "Oh, you must be so proud," Dr. Porter said. The babble of voices filled the air as Dewey stamped around in his usual restless way, turning in circles and swishing his tail.

Miss Simone joined in with the noise, explaining that Dewey would have some immediate duties to attend to when he arrived in her world; he would have to talk to the centaurs and persuade them to alter a few of their stubborn ways. As Dewey changed back into his human form, Miss Simone added, "So it was *you* we saw last night. It was the storm that set you off, wasn't it?"

Eyes downcast, Dewey nodded. "Something about the lightning and thunder scared me. I've never been afraid of storms before, and I like watching them, but this one was different."

Miss Simone shook her head. "The storm was no different to any other. But something in you had changed recently. Just about all centaurs have an irrational fear of storms, and somehow I expected one of you kids to show your true self last night once the thunder and lightning got started. I waited around behind the houses with my colleagues just in case, and sure enough, a frightened centaur showed up."

"That was me," Dewey said, looking mildly embarrassed.

"You ran off," Miss Simone continued. "We never did catch up with you. It was very frustrating. I knew it had to be one of you boys, but I didn't know which of you—Hal, Robbie, or you, Dewey."

Only half listening to the story, Hal looked around for Robbie, seeking his opinion on the virus and the fog-hole. But his friend was at Lauren's side, where he'd been since her impressive performance. *Figures*, Hal thought.

So he turned to Abigail. She had been clapping and cheering with everyone else, but seemed lost in thought. "Hey," Hal whispered. "Have you noticed the fog is lifting?"

"Yes," she replied. "And Miss Simone's noticed too."

"Right."

They said nothing more for a few moments. But then Abigail turned to him and whispered in his ear, "Hal, do you think we did the right thing, blocking the fog-hole?"

"I don't know," Hal moaned. Hearing this from Abigail was like a punch in the stomach. His own nagging feeling was confirmed. Something bad was in the air. "But it's been thirteen years since the virus struck Out There. *Surely* it's gone by now."

Abigail shook her head. "If that's true, then why did Miss Simone bother keeping the fog going all this time?" She sighed. "I realize I was wrong about her. I still don't like her very much, but I do think she's telling the truth now."

175

"So the virus could still be Out There," Hal said. His heart began to thump hard and a queasy feeling settled in his stomach.

"Who's next?" Miss Simone said, looking around. "Hal, Emily, and Darcy. Care to show us what you can do, Emily?"

Emily blushed. "Um, well . . . actually, I haven't been able to transform yet."

For a moment her parents looked horrified at this news, but after a moment, Mrs. Stanton smiled and winked. "You'll get there, my dear."

"Just a question of time," Mr. Stanton said, nodding.

Emily smiled back, but Hal could tell she was embarrassed, perhaps even ashamed of herself.

Miss Simone said nothing, just gazed at Emily with narrowed eyes for long seconds. Then she turned to Hal. "How about you, then, Hal?"

Hal felt all eyes turn to him. His parents held each other, nervous but expectant. He was reminded of all the times he'd stood up during school plays and recited carefully memorized lines to a hushed audience. He wasn't very good at speaking to crowds, even though he knew each and every person in the audience. And his parents *knew* he didn't like it, so they always had that same nervous but expectant look about them. He knew they were silently thinking, "We love you, but don't mess it up, but don't worry if you do . . . but try not to mess up anyway. Make us proud."

Now Hal felt the pressure of an audience again. And to make matters worse, he still hadn't fully mastered the ability to change at will. Everyone else could manage it, so why couldn't he?

He swallowed, nodded, and stared at a spot in the road. He thought hard. He imagined himself as a dragon. He imagined himself breathing fire. He even, for a moment, imagined himself flying up into the air with huge leathery wings pumping, but this immediately made him think of the damping effect the fog would have on him, and that in turn reminded him of the blocked fog-hole.

Why, oh why, had they blocked it up?

"Hal?" Miss Simone asked, studying him with concern.

"I'm trying," Hal mumbled, feeling his face heat up.

Darcy smiled and wandered over. She gave Hal a wink, then turned to the audience. "While he's trying, I have a neat trick of my own. Ready?"

The audience's gaze flicked across to Darcy, and Hal could almost feel the weight of that gaze leaving him.

"Now you see me," Darcy said, grinning—and then she was gone.

Hal blinked. No, she was still there, but extremely difficult to see. Darcy moved, and he focused on her. But immediately she was still again, and Hal blinked several times, sure she was there, but unable to adjust his eyes correctly. It was like staring out a window and realizing that, an inch in front of his face, a small spider was crawling across the glass. Adjusting his eyes to focus on the spider would cause the outside world beyond to become a blur.

Several gasps and a multitude of blinking eyes told him that he wasn't the only one having trouble focusing on her.

There was a rush of movement before him, a sort of ripple in the air as though he were looking into a clear pool disturbed by a breeze. Then he felt a light touch on his shoulder and a voice whispered in his ear. "Do it, Hal. Change. Don't think about it, just *do* it."

Then the touch was gone and he found Abigail glancing at him, looking puzzled. She was touching her arm where Darcy must have brushed by.

As Darcy played games with her audience, flitting here and there and touching shoulders, Hal stared once more at the ground. *Change. I can do this. Change!*

Wrangler was barking again, his tail wagging furiously. Miss Simone was laughing. "How lovely! Darcy is a perfect example of how difficult it is to communicate with dryads. It's even more difficult in the forests. Darcy is going to be such a help to us."

And then, as heads began to turn toward Hal, he felt a moment of panic and blurted out, "Miss Simone, we blocked the fog-hole!"

A long, quizzical silence followed. Darcy faded back into existence next to Emily and Lauren. Robbie, standing behind Lauren, frowned as if annoyed. Dewey looked like he wanted the ground to open up and swallow him. Fenton was nowhere to be seen. All the adults looked bewildered—except Miss Simone, whose face slowly darkened.

Thankfully, Abigail stood by Hal. She actually moved closer and faced the crowd with him, her chin jutting out defiantly as if demanding that Miss Simone split her increasing anger between the two of them.

"You . . . did *what?*" Miss Simone said quietly. Her fists were clenching and unclenching. "I thought you told us that you didn't block that hole."

"We didn't the first time," Hal explained. His heart hammered. "But we went back this afternoon and finished the job."

A ripple of concern spread through the parents. They began to murmur, looking around fearfully. Hal's mom touched her face and then looked at her hands.

"It's okay, though, right?" Hal said, raising his voice above the murmur. "The virus is long gone now, surely. And it didn't affect us when we went up to the top of the lighthouse."

"It didn't affect *you*," Miss Simone snapped, "because you're not quite human anymore. You're shapeshifters. You have the ability to heal. The microorganisms in your body are constantly changing, evolving, fighting off new bacteria and viruses. Why do you think you've never had a common cold or a simple sore throat?"

"How should I know?" Hal suddenly yelled. "You kept everything a big secret!" He felt his blood beginning to boil. "You told us just enough to keep us quiet, but not *nearly* enough to keep us from wondering. You told us nothing about what we would become, so we assumed the worst—that we were some big dark dirty secret, and that you wanted to take us away and lock us in cages and experiment on us, a load of doctors in white coats with clipboards making notes and nodding and whispering to each other and ordering more tests—"

"Hal, what on earth are you—" Miss Simone interrupted.

But Abigail jumped in. "And we knew nothing about where *you* came from, Miss Simone, until you showed up one day and started dropping hints about some other place full of strange creatures and forests and grassy hills—oh, and sunshine! Yes, how could I forget that? This other world of yours is full of sunshine and blue skies, and yet here we are, still cooped up on this foggy, depressing island, slowly turning into weird monsters and wondering what you're going to do to us." She scowled at Miss Simone. "And you wonder why we didn't *trust* you?"

"Abigail Porter!" her mother said, sounding flustered.

Miss Simone held up a hand for silence, her eyes fixed on Abigail. She turned her icy stare to Hal, then back to Abigail. Then she looked once more at the sky.

The moon was becoming clearer, brighter, more defined by the minute. And, Hal realized, the sky was becoming blacker. The hazy glow that normally surrounded the moon was vanishing, and—was that a pin-prick of light nearby? A star?

Hal stared and stared. He'd seen pictures of course, but actually seeing one, a *real star*, was something else entirely.

"If you blocked the vent," Miss Simone said evenly, "then we need to *unblock* it immediately. That means *now*, before it's too late."

She peered into the night sky, her brow furrowed.

"No, it may already be too late," she said quietly. "If the virus has made it to the island . . . if it's in the air already . . . it could take days, perhaps a week, for the fog to sanitize the air and make it safe again."

"Where are the chemical suits?" Mrs. Stanton asked, as she had earlier.

"You can't all wear chemical suits for a week," Miss Simone snapped. "Our best bet is to leave the island immediately. The children can stay—they're safe enough. But the rest of us must leave. We can return in a week, when the fog has been restored and the air is safe." She nodded, rubbing her chin, thinking fast. "Yes, we'll leave the island through the fog vent in Black Woods, and unblock it as we go."

"But the manticore," Hal protested. "It's in the woods. It's tried to kill us twice already! You can't go that way unless we go with you!"

"Yes, we'll protect you," Robbie said. "We can all turn into monsters."

"But we can't use that tunnel!" Mrs. O'Tanner exclaimed, sounding horrified. "We've been down there before, remember? I nearly broke my ankle. It's dangerous! Pitch black, jagged rocks hanging down, that slippery slope—"

"And don't forget the fog," Mrs. Franklin said. "Whether the tunnel is blocked or not, it will be filled with fog. Won't we suffocate or something?"

Hal wasn't sure he agreed with that, but he kept his mouth shut. At that moment, his dad cleared his throat to speak.

"Simone, you've always said the hole by the lighthouse is the safest one to travel through. You said it was just below the surface of the water, yes? You just duck under and swim through, right? That's where you were taking Fenton and his parents tonight, wasn't it?"

"Yes, yes," Miss Simone said impatiently, "but I only have a small boat, big enough to hold four. We'll have to make several trips, which will take time."

"Then let's stop wasting time and *go*," Mr. Franklin said firmly. "We leave now, tonight. All of us. I'm sick of this island anyway."

"But . . . we can't *all* leave," Miss Simone said, starting to sound desperate. She looked around, her eyes wide. "Listen to me. The children must stay until we're sure that—"

"Simone," Dewey's dad said in his deep, rumbling voice, "we're leaving. Now. Take us to the hole by the lighthouse."

Miss Simone's mouth opened and closed, but no words came out. Finally, she took a deep breath and help up her hands, speaking in a low, calm voice. "Let's not panic. We've held on for twelve years, and we can hold on for an extra few days. Let's not be hasty and take the children before they're ready. We can go and find the chemical suits, and that'll give us time to think before we—"

Mr. Morgan drew himself up to his full, imposing height, his face distinctly red in the brightening moonlight. "It's finished, Simone. Take us to the hole NOW!"

His sudden, angry bellow made everyone jump, and Wrangler gave a whine. In the silence that followed, Hal held his breath and wished over and over that he and Robbie had never laid eyes on the stupid fog-hole!

"All right," Miss Simone said tightly. "Have it your way."

"Let's get some flashlights and lanterns," Hal's dad said, suddenly taking charge. "Meet back here in two minutes."

As several men hurried off, Miss Simone shook her head and swept a hand through her hair. "This is not how I planned things," she said to nobody in particular. "Mr. and Mrs. Bridges are already prepared for this journey. I have a boat waiting for them. But it's only a *small* boat and I'm not sure I have time to row back and forth—what, five or six times before the virus reaches us? Some of us will have to swim."

*Swim*, Hal thought, thinking of the icy water.

There was an uproar at this. "We can't swim in cold water in the middle of the night with all those rocks in the water," Mrs. O'Tanner protested.

"We'll freeze," Dr. Porter agreed.

"Or drown," Emily's mom said.

"What do you suggest we do then?" Miss Simone asked icily. "If you won't use the tunnel because it's dark and dangerous, and you won't use the hole by the lighthouse because you don't like swimming near rocks, what do you suggest? Would you like to try diving off the cliff as I do, and swimming down to the third hole?" Miss Simone's eyes blazed.

"Oh, stop arguing!" Mrs. Morgan cried. "Let's just go! I can feel my skin starting to tingle."

Whether this was true or not, Hal couldn't tell. He suspected she was imagining it. Still, it galvanized the group into action. As the men returned with armfuls of flashlights and lanterns, Miss Simone grabbed one and began leading the way along the road at a fast pace that occasionally turned into a jog. Lanterns swung in the darkness and the air was filled with the sound of shuffling, hurrying feet on the paved surface.

"Biscuit!" Lauren suddenly exclaimed. "I can't leave Biscuit—I need to go and find him."

"Forget the stupid cat," said one of the adults roughly. "If you kids hadn't blocked up that hole—"

"He'll be fine," Lauren's dad said in a more gentle voice. "We'll make arrangements to collect him later. We'll have to come back anyway, to collect the cows and sheep and what-have-you."

Hal had a sudden ridiculous vision of herds of farm animals boarding a small boat, followed by a white cat with pale brown patches.

"Biscuit won't come to anyone but me," Lauren grumbled. "And he only has enough food for a day."

"He'll be fine," her dad said again.

The night sky was undoubtedly clearer by now, and although the dissipating fog took with it the usual cold moistness, in its place was a frigid, dry air that was even colder.

"Are we all here?" Miss Simone called from the front. "Is Fenton with us?"

"He's behind us," Hal yelled. He and Abigail were at the rear, away from disapproving adult glares. Behind them, Fenton's red eyes were pin-pricks in the shadows.

Miss Simone issued some instructions at the front of the group, then stood aside and waited while adults and children hurried by. Then she joined Hal and Abigail at the rear. Hal never felt more guilty in his whole life as Miss Simone glared at him.

"What a mess you've made of this," she scolded. "You'd better hope we make it to the lighthouse before the fog clears off."

"Do you really think the virus is still Out There?" Abigail asked.

"Yes," Miss Simone said shortly. "But never mind that now. We need to work on your transformation, Abigail. I explained that you children had to remain here in your world until your transformations were complete. Well, yours isn't complete, and yet here we are, about to cross over into my world." She sounded distraught. "You must complete your transformation, otherwise you may never get the chance again. *Do you understand?*"

Abigail nodded silently. She suddenly grew her wings and buzzed away before anything else could be said on the matter.

Miss Simone sighed. "And, Hal, I'm trusting that when you say you can change, you really can?"

"I really can," he said, panting a little as they hurried. "I just have a hard time making it happen. And I can't fly yet either. I've never tried."

She looked sideways at him as they walked. "So you're a dragon, yes?"

He nodded. "So you know, then."

"By the process of elimination, you can only be one of two creatures—and only one of those has wings. Emily must be the other."

"I'm surprised you didn't know which of us was which beforehand," Hal murmured.

Miss Simone grunted. "I *should* have known. But for the sake of fairness, I was asked to randomize the breeding assignments so that nobody got to choose a dragon or centaur over an ogre or harpy."

She put a hand on his shoulder and leaned closer, while remaining in step. "No matter what happens, Hal, you *must not* cross over to my world until you're ready. Flight is essential for dragons. If you can't fly, the other dragons will never respect you. They'll tear you apart."

"I have wings," Hal said feebly.

"Wings are just there to look at until you've actually used them," Miss Simone said firmly. "Remember what I told you about my friend, the flying horse who can't fly."

With that she jogged away with her cloak billowing and hair swishing from side to side. She caught up with Emily and began talking to her earnestly.

Hal was left with his thoughts. Ahead, Robbie gave him a glance, and raised his eyebrows as if to ask if everything was all right. Hal shrugged and nodded.

He worried about flying. It was hard enough transforming into a dragon, without learning how to fly as well. He resolved to give it a try the first chance he got. If he could only turn into a dragon right now—

But then he saw Emily, now walking alone with Wrangler. Miss Simone had gone on ahead to catch up with the parents. Hal increased his step.

"Hey," he said. "What did she say?"

Emily's reply was flat and emotionless. "She said that if I don't change in the next fifteen minutes, then I'll need to stay behind."

"Stay behind?" Hal repeated. "What—on your own? She said that?"

"On my own," Emily said, nodding. "None of our parents can stay here. Nor can Miss Simone. So, unless some of my friends stay with me . . ."

Hal squeezed her arm. "We're not leaving without you, Emily. We're in this together."

## Chapter Twenty-One
**The virus strikes**

The lighthouse was dark, but for once it stood silhouetted against a clear moon. The sight of the pitch-black tower against a starry sky and moonlit sea took Hal's breath away. He stared and stared, forgetting for a moment that the adults were arguing up ahead.

Alongside him stood Abigail and Robbie and all his other friends, equally silent and awestruck. Fenton slithered silently across the paved lighthouse grounds toward the tower, and in the next moment climbed the wall for a better look.

The fog had been clearing faster and faster as they had made the strange journey across the island, flashlights bobbing and lanterns swinging. Here at the coast, the evening was still but bitterly cold. Waves rolled and crashed lazily against the rocks. And the fog was gone.

Not just partially gone, but *gone*. It lingered inland, caught up in trees and lost in the meadows, but here at the coast it had escaped, having finally—after thirteen years of service—been allowed to fade away to nothing.

In the distance, on the horizon, the moonlight sparkled on the sea and the black silhouettes of buildings stood against a not-quite-black sky. The moon was bright, not quite full but brighter and sharper than Hal had ever imagined it. He saw stars. They twinkled just as his mom had always said they did. He'd never truly believed that, having seen nothing but photographs throughout his whole life, but here they were, twinkling, winking at him from far away.

The group had hurried through the vandalized gates without stopping, although Hal had seen a number of startled looks and more than one fatherly glare. As they approached the lighthouse, the children slowed to a stop while the adults continued on to a rocky outcrop. Hal and his friends stood admiring the night scene as their parents crowded onto a short dock, where a small boat was tied to a post—the boat that Miss Simone had brought along for Fenton's journey. An argument started up; the men wanted all the women to get to safety first, but the women wanted to go as complete families.

"It makes more sense if we go one complete family at a time," one of the moms insisted, her voice rising above the sound of crashing waves. "Otherwise we might end up with a bunch of women safe and sound in Simone's world, but a bunch of dead husbands left behind here—"

Then one of the women cried out.

Hal searched the darkness. The adults were just a mass of black shapes on the short dock, but lanterns swung and cast haphazard glows around the circle of faces. It soon became obvious that it was Robbie's mom who had cried out. She staggered and fell to her knees.

Men and women clustered around her. Then Dr. Porter's voice rose above the babble. "Move aside. *Get out of the way.*" There was a silence, then some hushed whispers, as Dr. Porter examined Mrs. Strickland. "She has the virus. She needs to get to safety *now.*"

Robbie broke from the group of watching children and bolted over to the dock. When he reached the circle of adults, his dad pulled him back.

"What's wrong with her?" Robbie yelled.

His mom was holding her face and seemed to be crooning while others held her upright. One of the men had removed his cap and was dipping it into the sea, then splashing the cold water in Mrs. Strickland's face. Meanwhile, Miss Simone was in the boat already, untying it and trying to make herself heard over the commotion.

"Get her in the boat! Get her in the boat!"

Hal rushed to the rocks. Panic surged through his body. *It's too late! The virus is here!*

The adults wouldn't let any of the children near Mrs. Strickland. Even Robbie was pushed back, although he yelled to get through. Then, in a flash, his huge ogre shape loomed over them, and everyone fell back at once.

"Maauummm," the ogre thundered, and hunkered down. As he reached for her, he became himself again, and thus it was Robbie's human eyes and clear human mind that saw up close what the virus was doing to his mother.

He yelled in anguish.

Then Mrs. O'Tanner covered her face with both hands. "Oh, no, no!" she cried. "It's happening to me too!"

Miss Simone had stopped shouting and was staring curiously at her own arms. She held them up to the moonlight and watched as her skin began to rise in large blisters. "We're too late," she said softly.

Hal stood rooted to the spot. He had never felt so useless in all his life. What could he do to help? He could breathe fire—the last thing anyone wanted. Even if he could fly, what use was that? He couldn't carry more than a few, and he didn't know where the hole to Elsewhere was anyway.

*If only they had a bigger boat.*

Or, more to the point, if only they hadn't blocked the fog-hole!

Hal cursed himself and wished he could undo what they had done. He could send Robbie hurtling across the island to unblock it, but it was far, far too late for that. The virus was already here.

He thought of his raft, somewhere out in the water. But even with that to hand, it was not enough. Besides, it was either floating way out to sea by now, or had been pulled under by the sea serpent.

And then Hal thought of something. He shouldered past Abigail, pushed Darcy aside, and weaved around the milling parents to where Miss Simone stood in the bobbing boat. "Miss Simone! The serpent! The sea serpent! Call it to us!"

Miss Simone hardly heard him. She seemed morbidly fascinated by her own bubbling skin. Her face was showing signs of the virus too, and her eyes were puffy and beginning to close.

"Massive allergic reaction," she said dreamily. "Whatever hidden allergies people might have, this virus triggers them all, leading to hives and angioedema and anaphylactic shock . . ." She put a trembling hand to her head and closed her eyes. "Prickly, sensitive skin . . . dizziness . . . labored breathing . . . soon my throat will constrict and . . ."

One of the men started a coughing fit.

"Miss Simone," Hal said desperately. "Listen to me. *Call the sea monster!* Call it to us. It can carry you all to the hole."

Miss Simone turned her head to him, but her eyes were all but closed now. She mumbled through swollen lips, "I can't call it. It's out there somewhere, but I don't speak its language."

Two more men started to groan. Three of the girls—Emily, Darcy and Lauren—were crying and vainly trying to splash water over the virus victims to cool their reddened, blistering skin.

Hal shut out the noise and tried to focus. How could he get the sea serpent to help? He knew it was smart. It had strict instructions to keep them on the island— but it could help if Hal could only make himself understood.

Fenton? *He* was a serpent. A serpent dragon, admittedly, but a serpent nevertheless.

He was about to search for the boy when Miss Simone collapsed. Gasping, she toppled backward into the boat. Hal jumped in with her, fighting to remain standing as the boat threatened to capsize.

"Miss Simone," he said, leaning over her. "Miss Simone, can Fenton talk to the sea monster? Can he talk the serpent's language?"

Miss Simone was having difficulty breathing. Her throat was impossibly bloated, and showed large patches of blue. But she managed to squeeze out a word. "No."

Hal felt that his last remaining hopes had just been dashed on the rocks. He tried to ignore the gasps and shouts and cries behind him. He knew that if he turned and saw his own parents succumbing to the virus, he would lose all chance of coherent thought.

Miss Simone grasped his wrist in powerful fingers. Startled, Hal saw that her fingers were webbed. Her skin was still blistering, but suddenly the swelling in her throat had diminished and her eyes were wide open. She looked different somehow, more vibrant. Her face had taken on a strange luminescence.

She smiled. "Hal, you're right. The sea serpent is the answer. Go fetch it."

"But you said Fenton can't speak the language—"

"Fenton can't," Miss Simone said. "But Emily can."

With that, she fell back and closed her eyes. Hal suddenly realized she had changed—dramatically. Her legs had been replaced by the tail end of a fish, with gigantic fins that spread and flopped over the side of the boat. The fishy scales spread up as far as her belly. Her magic clothes had transformed around her, and now covered her upper half only, with the rest draped like seaweed in the boat. Her cloak remained, but it too seemed different—long and stringy, almost like reeds, as if her clothes were an extension of her half-fish body.

"A mermaid," Hal muttered.

But the meaning of Miss Simone's words was still ringing in his ears. *Emily can speak to the sea serpent.* But she could only do that if . . .

He clambered out of the boat. "Emily! Get over here!"

"My dad—" she cried.

"The only way we can save them," Hal said firmly, grasping her by the shoulders, "is for you to change. You're a serpent of some kind, Emily. You can talk to the sea serpent in the water. Call it here and it will carry us all to the hole."

Emily wasn't taking it in. Tears were running down her face and she was shaking her head, trying to look over her shoulder at her poor mother, who was doubled up on the dock. A quick glimpse told Hal that only a few of the adults remained standing.

He ground his teeth and shook Emily. "You've got to *do* something," he said. "Emily, please."

But he couldn't even turn into a dragon himself when he wanted to. How could he expect Emily to turn into a serpent when she wasn't even aware she could change!

On impulse, Hal whispered in her ear, "Sorry about this, Emily. Let's find that serpent."

Then he gripped her around the waist and tumbled backward off the dock into the water, taking her with him. She had time to scream before the icy water engulfed them both—then they were both underwater with the ocean roaring in their ears.

Salt water immediately gushed up Hal's nose and caused him a moment of panic. Before he knew it, he had let go of Emily. He fought to open his eyes, but the salt stung and he blinked frantically.

Then he felt his body weight shift and suddenly found his eyes no longer stung. He opened them wide, surprised and pleased that he could see so clearly. It was a moment before he realized he was a dragon.

*Where was Emily?* He jerked his head around, searching. Being able to see underwater wasn't much good in the darkness of night, although the bright moon provided some eerie illumination at the surface. Luckily, that was where she was, flailing legs and arms amid white frothing seawater. She was already a startling distance away from him, the tide dragging at her and pushing her toward the rocks. Hal flicked his tail and twisted his body, and found it very easy to move through the water. He reached her in seconds, holding his breath with ease.

But instead of surfacing next to her, he gently tugged on one of her ankles and pulled her down into the depths of the water. He felt terrible for poor Emily—he could tell from her thrashing that she was half crazy with terror. She thought she was drowning.

And that was what Hal was counting on. As she ran out of breath and started bucking, something dramatic happened: she changed. It wasn't an instantaneous transformation, but it was fast enough to surprise Hal even though he had been hoping for it.

It started at Emily's shoulders. Her arms stopped flailing and came together, tighter and tighter until they were pressed firmly to her sides. Then a strange rippling occurred over her skin, and her arms fused with her body, her pale pink flesh stretching and becoming indented and scaly. All this happened in a split second, and the strange rippling continued down her torso to her legs, at which point her legs stopped kicking and pressed together, her toes pointed as the skin stretched and hardened. In moments she was cocooned like a caterpillar, with only her head free.

Amazed, Hal watched as Emily slowly drifted downwards. As she fell past him, her eyes locked on his. They were wide, her mouth open as if trying to emit a scream. Her face was white, and by contrast her hair looked like some kind of jet-black inky substance leaking slowly into the water.

But Emily's transformation hadn't finished. Hal looked again and realized her torso was now lengthening rapidly. And while it lengthened, it began to undulate, looking less like a fat cocoon and more like a giant serpent.

Emily began to rise and swim around, flicking her body back and forth, glancing back at herself with obvious shock mingled with—what? Relief?

"Go find the serpent," Hal tried to say, instead creating a lot of bubbles.

Still, Emily noticed him trying to speak. Her nostrils flared and she opened her mouth. A single large bubble popped out and rose to the surface. Obviously puzzled, Emily watched, almost cross-eyed, as another bubble popped out of her mouth.

Then she peered into the darkness of the sea. She seemed to be sniffing, or perhaps using some other sense Hal wasn't aware of, to seek out the gigantic sea serpent.

Watching her, Hal did a double-take. What kind of creature had the body of a serpent and the head of a human? She had no legs or arms, and at first glance it looked like a giant snake had tried to swallow her whole, feet first. It was a bizarre sight . . . and yet she already appeared to be adapting to her new body. And the prospect of drowning didn't seem to be on her mind anymore. Either she could breathe underwater, or she could hold her breath for longer in her new body.

One of Miss Simone's stories sprung to Hal's mind, the one about the snake folk and the rock slide . . . *Naga!* Emily was one of those human-snake naga creatures.

Hal swam to the surface, fearful that all was too late. How long had he been gone? It felt like ages, but couldn't have been more than a minute. As he emerged into the air above, sounds sharpened suddenly and he heard sobbing and yelling. Not a single adult was left standing. They were either sitting or lying on the dock, faces and arms swelled up, eyes puffed closed.

Hal clambered onto the dock. By the time he climbed to his feet, he realized he was human again, dripping wet and shivering. "I sent Emily to find the serpent," he gasped, gesturing toward the water. "But let's not wait. Let's get some of them into the boat. Robbie's mom can go in first."

Being first to be struck by the virus, Robbie's mom looked the worst. It was a horrific sight, and Hal tried not to look too closely as he and Robbie carefully put her in the boat next to Miss Simone, who was unconscious and taking up a lot of room with her mermaid tailfins.

"She'll make it," Hal told Robbie quietly as they worked.

Robbie said nothing, and no wonder—his mom was absolutely still and limp. Was she even breathing? Hal couldn't tell, and there wasn't a way to check for a pulse because her throat and wrists were so swollen. Her tongue protruded slightly, and this disturbed Hal more than anything else.

*It's too late*, he thought despairingly.

"Help us," he urged the others.

Abigail, Darcy and Lauren, who were still splashing water on their parents' faces in the vain hope it might help, climbed to their feet. They looked weary, their eyes red. Dewey sat with his mother and father, silent, whispering something to them. They were both unconscious.

Of Fenton there was no sign.

Hal dimly became aware of Wrangler barking non-stop from a high point on the nearby rocks. He didn't like the rocks, but at least it was away from the crashing tide. And he especially didn't like the scent of terror in the air.

Hal and Robbie, with the help of the three girls, carefully hoisted Darcy's mom and Fenton's dad into the boat. There really wasn't anymore room, but they returned for another anyway. "Your dad looks bad," Robbie mumbled.

They reached for Mr. Franklin, whose eyes popped open at once. He clutched Hal's arm and spoke in a hoarse whisper. "Whatever happens, son, I'm proud of you, and—" But he got no further, and collapsed into a coughing fit. After a moment he fell silent, unconscious again.

Hal and his friends lifted him into the boat and laid him out across the others. That was five now, including Miss Simone, and the small boat was already full. Eleven more adults lay on the dock.

*Bring out the dead*, a voice in Hal's head announced. Where had he heard that? In a play he had performed at school one time, set in the medieval ages of kings and queens. *The Black Plague*. That was it. It said in one of the history books that men would go around the village each day calling for the dead to be brought out. They were slung on the back of a cart and taken away to be burned.

Shaking off such morbid thoughts, Hal untied the boat and climbed into the water, holding the rope between his teeth.

"What are you doing?" Robbie asked. "You don't know where to take them."

Hal removed the rope for a second to say, "I'm doing all I can. Hopefully, Emily will be here soon with some help, but if not I'll be back as soon as I can."

He dove and found himself changing easily into his dragon form. At last *something* was going his way—finally he could change at will.

Gripping the rope between his teeth, Hal swam fast, pulling the boat and looking for something—anything—that might look like a passage to another world. Would it be a bright light? A black hole? He had no idea, and in the murky water he wasn't likely to see anything anyway. It was hopeless, and he knew it the moment he started swimming.

But he swam doggedly. He wished now they had made for the fog-hole in the woods. At least they all knew where that hole was. Thomas the manticore seemed like an idle threat compared to the current situation.

*My parents are dead, and it's all my fault.*

Hal blinked away tears, refusing to let his mind even go there. If he dwelled on the possibility that his parents were dead, he would probably end up sinking to the bottom of the sea in despair.

He swam for perhaps ten minutes, circling around, losing hope. At one point he thought he saw something: an unusually dark patch in the murky, moonlit water. But it was just a big fat fish that swam away as he approached. He then saw something bright and colorful and assumed it was another fish, but it turned out to be a green plastic ball about the size of his human hand, bobbing on the surface, lost to the world.

Hal felt very, very alone. He knew he couldn't face his friends again, not if it meant pulling the boat back to the rocks, his mission a failure. He stuck his head up out of the water and looked around. He was some way from the island. It skulked in the moonlight, black and shapeless. The lighthouse rose up, a sleek white shaft that reflected the moonlight.

At its base he dimly made out his friends and the remaining parents, a small group huddled together in silence.

*Waiting for me to come back and save them*, Hal thought.

He reached for the side of the boat, and as he did so he transformed back into his human shape and leaned in. Miss Simone seemed to be sleeping peacefully, surrounded by an odd glow. The others were not so peaceful, and Hal could hear rasping breaths.

*At least they're breathing.*

He took Miss Simone's limp hand and shook it hard. "Wake up. Tell me where the hole to your world is."

But no amount of shaking and prodding could wake Miss Simone. Hal looked once more to the island, then around at the cold, choppy sea, trying to find some clue that might point the way to the hole to Miss Simone's world. How did Miss Simone herself find it? Even though she had been through it on numerous occasions, how did she find her way to it when there was nothing to see but endless water. There were no signposts floating on the surface, nothing.

*Signposts . . .*

He frowned. Then, on a hunch, he gripped the rope between his teeth and dove, instantly becoming a dragon and using his tail and large paws to power through the water. He swam around, his eyes scanning the moonlit surface. After a while he found what he was looking for—the green plastic ball bobbing on the surface. It was easy to spot, and he swam closer to peer at it. It seemed ordinary enough, except that he wondered where it came from. It was doubtful anybody had thrown it into the water from the mainland if the virus was still present in the air. A survivor, perhaps? A child's ball, lost to the sea? But on the other hand, perhaps it was something more that that. Hal had been looking for signposts, and this was the closest he had come to finding anything remotely like one.

On impulse, he gently ensnared the ball in his mouth, then spat it out, shooting it high in the air. The green ball arced upwards and began to fall, but, impossibly, fell back to the same place it had left, smacking Hal on the snout.

Surprised, he tried again, this time angling it lower so it would fly farther away across the water. But it veered around and returned, once more smacking him on the nose before dropping into the sea to continue its bobbing.

Excited, Hal realized that this was a marker left by Miss Simone so that she could find her way back to the hole. But it was quite a distance from the island, so there had to be more, perhaps a line of them stretching out from the rocks. He positioned himself carefully, putting his back to the rocky lighthouse grounds and the green ball right in front of his nose, so that he was looking out to sea. Then, gripping the boat's rope once more, he dove and swam in a straight line directly away from the island. He kept his eyes on the surface.

After a minute he found another ball, and gave himself a mental thump on the back. This was it! He'd picked up the trail, and was heading directly for the hole.

He found another ball shortly afterward, and then another. They bobbed in what seemed like a perfectly straight line leading from the island. How manymore were there? He imagined Miss Simone first arriving through the hole and seeing the island in the distance. She must have left herself markers as she swam for shore, and they had been here ever since—these strange, inexplicable balls that floated on the surface but refused to leave.

After the fifth marker he found the hole. His eyes widened as he approached. There was absolutely no doubt that this was what he was looking for. It was a dull black smoky substance, as if someone had just dropped a gigantic clod of soil in the water and it was breaking apart. The cloud was at least ten feet across, without any definable edges, and it floated four feet below the surface, almost lost in the darkness. Miss Simone had said they'd need to swim down to it, and now Hal had another problem to resolve: How could he bring a boatful of unconscious bodies through an underwater hole and expect them to hold their breath?

Well, he'd just have to try. Perhaps if he was quick enough . . .

He reached into the boat and, with clumsy dragon paws, pulled one of the adults out. Mrs. O'Tanner groaned once, but made no other protest even though Hal's claws accidentally tore through her shirt sleeve and grazed her arm. He lost his grip and she toppled into the water. She woke, gasping, her face pointed skyward . . . but before she had a chance to flounder, Hal grabbed her around the waist, plunged below the surface, and made for the cloudy substance four feet below.

Hal dove through it without effort, and emerged immediately on the other side. Dismayed, he turned around, wondering if he'd missed it somehow. Was there a trick to going through a hole to another world? Thinking of Darcy's mom, he rose to the surface so she could catch a breath.

The boat was gone.

So, too, was the island. In its place was a land mass so huge that it surrounded him on all sides—flat grassy plains all around, rolling hills, a vast expanse of forest, and towering mountains in the distance, all under a black, starry sky. Hal was no longer in the choppy, salty ocean, but in a calm, freshwater lake, its clear, still surface mirroring the dazzling moonlight above.

This was Elsewhere, Miss Simone's world. *He had made it!*

Overwhelmed, hardly able to comprehend the changed landscape around him, he struck for the nearby grassy bank, clumsily keeping Mrs. O'Tanner's head above water. With no time to be gentle, he deposited Darcy's mom on the grass, turned, and dove once more. The cloudy substance was straight ahead. He shot through it, feeling nothing, seeing no change, but aware of a sudden salty taste in his mouth as he headed for the surface again. He saw the boat even before he popped up above water, and knew he was back.

Adrenaline rushing, almost shaking with excitement and relief, he reached for the next adult, his dad, and repeated his trip to Elsewhere, placing him carefully next to Mrs. O'Tanner before returning through the hole to the boat. As he returned from his third trip he was dimly aware of shouts and barking from the shore of the island, but he grimly continued his task until all five adults, including Miss Simone herself, were safely on the grassy bank of the lake.

With an empty boat, he turned to head back to the island. That was when he noticed something he would never forget: the monstrous white head of the sea serpent bearing down on him, its baleful yellow eyes unblinking.

Riding on its back were his friends and all the remaining parents. Some of the adults were upright, blinded by their puffed-up faces and swaying dizzily, but hanging on with grim determination. Most, however, were lying flat on their faces, unconscious, arms and legs dangling on either side of the enormous serpentine body. It was a curious sight. At the front was Dr. Porter, lying flat and motionless, with Abigail clinging to her for dear life; then there was Dewey, sitting between his parents, his dad barely awake behind him and his mom slumped at an awkward angle in front; then Lauren, desperately trying to stop her dad from sliding off on one side while her mom fought to stay on at the other . . . and so on to the rear where Fenton, still in his lizard form, rode effortlessly with his long black tail wrapped firmly around the sea serpent.

Then Hal saw Emily. She was in the sea, swimming *ahead* of the serpent with her hair plastered against her face. She cut through the water with ease, her snake body undulating below the surface, pushing her along.

"This way!" Hal yelled—but instead of words, he roared and belched up a ball of fire. For a moment the night was lit up with orange, and then it faded. But it served its purpose, and if there had been any doubt about where to find Hal in the dark of the night, now there was none.

As the eerie procession drew near, Hal dove underwater and waited by the hole to Elsewhere. Emily dove too, and her eyes widened as she approached. Hal urged her on, gesturing with dragon paws to aim at the strange black cloud and go on through.

Emily shot straight at it, closing her eyes just before she plunged in. Hal, floating to the side, was amazed to see her vanish—first her head, then her long, slender snake-like body, all in an instant. She had gone into the cloud on one side but hadn't come out on the other.

Before Hal had time to marvel, the sea serpent dove and headed his way. Hal backed off, awed by the giant. He had a moment to wonder about his poor friends and all the adults before the monster thundered by, its never-ending bulk covered with shiny white scales. He saw his friends, eyes tightly closed, cheeks puffed out, rising up from their seats. He saw a number of limp adults coming loose from their perches. He saw bubbles pouring from mouths, eyes opening in terror. He even saw Wrangler leaping clear and beginning to doggy-paddle for his life.

But the serpent was moving so fast that by the time bodies floated clear, momentum was already hurtling them through the water toward the black cloud. Most went through with the serpent in a haphazard fashion.

Others floated wide and missed the black cloud altogether.

Hal went after them immediately. He retrieved Fenton's mom and nudged her through the cloud with his snout. He used his tail to collect Mr. Morgan and shove him through. He seized his own mom's swollen hand between gentle jaws and tugged at her, swimming on his back with his mom trailing behind. He gently swung her through the hole, hoping and praying that someone was at the other side playing catch.

The water was suddenly clear except for thousands of bubbles . . . and four thin legs paddling at the surface. Hal had no time to be gentle with poor Wrangler. He rose up behind him, took the dog's scruff in his jaw, and probably a pinch of flesh too, and dove for the hole.

He had a moment of darkness as he went through, and then he was rising to the surface where numerous legs kicked. He released Wrangler and went for Dewey's dad again, who was floundering just below the surface. With a careful nudge, Hal steered him toward the bank, where the lake's sandy bottom rose up sharply.

When Hal finally exploded from the water, the sound of pandemonium hit him—splashing and yelling as parents, now wide awake, choked and spluttered, ducked and bobbed, trying to regain control in their half-dazed, semi-conscious states. Robbie, in ogre form, unceremoniously picked up a couple of adults at a time, one under each arm, and dumped them on the grassy bank before stomping back into the water to retrieve a couple more. Hal saw his own mom tossed onto the grass, and winced.

Dewey splashed noisily out of the lake with his mom somehow clinging to his broad centaur back. Meanwhile, Abigail was struggling to pull Dr. Porter clear of the water, her wings buzzing noisily, but she seemed unable to rise above the surface and kept sinking down to her waist, barely keeping her mom afloat. Hal knew she wasn't going to make it to land with such a heavy, sodden weight, so he ducked under the water once more, swam underneath, and surfaced with the doctor draped around his neck. Abigail, gasping, sank gratefully into the water and paddled ashore.

It wasn't until Hal stamped up onto the grassy bank and gently deposited his load that he took a moment to pause. He glanced around the lake. Half a minute ago the water had been filled with gasping adults, screaming children, a dog, an ogre, a centaur, a couple of sinister black reptilian things, and probably a few other creatures that Hal had been too busy to notice, not to mention the sea serpent itself, which surely must be close by somewhere, in the depths of the lake.

Now, however, all was calm in the water, the only evidence of a recent disturbance being a few broken ripples and somebody's discarded shirt.

## Chapter Twenty-Two
### Elsewhere

They all lay on the grass, exhausted. The rude dumping in cold water had revived many of the adults, and they were rolling around, moaning and grumbling. Hal studied each of them in turn, appalled at the sight of the swollen faces and reddened skin, but encouraged by the signs of life. Only a few remained unconscious, including Miss Simone, but Hal and his friends had already rushed around to check on them all, and knew they were okay. Abigail seemed as confident as her mom as they both checked for pulses and listened for heart beats; Dr. Porter had trained her daughter in that kind of thing long ago. And so, with sighs of relief, the children had slumped back on the grass and thanked their lucky stars that the situation wasn't much, much worse.

*Maybe everything's going to be all right*, Hal thought.

Human once more, he propped himself up on an elbow and sniffed the air. It was sweet, somehow fresher than he had ever known, clean and dry. He felt unable to stop himself from inhaling deeply. It almost made him feel giddy.

The slightest of breezes ruffled his damp hair and moved the long grass. The stars shone in the sky, bright and perfect, a dazzling array of patterns. Hal studied the moon, marveling at the way it glowed so big and round. Was that a face he saw looking down at him? Hal had heard about the face in the moon, and had seen pictures of it, but had never imagined seeing it with his own eyes. His dad had told him that the moon always looked toward the earth, never turning away—a friendly, watchful guardian.

Was this the same guardian that looked down on his own world? Did the two worlds share the same moon, or was it two different moons that happened to look the same?

Hal heard a splash and saw the gigantic sea serpent rising out of the lake for a moment, its bright white body cutting easily through the water. The lake was large, but Hal guessed the serpent wouldn't enjoy it as much as the open sea around the island. It would probably get restless! He wondered if this lake was its original home, before being sent through the hole to watch over the island.

Miss Simone stirred. She slowly sat up and touched her face, looking puzzled. Her long scaly fish-tail uncurled and huge fins unfolded and quivered. Studying her swollen wrists for a moment, she finally looked around at all the other patients. Her mouth dropped open.

"We're all alive," she whispered. A grin spread across her face and she pushed back her dripping hair, looking around. "And we're home," she finished, nodding with satisfaction.

"Emily found the sea serpent and asked it to help," Darcy said.

"She did?" Miss Simone asked, her eyebrows shooting up. She sought out Emily, who lay nearby. "Really? You transformed before we came through the hole? That's wonderful!"

Emily sat up, looking pleased with herself. No longer in her snake body, she drew up her legs, staring at them as if wondering how they had managed to return to normal after such a dramatic transformation. Her gaze settled briefly on Miss Simone's fish-tail, and then she replied modestly, "But it was Hal who made me change. I could never have done it if he hadn't pushed me into the water and then tried to drown me."

"Hal tried to *drown* you?" her mom said feebly, looking shocked as she joined in the conversation. She groaned and fingered her puffy eyelids. "I can't see. My eyes are swollen shut."

"I think it'll pass, Mrs. Stanton," Miss Simone said, sounding awed. "This is a first. When the virus first struck all those years ago, the reaction was far more severe and people died of heart failure, or couldn't breathe, or went into shock and simply shut down. We were lucky—the virus must have weakened over the years. This was a fairly mild case, all things considered."

"Mild case!" Mr. Morgan yelled indignantly. "Have you *seen* my wife lately? Her face looks like a sack of potatoes."

"Nice," Abigail murmured.

"But we're *alive*," Miss Simone said calmly. "Since we're not dead already, perhaps the worst is over. The swelling will subside and we'll recover. Is everyone conscious?"

Her long mermaid tailfin suddenly began to split down the middle, the scales fading and smoothing out. She quickly adjusted her dress, which had undergone a rapid and remarkable transformation of its own, and climbed unsteadily to her feet. Her green dress was soaking wet and her silky gown clung to her back, but as she walked across the grass to tend to the adults, her gown billowed suddenly and was, to Hal's amazement, inexplicably bone dry. Miss Simone ran her hands through her golden hair and, in the blink of an eye, it too was dry, somehow tumbling across her shoulders instead of plastering itself to her face.

*Neat trick*, Hal thought.

Abigail reached out and touched his hand. "You saved us," she said quietly. "You acted while the rest of us stood around panicking."

"I didn't do anything," Hal said. "It was Miss Simone's idea to get Emily to talk to the serpent."

"But you *got* her to do it," Abigail insisted. "And while she was doing that, you took the boat out and found the hole, and showed us where it was just when we needed it. If it weren't for you, we'd still be sitting on the rocks by the lighthouse."

Hal said nothing. Maybe she was right . . . and yet he didn't feel much like a hero. He realized it was because he was so laden with guilt. "We should never have blocked the fog-hole," he mumbled.

"Well, we did, and we're here. So everything turned out all right in the end."

"Did it?" Hal sighed and looked around once more. "What happens now? What happens to the cows and horses and sheep back on the island? They can't fend for themselves. Are we supposed to make them swim here?"

A laugh made him jump. It was Miss Simone; she was tending to Robbie's mother, one of the few who remained unconscious. Robbie and his dad sat close by, looking relieved. At first Hal wondered what she was laughing at, until she turned and looked at him.

"Don't worry, we won't make the cows swim," she said. "But it will be a bit of a journey for them nevertheless. We'll bring them through the vent, or the fog-hole as you call it."

"Biscuit!" Lauren exclaimed. "I hope he's okay. Are you sure the virus won't affect him, Miss Simone?"

Miss Simone looked puzzled for a moment. Then: "Oh, your cat. I'm sure he'll be fine. You can collect him soon, I promise."

She suddenly frowned as if remembering something, and gave Hal a long, curious stare. "Hal," she began, but then she was distracted by something, and when Hal followed her gaze he saw three pricks of flickering light appearing out of the nearby forest. Hal strained his eyes, but could make out only a vague shape moving toward them.

Miss Simone mumbled something to Robbie's dad and then clapped her hands to get everyone's attention. She addressed the adults first. "All right, please listen. I know you're all feeling pretty rotten, but I believe you're all going to be just fine once the swelling goes down. Still, I want our doctors to check you over, give you some medicine to soothe the skin, that sort of thing. Help is on the way." She gestured toward the flickering lights. "Just over there is a small settlement, sort of a lookout post tucked away in the trees. They were expecting me to bring the Bridges family through the hole tonight, so I guess they're pretty surprised to see so many of you."

She turned to the children, looking at each of them in turn. "My people can take it from here. They'll arrange transport, medicine, food, shelter, everything your parents need for a fast recovery. I should think they'll be fine in the morning."

*197*

The approaching dark shapes were beginning to take form. Squinting, Hal made out a group of squat figures moving through the long, lush grass. Immediately he was reminded of the short, stumpy people he'd seen during the storm at Robbie's house. These were Miss Simone's people?

"If you children would like to come with me," Miss Simone said, "I'll show you a couple of things while making plans at the same time. Also," she added, her eyes narrowing, "we have a job to do."

Hal went to check on his parents again. "Are you doing okay, Mom?" he asked, pleased to see that she was awake at last.

"I've felt better," she croaked. Her eyes were shut tight and everything on her face that could swell was swollen. She kept taking short, panting breaths.

"Just rest," Hal's dad said. He didn't look much better himself, but seemed reasonably comfortable, breathing easily. He was rubbing his arms and occasionally scratching at reddened skin. For a moment Hal stared, wondering if his dad was about to turn into a monster. A strange rash on an arm . . . Wasn't that how everything had started?

"Are you going to be okay if I go off with Miss Simone?" he asked anxiously.

"We'll be fine," his dad said. "Hey, son—" Blindly he reached out and grabbed Hal's shoulder, squeezing it firmly. "You did good, Hal. I don't remember much of anything, but I do remember everyone rolling around moaning and all the kids crying. Except for *you*. You were busy *doing* something, Hal."

Hal swallowed. "I was scared though," he mumbled. He suddenly felt deeply ashamed. "And I was too scared to come and see if you were okay. I was afraid you were—"

"You did good, Hal," his dad repeated softly. His strong, reassuring hand reached up and ruffled Hal's hair, then carefully stroked it flat again. "We're all going to be fine. It was a bit of a rough journey getting here, but we're here."

"We'll wake up tomorrow with the sun on our faces," Hal's mom said weakly. She smiled, trying to find Hal's hand. "We'll have to find some sunblock for our pale skin. And you'll have to remember to drink plenty of water. It gets hot here, and—"

She broke off, gasping for a breath.

"Rest," Hal said, feeling awful for her.

A few minutes later, he regrouped with his friends, or most of them anyway. Fenton was missing again. Hal knew the big boy had come through the hole; his sinister dragon form had been unmistakable even in those frantic moments underwater. But Hal couldn't remember if he had seen him since. Where was he now?

"Haven't seen him for a while," Darcy said, when Hal asked around.

"I saw him slinking off," Robbie said. "He's weird."

They waited nervously while Miss Simone's people arrived from the forest. They were not human. Hal counted seven of them, the three at the front holding aloft fiery torches. Shorter than Hal, and about twice as thick in limb and body, they looked powerful and heavy enough to walk straight through doors without bothering to open them first. They were like miniature versions of Robbie's ogre, able to throw boulders and snap branches without batting an eyelid. For a moment, Hal imagined himself rushing at one of these creatures with all his might . . . and bouncing off again.

But they weren't ogres. These people were scowling and broody, with pig-like faces and small, dark eyes. Large irregular teeth jutted out at odd angles, nostrils flared, and pointed ears twitched. They each wore rough, dirty clothing, dull leather boots, and a variety of belts, ropes and chains around their waists. On their heads they wore simple metal helmets shaped to fit around their ears—old and dull, dented in places. A few of them had similar metal shoulder armor, while a couple wore fine chain vests. All of them carried small bags or pouches over their shoulders.

*Soldiers*, Hal thought, thinking of pictures he'd seen in history books, of old medieval battles with swords and horses.

"Children," Miss Simone said, nodding at the lead soldier as the patrol marched past. "These are my friends. Goblins and humans get along perfectly, and we're perhaps the closest allies in our land. Goblins are extremely hard-working and loyal, and thoroughly trustworthy, if a little crabby sometimes."

One of the soldiers twisted his head around and bared his teeth in a snarl. But Miss Simone laughed as if they'd shared a private joke. "Now don't worry," she went on. "Gristletooth will take good care of your parents. He and his henchmen have all sorts of medicine in those bags. Let's leave them to their work."

Miss Simone started along the trail of flattened grass to the forest, and the children followed silently at a distance so they could talk quietly to each other. Hal wondered at first how the goblins had managed to leave such a wide, well-defined trail, but then kicked himself; obviously the trail was old, and probably used often. After all, the lake contained one of the few remaining doorways to another world.

"So this is where Miss Simone is from," Abigail said, walking beside Hal. "Imagine her jumping in the lake every day and swimming underwater, through the hole, and to the island—"

"And," Robbie said, "returning through a different hole. Remember when she dove off the cliff? I wonder how deep underwater *that* hole is, and where it comes out at this end."

Miss Simone slowed and allowed the children to catch up. "I'm sure you have a lot of questions," she said. "Ask me anything."

Hal thought of something immediately. "Are you human? You keep saying you're human, like when you mentioned earlier about how humans and goblins are allies—but, um . . ."

"You're a mermaid," Abigail finished for him.

Miss Simone nodded.

"And if you're a human that can turn into a mermaid," Hal went on, "does that mean . . . well, does that mean you're like us? A shapeshifter? If so, why did the virus affect you?"

"I'm a shapeshifter," Miss Simone confirmed. "Just like you. My parents lived in your world, as yours did. And like you, I was born and raised in a remote area away from ordinary children. I was one of twelve, and we went to a small private school in the middle of thousands of acres of privately owned land, miles from any other city or town. My parents learned to be self-sufficient, just like yours. Slowly but surely, our small community broke all contact with the outside world. It was very nice, actually, growing up there. But of course," she added, "we had sunshine and no threat of virus."

"And you changed into a mermaid," Lauren said, enthralled.

"At age eight. Right on schedule. My friends changed too, one after the other. And, when we were ready, we were brought into this land."

The forest loomed ahead. From deep within, Hal saw tiny pin-pricks of light. Campfires? Or fireplaces within homes?

"But you're not immune to the virus," Abigail pointed out.

Miss Simone shook her head. "I guess I'm *partially* immune. I felt better once I changed into a mermaid. The act of transforming rejuvenates cells and microorganisms. It's like they get to start over, fresh and new. So injuries tend to heal right away. Remember that, children—if you get hurt in an accident, just change and that might help you mend quickly."

Hal remembered when Thomas had stuck him with needles. He had felt dizzy and sick until he'd transformed into a dragon, after which he'd felt much better.

"But," Miss Simone said with a sigh, "our bodies grow weary as time goes by. As you get older, children, you'll find it harder and harder to shake off illnesses and cure yourselves of cuts and bruises. It's just nature's way of restoring normality to what she probably thinks are biological abominations." She turned and winked. "Otherwise we'd live forever, right?"

There was silence as the children digested this. Then Miss Simone fell in step with Hal and put a hand on his shoulder. "There's something I need to know, Hal, but . . . I'm almost afraid to ask."

Surprised, Hal came to a halt. "Ask me what?"

Everyone stopped. Miss Simone took a breath, leaned forward earnestly, and asked, "Did you manage to fly before we came through the hole?"

Hal slowly shook his head. "Sorry, no."

The disappointment on Miss Simone's face was plainly obvious. She let her hand fall to her side and stood up straight. Saying nothing, she turned and continued marching along the trail.

The children waited a minute before saying anything, watching Miss Simone walk off. Then Darcy murmured, "What's *her* problem? I'm sure you'll learn to fly soon, Hal."

"She doesn't think I'll be able to," Hal said softly, "now that we've come through the hole."

"I don't see why not," Emily retorted. "What difference does it make *where* we are? I think she's wrong about this. Hal, you know how to turn into a dragon, and you have wings, right? So it's not like you can't transform. You *can* transform. You just need to learn how to flap your wings a certain way and get into the air."

There was a murmur of agreement, and they all set off after Miss Simone, who was some distance away by now. Hal hung back, deep in thought, and Abigail nudged him.

"A dragon who can't fly," she teased gently. "What use are you?"

"About as much use as an oversized faerie," Hal said. "It's one thing to be freaks, but we can't even manage that!"

Abigail gave a wry grin. "If Miss Simone is right about this, and we really can't complete our transformations and do the things we're supposed to be able to do . . . well, big deal. Who cares? We're here, Hal. *No more fog!* A new life in a new place. Forget Miss Simone, the old sourpuss."

They finally made it to the forest. Hal glimpsed small cottages through the trees, their walls illuminated by lanterns that hung from hooks or were perched atop poles. There were one or two crackling fires in little clearings between houses, where goblins were roasting things in little pans.

"They're nuts," Miss Simone said, as if reading his mind.

"Oh, I don't know," Hal said. "They seem quite sane to me."

Abigail giggled and Robbie guffawed, but Miss Simone looked puzzled for a moment. Then Emily explained the joke, and Miss Simone smiled politely.

Instead of heading into the small village, they circled around the perimeter and walked right by it. Hal glanced at his friends. They looked just as surprised, and a little disappointed too. It was a quiet, friendly-seeming village with perhaps ten or fifteen cottages, hardly a village at all. But then again, Hal had grown up on an island with even fewer occupied houses, so to him it was just the right size. What had Miss Simone called the place? A settlement? An outpost of some kind?

"We're not stopping?" Hal asked her.

"Not just now. We have a job to do. But we'll be back here later."

So they left the smell of roasted nuts behind and plunged into the dark forest. They soon came across a meandering path lit by hanging lanterns. The ground was well trodden, and scattered with a fine layer of pine needles that cushioned their footsteps. Hal's feet, which were still bare except for the curious stick-on soles, felt a comfortable tingling, tickling sensation as he walked.

"Look at these moths," Robbie whispered, awed at the size of them as they buzzed around the lanterns. He spotted one the size of his hand. "I saw a huge spider back there, too—its web stretched right across—"

"Robbie, stop," Emily commanded from behind him.

After five minutes of silent passage through the forest, walking in single file along the narrow path and ducking occasionally to avoid the hanging lanterns, they came at last to the end of the trail. Here it was curiously foggy, and they could hear a huffing, wheezing sound, accompanied by a constant rattle and *click*, rattle and *click*. It was a curious, rhythmic sound, obviously a machine of some kind.

They rounded a tall thicket and came suddenly upon a strange sight. Here a sheer rock face loomed over them, disappearing into the foggy night sky. It seemed completely out of place in the heart of a forest, but Hal realized, as he looked around, that in fact the forest ran right up to the foot of one of the mountains.

But it wasn't the rocky wall that was strange, nor the mouth of a cave that yawned dark and wide, roughly twenty feet across. What was strange stood directly before the cave: a complicated, rickety contraption made of wooden beams and metal rods, standing four times Hal's height and just as wide, with wobbly cogs and wheels and greasy pulleys that turned continuously, pulling around chains that crisscrossed here and there. That was the rattle and *click* sound. The huffing and wheezing was caused by a gigantic set of bellows that expanded slowly and then squeezed flat, then expanded again . . . as if it were breathing. On top of these sounds was the hum of an engine that whistled and hissed and puffed out steam.

The children were enthralled. "It's like music," Emily said, delighted. "Listen to it—*huff click whirr, rattle fizz pop*. It's like—"

"It doesn't pop," Darcy said, laughing. "And it's more like *rattle click hiss, whirr puff bang*."

"But what's it for?" Lauren asked.

"I know," Robbie said suddenly. His eyes were shining as he glanced around. "We've been walking for, what?—forty-five minutes or more? That's how long it takes us to get from the lighthouse to Black Woods. I don't know if this forest is like an alternate version of Black Woods, but the point is, if we were back on the island, we'd be at the fog-hole by now."

*The fog-hole.*

Hal blinked, and his mouth dropped open. *Of course!* He edged closer, first checking to see if that was okay with Miss Simone. She simply nodded, stepped aside, and waved him past. Hal hurried over to the machine, his friends falling over themselves to catch up.

At the far side of the machine, facing the rock wall and pointing directly into the mouth of the cave, fog squeezed out of the huge bellows. The thick, silent substance poured into the darkness and disappeared as the machine rattled and huffed and whistled.

But the fog wasn't just confined to the cave. It swirled and drifted up the side of the mountain too.

The machine gave an alarming creaking sound, and Hal turned to see a greasy, sweaty goblin scowl and whack something with a hefty wrench. The creak eased at once, and the goblin muttered something that was completely drowned out by the small, noisy engine. He didn't appear to know he had visitors.

"It's been running for thirteen years," Miss Simone said from behind them. "Sometimes it breaks down, and then the engineers rush about like mad trying to fix it. Sometimes they do major maintenance work, bringing in a smaller version of the machine to keep the fog going while this beast is shut down for a while. But for the most part, it's been running non-stop since before you were born."

She pointed out various leather pouches that were hung on the side. Each had a tube running out of the bottom, evidently supplying some kind of liquid to the inner-workings of the machine.

"That large bag there contains a special formula that filters the air and makes it safe. It has a slow, cumulative effect, which is why I said it would take a week to make the island safe again. This other, smaller bag is for creating pockets of vacuum in the air. That's what dampens your flight." She glanced at Hal with a raised eyebrow. "For those of you who can fly, I mean."

Hal decided to ignore the remark. "What's that lever for?" he said, pointing.

"That's just a speed control. It speeds the machine up. When there's a storm over the island, the fog gets blown around and we have to speed up the machine to pump more through. Better to be safe than sorry."

She stepped around the machine and waved at the engineer, who was bent over the engine with a scowl on his face, intent on an oily chain that spun smoothly around a set of cogs. The goblin didn't see Miss Simone at all, so she tapped him on the shoulder. He jumped, straightened up, and nodded in greeting. Then he spotted the children and stared at them, his eyes first narrowing with suspicion, then growing wide with surprise. The wrench fell out of his hand.

Miss Simone smiled at him. "The children are here now," she said above the noise. "You can shut it down."

The goblin turned his stare on her. "Shut it down?" he repeated in a deep, throaty voice.

"Yes. Shut it down."

The goblin continued to stare, astonishment plastered across his gnarled face. Then he gave a huge shrug and turned to the noisy engine. After a moment's hesitation he reached out, flicked three switches, and pulled a lever down with a sharp yank.

The engine sputtered and died. The machine kept going almost as though it hadn't noticed it had been switched off, but without power it began to slow down. Its wobbly wheels and chains squeaked and rattled to a gradual stop, and its bellows wheezed slower and slower until, finally, they gave out and expired. Something came undone and fell off with a clang.

Then the machine was still.

One by one, the children turned back to the cave entrance. The fog had already stopped belching, and the air around them became still as the fog slowly lifted.

The goblin mopped his forehead and sat on a small chair, from which a lantern hung. "Can't believe it," he grumbled, gazing at the silent machine. "Never thought I'd see the day . . ."

"Noticed anything unusual lately?" Miss Simone asked him.

The goblin nodded, frowning. "Fog's spitting back out. Like there's a blockage, see? Remember that roof-fall last year? How the fog backed up on us?"

"I remember," Miss Simone said, nodding. "Well, the vent is blocked again, for sure. The children did it."

The goblin nodded, and spat on the ground. "Explains everything," he complained, gesturing to the drifting fog. "Kids."

Miss Simone grinned. "Don't mind him," she whispered to the children.

"'Course, there was an incident a few days ago," the goblin said quietly, looking embarrassed. "Maybe a week ago. Can't remember. Anyway, someone clubbed me." He rubbed the back of his head. "When I came to, I didn't notice anything unusual, 'cept the footprints."

"Footprints?" Miss Simone said, frowning.

"Harpies," the goblin muttered. He spat in disgust.

Miss Simone was perplexed. "And?"

"And nothing. Nothing was taken, nothing was broken. Just prints, that's all."

"They wouldn't have come here and knocked you out for no reason," Miss Simone said grimly. "Why didn't you tell me about this?"

"Nothing to tell," the goblin said, sounding a little sulky now. "They didn't break the machine this time. They didn't try stuffing up the cave. They didn't do nothing."

Hal snapped his fingers. "Thomas! Don't you see? The first time Abigail and I met Thomas, he told us he'd woken up in Black Woods and didn't know how he'd got there. He was lost."

"He was *kidnapped*," Miss Simone said, nodding. "Yes, the harpies would have known about him; they're always snooping and spying on us. Of course they know all about the shapeshifter program. Everybody in the land does. I suppose they thought it would be funny to dump a manticore on the island and see if it picked off any of the subjects." She thumped one of the supports of the fog machine, her eyes flashing angrily. The goblin backed away, looking wary, and Hal wondered, not for the first time, exactly what Miss Simone was capable of when she got angry.

After a moment she calmed a little. "I wonder if they knew it was Thomas himself they had kidnapped."

The goblin snorted. "There aren't many manticores around this area. Maybe he's the only one they could find close by. You can't get much nastier than a manticore, 'cept for a dragon, and no-one's gonna mess with those. Ogres are too big to fit in the tunnel." The goblin nodded. "Makes sense."

Miss Simone still looked cross. "Well, children, now we have something important to do. You see, this tunnel is our best route through to the island, and we're not finished there yet. We need to clear the tunnel and make it safe so we can pass back and forth, fetching animals and whatever possessions your parents want to hang on to. That is, once we re-start the fog machine tomorrow. A foggy island is a safe island."

The goblin groaned. "You mean we're not done with the machine yet?"

"No. But we'll leave it switched off for the night until we get that blockage removed. Tomorrow we switch it back on. Then we wait a week for the island to re-fog before we venture back." She paused. "But in the meantime, tonight, we need some of you immune youngsters to go through that tunnel and clear the vent of any obstruction, and catch young Thomas while you're at it."

"*Catch* Thomas?" Robbie exclaimed.

"What with—butterfly nets?" Abigail snapped.

"Something like that," Miss Simone said. "Now, who's going to volunteer?"

## Chapter Twenty-Three
### One last journey

Hal wasn't quite sure how he got roped into the task of capturing Thomas the manticore, but somehow he found himself facing the mouth of the cave and his friends looking at him as if he had volunteered, which he hadn't. He'd simply been the last one to refuse.

"Where's Fenton?" Hal asked, suddenly irritated with the big boy. "Just when I could do with his help, he's not around."

"I must admit I'm a little worried about him," Miss Simone said, her face half hidden in the darkness. The tall trees blocked out the moonlight, and the only illumination came from several hanging lanterns. Huge moths were beating against them over and over. "He seems to be stuck in his new body. Either that or he likes it so much he doesn't *want* to change back."

She nodded toward the tunnel. "Frankly, though, I'm more worried about Thomas. He's been stuck in that manticore body since he was six, and I'm afraid the human part of his mind has long since given in to the prevailing presence of the manticore. Still, we can always *try* to reason with him."

"Why haven't you tried before?" Abigail asked, wandering over to the tunnel and peering inside. It was pitch black.

Miss Simone sighed. "We have, Abigail. When he fell off the cliff all those years ago, it was because he'd changed unexpectedly. Not just a few odd changes here and there, like a rash or strange tuft of hair. No, Thomas changed *completely*, in one single moment."

Hal edged away from the cave entrance, welcoming the delay. He leaned against the hulking fog machine and hung onto Miss Simone's every word. The terrible event unfolded in his mind . . .

Mrs. Patten had been right there when it happened, Miss Simone explained. Thomas had been playing in the backyard when he came across a groundhog. It snuffled around, minding its own business, not noticing the red-headed child who stood watching it. Thomas was so excited that he wanted to run after it, play games with it, maybe even catch it and take it home. But the groundhog scampered away into the bushes. Thomas took off after it, at first disappointed, then growing angry as his clothes caught on bushes and thorns grazed his arms.

Mrs. Patten went after him, calling him back to the yard. But he ignored her, and she grew more and more concerned as she struggled through the woods. Then she heard a wailing, and it chilled her to the bone. She followed the wails, and came upon her son's clothes, ripped and torn, stamped into the mud. And standing over the garments was the manticore, all rippling muscle and claws, red fur and blue eyes, rows of needle-like teeth, and a terrifying segmented tail with a ball of quills on the end, from which protruded a vicious-looking shiny black point.

The manticore—*her little boy*—looked at her with shock and horror, and a single word escaped from its thin black lips: "Mom?"

Mrs. Patten lived to regret what she did next. She screamed.

The manticore's eyes widened and tears welled up. It backed off. Then it turned and ran, plunging into the bushes and disappearing once more.

Immediately Mrs. Patten realized her mistake and took off after her son again, sobbing with regret, calling his name, trying to calm him. But then she heard another wail, this time one of sheer panic—and then there was silence.

Mrs. Patten emerged from the woods on the edge of the cliff, and her heart almost gave out as she realized what had happened. She dropped to the ground, crawled out to the crumbling edge, and peered over, but by then Thomas was gone.

Miss Simone let her words hang in the cool night air. Then, seeing that Emily was fighting back tears, she squeezed the girl's shoulder and smiled ruefully. "You now know that Thomas didn't hit the rocks when he fell, despite what you were told all those years ago. He didn't drown either. You see, purely by coincidence—call it luck, if you like—I had come through the nearby underwater hole and was splashing around just below the cliff where Thomas fell. I heard the screaming and wailing from high above, and came to investigate. Imagine my surprise when a large red-furred beast came tumbling over the edge, bringing with it clumps of bushes and clods of dirt."

"But what *happened* to him?" Hal asked, remembering what Thomas had said about being pulled under. Surely Miss Simone hadn't tried to drown him?

"Well, he fell into the water and went under," she went on. "I followed him down and there he was, a huge, impressive, but extremely dangerous floundering creature, sucking in water, huge bubbles rising up."

"Didn't you try to save him?" Lauren asked.

Miss Simone sighed. "Think about it, children. Imagine a drowning manticore—legs thrashing, claws everywhere, tail shooting off quills left, right and center, stinger jabbing."

"Oh," Hal said.

"Yes," Miss Simone agreed. "I couldn't get close to him without getting myself killed. He would have surfaced eventually, but he had dropped from such a great height that he was deep, deep underwater, and even if he made it to the surface, I doubted he could swim anyway. And there's nothing to swim *to*, just a sheer rock face. So I made a decision, one that saved his life, but caused a lot of distress to his family and friends."

"You grabbed his ankle and pulled him deeper into the water," Hal finished, knowing this to be true, but perplexed as to how that helped matters.

Miss Simone looked surprised. "How on earth did you—? Well, yes, that's exactly right. As I couldn't get close enough to Thomas to wrap my arms around him and help him up to the surface, I grabbed one of his ankles and dragged him downwards. Thomas began kicking immediately and I was stuck with a few quills. I began to get drowsy. But I didn't need to drag Thomas down very far, just a hundred feet or so."

*A hundred feet!* Hal couldn't imagine swimming that far on the *surface* of the water, never mind *downward*.

"That's where the hole was," Miss Simone explained, seeing a number of blank faces. "I deposited Thomas through the hole, then followed him through."

She looked across at the goblin, who was sitting there listening intently. He jumped guiltily when Miss Simone fixed her gaze on him, then relaxed when she asked him a simple question. "Do we have a large net here somewhere?"

The goblin scratched his head. "Um, not *here*. There's a big 'un in the storage shed though. Want me to get it?"

"No, I'll wander back myself and arrange a few things. I want to show the kids something anyway."

To Hal's relief, she led them away from the cave entrance and back to the path. Walking once more in single file along the meandering trail, ducking to avoid the lanterns, he wondered what time it was. It felt late, way past his normal bedtime, and yet the goblins seemed to be milling around as if the evening was young. He guessed it was around ten or eleven. No wonder he was exhausted.

"I don't get it," Robbie said loudly from behind him. "Miss Simone, you said the hole was right there at the foot of the cliffs where Thomas fell. But we followed you one day after school, and we saw you dive off the cliff *miles* outside Black Woods. Well, a good walk from where Thomas fell, anyway."

"Well, of course," Miss Simone said. "Do you think I'd be stupid enough to dive off the cliff where Thomas fell? Those rocks are deadly. It was a miracle Thomas happened to miss every one of them. No, I chose a much safer spot to return home where I could dive in, then swim along the coast to the hole. Much easier than struggling through the woods and risk bashing my head open on the rocks below, wouldn't you agree?"

Robbie grunted something and fell silent.

The children followed Miss Simone back to the cluster of cottages in the forest. She led them between buildings, nodding her head at several goblins as they passed. The night was getting unbearably cold now, and the crackling campfires looked extremely inviting, especially with the smell of roasted nuts wafting through the air.

Miss Simone wasted no time. She led them to a brightly lit area at the center of the village, a circular patch of land enclosed by a wrought iron fence. There were five separate openings in the fence, each with stout gate posts but no actual gates. It seemed that all paths led to this place, and yet there was nothing to see except neatly cropped grass and a large, murky puddle.

Everyone stared, perplexed. "What is this place?" Hal asked at last. "A miniature park?"

"This is the third hole," Miss Simone said. "It's a curious one, this. It was easy the first time I went through it to your world. I just jumped in and ended up in the sea near your island. Being a mermaid, that's just fine with me." Her brow furrowed as she tried to form the words to explain. "But when I tried to come back through, it didn't work. I approached it from *above*, you see, swimming *down*, and when I passed through, I nearly brained myself on solid ground, the bed of this puddle, you see? I just couldn't seem to get through. After I while I figured out that I had to swim *up*, approaching it from underneath. Then it worked; my head popped out of this puddle and I was home again. It appears that certain holes have certain, uh, *rules* depending on location or position."

Hal peered into the puddle and saw a strange blackness within, a swirling mass that seemed to have a life of its own.

"When I pulled Thomas down below the water under the cliff, I made sure to drag him all the way down below the level of the hole. Then I let go and he floated right up through it, and emerged from this puddle, coughing and spluttering. Of course it was a shock to the goblins when a manticore popped up out of the puddle. Instant panic, and that probably didn't help matters—Thomas ran for the trees before anyone could do anything. I came through moments later, woozy from the poisoned quills. We organized search parties, but Thomas was long gone. I heard reports that he was seen the next morning, skulking away from a river that runs through the forest, but otherwise he disappeared and wasn't seen again for months."

Miss Simone walked off suddenly, and the children hurried to catch up. She led them to one of the campfires, and several goblins turned to face her as she approached. One of them tipped his helmet politely, and gestured toward a beaten up, blackened pan with hundreds of holes punched in the bottom. In the pan was a single layer of chestnuts, each with an X carved into the shell. They smelled delicious and were beginning to smoke.

But Miss Simone declined, and instead asked the goblin if he would bring her a net. "A large one," she said. "Take it to the fog machine, if you don't mind, and get some more help. We have a manticore to catch."

Hal's stomach turned over at the reminder. He followed in silence as Miss Simone led the way once more along the meandering forest trail. This time Robbie banged his head on a lantern and complained loudly.

"You have to realize that goblins are very short," Miss Simone said, laughing. "And they have to light these things every night, and put them out again before turning in."

As they approached the cave entrance, Hal asked Miss Simone about Mr. and Mrs. Patten, who had mourned the loss of their son and disappeared shortly afterwards.

"At first they truly believed he was dead," Miss Simone agreed. "I guess it was a natural assumption. News spread fast, too. By the time I returned to tell them that Thomas was alive, everyone on the island was in tears. But as it turned out, it was for the best. It explained Thomas's disappearance without revealing that he had turned into a monster. Of course I took the Pattens aside and explained the truth to them—and brought them through the hole to my world."

"But we all thought he was dead!" Abigail said, suddenly angry. "How is that for the best?"

"He *is* dead," Miss Simone said. "Or as good as dead anyway. His mind is not his own anymore. He's a manticore with a few human memories. Perhaps if we'd been able to find him earlier, we might have helped him, but he completely disappeared. And trust me, one thing you don't want to go hunting for is a manticore. What if you come across the wrong one? What if you come across a whole family of them?" She shuddered. "Perhaps there's hope though. There's *always* hope. That's why we need to find Thomas while we have a chance, and bring him back to us. We need to talk to him, reason with him, see if there's any hope of saving him."

The sound of stamping feet filtered through the forest, and half a minute later a group of goblins marched into view—four of them, carrying a large, heavy net and a couple of long, sturdy poles. They dumped it all at Miss Simone's feet and set about untangling it.

Miss Simone turned her gaze to Hal, and nodded. Hal again felt his stomach turn over. *This isn't fair! Why can't she send her goblin army through to capture the manticore?* "Does the virus affect goblins too?" he asked, somewhat sullenly.

"No," she admitted, "but Hal, you're a dragon. I'm not afraid for you. The poison quills may weaken you, but you can shake off the effect easily. Only the stinger is likely to be harmful, so be careful."

She looked at the net on the ground. The goblins had laid it out in a large square and were now looping a rope through it.

"Besides," Miss Simone said, "I don't want you to *tackle* the manticore. Just provoke him. Bring him through the hole. We'll capture him at this end."

With a heavy heart, Hal took a breath and stepped up to the cave entrance. He heard footsteps behind him and a hand caught his elbow.

It was Abigail. "I'm coming with you," she said.

Robbie stepped up too, and cleared his throat. "Me too. You could do with an ogre's strength."

Hal felt better already, but as he stared at Abigail, who still wore her strange green frock, he came to the conclusion that he didn't want her to come with him. It was too dangerous. A few quills and she'd be lying on the ground unconscious, unable to defend herself or escape. And Hal would have enough to worry about without trying to protect her too.

Robbie, too, might inadvertently make things more difficult. Sure, he was an ogre, but even ogres had soft hides. And he was so big that he wouldn't fit through the tunnel as an ogre, so would have to revert back to his skinny human body.

He put a hand on Abigail's shoulder and shook his head. "Sorry, this is *my* job. Thanks, though."

Abigail's mouth dropped open. She looked as though she was about to say something, but after a moment closed her mouth and studied him thoughtfully.

"Let's go, then," Robbie said.

"No, not you, either," Hal said. "I think Miss Simone could do with your help at this end."

"Yes, I could," Miss Simone said. "In fact I'm counting on you, Robbie."

So, grateful to his friends, Hal grabbed a lantern and headed into the darkness of the cave. He heard a number of muted calls—"good luck" and "be careful"— and then he was climbing a gentle slope at the back of the cave, holding the lantern high. The lighting was a dull orange color, and it flickered a lot. His shadow danced.

It was cold in the cave, even colder than the night outside. The air was almost frigid, and goose bumps rose on his arms and legs. His thin pants and shirt, and virtually bare feet, seemed ludicrous in the dark, cold, damp tunnel; he needed a thick coat and solid walking boots.

The air smelled musty, very much like a day of drizzle on the island. There was no sign of fog though. If the fog-hole was blocked, where had all the fog gone?

After several minutes walk along a fairly wide tunnel, he came to a narrow section. This continued for at least thirty feet, and the walls closed in even more as he started up a steep rise. The floor was pure rock, uneven but smooth, slippery in places where moss had grown. Ice cold water trickled down the walls. Hal's breathing sounded loud in the tight, enclosed space, and when he stumbled and bumped the lantern against the slanting wall, the sound echoed all around. He heard the fluttering of small wings over his head and instinctively ducked. *Bats!*

He pressed on, heart thumping. The tunnel turned and twisted, dropped a few feet, rose again, widened out, then narrowed again. *An ogre would never fit through here*, he thought suddenly, mentally patting himself on the back for refusing Robbie's help.

*But then again, neither would a dragon.*

He thought his eyesight was playing tricks on him as he approached what appeared to be a black spot ahead. As he got closer, the light from the lantern should have lit it, but instead the black spot remained pitch black until he was standing right next to it. Around him the lantern's flickering glow bounced off the rocky walls. But ahead, stretching across the full height and width of the tunnel, a black smoky cloud breathed in and out, rolling and turning in on itself as it expanded and contracted.

Hal stood for a minute just staring at it. Then he reached out and put his hand through. There was no sensation whatsoever.

He took a breath and stepped through the cloud, keeping his eyes open. There was utter blackness for a moment, then a flash of something—stars in a night sky?—and then he was through, stepping down heavily onto a hard floor that was a foot or two lower than he expected. He was standing once more in a tunnel, but this tunnel was different. It was large, and filled with fog.

Hal glanced back at the hole, making a note of its location. In this cavernous tunnel, the hole floated above the floor and it was possible to walk around it. How on earth was he supposed to find it again, in the darkness, with a manticore chasing him? With fog everywhere?

He sighed. This was madness. Still, he continued on, plunging into the fog and feeling his way along. The lantern was useless now—the light just bounced back at him. Having a sudden brainwave, he returned to the hole and put the lantern on the rocky floor directly underneath. Now he had a marker to help guide him on his return journey.

Treading carefully, Hal felt his way along the tunnel in total darkness. He could not see the fog, but he could smell it. It filled his nostrils, a damp yet oddly pleasant smell. He'd lived with fog all his life, and it was strangely comforting to return to it.

Hal didn't know how long he walked, or how far, but it seemed to take forever. Finally he saw faint pricks of light ahead. There were gaps in the fog-hole blockage, tiny cracks where the blankets had shifted. He reached for one of these gaps, and widened it enough to stick his head through. Fresh air at last! And, despite being in the middle of Black Woods at night, the moonlight poured into the little clearing. High above, stars twinkled in a clear black sky.

He transformed himself into a dragon, at once feeling safer as he burst out of the fog-hole amid an explosion of blankets, branches, leaves and dirt. He cleared the way with his huge paws and watched as fog poured once more into the air. He suspected it would continue for a little while until it cleared out of the cavernous chamber and tunnel.

Hal looked around. Bright as it was in the moonlight, it was still night and he couldn't make out much at all. He didn't relish the idea of venturing into the thick woods, so he transformed back into his human body and stood in the center of the clearing, feeling extremely vulnerable.

"Thomas!" he yelled. "Thomas! I want to talk to you."

His voice echoed, but all he heard in return was the grunt of a bullfrog.

"Thomas!" he yelled again.

Then he felt a number of sharp, stinging needles thud into his neck and shoulders. He gasped and ducked, but it was far too late. Behind him, the manticore watched warily, hunkered low to the ground, its tail high over its head and bristling with quills.

Hal felt woozy in a matter of seconds, and he fell sideways. He didn't feel anything when he hit the ground, but he saw leaves fly up around him. The woods began to spin. Dimly he was aware of time stopping, starting, stopping again, like his life was sputtering and grinding to a halt. One moment the manticore was twenty feet away, rising to its feet; the next, it was standing over him.

Hal fought to keep his eyes open, but they kept closing. His limbs were heavy, impossible to move. There was a rushing sound in his ears.

*Change*, he told himself.

He felt annoyed that he was in the exact same position now as when he had first met Thomas. Then, as now, Hal had been stuck with quills. Then, as now, the manticore had raised its stinger to strike. And, once again, Hal felt himself changing as he lay in the dirt.

As the change occurred, he forced himself up and swung a heavy fist at the manticore. Once again, as before, he hit the creature with a glancing blow to the face. Thomas staggered back and Hal climbed to his feet, already feeling the effects of the poison wearing off. He raised himself to full height and spread his wings. Then he roared angrily, and a huge blast of fire erupted from his throat. It lit up the trees and blackened the manticore's whiskers.

Thomas backed off, his eyes narrowing. "This isn't fair," he growled. "I've brought down a dragon before. What makes *you* so special? How do you keep getting up?"

Hal wasn't in the mood to chat. He swung around, putting his back to Thomas, and relished the brief moment when the manticore thought the dragon was turning to run. In that moment, a huge grin started to spread across the manticore's face, but then Hal's club-ended tail whacked Thomas so hard across the head that he flew through the air and slumped to the ground.

Breathing hard, Hal stared down at the manticore. It was still. Hal could see its chest rise and fall, and he nodded with satisfaction. *Unconscious is good.*

Hal carefully clamped his jaws around the manticore's long, thick tail, careful not to touch the black stinger that was partially hidden by poison-tipped quills. Then, walking backward, he stamped over to the fog-hole, dragging the manticore along. He wasn't in the mood to feel sorry for any bumps or scrapes Thomas might endure on the journey to Elsewhere; Hal simply backed into the fog-hole and gave a hard yank every time the manticore got snared on anything.

Once inside the tunnel, Thomas slid easily along the moist, rocky floor. Walking backward in dragon form was not so easy though, so Hal gave up on that idea and began pushing the limp creature instead, hooking his large snout under the manticore's body and giving it a good hard shove every few steps. This was certainly easier, at least for now. But what would he do when the tunnel got too narrow and he had to turn back into his human body?

He made it back to his lantern marker without incident. Above it, in the steadily thinning fog, the black cloud breathed endlessly a foot above the rock floor.

Then Thomas woke up.

He was dazed at first, but when he became aware of his surroundings he jumped to his feet, staggered, and spun around to face Hal. He looked angry, but frightened too.

"Where are we?" he said in a nasally, high-pitched voice.

Hal didn't answer. There was no point, since he couldn't form human words. But an idea came to him. He put on what he thought was his most threatening scowl, hunkered down, spread his legs wide, and let out a bellowing roar.

The manticore backed up and knocked the lantern over, and it went out.

In the sudden darkness, Hal heard a whimper of fear. Seizing the opportunity, he roared once more, only this time belching up a huge burst of flame, long and hot. In the flickering orange glow, Thomas turned to run, and disappeared into the black cloud. Hal shot another long, hot blast of fire into the cloud just for good measure.

He waited a few minutes before changing into his human body and stepping through the hole. The lantern was useless, so he was in utter darkness. If Thomas was waiting for him in the tunnel, there was very little Hal could do about it.

He began to feel his way along the narrow tunnel towards Elsewhere, hoping that Thomas had kept on running.

\* \* \*

When Hal finally emerged from the cave entrance, a cheer went up. There were his friends, crowding around him, clapping him on the shoulders and ruffling his hair. There was Miss Simone, smiling broadly and nodding. And there were the goblins, standing around looking almost cheerful.

But best of all, there was Thomas, trussed up safely in a net, looking very annoyed.

"Robbie leapt on him," Lauren said, nudging Robbie's arm. "Thomas came hurtling out of the tunnel, then stopped when he saw everyone standing here, and turned to go back in. But Robbie was waiting. He had the net spread wide, and he jumped on top of the manticore and wrapped it around him. Then the goblins piled in, and it was all a bit of a struggle, but finally Thomas gave up."

Hal gave a shudder. If the manticore had been allowed back into the tunnel, sooner or later it would have come across a poor, defenseless boy in a pitch-black tunnel.

"Nice one, Robbie," he said, nodding. "You saved my bacon."

Robbie looked pleased with himself. But more than that, he liked the attention Lauren was giving him.

Abigail linked her arm through Hal's. "Come on, O Brave One. While you were away, a goblin arrived to say that our parents are feeling much better. They've set up campfires and things by the lake. Apparently there's good food to eat."

Hal's stomach immediately began growling. "And roasted nuts?" he asked.

Miss Simone nodded. "Always."

Thomas was taken off to be locked up somewhere. Still trussed up in the net, he hung between two long poles which the goblins carried on their shoulders. Weary but happy, Hal and his friends followed Miss Simone all the way back to the lake, where a ring of small fires warmed the air and cast a comfortable glow over the grassy bank. Hal found his parents bundled up in many layers of blankets, drinking soup from a huge pot and munching on thick, warm bread.

The mood was cheerful. Whatever medicine the goblins had given the virus victims, it seemed to be working. The puffiness had subsided, the burning sensation soothed with some odd-smelling cream, and all were enjoying dinner under a clear, starry, but icy cold sky.

Miss Simone kept on talking even after Hal and his friends had snuggled under blankets by the fire. "And tomorrow we'll move you into your new homes, introduce you to everyone, and show you around. You children have a lot of important work ahead of you, but you're also going to enjoy exploring this land."

Hal's eyelids were growing heavy. He glanced across at Abigail. She was sound asleep already. So, too, were Lauren, Darcy and Dewey. Robbie was staring at the sky. Only Emily seemed to be paying full attention to Miss Simone.

"In time, my children, you'll join me and others in our research. The fog on the island makes the air safe, and we're working to expand on that idea, to figure out a way to clean *all* the air in your old world and restore life. We've been unsuccessful so far, but, perhaps in time, we'll find a way."

Hal closed his eyes. Right now, all he cared about was sleeping.

"We need young Dewey to meet with the centaurs very soon," Miss Simone went on. "Emily, the naga folk need to be pacified. And as for the harpies . . . "

Hal felt himself drifting off, but then a strange feeling of being watched caused him to look around. In the darkness by the lake he found two bright red eyes watching him.

"Fenton," Hal whispered, already dropping off again.

He dreamed of fog machines and manticores, of goblins and mermaids. At some point his visions turned dark and he saw the faces of his parents swelling up with blisters and rashes. He then found himself being chased by a pack of flying dragons, all laughing at him, jeering as he ran across the fields in desperation. He tried to fly, but no matter how hard he flapped his wings, he simply *could not* take off into the air.

He jolted upright, gasping, looking around in fright. But everything was all right—he was with his friends and family, safe on the grassy bank of the lake, under a glowing moon and clear, starry sky. He relaxed, sinking back into the grass, his eyes already closing.

He woke several hours later as a warmth spread over his face and something shone bright and orange through his eyelids.

He opened his eyes, blinking. It was morning.

And the sky was blue.

## DATE DUE

Made in the USA
Lexington, KY
14 November 2015